The Surv

Book 2

The Finale

Francis Wait

Have a good read
John
Best Wishes
Francis

First published in the UK in 2015 by MyVoice Publishing

Copyright: © Francis Wait
Francis Wait asserts the moral right to be identified as the author of this work

Published by: MyVoice Publishing,

ISBN: 978-1-909359-46-8

All rights reserved. No part of this book may be reproduced without the permission of the author, stored in a retrieval system, or transmitted in any form or by any means. Electronic, mechanical, photocopying, recording or otherwise, without the permission of the author.

This book is sold subject to the condition that it shall not, by way of trade or otherwise, be lent, re-sold, hired out or otherwise circulated without the publishers prior consent in any form of binding or cover other that that in which it is published and without a similar condition including this condition being published being imposed on the subsequent purchaser.

All characters in this publication are fictitious and any resemblance to real persons, living or dead, is purely coincidental

Dedications

I would like to thank the following people for their help during the process of writing this book.

Tony Flood, The Author of 'The Secret Potion' and 'My Life with the Stars' (both available on Amazon) for all his help, encouragement and suggestions in the writing of my book.

Liz Wright, the author of 'Belle Tout - the Lighthouse that Moved' and 'From Fancy Pants to Getting There', (both available from Amazon) for her editing advice.

Christine Dudley for her alternative ideas regarding some of the more difficult parts.

Steve Lee for reading the book and his invaluable advice.

Publisher Rex Sumner for pointing out that the first edition needed amending and suggesting different locations.

My wife Angela for her forbearance when I disappear for long periods during the writing process.

The Survivalists, Book 2, **The Finale**

Yellowstone Park

Millions of visitors head for the Rocky Mountains at Yellowstone to marvel at the steaming geysers, bubbling mud pots and thermal pools. Few of them realise the scale and depth of this natural wonder. A Super volcano is not formed above ground but rather below it. This natural phenomenon is actually a Caldera which is formed after a volcano erupts, blowing the top of the mountain away. The resulting depression fills first with lava and then with water which forms lakes and thermal pools. The caldera at Yellowstone extends for seventy miles by thirty and is approximately six miles deep.

Scientists and archaeologists have discovered and recorded that this caldera has blown at least twice at 600.000 year intervals, the last time 640.000 years ago. It is now overdue for another eruption. If it does blow, it will spread billions of tons of rock and dust into the atmosphere blocking out the sun's rays and creating a global wide nuclear winter. As a measure of how much dust will be expelled, the last time it happened, two meters of dust was deposited in Iowa which is a thousand miles away. The dust so high in the atmosphere will block out the suns rays and temperatures on Earth will plummet until no crops can be grown and billions will starve to death. The last time it happened nothing larger than a dog survived.

Reports have been coming in of activity in this region with small volcanic movements happening more and more frequently. The earth in the region of the lakes has risen out of the ground by about a yard, giving rise to speculation that the magma chambers far below the surface are moving, creating unheard of pressures which could ultimately blow in one enormous explosion.

If this happens it will be catastrophic for all mankind and it is possible that out of the world's population only a few thousand people might survive.

The Survivalists, Book 2, **The Finale**

Francis Wait

The Story so far

The phone rang in the middle of the night, and bleary eyed, James groped in the general direction of the bedside table, and picked it up, fearful that something awful had happened to either of his children. "Hello," he said irritably "Who's this ringing at this ungodly hour?"

"Is that James?" The voice sounded vaguely familiar.

"Yes," James snapped. "Whoever you are, what on earth are you doing ringing me in the middle of the night?"

"James, mate, it's Rex. Remember me from our army days?"

How could James ever forget? In the invasion of the Falklands he'd crawled out in front of enemy fire and dragged a badly injured Rex to safety.

"What's this all about?"

"Listen. I've got something vitally important to tell you. Since you saved my life, I've owed you one, big time, now I've got the chance to save yours."

"What on earth are you talking about?"

"I need your e-mail address right now. The message I send will explain everything, but you have to act on it as soon as you can. I can't stress how important this is. The US Government is keeping a lid on something that may end up being globally catastrophic. They know I have access to this information, and it wouldn't surprise me if someone was watching me right now, so I can't talk for long. I'm phoning from an outside line here in the States, and when I've got your e-mail address I'll send you some mail from an Internet café in the hope it can't be tracked down."

James frowned, "Have you been drinking Rex? This is just ridiculous."

By now Patricia had woken up. "Who's that on the phone? It isn't about the kids is it? Are they all right?"

"No, its Rex, remember him? I saved his life when we were in the Falklands. I think he's having a bit of a funny turn."

"Well put the phone down and get back to sleep." She mumbled angrily.

v

Rex must have heard the conversation, "James, James, listen to me," he yelled, "This isn't a joke, I'm stone cold sober, this is for real and if you and your family want to stay alive, you must give me your e-mail address and I'll send you a message that will explain everything."

Still unconvinced that this wasn't a big wind up, James reluctantly told Rex how to get in touch.

"I'm going to send the message right now and I'd urge you to act on it straight away"

"All right, I will. Thanks mate." By now, James just wanted Rex to get off the line.

"Oh come on, let's get back to sleep," muttered Patricia as she snuggled down.

But James couldn't get the call out of his mind, so he went to his study and switched on the computer.

"What are you doing?" Patricia was standing behind him.

"Rex says he's sending a vitally important e-mail, and we must act on it, as our lives depend on it."

"He must really be having a funny turn; what utter rubbish. Leave it and come back to bed."

The computer pinged and 'One new message' appeared in the corner of the screen. James clicked on the anonymous words, 'From your Pal.'

They both read the contents.

"Oh my God," exclaimed James, turning to Patricia and holding her tight. "This looks as if it's genuine and if it is we've got to change our entire lives."

This message had struck fear into Jim's breast as the prediction was that dust from a catastrophic volcanic explosion in The Yellowstone Park would spread over the planet and nuclear winter would descend on earth. No crops would be grown for at least ten years and billions were going to die of starvation.

He can't abide the thought that the leaders of any civilization will use their power to make certain they survive; and emerge when the crisis is over to take up the reins of power again, because they contribute nothing to a community who can only live by hard work and the power of their hands. He recruited people who would be useful in a new society which they could form when the disaster is over. People such as teachers, doctors, builders, and farmers.

At first everyone is reluctant to go along with his ideas but he manages to convince his family and some friends to sell all their possessions and move into the outback in Australia and build a large indoor farm with water running deep underground and erect a large windmill to supply their power. They are in the process of building when disaster strikes! The police get wind that they have bought arms to protect themselves from the inevitable chaos and breakdown of society, and Jim is forced to flee to the home of a smuggler they know. The police track them down and when they find them they raid the smugglers home. One person gets shot and killed, and Jim's wife Pat declares that she wants nothing more to do with the scheme. Can Jim convince her to come back on board, as without her the whole enterprise would be threatened?

*The Survivalists, Book 2, **The Finale***

Chapter One

Ray with Dick by his side watched the plane disappear and head off, then he turned to Leah who was standing near and said. "I want you to figure out a way for us to get that Abbo on his own, and make him an offer to keep his eyes closed." Then he said to Dick, "I want you to get rid of that electrician all the time that copper's here. The more I see of that guy the less I trust him, I thought he was OK when he first came but now I've got my doubts."

Leah broke in with her characteristic sarcasm. "What do you want me to do darling? Make him an offer of my beautiful body and tempt him with a repeat performance if he's a good little guy?"

Ray sighed. "I thought you were a little more inventive than that dearest, do your best, I'm sure you can think of something." He snapped his fingers. "I know, the best we can do is offer him some of the best incentive in the world." He rubbed the tips of his fingers with his thumb. "Money; I'm sure he'll have a price."

"How long does the electrician have to disappear?" Dick asked.

Ray was clearly unable to answer the question, he shrugged his shoulders. "You know, on second thoughts bring him over to the construction workers and I'll talk to them all at the same time." Dick strolled off down the road to call him, and Ray went over to the site to call the workers down. They had started to lay the shuttering for the concrete floors on the top of the ground floor and it looked to him that they would start to pour the concrete as soon as they had enough men to start the heavy job of mixing and pouring in one smooth operation.

When they had all gathered and the electrician had joined them, Ray started to make them his offer. It was noticeable from the start that the electrician was going to make a nuisance of himself, as his first question was why he was being asked to break the law. Ray tried to explain that it wasn't actually breaking the law, more bending it a little, a fine distinction in Australia. Then the inevitable question came. "How much?"

At least Ray was prepared for this and made an offer that was as much as they could earn in a month. The electrician hung out until they agreed on six weeks salary, although, as Ray pointed out darkly. "If this gets out now, or in the future, I'll come looking for you with all the resources at my disposal and one result will be that you won't work anywhere for a long time afterwards."

He omitted to enlighten them as to what that meant but left it to their imagination. The men accepted his offer and looking at his watch the leader said. "It's about time for a break lads, so let's go over to the caravan and have a sit down." Ray went back to his caravan to see how Leah was getting on and passed Julia talking quietly with Dick. She called him over as he passed and asked what they should do when the police arrived. He told her to act as normally as possible and just do what she would usually do when they came. All she had to do was claim she didn't know what deliveries had been made in the last week or so. He finished. "Just plead innocence, you don't know anything, but don't lie at all or try and make up stories because you think it might sound better. They can catch you out that way, it's much better to say I don't know, than anything else."

He left them and went in to see how Leah was getting on with her plan and she smiled with achievement." I think I've got it covered now, we've got to split them up somehow so someone can get to talk to the Abbo, and I think I can do that"

Ray looked questioningly at her and asked. "What do you reckon you could be doing about that?"

She smiled slyly. "I've got a couple of things up my sleeve to try, so give me a few minutes, and I'll be out."

He went back outside and saw that Dick and Julia were still waiting for him so went over to sort things out with them. Julia smiled when he approached and said. "I know, act all surprised when he asks me any questions. And pretend I don't know anything that goes on around here."

Ray nodded in agreement and would have answered but a shout from their caravan alerted him to something happening with the construction workers, he ran over quickly and when he entered the door, he was greeted with a scene of destruction and in the middle the electrician sat nursing his jaw. A quick glance round told him that the foreman was responsible as he had his hand in front of himself and was massaging his knuckles. "What the hell are you lot playing at?" He asked angrily, "Can't you think of anything better to do than start fighting just before the police arrive?"

"Yeah, well if you knew what had been said just now you might be thanking me instead of shooting off at the mouth like that." The foreman shook his hand to loosen it and then massaged it further. "He started to gee everybody up to ask for more money, he figured he could hold you to ransom as you had no time to argue with him."

Ray looked at the electrician who by now had spat a tooth out and was regarding it sombrely as he explored his mouth with his tongue. Bending down he spoke into the man's face from a few inches away. "When I spoke to you out there we made an arrangement, then we shook hands on it. I'm a man who always keeps his word, so what gives you the right to go back on a deal?"

The man flinched back as much as he could as Ray had got too close to him and invaded his body space, and he looked worried that Ray might hit him again. "I only wanted to get a bit of extra cash," he whined, "You know you can afford it, and it just makes it easier to make ends meet. I didn't mean any harm in it."

"I've already told you what's going to happen if you start rocking the boat so you'd better start forgetting all those ideas about extra money right now." Ray said angrily. He took hold of the front of the mans shirt and thrust his face to within inches of his. "Now get this straight, I'm in no mood to take any nonsense from you, so get out there and act like you said you would and don't forget what I said to you earlier. If anything goes wrong here today, you're going to be the one I'm looking for and I can assure you mate, that's the last thing you want." He pushed the man back so his head hit the side of the caravan with a thump. "Do I make myself clear?"

The electrician rubbed the back of his head and looking at Ray he nodded his head slowly. Satisfied, Ray stood and glared round the caravan. "Is there anyone else who fancies trying their luck?" To a man they all shook their heads. Ray said. "Right I want you out there working pronto, I want this camp looking normal when the police arrive. You." He pointed to the foreman. "I want you to hang on for a minute, I want a word."

The men filed slowly out and went off to start work. Ray gestured to the table and chairs and they sat for a moment while Ray got his senses back and then he looked at the man and grinned. "Thanks a lot for handling that, it could have got out of hand if you hadn't stopped it so quickly."

The man looked at Ray quizzically. "Look mate, I don't know what's going on here and to tell the truth I don't think I want to find out, but it's got to be something queer, and you're going to get a lot more curiosity about this place. Now those coppers are coming out here for a reason, and I think the reason's got a lot to do with that load that came out here the other day." He looked Ray straight in the eye. "I've got a pretty good idea what it was, and I want it to stay an idea, I just hope you've got it well hidden away, because if it's found you are going to be in a lot of trouble. The other thing I'll say is that if I make a deal, I keep my end of it and I expect the other guy to do the same." He stood and went to the door. "I'd better get back before that load of idiots over there muck the work up."

He turned to go out of the door and suddenly stopped, his eyes bulging out and his mouth dropped open, a voice came from outside. "Are you going to stop blocking that door and let me in? And put your eyes back in their place, this getup isn't for your benefit." He stepped back slowly and Leah pushed past him to enter and Ray's eyes did the same as the foreman's had moments earlier. She had dressed herself in the skimpiest outfit Ray had ever seen her wear. Her skirt barely covered her long legs and the skimpy blouse hung loosely over her breasts, it was translucent and Ray could see her nipples clearly through it. Her breasts jiggled slightly as she stepped through the door on the highest pair of heels possible.

"What the hell do you think you're doing, wearing something like that?" Ray gasped, "You'll cause a riot walking around dressed that way."

"Don't worry about that, these guys can see more than this any day down the beach, if they could drag themselves out of the pub to go there. This is to take that coppers eyes away from searching too closely, so you can get to that Abbo and make a deal. I figured the copper would like to sit and watch me rather than search the place."

"I'd like to sit and watch you myself." Ray joked, he leered at her, "When he's gone I've got an idea about what to do to pass the rest of the evening away."

"Put em back in lover boy, we've got to get rid of this bloke first." She pushed him back into his seat. "How long have we got before he comes anyway?"

Ray involuntarily looked out of the window. "Not long, I should think. The last I heard it was three hours and that times about up now."

Leah walked over to the window and as she looked out she said over her shoulder. "Have you got it sorted with those guys over there?"

Ray shrugged. "As far as I can; that sparks is going to cause some trouble unless we're very careful, I didn't know what I was letting myself in for when I took him on. I think I'll have to get rid of him one way or other, but I can't do it yet, he's got a big mouth. I can control him when he's here but if he leaves I won't be able to shut him up quite so easily."

Leah turned and said shortly. "You never want to listen to anyone else do you? And if you'd asked I could have told you what he's like. That guy loves causing trouble and he's never going to get any better. He was a greedy bastard when we hired him and he's greedy still. I think you'd better leave him to me when this is over, I'll see what I can do to control him, and I've got one or two ideas about the way to treat him."

To tell the truth Ray was only too pleased to leave the problem to her, he knew that women are much more used to being direct than a man and if she wanted to take on the sparks, as far as he was concerned she was welcome. His musings were interrupted by her turning away from the window and checking how she looked. He became aware of a new sound outside and he heard the noise of a car engine, he walked over to the window and could see the police car had turned up. He went outside in time to see the window slide down as the policeman looked out. He bent down to it and was greeted by a blast of ice cold air as the air-conditioned interior vented to the outside. He was about to speak to him when the mans eyes slid past him to watch Leah coming towards them. She reached the car and bent down to say hallo to the man and his eyes were drawn irresistibly to her neckline. The blouse gaped open and he could look straight down to see her breasts swinging gently a few inches from his nose, he stared at her transfixed and a sweat broke out on his forehead that couldn't be entirely put down to the heat.

Ray looked down and from his viewpoint he could see her breasts in all their glory and the nipples swelled slightly as she felt the close scrutiny the policeman gave her. Still holding her stance she spoke. "Well hallo there, and to what do we owe the pleasure of this visit from our wonderful police force?"

The policeman finally managed to tear his eyes away from the view and remembering what he had come for he started to open the door, she stepped back slightly to let him stand but gave him no room and he was forced to brush against her as he stood slowly by the door. He mopped his brow with a tissue and reaching down he picked up his cap from the seat and placed it on his head, settling it with a pull on the brim. He tried to step back to make some room but his back pressed up against the car and Leah followed him, still giving him no room, he looked around wildly and seeing the Aborigine had dismounted from the car he called him over, trying to look officious at the same time.

Before he had a chance to give any orders Leah said. "You must be exhausted officer, why don't you come in and we'll get you a nice long cold beer."

Ray started to grin at the hapless officer and the man looked at Ray over her shoulder and said to him. "I'm er, I'm on duty and I'm not supposed to drink."

Leah put her hand out and laid it on his arm, the man started and flinched away as if he had been stung. "Oh come now." She said. She looked around the compound. "There's nobody here to see you have one little itsy bitsy beer is there?"

He shook his head, lost for words and she took his arm to lead him towards the caravan, taking the opportunity to press herself against his elbow with the side of her breast. She went up the two steps to the door and he paused turning his head and called out to the aborigine "Take a look around while I question these people." He added sternly. "And don't accept any free booze while you're here."

Leah led him straight to the caravan and seating him facing the large fridge in the corner, she stepped over to it with her behind swaying. When she reached it she opened it and looked inside. She called out over her shoulder. "The coldest beers are always at the bottom aren't they?"

She bent over from the waist down and the mans eyes almost popped out of their sockets as the skirt rode up to reveal her rounded bottom with the merest scrap of cloth between the cheeks. She selected a beer and turned with a smile, he licked his lips as she set it down and opened it, then sat on a chair opposite him and crossed her legs flashing her panties at him again. She filled the glass to brimming and said; "Now I want you to tell me all about why you're here."

Outside Ray had been watching through the door and knew that Leah would have everything under her control, and he marvelled at the stupidity of man who could let the sight of a sexy woman put them off and distract them from their true purpose. He knew he would have done exactly the same as the man himself if it had happened to him, and felt mildly sorry that the policeman would let it happen and not be any the wiser for it. He turned to the Aborigine and said. "What do I call you mate?"

The aborigine had been watching the turn of events and could see as well as anyone else that he was going to get no sense out of the policeman for a while yet. He turned his dark eyes to Ray and said. "You can call me Jimmy, if you want."

He started to walk away from Ray and looked around as he went, but stopped when Ray came alongside him and said. "Fancy a beer Jimmy?"

"You heard what the man said." Came the surly response. "I ain't to have no beer."

Ray waved his hands to stop the words coming and said. "He won't know if you just have one will he?"

The man licked his lips, Ray knew he had him hooked and all he had to do was reel him in. He followed him over to the other caravan and Ray poured him a beer from a Darwin stubby. He left the bottle on the table and the man picked it up and studied the dew forming on the side of the glass and with one swift motion drunk the whole glass down and placed it back on the table. Ray grinned and said. "I reckon you must be a bit thirsty."

"You don't know the half," the man replied, "That bastard over there drinks his in front of me and then says I've got to brew up in a Billy for myself."

They chatted for a while and at last Ray broached the subject of why they had come; he knew already but it was the easiest way to bring the question up. The man told him that they had had a tip off from an unknown source that a delivery of guns and ammunition had been made here and they were here to find them. They talked this over for a while and then Ray made him an offer, which he knew the man wouldn't turn down. It took Jimmy only moments to work out how long he could live from such a sum and they agreed that he would go and have a good look round with his eyes closed. He left the caravan when he had finished the bottle and ran up the slope to start circling the compound. He came back three hours later and went in to report to the policeman; by this time the man was quite drunk and almost ready to start trying to paw Leah. Jimmy told him he had found nothing anywhere in the vicinity. The policeman snarled at him to get out and look around again completely forgetting that if he had wanted to find anything he could have found it.

Jimmy shrugged and looking at the policeman he went outside where he said to Ray. "Don't ever tell me the white man is superior to the black man, especially when I have to work for a stupid racist like that. I wouldn't have found those guns hidden on that cliff face for all the money they give me because of him. You could have saved the cash if you went about it the right way."

Ray studied him through wary eyes, 'so the man was good, and he'd found the hiding place with very little difficulty'. Jimmy could see the expression on his face and smiled. "It'll be alright in about four or five weeks when it's had time to settle down a bit, right now anyone half decent could spot it."

Ray breathed a sigh of relief and sat down at one of the tables scattered around, Jimmy came and sat down with him and Ray spoke and offered him another bottle, the man's eyes flicked to the caravan where the sound of the policeman's voice could be heard sounding louder as he drank more and more. "Don't worry about him." Ray said. "It won't be long before he passes out the way he's knocking it back, it wouldn't surprise me if she's not spiking it as well to knock him out sooner."

"Yeah, well in the circumstances I suppose another beer won't be missed will it?" the man replied, "by the way," he went on, "I'll accept half what we agreed, it's worth it to see that bloke being taken for a ride."

"Every man's worth what he's paid," Ray answered. "You've done me a service and you're going to get what I promised to give you. A deal's a deal."

The smell of cooking came from the contractors caravan as Julia got to work and Ray looked at his watch to find the time had gone by and it was coming up to evening and time to eat. The contractors strolled over to the showers they had erected and soon they had a gathering round the table. Leah appeared at the top of the steps to come down and was greeted by a series of wolf whistles and some clapping as they admired her dress. She held her hand up with the fist clenched in triumph and looking at Ray she said. "He's passed out, and he won't be coming round for a long time."

The men hooted at this as the traditional enemy of the drinking classes suffered another defeat. Ray popped his head round the door to look at the recumbent copper lying on his side on the floor snoring. Leah entered the caravan after him and sat down and gestured to him to sit as well. "He asked me about Jim and Pat before he got too drunk, he seemed pretty sure they weren't here legally."

Ray swore. "Now it's another thing to worry about. What did he say exactly?"

"All he said was that he'd like to meet them and see their passports."

"Did he know they were here?"

"I told him they only came out occasionally, but that they owned the company that's building this place." She smiled mockingly. "I didn't bother to tell him we all owned a bit of the company as well. He'll have to go to Company's House in England to find the true shareholding."

Ray grinned. "You seem to have stitched him up good and

proper." He leered at her dress. "I'll have to find some way to say thank you won't I? Got any ideas?"

"That's not going to thank me in the way I want," she answered, "I want to get away and stay in a nice hotel and have food and showers laid on for a bit instead of all this sweat and hardship out here." She smirked, and looking at his crestfallen face she went on. "But before that happens what did you have in mind?"

The following day it was a sad and sorry policeman who stumbled down the steps. He almost ran to the toilet block and could be heard retching as he bent over. Leah gave him a towel and let him use the showers but it did nothing for his temper and he snapped at Jimmy to get in the car and before he left he turned to the grinning crowd of people watching him depart. He pointed his finger at them and said. "I know there's something queer going on out here, and I'm going to find out what it is if it takes me a year."

A disembodied voice came from the back. "With his intelligence, you'd better make that ten."

He stared at them, trying to put a face to the voice but failed, then climbed in to the car and gunned the engine in his temper as he sped down the track to go back to 'civilisation' as he had called it. After the dust had settled Ray turned to the men and called out. "OK, men the shows over, lets get on with some work, I want to see that concrete laid for the upper floor as soon as possible."

It was two weeks before Jim flew in with Andrew and Pat, and the concreting had been going well under Ray's supervision. They had hardly touched down before Ray had arrived at the plane to welcome them. How did it go then?" Ray asked.

Jim smiled, "It went better than I thought it would," He answered. They took everyone to court for various things; when Blackie went into court we all thought he was going to get done for smuggling, but he turned it right round by asking if they had found any drugs, or for that matter anything illegal anywhere. But that copper Tom Wilkins hadn't found anything at all, he was in court and when it all came out the magistrate was scathing, and said if he comes before him again with half baked theories he'd make sure he lost his job. But Blackie had better make sure he looks out for himself in the future because that sergeant will be after his blood."

Ray asked "But where did Blackie hide all the stuff then?"

Jim shrugged, "I haven't got a clue, he didn't say and I didn't want to know. All I wanted was to be out of there, and luckily I did."

"How did you manage that?" Ray asked.

"Well I'm not actually sure what happened, they put me in front of a magistrate and he looked at all the stories from me and the prosecution, and then said the verdict was unsafe because the Defence Solicitor hadn't taken enough trouble to defend me. He said she didn't stress that I hadn't loaded the trolley with the fruit; it wasn't mine in the first place; it was Dianne's, and also we had it for medical reasons. And we probably wouldn't have brought it in, in the first place had we had warnings about it. And from my point of view they didn't prove it was diseased anyway. Although that wasn't a feasible argument."

"Well all I can say is you're one lucky bastard," Ray said admiringly, "so what's the position with you being here in Oz?"

"I get the normal six months visitors stay then I'll have to apply to continue longer, but if I'm in business here I should be able to get my application through fairly easily. Andrew can still stay with Victoria if they get married. So it's not a bad lookout for the future although I'll still have to keep my nose clean. Now you'd better bring me up to date on the progress you've made here."

Ray started to tell them how he had offered the Aborigine some cash not to find anything and caught Jim staring at him with a puzzled expression on his face. "How much did you offer him?" He asked.

Ray said. "Well, I offered him enough to last him for about three months without working."

Jim, Andrew, and Pat looked at each other and started to laugh. "OK." Ray said, "What's the joke?"

"You've been taken for a ride mate." Jim answered, "When he heard about it, Blackie knew he could get involved as the carrier, so he took his own action to stop that Abbo finding anything. He paid him off before he came out here, so your guy's been paid twice for that service he did for us."

Ray raised his eyes to the sky. "If I see the little sod again I'll skin him alive," he grated, "no wonder he offered me a discount because the copper treated him so bad, I thought it was because I treated him right." He thought for a moment. "So all that business about Leah getting the copper drunk and putting one over him was for nothing," he looked at them, "One thing's for sure, it had better be one of you that tells her that, I'm going to make myself very scarce when she finds out."

They had arrived back by now and as they got out of the Ute they stopped to ponder on one aspect of this incident that remained unsolved. When it came to the question of who had informed on them, no one had a definite answer. They had some suspects but not one person who could gain very much from their actions. "Perhaps it's just because they don't like us or something." Jim said hopefully.

Even Pat who had an unerring instinct for getting to the root of a problem with a combination of observation and what she called 'feelings' had no idea of whom it might be. Leah came out of the caravan with a broad smile on her face and suddenly Ray found he had some urgent business with the contractors and disappeared in their direction. She watched him go with a puzzled look and then greeted them with the words. "Boy, have I enjoyed myself since I last saw you," she grabbed Pat by the arm and said, "Come on in, I'll get something to drink and bring you up to date on events here." She led Pat towards the caravan saying. "How was it at Blackie's? I heard the landing strip wasn't up to much, was it difficult to land there?" Pat looked helplessly over her shoulder as she went but could see no help from anyone else, they were all grinning and backing away to put as much space between the caravan and themselves as they could.

They went inside and a short while later there came an almighty crash as something hit the side of the caravan and Leah could be heard screaming at the top of her voice, Jim laughed, "I don't think I'd like to be in that Abbo's shoes if she comes across him when she's in town."

He looked at the others and said. "Well, I think the shows just about over; we'd better get a bite to eat and then get on with this building." He glanced over to where Ray was pretending to work while keeping a close eye on the caravan and went on. "If we get over there we can start pushing this concreting on. I want to see it all finished before the months out, and then we can fit the top floor. A lot of that's going to be glass for the extra light."

Andy frowned. "Do you think it's a good idea to have a lot of glass on top of there, we'll never be able to defend it if we're attacked?"

Jim grimaced. "I never intended to ever defend that floor, it's disposable. I've ordered enough glass anyway to rebuild it if necessary. The bottom floor if you look, is solid concrete and brick, it's not impregnable but I'm relying on the fact that if anyone comes they won't think of bringing anything like rockets or stuff like that. And it's far enough away from supplies of those that I don't think it'll come to using them anyway. And also." He held his finger up to stop Andy. "If someone wants to attack us it'll be to take it over or make us work for them, either way it won't do them any good to destroy it because if they do they lose anyway. They need to take it whole."

Andy shook his head at this; "I think you're not reading this situation right Dad, there's enough people out there who would destroy something they can't have, just so you can't have it either."

"All right Andy I agree with you." Jim replied. "But what have I said to you before? If it comes to it, the best defence we'll have isn't to sit inside cowering away, we've got to get outside and carry the fight to them, or otherwise we're a sitting target for whoever comes. History should tell you that no one can defend a building anyway, nothings impregnable."

This was music to Andy's ears and he went happily off to find the electrician and start laying cable down the road to set up the CCTV cameras. Jim and Dick went over to join Ray and start work. By the Friday they had made satisfactory progress and when the contractors started to pack up to go home, Jim pulled Ray to one side. "When these guys have gone I know you want to go and get the Prof and Colette but we've got a job to do first. When I went to Blackie's we loaded all the ammo on the plane instead of him delivering it and it's still there. We've got to get it out and up to the cave before you can leave."

Ray turned to him with an astonished look on his face. "You

left it out there sitting in the open all that time. What would have happened if the police had come back out here? You'd have had no chance of talking yourself out of that one."

"It's called hiding it in plain view. Face up to it mate, nobody even thought to look in the plane at all have they?"

They took Dick and drove down to the plane, the ammunition was held in several large and heavy boxes under a tarpaulin in the back behind the seats. They hauled them out and put them on the Ute under the same tarpaulin and drove back to camp. Andy drove back up the road to join them with the electrician, who jumped in with the contractors for the long journey home. When they had gone, they drove the Ute back up the cliff and unloaded it there. This done, Jim gave a sigh and looked at Ray. "You might as well get off and pick up the others in the plane; we'll see it all gets stowed away properly."

Ray blinked in surprise but raised no objection, climbing down cliffs wasn't high on his list of pursuits so he went off happily to take the plane and pick the others up. When he had gone Andy said. "Why did you let him go off on his own Dad, I need the experience of flying?"

"Maybe." Jim replied but you would have been one body too many today, because that Biologist and his wife are coming and maybe some of the kids. I don't know how many but I know they'll all try and get in. So he'll have at least six adults on there plus kids as well, I don't know how much that lot'll weigh but maybe someone's going to be disappointed anyway. If you were there it's just so much extra baggage."

"Who's the sixth person then? I only count five adults." Andy looked questioningly at Jim, who smiled knowingly.

"Have you forgotten so soon about Victoria?" He asked.

"Aw, Christ Dad, she's coming and you didn't even bother to let me know?"

"Yeah, well I thought it would only put you off your work, you'd be mooning about like some lovesick calf and we'd never get any work out of you."

Andy slammed his tools to the floor. "I'm going to go and get ready, and I've got to have a shower and shave and get some clean clothes on before she comes."

Jim put his hand on his chest to stop him walking back down the hill to the camp. "Hold on there son, she won't be here for hours and we've got to get this ammunition down to the cave before we go anywhere."

Staring at his father with his face suffused with anger he looked then to be the image of himself when he had been younger, but now Jim wasn't as forgiving as he had been so he said. "Come on, lets get this stuff down to the cave and under cover, then you can have as many showers as you want."

It was with bad grace that Andy stayed to help and lug the heavy cases down on the scaffold that Jim had erected, but finally they had all the ammunition in place and the entrance sealed once more. When he surveyed it from only a few feet Jim found it hard to spot anything that would identify it, but he was reminded that the Aborigine had spotted it easily. He marvelled once more at the difference in cultures and how many Australians never gave them any credit for their long-lived race, quite forgetting the Abbos had been in Australia for possibly eighty thousand years. They were clever in a way the average Australian could hardly comprehend.

Andy went over to the Ute and started the engine. "Come on then." He called to Jim and Dick who grinned at each other, and walked slowly over to join him for the ride back. He revved the engine impatiently and was off down the hill as they were trying to seat themselves. "Take it easy son," Jim said, "You've got hours before she arrives."

"You'd better get us fitted up with a better form of communication before long," Andy answered, "If you got a satellite phone things would be more comfortable around here, we could get on the internet then. You know we don't get hardly any reception on the cell phones this far out."

"I was waiting to install it in the building so we wouldn't have to keep shifting it about, is all," Jim snapped, "Someone's got to watch the cost of things around here, you don't realise how quickly the money goes."

Dick who normally kept his peace when they started to argue said. "When we get the first floor finished, there's no reason we can't start working on the indoor farming bit. And also the fruit out there will be ready soon so we could have a few days picking the crop and then sell that. At least it'll bring in some cash."

Andy stopped the Ute with a squeal of the brakes and a flurry of dust and jumping out he slammed the door and went running in to his quarters. Pat and Julia appeared in the door. "What's up with him?" Pat asked.

"He's just found out Victoria's coming out today," Jim grinned.

Pat raised her eyes to heaven. "I suppose that means nobody's going to get in the shower for a while then."

They heard the plane coming in eventually but not before Andy had almost driven his mother mad with demands for clean clothes, well pressed of course and changed them several times until she was driven to say. "If you change those clothes once more I swear I'll bung the whole lot back in the wash and you can do them yourself."

When it arrived, they watched in amazement as a total of six adults and five children climbed out, happily chattering and laughing with relief that they had arrived safely. Victoria introduced them to Martin and Liz his wife the biologists with their two children Stuart, 15, who tried to affect a blasé demeanour in front of the younger children, and his younger sister Becky, 14, who looked excitedly at all the preparations they were making. She was soon asking questions of whoever would answer them and seemed quite taken with the idea of what they were attempting to do.

They had prepared food and after they had eaten Jim took the two biologists on a tour of the works. They had, by this time laid concrete over most of the ceiling on the ground floor and within a week Jim estimated they would finish that completely. It stretched away into the distance and Martin commented on how vast the floor area was. Jim explained that they intended to house animals as well and also they had to have a large storage area for commodities they couldn't make themselves. The pre-packed foods would take up a large area also, although as he pointed out, when they were eaten the space would get bigger. While they were looking, the children were running around playing and making friends with each other. Martin wanted to see all the preparations so Jim took them right to the back and showed him they had laid a service pipe to the windmill up on the hill to run both water and electricity down to them. Then they went up a ladder to the first floor and he showed them the area that would be housed in glass. At the end of the tour Martin turned to Jim and commented. "All this is based on the assumption that a volcano is going to blow up some time in the future; do you honestly think it's ever going to happen?"

Jim took his time before trying to answer the question. "I know that that Yellowstone Caldera is definitely on the move and it's still giving out small eruptions. My mate told me that it can go on for some time like that until one day when the pressure builds up to a peak and it can blow like no other volcano has ever done in the last 640,000 years. If it does go, there's no other place on Earth that I'd rather be than here, because we'll have the best chance that any person can have. Also, I've given it a great deal of thought over the last year, and I've come to the conclusion that it doesn't really matter if it does or not. Think of what we've got here, we've got a community with a great deal to offer. We can be self-sufficient and we can make a profit from what we produce as this place can turn out far more than we need to live. The children can be happy here without ever getting involved in all the things that are on offer for them in larger towns, like drugs and so on. They can have a good education because the teacher we have can give them personal study periods with no bother about teaching to large classes. We've got our own Doctor if we need medical treatment. If disaster does strike, and it's always possible, we have a very good chance of surviving if we live our lives here until the danger passes. There's sufficient water for agriculture and electricity for running everything, so it could be a good life either way, and we'll have covered all the options."

Martin looked at Liz who was regarding them with large solemn eyes and they then seemingly reached an agreement and he turned back to Jim and said. "We talked this over before we came here and we agreed that if we were satisfied on this trip we'd throw in our lot with you, but." He held his hand up to stop Jim from speaking. "I want to make it clear that we reserve the right to leave if we want to and to take out our investment when we do go. I think that I personally can make a great contribution to your efforts here if you follow my advice. I don't think that this is going to last any more than a few years if that volcano doesn't blow; people get disillusioned very quickly when nothing happens. It might work if you try and make a community here, but the trouble with that is the young ones won't want to stay. But as I said, I'll give you some time; I can do some valuable research while I'm here."

Jim let the air out of his lungs, he had unconsciously been holding his breath and the relief was palpable, he was aware of the potential this man had and was pleased to hear that he would stay. He held his hand out and said. "At the moment I'll take you on those terms." He shook their hands and went on, "I think you'll get to like it out here anyway. At the moment everybody gets on pretty well."

He turned and surveyed the vast room and said. "You'll have to see Victoria and start drawing up plans for this area; it's all going to be your responsibility."

"They're already drawn up, I got the dimensions from her and started on them before I came out here, I can let you have specifications for all the equipment we'll need. I'm transferring capital into your bank account as soon as we draw up an agreement and get it signed and into the bank and we'll start moving out here in two weeks when I finish this term in the college."

Jim whistled. "You don't let the grass grow under your feet do you? I expected you to be humming and hawing for weeks while you made up your mind."

"I was interested in this project from the first time I spoke about it to Victoria," Martin answered, "I know it's not quite the same but I've always been interested in the idea of space travel and living on another planet, this is just the scheme to learn something about the difficulties of supplying food for something like that. Maybe if we can do that here, we can do it in space."

Jim shook his head, he couldn't believe that the man really thought that space travel was a possibility; he had seen some figures that suggested that a vehicle hurtling through space at twenty thousand miles an hour would take over a hundred thousand years just to reach the nearest star. Martin saw the expression on his face and exclaimed hurriedly. "I didn't mean about going to the stars, I meant going to the other planets, it would be possible to colonize

Mars under the right circumstances."

"Oh." Jim clearly wasn't impressed.

"Well." Martin was obviously used to people doubting his ideas. "No matter, I was merely making the point that the technology is much the same, so research here could help when we do explore the planets."

He touched Liz on the arm. "Shall we see if we can make any suggestions before we go?"

She nodded, and Jim found she was one of the people in life who rarely spoke unless she had something important to say. Martin turned back to Jim and said. "We'll just wander off for a bit and assess the situation, and maybe we can make things a bit easier." Jim smiled and left them to their own devices while he did some measuring at the front of the building, he had had an idea for some time now and the arrival of the policeman had crystallised his thoughts and he intended to make preparations that only the people who were involved in living there could know about. He expected that some people wouldn't let it go and wanted to make sure that they couldn't get caught again if they came snooping around. He intended to put a series of rooms across the back end of the building for storage and processing all the waste products and also to enclose the indoor farm. He had worked out a way of making it really difficult for anyone to enter the front of the growing area from the front living quarters. He had discussed this with Andy and Ray and agreed that it would be best to do it when the contractors had finished all their work to lessen the chances of someone discovering what they were doing.

Andy and Victoria strolled in and Andy said. "Well dad, you'll be pleased to know we're going to tie the knot next week and then Victoria can come out here and live, we want to take a week out and come out with Martin and Liz to start living here full time."

"Does your mother know?" Was the only thing Jim could think of saying. He realised he knew next to nothing about this girl who intended to marry his son, and asked her. "What about your parents, have you told them what you're doing?"

The answer to both questions was in the affirmative so they went out to find everybody rushing around to prepare for a celebration dinner or 'Barbie' as Ray insisted it be called. While this was going on Jim called Blackie on the mobile phone and asked him if he wanted to come into the town and help celebrate the wedding. At the same time he asked him to send two of his Abbo friends to stand guard whilst everybody was away for the wedding. There was no time to organise a big affair but Pat insisted she was going into town for the week and she would have the best available wedding come rain or shine, and in the event that was what they had in the way of weather, as the long awaited wet season started to kick in with some king sized rainfalls.

Within the next week the contractors came out and finished the concrete on the first floor and departed with pockets bulging. The team who would erect the glass roof were due to start the following week if they could get there with the road almost impassable. In all his life Jim had never seen such a sticky mess that the road turned into, but luckily the plane was still operative as they had had the foresight to lay shale over the whole strip and if they didn't use it too much the plane could scoot over the top without bogging down. Jim had sighed and wished he could have had the hovercraft delivered but it was still being constructed and would be brought to them later.

They flew down for the ceremony that Friday although Ray had to make two trips to ferry everybody down. The Aborigine guys had arrived to stand guard so Jim left them the keys to all the caravans except the one that had the booze in it, and left strict instructions to touch nothing and they would get a bonus if everything was there on their return. The wedding had to be conducted indoors much to Pat's chagrin as she had set her heart on it being outside, but torrential rain put paid to that idea. They regarded the river that flowed through Katherine and could see the level rising rapidly and the residents had started to make preparations for flooding. Victoria's parents had managed to come and were pleased to meet everybody connected to her. Ray insisted on being best man much to Dick's displeasure as he thought he should have held that position. Leah not to be outdone was matron of honour and several of the children were pages. They held a great reception after the wedding and Jim got pleasantly drunk with Pat glaring at him in the background, but she knew better than to try and say anything to him at that time. He acquitted himself quite well when he was called upon to make the traditional speech and the party went on much later into the night after the newly married couple left for a honeymoon to somewhere unknown to everybody. When they returned the following week Ray flew them all back and then they arranged for the team coming to erect the roof to be flown out the first day the weather permitted. Luckily they had had the materials delivered for the roof some weeks previously because the state of the road would have meant a long delay. Most of the road had been washed out along the route and it held up the delivery of all the materials Martin had ordered for the indoor farm.

They carried on working as much as possible during the wet but it was several weeks before the roof got erected. While it was being done they concentrated on building the living quarters at the front of the building and fitting them out was easy work to Jim as it was no more than a house tacked on to the front of an industrial building. The materials Martin had ordered came while they were erecting the living quarters, as a spell of a few days meant the road dried out sufficiently to harden enough for lorries to drive to them. They were loaded on to several of them in flat pack form and when they were all unloaded they carried them in painstakingly and left them for Martin, Liz and Victoria to assemble. Most of it was no more than steel troughs stacked several feet high which would be filled with compost and used to grow all their food.

The electrician was still with them and Jim had spoken to Ray several times to try and get another man to join them and possibly one more farmer who knew something about cropping inside. In the event it was Martin who overheard them discussing this and suggested they try his college as farmers in Australia saw no need to farm inside and wouldn't understand so they had canvassed around and came up with a former student who had several years teaching under his belt. He had agreed to join Martin and Liz and bring his family for a trial period. Jim was worried at this time as the electrician was installing all the cable needed to run the complex, and Jim thought that if only he knew where everything was it would cause difficulties later when repairs were needed. He knew he was prejudiced against the man but felt that if he didn't like him he would prefer he was gone.

With the roof finished they were able to start putting the finishing touches to the building and they installed all the fittings for processing the sewage and producing gas. The farm had been completed and an airtight door with an airlock had been fitted. The new recruit was designated to attend to the animals when they were brought out and given strict instructions on the care of them. This was basically to ensure they stayed free of disease. He was given one more job until they brought the stock in and that was to run the irrigation system around the building. At first glance it looked easy as they had bought all the pipe in plastic to ensure low maintenance but it proved very difficult to run as all the fittings had to be solid brass and he found it difficult to work; eventually Dick offered to help him and they proved to be a good team. The containers with all their possessions had arrived and been stacked to one side to be left until they knew what was going to happen.

Jim sat down one evening with Ray and had a look at the accounts and they found that they had probably a quarter of the original investment left and the building was almost finished. So he called a meeting of the committee for that evening to run over the finances. They met in the old contractor's caravan, which was now being used as a storeroom. Jim looked around the room, Pat was there and Dick, Ray sat opposite with Leah and Julia sat opposite them. Andy made himself comfortable at the other end of the table from Jim who sat at the other end and called them to order saying. "This is an official meeting and I want reports from all of you on the progress we've made, or not made as the case may be."

Dick spoke first. "We've made great progress with the building programme, and we could finish everything as far as construction goes within about two months. There is one thing I want to ask. When are we likely to see an electrician coming out here? We really need a handy man as the guy we've got is nothing but trouble"

Ray started up at this. "I hope you're not implying that it's my fault that he's here, I did my best to get a responsible guy, and you can't lay the blame at my door."

"All right, Ray," Jim butted in, "I don't think Dick was saying anything of the sort, he only said he wanted to get another handyman out here, and I tend to agree with him."

"I think I've arranged that to everyone's satisfaction," a voice said quietly. They all turned to stare at Leah, who smiled when she saw the puzzled looks on their faces. "I went into town a couple of days ago as you know, and I knew about this problem when I was there, So I gave this guy I knew a ring and he's coming up tomorrow to give us the once over."

Ray turned and looked at her. "Kept that bloody quiet didn't you?"

She smiled her sweetest smile at him and Jim quailed inside, he had seen that look before and dreaded it when she got in that sort of mood, as she could be so unpredictable. She said innocently. "I didn't think you'd mind as it was getting you out of that hole you dug for yourself when you hired that waster out there." She pointed out of the window at the electrician who had seated himself so he could watch the shower stalls where Victoria's feet could be seen under the screen as the water splashed around them. "He sits out there every time he can when the women go in for a wash, Christ knows what goes through his mind, but it's creepy when he stares at us women all the bloody time."

Ray stood as if to walk out and confront him but Leah pulled him back down. "Don't go making a bloody fool of yourself now dearie," she commented, "He's been doing it for months, and it's better to have him in plain sight so we know what's going on."

Ray sat down again reluctantly and said. "You could have said something before now couldn't you?"

"Maybe I could have darling.""But you've been so busy flying that bloody plane around I haven't had a chance to tell you anything have I?"

It had the ring of truth about it as Ray had been flying it quite a lot just lately but they had had to have a great quantity of supplies and the quickest way had been to let him fly them in. But Jim knew the time that Leah claimed she had hired the electrician had been the time she had flown in with Ray to see Schoonheid about some business, so she could have told him then. Ray had obviously thought the same thing as he half rose to face her and the anger showed clearly on his face.

"Just who is this guy you've found so easily then?" He asked. Clearly by now spoiling for a fight and ready to veto any person she asked, whatever the man was like.

She waved her hand airily in the air in front of his face. "Oh, you'll find out soon enough, I think we should get on with the rest of the days business before you forget why we're here."

Rays face went from red to bright red and he was about to explode when Jim defused the situation. "It's OK Ray, Leah spoke to me about this and I agreed to give the guy an interview for the job, that's all. Now I think we'd better get on with the business we came here for or we'll never finish this meeting."

Ray subsided back into his chair clearly dissatisfied with the turn of events and from the look he shot Leah it was clear the matter was far from over. Jim turned to Pat and asked her, "How is it coming along with supplies?"

She had some papers in front of her but laid them on the table while she spoke. "It's very simple from our point of view." She smiled and looked around at them. "As you know Julia has been helping me on this one and we've got the storage rooms at the back ready, we looked at all the items we use in our life, and we had to think what we could do without as there's no way we could bring everything we need for ten years. So we had to make a list of everything we use now and split it in half to decide what we can't supply. I'm afraid you're going to miss quite a lot of things in the future that you take for granted now. Clothing for a start, we've had to take a leaf out of Robin Hood's book and buy cloth in bulk, it's not exactly Sherwood green but we've bought a lot of cloth and we'll have to make our own clothes when what we've got runs out.

She heard the groans from around the room and said. "Think what the early settlers who came to Australia had to put up with, they had to make do with what they had and could make, and we're going to have to do the same." She paused to wait for them to settle down, then went on. "As far as food goes, I'll have to leave that to the experts but that pre-packed food Andrew has ordered apparently arrives next week and we'll have to store it somewhere dry as it comes in cardboard boxes direct from the factory."

She consulted the papers on the table in front of her. "There is one thing I want to say before we go on and that is. This crisis hasn't happened yet so we can carry on using a normal supply of the necessities of life but I'd like to quote one statistic to you to illustrate my point. Have any of you seen how much toilet paper we're getting through?" She stared at each of them in turn. "No. Well let me tell you, on average it comes out at one roll per person per week." Her gaze lingered on Leah. "And some of us seem to use at least twice that amount." She was rewarded with a reddening of Leah's face. "Anyway, that means approximately twenty five rolls a week we're buying. Multiply that up for a period of ten years and it comes out at more than twelve thousand rolls. Can you imagine how much storage space we would need just to wipe our behinds in comfort? So we've decided to make everyone use some towels and a bidet and if any of you want to know what a bidet is come and see me after and I'll tell you."

She held up her hands to stop the babble of noise that broke out. It was mostly sniggers from the men and arguments from the women but she persevered and when she had some silence she went on. "We should start earning some money back from the farming part of this business soon as the fruit ripens, I'm not into the finance side of it but we have to start using our skills to get back some money into the kitty or it's going to be a hard slog from now on. There are also a lot of items that we simply can't store and we'll have to stockpile enough and later, improvise. We," she gestured in Julia's direction. "Have been talking this over for a long time now and the consensus of opinion is that if indeed it does happen, we're going to be back in the dark ages in about ten years and unless we use the knowledge that we've acquired we won't survive in any degree of comfort at all."

Ray had been listening to this with some interest and now he interrupted her. "You know I've done a deal for all the computers and everything to go with them, we'll have the knowledge with us so what's the problem."

She turned to him with a sigh. "Look Ray I know you've done well with the equipment side of it but have you stopped to consider that the people who are going to be using it in the future won't understand half the terms it uses, most people over the age of fifty have to be taught how to operate the things in the first place. I understand that the knowledge is in there but accessing it is another matter."

"I think we should stop this argument right there." Leah interjected. "We've all got some computer experience and they'll be with us if anything happens and that's the last word. I personally think we've got to go on from that and sort out what we can store and what we'll have to manufacture ourselves."

Pat nodded her agreement with this view and started to tick off on her hands the points as she made them. "First, the main things are food and clothing; I think we can say that those are taken care of. Medical supplies are the next priority, Colette assures me she can stockpile quite a lot and Victoria said to me that she intended to create an extensive herb garden so we can maybe make some herbal remedies. We can operate a limited medical programme but for anything that requires up to date facilities it's going to be impossible, and like in the old days if you get cancer or any of the lesser known ailments you either die or get better. We've got electricity and water so they aren't a problem. It's the little luxuries we're going to miss; I'll make sure we have enough soap." She grinned at Leah when she said this. "And toothpaste, but it will run out one day and then it's back to the drawing board. I've been told we can make our own gas to run the motors so that'll be a bonus if there's anywhere we want to go when we leave here. That's about all I can think of for the moment so I'll hand it back to Jim."

She sat down and looked expectantly at him. He stood up and asked. "Has anybody else got anything to say?"

Leah had been following this exchange with interest and now she stood and said. "I know that my job here is almost over and when everything is built I'll have to look for a new one. In the beginning when we first agreed to go into this, my better half." She said with enough emphasis to show it was sarcasm. "Said he was going to get a computer expert in to look after the computers, well what I want to say is that the guy I spoke to earlier can do that job as well as the electrical work around here. But I want to offer to teach any one who wants to learn, all about programming the things, because I've done several courses on them and I'm well qualified to teach them as well."

She looked out of the window as she spoke and frowned slightly, Victoria had finished her shower and had walked over to the complex, and disappeared inside, the electrician had gone as well, so she assumed that as the show was over for him he'd gone to his caravan. But she couldn't spot him at all. Ray was talking now and she had to drag her attention from the window and concentrate to make any sense of what he was saying…….. "Be necessary to teach them about computers," she stared at him trying to make some sense from what she had heard and he assumed she thought it was rubbish.

"Why don't you answer?" He snarled. "Or am I flapping my gums in the wind for nothing."

She rubbed her hand over her forehead to give herself some time and finally cleared her head. "Well of course they have to learn about computers, not only how to use them but more importantly to be able to fix them both in the hardware and the software, if they can do that they can give any community a head start in the future. And while I'm thinking about it." She turned to look at Jim. "Have you done anything about getting a good broadband radio, one that's capable of broadcasting worldwide an all frequencies, especially short-wave, if there are any survivors after a catastrophe, the one sure way of communicating is by radio. The satellites up there will probably be inoperative by the time we want to use them."

"It's coming in a few days time." Jim answered, "I ordered it a long time ago, anybody else got anything to say?"

Ray held his hand up and said. "I do." He stood slowly to his feet and looked around at them as he did. "This won't take long," Julia smiled and said, "I've heard that before, usually before a long interminable speech from some school governor who's trying to impress everybody about his knowledge of the school system and how to run it efficiently."

They all smiled as she normally never opened her mouth except to make some acerbic comment about someone's stupidity.

Ray went on, "I really mean this won't take long; as we don't need a lot of the site equipment now I intend to take some of it into town in a few days and sell it for what we can get for it. We paid quite a lot out before and we should get a reasonable amount back for it. That contractor said he'd be interested in a few of the items and the rest should be easy to get rid of. I think we ought to keep one digger so if anything happens we can use that. I've got some brand new batteries for the Ute's and if we don't use them they'll keep for a long while. The computer equipment is on line to be delivered as soon as the space is available to install it. Which if my reckoning is right means that we can have it up and running in about two to three weeks."

He sat down immediately he had finished to signify he was done and looking around and finding no one had anything else to say he spoke himself. "All I want to say right now is that it all looks as if it's going to work out OK. As you know the growing medium for the seed beds was delivered last week and I spoke to Victoria earlier and she reckons to start a lot of the plants as early as next week, she's going to sow them up in trays and then move everything into the growing troughs in a week or two so we should start to get self sufficient in the food line soon after that as we're providing optimal conditions for quick growth. As you know we're going to start selling the produce in town to provide income for the time before we need to 'batten down the hatches' I think we'll start to see some profit coming back very soon from now, and we still have a balance in the bank to tide us over in the bad times," he looked at them again, "Any more comments?" One by one they shook their heads and he stood up and said. "That's it then, let's get finished here and get something to drink and relax."

Victoria looked around the vast space of the floor; they had started the erection of the staging for the plant growing area and they rose in tiers before her, five to a tier in rows that marched away from her into the distance. There were hundreds of them each consisting of an aluminium tray about a foot deep which was intended to hold the growing medium, they all had drainage holes in the bottom and weren't fixed down but left lying on the top of projections on the framework. This was intended to make it easy to lift them into different positions so each tray could be lifted into the light. Some of them had a simple ratchet and chain to make it easy to turn and so lift the trays to the top in rotation. The watering system hadn't been finished yet and there were rolls of piping scattered over the floor. At present the whole floor resembled a scrap yard, and only the growing troughs, which were in place, gave it some semblance of order.

It wasn't these that interested her at the moment and she walked over to the benches that had been placed round the outside so they could have somewhere to work on the seed trays. These consisted of a framework and the top surface was simply slats to allow the compost material to fall through to the floor where it could be swept up. She picked up a box that was lying on the top and looked inside. It contained several hundred packets of seed and they intended to eventually bring them all into production. She had waited a long time for this moment and now wanted to get on with it as soon as possible. As far as had been likely they had tried to purchase seeds that grew close to the original plant, as they could only with difficulty propagate hybrid varieties because they had been specially bred and only grew one year and then the seeds reverted to the type they had previously grown.

She sighed and thought to herself that maybe when things had settled down and they had a routine that they could possibly experiment and grow their own hybrids, but she understood that it was a lengthy process and better left to someone who knew exactly what they were doing. Bending down she picked up several seed trays and started to fill them from one of the sacks of growing medium that were lying ready by the side. Her hair was still damp from the shower as she preferred to let it dry naturally and it hung to her shoulders in long waves. She had only thrown a long robe on and had no underclothes under it as the weather although damp and rainy was still very warm. As she bent over the table a long tendril of hair fell over her forehead and she pushed it back with the back of her wrist so as not to get it dirty from her hands.

She hummed a tuneless ditty as she worked and methodically filled the trays, her fingers busy with the familiar work. Her elbow knocked into a tray as she worked and it fell to the floor with a little clatter and she bent down to retrieve it, she had bent from the waist and the movement stretched the robe over her round buttocks. Her fingers had just touched the tray to pick it up and she suddenly felt a hand placed right in the centre of her rear and a finger stroked gently up the cleft of her behind. She jumped as if shot and turned with a smile thinking Andrew had been responsible for the gesture, the smile died on her lips as she saw the leering face of the electrician. She swung her hand without thinking and slapped him in the face; he put his hand to the spot and rubbed it gently as he regarded her with some amusement.

This only served to infuriate her and she started to put her hand up and hit him again, her eyes blazing. It was a blow that never landed as he put his hand up swiftly to stop her. He grasped her wrist and the movement pulled her close to him. Keeping hold of her hand he put the other out and before she could stop him he grasped her breast and squeezed, then slid his hand round her back and held her tight. She could feel his swollen member pressed against her and for a moment she felt helpless to do anything to stop him. His hand went down her back until he could reach her behind and then he pressed himself against her by pulling her tight against himself. His face was now only inches from hers and she could smell the stale beer on his breath.

She opened her mouth to scream but he pressed his mouth over hers and stopped the noise by clamping his lips tightly on her mouth. She felt his tongue start to probe into her and thought for a moment of letting him put it inside so she could bite him but the thought nauseated her so she ground her teeth together in a grimace and tightened her mouth in a thin hard line. He finally stopped trying to kiss her and took his mouth away. Up till this point neither of them had spoken but now he broke the silence and said. "Come on darling, I only want a bit of fun and I know you're up for it, the way you keep on flashing yourself around here."

Victoria was astounded and couldn't think for a moment, her mouth dropped in astonishment and if he had let her go she would have laughed in his face. Then the shame and embarrassment at having a complete stranger fondle her like a piece of merchandise came over her. "Let me go you filthy pig." She hissed. She started to struggle to get away but he just held her tightly and laughed. She finally realised why he was laughing as she was still pressed tightly against him and it only gave him more pleasure when she struggled. Her other hand was still free and now instead of trying to push him away, a move he easily resisted, she tried to scratch him on the face but he stopped fondling her behind and grabbed her other wrist and swung her round so her back was pressed against him, he was much larger than her and so he could hold both her wrists in one hand while he felt her breasts with the other.

She felt her robe rip in the front as the flimsy material gave way under his probing, and she felt his sweaty hands fumbling her breasts and pinching her nipples. She realised she needed more help and opened her mouth to scream, but her body gave her away as she took the first deep breath to get some air in her lungs and he swiftly let go of her breasts and putting his hand over her mouth said quietly in her ear. "One peep out of you and you'll regret it for the rest of your life." He reached down and picked up a knife lying on the bench and started to press it on her cheek, drawing a little blood in his haste. "Do you want me to scar you for life?" He didn't wait for an answer, and started to drag her roughly towards a pile of sacking lying behind a stack of crates.

Her feet were scrabbling on the floor as she fought to keep her balance but he simply hoisted her a little higher and carried on dragging her, keeping the knife pressed against her neck. She felt it was useless to struggle but feebly tried anyway. His big body gave him an advantage over her as she was slimly built and he could drag her easily along. They reached the sacking and he threw her down out of sight of the doorway. Bending over her he snarled. "Come on darling, it's only one slice of a very big cake, you've got enough to keep a dozen men happy."

She stopped struggling for a moment and looked him straight in the eye. "You've forgotten one thing you filthy bastard," she hissed at him. "A woman's got to do it when she wants and not have some sweaty man all over her when he happens to feel like it. Now get your filthy body off me or I'll start screaming rape and when they come God help you because you'll be lucky to get away with your life."

He looked at her wildly and couldn't resist looking over his shoulder furtively, then he turned and said. "I'll only tell them you led me on because you wanted it, and asked me to do it." He pressed the knife harder against her, and threatened. "Now get your legs open before I take it into my mind to cut a little deeper with this." He pressed a little harder with the blade and she felt the blade cut a small snick in her neck and the blood started to run slowly down on to her shoulder.

Her eyes widened as he did this and panic started to set in, her breath was coming now in deep draughts and he glanced down in pleasure as she breathed and her breasts swelled each time. Fumbling the robe open, he once again grasped her and started to massage her breasts. To her shame she felt the nipples swell involuntarily and he took this as a sign that he was turning her on. "Come on darling you can see we're getting along famously now." He whispered in her ear. He thrust his knee down between her legs and opened them, and then he put the other one there and widened his knees. She felt helpless to stop him as he kept up the pressure and finally he had her legs wide open under him. She tried once more to reason with him and said. "Please stop, you're hurting me, and I'm going to tell everybody what you've done. Andy will kill you when he finds out."

She might as well have tried to reason with a brick wall, he only had one thing on his mind now and letting her go didn't enter his head. He was going to have her and she knew that no power that she had would stop him. For some reason the old quotation from a Chinese philosopher flashed into her head, 'If rape inevitable, relax and enjoy.' 'Some comfort,' she thought sarcastically. 'Just typical of a man to think of that.'

The thought of sex with this man sickened her and no way could she see herself relaxing and enjoying this experience, she cast about in her mind for some means of stopping him but there were no tools or anything hard to hit him with nearby, there were crates and sacking around and for a moment she thought of trying to smother him with a sack but knew it was useless. He reached down and pulled her robe up exposing her legs with their downy pubic hairs above her cleft, and then he reached back down and touched her between the legs roughly rubbing his fingers up and down to try and lubricate her. She felt his fingernails scratch her slightly and hoped against hope that he had at least cleaned them. Then thought how stupid it was to think of something like that at a time like this. He took hold of his belt and loosened it then reached for his zip and undid his trousers and she felt his manhood on her leg, it felt huge and frightened her to think of what was about to happen. She knew if she screamed now she could get herself killed as he was in a frenzy of lust and wouldn't stop for anything even if she resisted any more. She tightened her legs as much as possible to make it difficult for him to penetrate her, and she lay like a board under him. He hardly noticed and continued trying to thrust himself into her, but with no help from her she knew he wouldn't be able to do it easily. Then he reached down and quickly put both hands under her knees and raised them higher until they were alongside her cheeks. In this position she was virtually helpless and tears of frustration started to roll down her cheeks. The knife was once more pressed against her neck and he grinned into her face as he prepared to enter her, he smiled in pleasure and started to wriggle around to get into the best position to push, and she felt the tip of his member on the lips of her womanhood. In this position she felt ashamed and humbled to have to submit to this indignity, but still tried to keep herself from responding in any way.

    He knew what she was doing and growled. "Come on, open up, it won't hurt you so much if you do."

    She bit her lips and continued to keep herself as stiff as she could but knew she couldn't go on much longer resisting him, his manhood was still pressed against her vagina and she felt him wriggle until it reached the point of entry, he thrust suddenly and she felt him enter her roughly, a scream escaped her and he pushed his hand over her mouth to smother it. The looked at her exultantly, and started to push in and out, a look of satisfaction on his face, she could feel every thrust and tears rolled down her cheeks as she closed her eyes to shut out the grinning face of her tormentor. She felt rather than heard the thud as it happened and suddenly she was free as his weight was pulled off her body. Opening her eyes in surprise she saw Leah standing over her with a length of timber in her hand and the man rolling on the floor beside her, his hands pressed over the back of his head which was oozing blood between his fingers.

Leah smirked as she glanced down at Victoria's body stretched out on the floor her naked legs still apart, Victoria quickly pressed them together in shame and pulled down her robe to cover herself. Leah glanced at the man and said to Victoria. "You didn't look like you were enjoying that very much dearie."

"Thank God you turned up." Victoria gasped. She glanced at the electrician who was still rolling around with his hands on his head; she went on "That bastard was raping me."

"I gathered that." Leah commented dryly. "When he disappeared at the same time as you I started to wonder what was going on and I didn't figure you for the kind of woman to cheat on her man just after marrying him. The problem is, what are we going to do now?" She poked the man with the length of timber. "I said, what are we going to do now?" Her eyes went to his penis which was still exposed although much smaller now, and dribbling a little on the end with some fluid. "Cover yourself up for Christ's sake." She snapped. She tapped him again with the wood. "I should let you go out and face the rest of them, you dirty bastard, maybe they'd cut it off for you and then make you walk to town."

He cowered away from her, all thoughts of sex gone from his mind, now the only thought he could muster was survival and intact as well. She swung back to Victoria; "We've got to think quickly here, we don't have much time, if we tell everybody about this all hell's going to break loose and this one here." She tapped him again with the wood, only harder this time so he winced. "Is going to be lucky to get away with his life."

Victoria stared at her in surprise. "Do you mean we let him go without punishing him? She scrambled to her feet and tried to close her robe, which was still gaping open at the front. "If I had a knife in my hand right now he'd be walking funny for a long time, and he'd find it difficult to go to the toilet."

The man was listening to this as his head started to feel a little better, and his eyes swung from one to the other, as hope raised his spirits. He started to try and get to his feet as well but Leah tapped him again with the wood and said. "You stay down there for a bit mate; I want you where I can control you for a while."

He sat down and put his hand on the back of his head to feel it and grumbled. "You fetched me a fair crack there missus, you could have killed me."

Leah bent down a little so she could look him straight in the eye. "You're very lucky I didn't kill you mate, I felt like doing it, so shut up for a bit or I might give you another one, only harder this time." Something in the tone of her voice made him realise how thin the ground he was walking on really was, so he subsided back to the ground and stared at the floor.

She stood and looked critically at Victoria. "All right, I'm going to give it to you straight, Vicky, this is a bad business and it's not going to be easy, but if you go out there shouting rape what do you thinks going to happen? First of all that man of yours is going to want his piece of flesh out of this one's hide." She indicated the electrician. "Then it's going to start, every person on this site is going to know what happened to you and it'll be a topic of conversation for years to come. Your husband's going to be very sympathetic at first but then the doubts will start; did she let him do it? Did she enjoy it? Was he better than me? It'll put a wedge in your marriage that time will never heal. And you won't have any wish to have sex for a long time anyway, this is sure to put you off that."

Victoria stared at Leah in astonishment. "You really want him to get away with this?" She held her hand out. "Give me that piece of wood," she said determinedly, "I want to have something to take away from here that'll give me some dignity. I'll fetch him a crack he won't forget." She put her hand between her legs and grimaced. "I can still feel his filthy prick there." She shuddered involuntarily. "You don't know what it's like to have something like that animal there, rutting away on top of you like a pig with no feelings."

That's where you're wrong dearie." Leah replied. "I know only too well what it's like, but I can tell you the memory will fade, but it won't if you run out of here like a scalded virgin."

"It happened to you?"

"In aces and spades," Leah said sorrowfully. "Between me and you and this bastard down there, only trouble was it was three of them, not just one." She paused and looked at Victoria. "One thing

I can tell you, I thought they were going to kill me there and then. I've never told anyone till now." She shook her head at the memory. "They took their time and held me down while they took it in turns; it lasted about six hours all told."

"Did you know them?" Victoria questioned her, partly to let her get over the trauma of talking about it.

Leah took her time to answer this time and finally said. "Oh yes I knew them all right."

"But if you knew them why didn't you report them and get them charged?"

"For the same reason I'm telling you to keep quiet about it, it's going to cause more trouble than it's worth if you try to get him charged, and at the end of the day he's only going to claim you let him do it. That makes you out to be the one in the wrong, not him."

The man had been listening to this in between moaning to himself about his injuries and now raised himself more upright. "If you let me go I won't let on about any of this to anyone, I'll be as quiet as the proverbial church mouse."

The two women turned to stare at him, and Leah spoke for them both. "Too true you'll keep quiet, because if you don't I'm going to come looking for you, and I'll keep looking until one dark night on your way home from the pub you'll find yourself looking down between your legs and wondering how you're going to get a piss when you get home because it won't be there any more. Now here's what we do…. You!" She pointed at him. "Go out there and say to Pat you fell over and hit your head on a steel bench, that you don't feel well and you want to go to hospital. I'm going to see Ray and tell him to fly you in. When you get there, you stay there and don't turn up here ever again. I'll try and get someone to run your car into the town, but if it doesn't arrive hard luck. Now get yourself together and get out of here."

The man scrambled to his feet and started to shamble out still holding his head, he had only gone a few paces when a thought struck him and he turned and looked at them. "What about my wages? I've done a lot of work here"

Leah looked at Victoria, then sneered. "Forget it mate, you just paid for a bunk up, let it be a lesson to you."

He took the time to leer at Victoria and said. "Wasn't much of a bunk up as it goes anyway." Then he turned and would have walked away but Victoria, who had listened to this last remark with rising anger in her, snapped at him. "I'm glad you didn't enjoy it, you filthy bastard, if I wanted to, I could be the best lay of your life, but you'll never know what that feels like, so dream on."

He regarded her sourly for a moment then walked away slowly still holding his head where Leah had hit him. Leah turned to Victoria and looked at her with a little respect in her eyes. "I'm glad you stuck up for yourself there but we've got to get you a bit presentable before anyone sees you and starts asking questions. For a few moments they tidied her clothing as best they could and then Leah looked at her and said. "I suppose that'll have to do for now, I think the best thing is for you to go and get another shower as soon as possible and act as if nothing's happened. I'm going to see Ray about flying that guy into town so we're rid of him as quick as possible."

Victoria laid her hand on her arm and clasped it saying. "Thanks for what you did, I'm glad it was you that came and not one of the men, but it still galls me that that guy gets away scot free with what he did, if I had my way he'd be behind bars for a long time."

Leah nodded. "I'm glad it was me that found you, and you'll understand soon enough why a lot of women don't report rapes. Just remember, whatever you feel like now, he's not actually taken anything away from your spirit, and your body will forget in time. But at least it's only us that knows what went on here tonight, and." She added coldly. "Don't think he's going to get away scot free, I'm going to put the word out when I'm in town next time. He's going to find it harder to get work in the future and he'll never know why." She laughed. "But I will." Then she walked down the room and down the stairs. Victoria watched her go until she disappeared down the steps and then her legs gave way and she sank down and gave thanks for her deliverance.

Chapter Two

Jim looked around and cursed yet again, the rain never seemed to let up at this time of year and it had turned the ground into a quagmire, everywhere they walked in the open air had its own fair share of mud. It oozed over their boots and clung to every piece of clothing. He swore it had a mind of its own and knew how to work its way steadily up ones legs until there was no escape from the sticky embrace. They had laid planks from place to place in the compound but they had all but disappeared under the surface and now when they walked on them water splashed up to wet their legs. He had one thing to be thankful for, if thankful about someone else's misery could be cause for celebration, and that was the fact that elsewhere in this part of Australia they had had floods and no traffic was moving anywhere for the moment. Luckily they had managed to get some of the plants growing well and had sufficient food to eat. He surveyed the building in front of him with satisfaction; they had completed the main food growing area and the farm where they intended to keep the few animals they had decided to bring in was ready for their occupants.

It had been a stormy meeting several weeks ago after the electrician had left so suddenly. He was still unsure what had happened that night but he knew for certain that something had. The only two who had any knowledge of the events of that night had been close mouthed about the whole affair. He knew that both of them had been closeted with the electrician for some time because he had seen Leah go into the building after the other two had disappeared. The next thing that happened had been the electrician coming out with a story about falling over, which to his eyes had been preposterous as no-one got a bump like that by stumbling.

When they had taken him to hospital and the man had decided not to come back, Jim had felt the god's were conspiring against him; the one piece of luck they had had was that the man Leah had chosen to replace him had turned up a week later and had been enthusiastic about the aims of the group and had put a great deal of money in to take part. He had brought with him two more children and a wife who Pat had taken to immediately and swore was pregnant again. Ray had recognised the man immediately but made no comment when he had arrived.Leah and he seemed to get on like a house on fire, He could handle computers as if they were made just for him and had set up several of them so they could use them.

The man had also taken to the electrical work like a duck to water and had soon enough checked out the other man's work. Now he was busy working on the living quarters they were erecting in front of the main work area. As they had some money coming in from the fruit farm now, they had decided to go for luxury in the fittings and the rooms were of a better standard than normally they would expect. They had divided the whole complex into small apartments for each family and had erected a large kitchen and dining area to service them. It also had a communal living room and smaller rooms to one side if the occupants wanted to watch TV or use computers and videos.

'The student teacher/farmer that Martin had promised had arrived as well and had made some valuable comments about the storage and space for the animals, they had implemented these and he had been helping out with growing feedstuff for them.

They had also installed a shower room and sauna so they could congregate and clean themselves. They had followed the original idea and made this area communal, as segregation in their situation seemed pointless. When they had had the meeting about it they had agreed that hiding bodies only created problems and if they were open about their lives they could live together in a happier way. Jim was waiting to see what would happen when they really started to live that way but could see no real problems happening as the shower block they had now was communal, and had to some extent become a meeting place where everybody could chat in comfort. They had also taken the trouble to set up a second set of computers and monitors in the main farming building, this had been Roy the electricians idea, as when he heard they might possibly have to defend the place he had put the opinion that they were almost bound to end up defending the solidly built farm from inside. They could now access the cameras outside from that room and the whole place could be run from in there if anything happened.

Victoria had been unsettled now for some time and Jim and Pat had had trouble trying to find out why, but Julia had decided to befriend her and worked with her most days when she had some time from teaching the children. Andrew was fortunately a placid sort of young man and never caused any trouble with her, but the atmosphere between them was clearly troubled. The upside of this was that Victoria worked all day and every day and the food production had soared.

Pat and himself were aware that Andrew had been spending a lot of time in the company of Leah and they worried about the consequences, as Pat had said only the previous day. "It's a very unusual couple of the opposite genders that can have any relationship where sex doesn't come into it, as friendship between opposite genders is based on sex anyway."

He wasn't absolutely sure she had it right but he had to admit that he knew of very few friendships where the couple were close without sex coming into it. He crossed his fingers and hoped that it wouldn't cause too much trouble if anything happened. 'If it hadn't already' he added silently to himself. The two of them had made the run to town several times to take produce in and bring materials back, and who knows what went on when they were out of sight of the camp. Ray had shown little interest in what Leah was doing anyway and Jim wondered if he hadn't found someone himself on his frequent flying trips into town. He shrugged his shoulders and decided to worry about it when it happened and not before.

The only problem had been the high cost of the fuel. Martin had started a primitive gas production plant with the waste products and he hoped to start producing gas later. They had bought conversion kits for the Ute's and intended to convert them to run on the gas as soon as they could produce it relatively easily. If they were successful Jim knew they could turn a modest profit into a handsome one. He smiled to himself and wondered what the government tax officials would say if they knew they weren't getting their fair share of tax on fuel. The idea appealed to everybody, as they never had any money spent on roads out to here, and they had to undertake any repairs themselves. He looked down again at the mud oozing around his boots; if only they could run the road to town every week with a lorry load of produce he would be happy. The hovercraft they had ordered had been delivered but they had had no chance yet of learning to drive it. He wanted to use it to take their produce to the nearest point on a blacktop road and transfer it to a lorry for transport into town.

As the community had grown they had been able to complete much of the project faster and now the only people who weren't living there were the Prof and Colette. They had been working in town and the money they earned had gone into the central pool after they had taken out expenses to cover living costs. They had had a meeting a few days previously and now they had decided to call them in to live on site as they were in a viable position financially. Although it would take some years they would achieve the point where all the original investment would be returned to the bank, and it was a distinct possibility they could end up creating more money than they had invested. He knew that the main reason for this was that nobody was drawing wages at present but they had at least got all they wanted for the time being and many of them were happy to be there and gain experience of the unique situation. When they had spoken about financial matters at the meeting it had been a surprise to him to find that most of the members had little interest in making money, they had been more emphatic about creating a better way of life. But they knew that the next generation they were building might not feel like that so Jim had been attempting to find ways of letting them have some freedom in the future, without compromising the security of the whole project.

They had all agreed that they would try and make money and resources available to the young ones to allow them to attend colleges and University if they wanted. He did a mental count up of children and found if his figures were correct that they had now got fourteen children if he counted the pregnancies as well. He thanked heaven that Julia coped as well as she did with the aid of the computers and with the Internet connections they had managed to install, the children stood a fair chance of being highly educated by the time they reached the age when they could attend college. When the Prof arrived soon they would have two very able teachers to bring them on.

He was brought out of his reverie by the sound of Leah's husky tones. "You won't make any progress in this life if you stand there dreaming about it, you've got to do something first to change it."

He blinked and sighed. "I suppose you're right Leah, but the first thing I have to do is get my priorities straight, and make a plan of action, then I can make progress. Now I'm sure you didn't come over here to talk to me about inane things like this, what's up?"

"Simple." she answered. "We've been talking things over." He shot her a glance, and she went on hurriedly, Victoria, myself and that farmer," she paused, "Lee." shaking her head she said, "Never sounds right to have a man called that when he's a farmer, get it, farmer Lee, sounds like family." She waited for a reaction from him and when none seemed to be forthcoming she gestured with a wave of her hand that it wasn't important and carried on. "Anyway, we got talking and we thought that we should be doing something about bringing some animals in now as we're buying milk in cartons when we should be producing our own, and then there's the meat situation, most of the meat we have now is expensive, and we either have to have refrigerated transport to bring it out, or we use cans. Neither of which is a good answer, and also Lee thinks that we've got to get some animals out here in case anything does happen, because we have to be sure they're disease free. And we have to have time to allow the diseases to develop; we can't afford any slip ups as we could only have one chance." She stopped talking and looked at him expectantly.

"So you want to go into town and buy some? Is that it?"

She smiled sarcastically. "Never fails to beat me how the average male is so quick on the uptake."

He bridled at this and snapped. "I was merely clarifying a point; I wanted to make sure we both understand what we're talking about."

"OK, OK, I was only joshing you for a bit of fun, don't get on your high horse and make an issue of it." Her reaction was the same as many peoples would be. A show of anger in return for anger shown. They faced each other angrily for a moment until they realised what they were doing and simultaneously they broke into a smile. Leah put her hand on his arm and squeezed it. "I bet that's how some wars can break out when people get a bit irritated with each other and push too much."

He smiled ruefully. "We all get a bit fraught sometimes Leah, of course I agree you can go," He looked around at the sea of mud which surrounded them. "Just as soon as this clears up a bit, I don't want you out on the road stuck in the middle of nowhere with animals on board."

She nodded in agreement. "I want that Lee to come with us as he probably knows enough about animals to know what's good or bad."

Jim frowned a little when she said that. "I thought he was an all round qualified farmer?"

"Yeah he is, he did a stint at college about animals on the farm so that qualifies him for the gold award for expert. I've been round all the rest and he's the only one who claims to have any knowledge of the little beasties we want to buy."

"Talking of that, what are you going to buy? As I seem to recall we were thinking on the lines of buying females and artificially inseminating them."

Leah shook her head and answered. "Sounded like a good idea at first but it's a specialised field and we'd need a laboratory to do it, with facilities for liquid nitrogen freezing. There's no way we could do that with the limited knowledge we've got, so we're down to the old fashioned method that Noah used; two of everything." She flashed her eyes mischievously at him. "Still, it gives the teachers the opportunity to teach the kids about the birds and the bees, and it might provide some light entertainment for the adults as well. After all I don't think we're going to get any films of that sort if we stockpile a load of films to pass the time in the evenings."

Jim raised his eyebrows. "That's something I'd never thought about up till now; I've been too busy with all this construction. I suppose I'd better get somebody on to it right away."

She cocked her eyes at him. "What do you mean? Films, or that sort of film?"

It was his turn to grin mischievously. "Everybody to their own taste I suppose, but we've got to do something to pass the long nights in here. Once in a while it can do a lot of good to see something like that. Too many people say there're bad because they don't want others to think they enjoy that sort of thing. And that's a bloody two faced way of looking at it if you think about it."

"Mmm." Leah sounded uncertain. "I think you'd better put it to the vote before you start that sort of thing; me, I can take them or leave them but some of the others might not feel that way, and on that subject, if you want to get at the truth I'd have a secret ballot about it. It's a subject that creates a lot of emotion in some people, and they certainly won't tell the truth if they think others will think badly of them for voting yes."

"Instead of going to all that trouble, why don't you sound out the women quietly about how they feel about it and I'll do the same with the men. Let's see what we come up with. I think there might even be a case for allowing couples to have them out for private viewing, not everybody wants to see them with a load of other people trying to see their reactions. Frankly, I think a lot of the men would rather see a good action film and the women a good romantic film; that seems to be the way the sexes think when it comes to entertainment."

She bristled at this as he had expected. "You men like to stereotype women don't you, why don't you think women would like a good action film the same as men?"

Jim felt that this discussion would go on and on if he allowed himself to be drawn so contented himself by saying. "I'd never try to put you in a slot Leah, but this is my final word on the subject. Tell me you didn't enjoy watching, 'Love Story,' and having a good cry at the end."

She was beaten on that, as it was one film that women seemed to enjoy better than men. "You men have got no feelings if you can't enjoy that film." She then changed the subject showing she had no further interest in carrying on the conversation, much to Jim's relief. "So I take it it's a yes about going to go and get those animals? I've got to go and see Schoonheid about some more materials to finish off the living quarters and some of the others want to go into town anyway."

"Have you thought about the state of the roads out there?" Jim asked. "Look at the mud we've got around here and think whether it's a good idea to go into town at this time."

"The weather forecast is real good for the next week with no rain to speak of and if the temperature stays up it won't be long before it's dry enough to go into town." She ran her fingers through her hair. "Some of us around here want to get into the hairdressers and have some care taken over us, or we'll all end up looking like scrag ends of meat."

Jim could hear the start of an argument behind him as he listened to her so answered quickly as he turned. "Do what you think is best and go if you want and take the farmer with you to buy those animals, even if he is called Lee." He grinned and went off to where he could see Dick, Ray, and Andy, standing in a circle waving plans at each other arguing with red faces. He managed to get the problem sorted out as it only involved minor alterations to the construction and was more about the men arguing over who wanted to be boss.

The next few days were hectic for Jim, as all the women had decided to go into town and treat themselves to a few days off; it left Jim, Andy, and Ray to look after all the children while they were away. They decided that as the women were enjoying themselves in town they would take a few days off and go out a way into the outback and camp out and show the children something of the countryside around the area. Dick had drawn the short straw and had been left in the compound to irrigate all the plants and keep an eye on the quarters, although as he had been reminded enough by Victoria and Leah. "The whole shooting match as far as watering everything is concerned is controlled by the computer, you're contribution comes in if it breaks down. Then you can turn the tap on by hand if you think you can handle it." He had also been given the job of transplanting plants to their growing trays which was not a job he relished, but he knew it was necessary and did it as smoothly as possible.

As the children had been confined to camp with Julia keeping a close eye on them they behaved as if they had been let out of prison and enjoyed themselves with a vengeance. That meant that after a few days Jim looked at the others one evening and said. "Let's take them back home, I'm being driven crazy with all the demands they're making on us. I can't cope much longer."

Andy looked over to where the oldest of the children were whooping and running crazy amongst the trees. "To tell the truth," he said, "I didn't expect these kids to enjoy themselves so much out here; I thought they'd all be suffering withdrawal symptoms from being away from the computers for so long."

Jim did an old fashioned double take, then stared at Andy for a long moment. "Am I hearing you right? You're the original computer games player and that brother in law of yours qualifies for number two. Between you I reckon you qualify for players of the year for the number of hours you spend tapping those keys and pushing buttons."

Andy grinned superciliously. "People like you never will understand what we get out of playing those games will you?"

"You might look at me and think I'm old fashioned and stupid but you spend a lot of time playing games when you could be interacting with other members of the community, for a start you should be paying a lot more attention to that wife of yours she's looking a bit too peaky for my peace of mind."

Andy stood up quickly, a little too quickly, Jim noticed. He faced Jim with the colour rising in to his face. "Leave her out of it, will you. If we've got any problems, we'll sort them out ourselves and we don't need any of your old fashioned lectures about what to do."

Jim could see he had got himself upset over his words and wanted more than he could say to help him with any problem but knew better than to try now, as he would only stir things up and make them worse. So he immediately backed off and stood himself. "Don't get upset by me son, I only want what's best for you. Now let's make a start on closing down this camp and making tracks for home." They turned and called all the children over to make a start on packing up the camp.

Pat looked out of the front windscreen of the Ute as they travelled through the featureless Australian countryside. The air conditioning had been turned on full blast and still it laboured to conquer the heat that blasted through the vehicle, she wished she could open a window but knew it was impossible as the heat just permeated right through and would have made life unbearable. She was sitting in the rear with Julia and Leah for company and Victoria was in the front next to the farmer Lee who was driving. All the rest of the men and women who were going into town had been crammed into two more of the Ute's with all the produce they had brought into town to sell. They had quite a load this time and it would pay them a handsome profit if it arrived as fresh as they could keep it. They had built up a reputation for selling quality produce in the local supermarket and they knew it would be welcome when it arrived.

She smiled to herself as she looked at Lee driving with a fierce concentration as they bounced along on the rutted track. It had only just dried enough to negotiate and he had a hard time keeping it going through ground that was not dry but slightly muddy. He had offered to drive when they had started out and obviously thought that the best place for women wasn't behind the wheel of a Ute. He had been driving for several hours now and had refused all offers from the women to take over and give him some rest. She sighed and turned her attention back to the laptop computer she had on her knees. Julia looked at her questioningly and put her finger on the screen as she studied it. "Well how is the situation then?" She asked. "You keep on studying that thing and sighing but we've got no information over here." She indicated Leah who was listening to them. "Maybe we could help out if we knew what you were doing."

Pat smiled in apology. "Oh, I don't know what to make of it, everything we do to estimate how much of certain items we're going to need, gets lost when we do it again. I suppose we make the mistake of guessing all the time instead of counting what we've bought since starting."

Julia smiled back at her. "Simple arithmetic will get you out of this problem, now it just so happens." She reached inside her bag and took out a notebook and opened it to reveal the pages were covered in script and columns of figures. She went on. "I set the children an exercise in the classroom last week and I used the figures for purchases made and the time the people are in the compound minus what we have in stock." She smiled depreciatingly at Pat. "All the figures are there in the books, it's really quite simple. I've got here an estimate of all the stock I think we're going to have to have to survive ten years inside that building, but quite frankly I hope we never have to, as some of the items can't be stored more than a short time. And by short I mean much longer than five or six years."

Pat looked at her in amazement. "Are you telling me that I've been struggling with that computer all this time trying to input the information and figures and you got the children to work it out instead?"

Julia looked smug. "It gave them something to think about, and anyway they'll be more conscious of waste now, because they understand how we only have limited resources." She held the notebook up. "These are only figures I brought to show you and compare what you've worked out, but back there we entered all the figures and facts on a database as an exercise for the older ones so you can access them in anyway you want. Actually you aren't too badly off for supplies as you have bought quite a lot over the time we've been here and we only need to top up in a lot of instances. The one thing that worries me is the medical supplies; I hope Colette knows what to do about them as we should be stocking up right now to ensure we have all we need."

Leah, who had listened to this with interest, leaned forward and said. "I don't think you need to worry on that score dear, I spoke to her when I saw her last week and she's been in touch with a supply firm and ordered as much as she can, of course in her line of work it's all speculation as to what she'll need."

Pat nodded and added. "I heard much the same from her myself when I spoke to her." She would have carried on but there was a curse from Lee in the driver's seat and the vehicle swerved dangerously to the right and stopped almost immediately. He banged the steering wheel with the palm of his hand and cursed the Ute roundly.

Although they suspected what had happened, the women wisely held their tongues until he climbed out and went to the front of the Ute. They watched as he bent down and examined the front wheel shaking his head, then he straightened and kicked the tyre before going to the back and opening the rear door of the cab scrabbled under the seat to find the jack. He glanced up as he did so and said tersely. "Bloody flat tyre, it's the shale used on these tracks, cuts the tyres to pieces."

It was left to Leah to answer sarcastically. "Never would have guessed ducky, it's never happened to anyone else out here, must have been the way you were driving."

He shot a venomous look at the back of her head but that gave him no clue as to whether she was being sarcastic or merely joking. She turned to look at him and said in her sexiest voice. "Do you want me to show you how to change the wheel or can you manage it on your own?"

He slammed the door shut with a crash and stamped to the front of the Ute muttering to himself. By this time the others had caught up with them and strolled over to see what the problem was. Pat looked at Leah. "You pushed him a bit there didn't you?"

"He was asking for it wasn't he? Fancy trying to drive all the way to town with four other drivers in the truck and Mr macho won't let anyone else have a go. If you ask me the tyre wouldn't have blown if he'd not been so tired and driven down that rut."

Pat kept herself in check as she felt that it was only a negative way of dealing with the problem and anyway she knew that Leah was probably right to criticise, the man had been tired and should have handed over to someone else.

Ever the peacemaker Victoria said. "Shall we get out and help?"

Looking out through the windscreen they could see Martin and the Sparks leaning over trying to assist. Leah shook her head. "Let them deal with it, it won't take long, I checked before we left, the spare is pumped up and ready to go, they've only got to replace it."

She was proved correct and the tyre was replaced within about fifteen minutes. Lee walked to the back and threw the jack back under the seat and went to climb back into the front and drive again, he stopped in surprise when he saw that Leah had taken the seat and she stared at him from behind the wheel. "It's OK, I'll drive," he said.

Leah smiled patiently as if she had a child in front of her instead of a six foot muscled man. "It looks like I'm going to have to put you straight on a few things matey, first of all you belong to a community here and you aren't self employed. Now it might have escaped your notice but the only thing you've got over most of us females is your size and strength. We take it in turns to do work around here and that means us women, frail things that we are, drive Ute's. Now I don't want to get into the old argument about who's the best drivers, men, or women. But one thing I am dead sure of and that is that I can drive this vehicle and I intend to do so. And when I'm tired I'm going to hand over to one of the other people in here. That way all of us stand a better chance of arriving fit and well and none of us are going to be too tired to do our work when we arrive. You have got to go and buy some animals when we get there and I want you to be able to do that, not stand in some bar guzzling beer because you think you're too tired to work. Do I make myself clear?"

He had been standing open mouthed while she had said this and now he blinked slowly while he thought over what she had said, his brow furrowed and he went to say something but was beaten to it by Leah again. "Oh, and don't give me any of that shit about it being a mans job to work on the farm and a woman's to cook and clean, or I might find it in me to make sure you end up cleaning the toilets a couple of times a week."

This was too much for him and he burst out. "You can't make me do that, I'm the farmer round here, it's my job to look after the animals and grow things."

Leah grinned wickedly. "I really hope you try and put that to the test matey; then we'll see who does what around here."

Pat leaned forward and said tiredly. "Leave him be Leah, I want to get to town today and I don't want to camp out here if I can avoid it." She looked at the man. "She is right about one thing though, you aren't the only one in this, we're all in it together, and trying to be the big hero all the time isn't the way to get things done. You were tired when that tyre went and maybe it could have been avoided. Now lets all take it in turns to work and things will go easier, so will you get in and allow one of us weaker sex to drive."

The man was an Australian and evidently not used to being talked to in this way by a woman, his mouth opened and closed several times as he thought about a rejoinder and started to say it then discard it as not cutting enough. Finally he climbed reluctantly into the seat vacated by Leah and found something to say. "Well, you women can't play footie, that's for sure."

They all stared at each other in amazement and surprise, then they howled with laughter; he stared at them and grinned nervously with them. He was awkward as most people are when everybody else is laughing and they aren't sure the laughter isn't at their expense. At last as the laughter died down a little Julia looked at him and said. "Don't worry sonny, we'll turn you into a proper man by the time we come out of this, always provided you listen and understand what we're telling you."

Without turning her head, Leah said. "Fat chance." Then started the engine and drove slowly forward. He subsided into the corner and sulked for most of the rest of the journey, occasionally snorting if a clutch was dropped too quickly or a gear grated a little.

For the rest of the journey Julia and Pat were busy conferring over the list that Julia had produced and at length Pat leaned back and said admiringly. "I have to give it to you Julia, you've done sterling work on this; I just wish I'd known about it before so I wouldn't have had to worry."

"You wouldn't have been so impressed if I'd started it and it had all gone wrong, would you? When I began I didn't know what the children were going to do with the facts and figures, it was only speculation at first. It was only later I realised that they had actually done a good job of it."

Pat smiled. "When we get back I'll see if I can work up a little surprise for them so I can say thank you properly." She held the lap top up. "I can put in my order for supplies with a much better idea of what we need now. I reckon we could get it all in one or two more lorries, then if we do get into this situation we can batten down the hatches."

Lee had been listening to this exchange with some interest and leaning forward a little so he could see them clearly he said. "You really are serious about this happening aren't you?"

Pat stared at him for a moment, then asked. "Why did you join if you didn't think it was going to happen?"

He shrugged. "I wanted to get some experience in and I knew that I could learn a lot from Martin, he's a first class biologist and I also had the idea they were going to carry out a lot of research into intensive farming methods, when I leave here I'll be able to get a job anywhere."

Pat frowned. "But how do you know that the volcano won't blow up? It's on the cards that it will, it's done it twice before in earths history that we know about."

"Yeah, come on lady, I've heard the figures, six hundred thousand years apart. That means it could maybe blow in the next thousand years or so, you might as well speculate on when the next asteroid is going to hit earth and cause the same thing."

"I agree with what you're saying." Pat said earnestly. "But let me ask you one thing, where would you rather your children grew up? In a good stable community like ours or in some place like the Gold Coast, where they've got access to drink and drugs and all the pitfalls of life in those places. Where you stand the chance of losing them before they get old enough to understand life itself."

He clearly wasn't convinced but didn't seem to have enough brains to know why he disagreed so he sank back into the seat and kept his silence till they arrived in town. It was late in the evening but Leah had telephoned before they arrived and so they delivered the goods to the buyer who placed them directly into his storage area and promised to meet them in the morning to go over the figures with them. Then they drove straight to the hotel, and booked in for the night to get some sleep. As they went up to their rooms Pat watched worriedly as Lee headed for the bar. "I think we're going to have some trouble with that young man." She commented to Julia who was standing beside her.

Julia agreed a little cautiously. "Give him time to settle down." She answered. Sometimes it can seem a bit restrictive to be told you might lose all the things you want, and have to settle down to life on a farm in the middle of nowhere."

"Come on you two." Said a voice from behind them. "I've managed to get a bottle of vodka from the barman and some cartons of orange juice, I want you to come and help me with Victoria, she's been a bit down in the mouth recently and she needs cheering up." They turned to find Leah standing there with a man carrying her case and Victoria behind her looking a little shamefaced to be the centre of attention. Leah was waving the vodka in the air like a trophy and glancing back at the man she said, "Lead on Mcduff, take us to our room."

The following morning they met in the dining room for breakfast somewhat worse for wear but at least able to function, but Pat had to ask the waiter to get a call into Lee who hadn't put in an appearance. When he finally arrived they had finished breakfast and Pat was getting increasingly anxious about whether he would be able to concentrate on buying the animals. He was obviously nursing a hangover but several cups of coffee and some painkillers seemed to put new life into him and they set off to the breeding farm in a better state of mind.

Several hours later and some hard bargaining behind them, they drove away the proud owners of a small menagerie of farm animals. After some discussion they had bought two each of all the females in a state of pregnancy and two males of each species. This would give them a choice of two different fathers and two different mothers within each species giving them four different bloodlines to follow. As Lee had pointed out. "It's not really enough but without a large herd to play with we'll have to accept some inbreeding at some stage, and until we get locked into the compound we can use the artificial insemination service from here in town to keep the risk of inbreeding down."

Leah asked. "Why buy males then? If you intend to inseminate them."

He looked at her in puzzlement, as if her question had a flaw in it. "If anything happens and we do have to batten down the hatches out there, we possibly won't have the time to go and buy fresh stock, then the fat would really be in the fire wouldn't it?" He grinned, an evil grin, to see if he could upset her. "We can always eat them if we don't need them."

The thought appalled her, and Victoria looked positively sick. The pair of them looked at each other and then Leah said. "That's just the kind of thing I'd expect someone like you to say, but if you think you're going to get back at me by saying that, you're wrong." She leaned right into his face. "I'll match you bite for bite on anything you want to eat, and then I'll make you clean the toilets for desert."

He glared at her angrily as he realised that once more he had bitten off more than he could chew, then he answered. "I've cleaned up shit all my life from these animals, so don't think you can scare me by saying I can clean up a bit more."

Leah held his eyes while she digested what he had said and then turned to Victoria and said. "I saw a bar down the road a bit; let's go for a drink while these guys are sorting out payment and delivery." She marched of with a straight back and Victoria trailing behind.

Pat and Julia looked at each other commiserating, and then turned to the task in hand. They had bought some cows, pigs, sheep, and horses. They had also invested in some chickens that were promised to be excellent layers and good to eat. So they could look forward to a varied diet of dairy products and have some meat for those who were inclined to eat it.

It was time for lunch when they concluded the business and exchanged documents and cheques, and they went back to the hotel for a meal. When they arrived, Lee headed once more for the bar and started to down beer after beer as if he had never had a drink before. He only slowed when they insisted he come for something to eat and his wife who had joined them looked ashamed when he ordered a large pitcher of beer to go with the meal.

After they had eaten, all the women went down the road to the beauty salon as Leah had promised them that they were all going to have some pampering. Lee looked at the rest of the men and said. "Anyone for a drink lads?"

The others glanced at each other and shook their heads, so he ambled off on his own into the bar. When he had gone Martin looked at the Sparks and raised an eyebrow in question. "What do you think of our farmer, he seems to like his drink doesn't he?"

The Sparks shrugged, his name was Roy, but no one seemed to refer to him by anything but Sparks and he appeared to be quite happy with the situation so they just called him that. Ray hardly spoke to him but it didn't seem to matter to the Sparks as he got on with all the others and so wasn't short of friends. His wife Alison was a friendly woman who was visibly growing bigger with each passing week and found the two children she already had something of a handful, but Pat had stepped into the breach and was now a secondary mother to the pair of them. He looked over into the bar where they could see Lee standing at the bar with a fist closed around a glass of beer. "Some men are like that I suppose," he volunteered, "It didn't seem to worry him when he was back at the farm, and if a man kicks over the traces now and then I can't see the problem. In fact….." He stood as he was talking. "I'm going to join him for a couple myself, as long as the missus is spending some money trying to improve her looks, I might as well use it for a useful purpose."

Martin glanced over his shoulder in the direction of the door where the women had disappeared in search of the beauty salon, then heaved himself to his feet when he had ascertained the coast was clear. "Might as well come with you then," he said, "Don't want you drinking on your own do we?"

As it happened, the drinking session didn't last long as Lee had consumed too much in too short a time to last very much longer, they heard him with some shock start to tell all and sundry about the project in scathing terms and managed to turn the conversation to other matters before the drink overtook him and he staggered a little as his eyes glazed over. They grabbed both his arms and wrestled him to the door and up into his room before too much damage was done, but not without Schoonheid who had been standing there hearing what he had had to say. As they left, Schoonheid scratched his head and said musingly into his glass. "Funny old situation over there, first they say its research and now this guy implies there're looking forward to the end of the world. I'm going to get to the bottom of this if it kills me." He grinned nastily to himself. "There must be some way of turning a profit out of this, especially as I don't get any more sales from that bitch Leah, now the building work is finished." He looked up as the manager of the supermarket came through the door and called him over to buy him a drink. They said the customary. "Cheers." and then, "up yours," before the conversation got round to the activities on the farm that Fred had owned.

As the conversation progressed, Schoonheid took note of one key sentence he spoke. "I've had to buy extra supplies and send them out there, I don't know what there're doing but the amount of food they've had, couldn't be used by that many people in five years, and it's not only food, it's household supplies as well."

Schoonheid was intrigued, he had heard rumours going around that they were stocking up but he hadn't heard the scale of the operation until now. "So you reckon there're stocking up for a war or what?" He questioned.

"Don't ask me mate, but I tell you one thing, I reckon they could live out there for the next seven or eight years without buying anything else, I've just had another order from them and it's going to take a big lorry to deliver it, I can tell you." He shook his head in wonderment. "I know one thing, I stand to gain a lot of money from them now, but they needn't buy anything from me for years."

"What do you reckon they're going to do then?" Schoonheid persisted.

The man raised his eyebrows and grimaced. "I tell you mate, if you ask me they've got to be looking forward to a long time with no contact with the rest of the human race, it's almost as if there's going to be a nuclear war and they reckon on staying underground while the rest of the world stays on top and dies out with the radiation."

Schoonheid looked at him disbelievingly. "You've got to be kidding, I thought that scenario was long past, and everybody had signed those documents for non proliferation of nuclear material."

The man looked at him darkly. "Some of those Arab states have got enough to turn out some bombs, haven't they? What if one of those decides to start one of them there Holy wars with America or even the Jewish people? That'd be sure to start a world war wouldn't it?"

The thought had never crossed Schoonheid's mind before this moment but he nodded sagely to the man, trying to convey the impression that he thought of nothing else. But he finished his drink in one gulp and said quickly. "Well I've got to go, time waits for no man, and I won't make a penny standing here gassing." He turned and marched forcefully out of the door with the mans eyes on his back as he went. If he had followed his normal course of action he might have gone to the office and pestered his secretary all afternoon until she gave in and entertained him in the back room, but this time he got on to the phone directly he got back. He stayed on it the whole of the afternoon calling people in many different places. Although his information was sketchy he had learned enough to guess a great deal and he thought he knew what the community were doing. What he was trying to ascertain was, would it be possible to profit in some way?

It started off in a very low-key manner, the women had all returned from the salon and eaten a meal, and the men were quietly drinking and chatting in the bar. The women with the exception of Pat were in the television room listening to the news, and when she walked in she found them all glued to the set. She started to tell them that she had spoken to Colette and the medical supplies should be delivered the next day, the men in the camp could cope with the unloading and Colette was to come during the next week with Prof to settle into the community. She was going to be happy about getting her family together for the first time since leaving England and the medical supplies along with the extra rations and materials they had bought should make them self-sufficient at last.

She was waved to a seat and with a gesture of the hand, Leah indicated the television set, the news was on and the announcer was saying. "We are getting reports of a volcanic eruption in the Yellowstone park area of the United States, first news is that it isn't a very large eruption with very few casualties. These are mostly tourists who happened to be there and some park wardens who were trying to clear the area. But scientists are worried that there could be more to come, the whole area has been watched carefully for some time as it has long been thought that it could be the site of a so-called super volcano."

Pat put her hand to her mouth in horror; this was just what had been predicted by Rex all that time ago. She had never really believed it would happen as they said, and to her, it had been a way of getting together with her children for a nice life in the Australian countryside. But this news was devastating and all the predictions were going to come true! Leah tore her gaze away from the sight of the eruption being shown on the television and stared at Pat with eyes that were filled with horror and dread. They both understood that from now on there would be no going back, they still hoped that it would be a minor eruption but Pat had that feeling deep down that told her this was the big one and they would have to save as many of the community as they could.

The announcer went on. "The pall of smoke and ash has reached a height of five miles and is spreading across the sky as we speak to you and it is so thick it blots out the sun when viewed from underneath. It is difficult to breathe as the ash is fine and clogs the lungs when one's mouth is open." He turned his attention to the screen alongside him which showed a picture of the column of smoke and ash rising in the air. "As you can see it is billowing out at a tremendous rate and has been doing this for several hours now, and it is being spread by the jet stream over all the US. One wonders how it can keep up this rate but scientists say that it is possible to go on like this for a very long time." He touched his ear in the gesture that announcers use when the earpiece is being used.

He nodded and then turned his attention back to the screen. "I've just received news that the scientists monitoring the eruption have detected new movement in the area and they speculate the there could be more eruptions to follow, they advise any persons in the vicinity to evacuate the area as quickly as possible, the police will be on hand to help any persons stranded. We're trying to get an interview with one of the team who are monitoring this outbreak and we will return to you as soon as possible with an update."

The screen went blank for a moment and started to show the smiling face of the weather reporter. Victoria, who had the remote control, switched off, much to the annoyance of another resident of the hotel who had been watching as well. She handed it silently to him and said to them calmly. "I think we ought to have a conference about this development as soon as possible."

They filed out and calling the men from the bar went to the room Pat and Julia were sharing. When they arrived they all took places as best they could in a room designed for two. Glancing around Pat saw the only person missing was Lee. Martin saw what she was doing and called out. "Lee's indisposed for the moment, but he'll be alright in the morning."

Although she knew the nature of the indisposition Pat felt it prudent not to dwell too much on it and merely acknowledged the fact. It was a short meeting as they all agreed that the best thing for them was to return to the farm and await delivery of the medical supplies and the rest of the order that Pat and Julia had give to the supplier. Leah looked around at all the women with their new hairdos and shining healthy faces from the treatment they had received that afternoon and said wryly. "Well all the cosseting you girls got this afternoon looks like going to waste after all, seems like we'll be doing our own from now on."

Pat could see this conversation was going to do nothing to help matters so she broke in. "I think the most important thing is our survival, so we should start by concentrating on that. Looks don't matter much if you don't live to enjoy them, and I want to make it clear that this catastrophe is the reason we're all here. Let's get back to camp and start on all the preparations for surviving shall we?" She looked at the men and asked. "Have any of you thought to fill up and supply those Ute's outside?"

Martin and the Sparks held their hands up. "We serviced them while you women were getting your own service," Martin grinned, "There're all tanked up and ready to go."

Pat breathed a silent prayer of thanks and said. "Who thinks we ought to make a start right now?"

Most of them held their hands up but Bev protested. "What about my man? He had a bit too much to drink today and now he's out for the count, he won't be in any fit state to travel till tomorrow."

Martin answered for Pat. "We'll just have to sling him in the back seat and he can sleep it off on the way back, he won't feel too good in the morning but we've all been there and done it."

Pat opened her mouth to reply but was forestalled by the sound of her mobile; she knew who it was the instant it rang and sure enough it was Jim, when she answered he only said. "Have you heard?"

She nodded as she answered yes in the manner of people who think the other party can see them, then added. "We're thinking of coming straight back now, if we leave in half an hour we can get back about three in the morning."

"Good idea," Jim said, "I don't know how long it can take to explode completely and maybe it won't directly, I don't even know yet how long the fallout will take to get down here, I read somewhere that if it's a long way north it could take weeks to cover the southern hemisphere. But I'd still be happier with everybody here."

She told him they would leave directly and looked at them all as she spoke so they knew what was happening. No one spoke up to object so she said goodbye and rang off. "So that's agreed then, we go back," she said briskly, "Let's get going shall we? I'm going down to the reception and pay our bill; I want everybody packed and ready to go in twenty minutes," she touched Martin on the shoulder, will you do me a favour, and get Lee into the Ute for me?"

He nodded a little reluctantly and Pat supposed he was wary of the consequences of trying to move him whilst he was still belligerent with the drink. Bev came over and said. "It won't be any worry, I've had him like this at home and all he wants to do when he's drunk is go to sleep, I'll make sure he's no hardship to you." She looked around defiantly. "I've known lots of men who let go once in a while, they don't mean no harm by it." She looked at Martin and the Sparks. "I bet if the truths known you've both had a bit too much sometimes."

"I'm not making any accusations here Bev." Pat broke in. "I personally would prefer it if there was no drink at all, but I can't stop other people having it, and I don't say one man is better than another because he doesn't drink." She smiled in self depreciation. "My man's been known to go overboard now and again so don't think we're putting you down because Lee got pissed. It's only because it's a bit awkward right now."

Somewhat mollified Bev nodded her thanks and went to start the task of getting a large man like Lee into one of the Ute's. They finally managed it with the aid of the two men and Pat helping, and then Pat went into reception and asked for the bill. The receptionist, although surprised managed to have the acumen to insist they paid for the rooms till the following morning, which under the circumstances was acceptable to Pat as she knew they were letting the hotel down by leaving at such an awkward time. She scribbled out a cheque and had Leah countersign for authenticity, then they all trooped out for the return journey. They completed it in what seemed to Pat to be record time and when they arrived it was early morning so they just went in to the large building, sought out their beds and tumbled in to sleep as best they could.

When Pat woke later she found that Jim had gone from the bed and went in search of him after her ablutions, she found him in the communal kitchen conferring with Ray, Dick, and Andy. The kitchen had a few extra people in there as some of the other men and women had risen and come in for breakfast, Jim looked up as she entered and said. "I wondered when you were going to show your face, we're having a little meeting to agree on what's needed to finish this place off as quickly as possible in the light of the events that have happened. Now I want to know what supplies you've ordered and when we can expect delivery, also I've been trying to reach Colette on her mobile but I haven't had any success at all, it's vital she gets those medical supplies out here as soon as possible because I think we're going to be in need of them soon. So as soon as this meeting's over I want you to start trying to get in touch with her."

He would have gone on issuing orders to all and sundry when Pat replied angrily. "Why don't you let me get something to eat before giving me all this hassle, I'd have told you last night but I don't think you wanted to be bothered about waking up." The rest of the women all seemed to want to get into this argument and started to interrupt at this, but suddenly Julia screamed. "That's enough!! You lot behave like a load of schoolchildren in the playground, now lets get some order into this meeting now." They all subsided in embarrassment and wonder at Julia shouting like that, she normally never raised her voice, and this was something unusual. When the noise had quietened down under her steely gaze, she said. "That's better, now, lets discuss this in a civilised fashion and I'm sure we'll get everything sorted out easily," she turned to Jim and waved him up, "Now tell us what you have to about the situation, then let somebody else have their say."

Jim grinned at Julia taking such a forward stance but nevertheless he stood and spoke. First he looked around at them one by one and then started. "You all know by now the situation as it stands, there has been an eruption but not a very large one, it's entirely possible that it will end in a few days and even if it doesn't we aren't sure its what we've been expecting. I personally think that it's a case of better safe than sorry, so I want us all to go on an alert situation.

The Survivalists, Book 2, **The Finale**

There are several things that have to be made ready, first of all the living quarters aren't quite finished but that's not so important as we will have a lot of time later for that sort of thing. We need some more supplies but I assume." He raised his eyes and looked at Pat for confirmation, and she nodded in his direction. "They are ordered and will be on their way soon enough; the next thing is Medical Supplies, these are so important I think it will pay us to go and search for Colette if we can't raise her on the phone, she promised they were ordered so lets go on the assumption, for today at least, that they are.All the necessary things apart from that are here, the last item is defence, now I know some of you don't think it's going to be necessary but I'm asking you to humour me. You know that we've installed CCTV cameras in a couple of places around here about four miles out, and also round the camp, I want someone to be watching the monitors on a 24/7 basis from now on, if any strange vehicles or people approach there's a button next to the monitor that will ring an alarm bell inside and outside. If it goes off I want everybody in the doors and, the doors locked as quickly as possible." He looked at them grimly. "This rule is absolute, I don't want any of you chasing around looking for little dolly's or teddy bears, or chasing a chicken to get it in; you drop everything and run inside. Is that clear? Get inside as quickly as possible." He looked at the men. "The last thing is the defence of this place; when this meeting's over I want you men to go with Andy and bring our means of defence back with you," he looked at the women and said, "I want this place to get tidied up and ready for living inside from now on and also at first I want you to take the watches on the monitors for the time being while we prepare everything outside." He sighed and said almost in an undertone to himself. "I hope we've got everything ready that we can, because if it does happen we only get one chance at doing it right."

    Lee raised his hand slowly, his face told the story of his binge the previous day, his face was puffy and his eyes bloodshot. He licked his lips which were a sure sign of dehydration from the excessive drink he had consumed, clearing his throat noisily he asked. "Are you sure this is the catastrophe or is it going to be an exercise trial, only some of us have things to do back in town before this gets closed in. And anyway," he went on defensively. "I don't know whether I want to be locked up out here for years."

Jim stared at him with frosty eyes, and would have told him to pack his bags and get out immediately, and had just opened his mouth to say just that when Leah stepped forward from her position by the window. "Do you want to jeopardise everything, your life and the life of your wife and your kids because you don't like the idea of being cooped up here? We all know that it might not happen, but if it does and you're in some place that you like to call civilisation, you're going to die. End of story, that's why we're all here."

It was left unsaid but behind the harsh words was lurking another truth that until now, no one had faced because it would be deeply unpalatable, that was, what would they do if someone left and then decided that maybe they wanted to come back?If that happened there was no guarantee that they would come alone, it was a truth that maybe only one person in the whole camp had decided to face. Andy stepped forward and regarded Lee dispassionately. "How far are you going to get, walking down that road with your wife and kids and her pregnant as well? And just maybe, we don't want you to go spreading word about us here."

Lee's eyes opened wide in surprise and shock. "Are you saying you'd keep me here against my will?" He swivelled round and pointed out of the window. "That estate car over there is mine, and if I want to get in it and go I bloody well will," he leaned forward and pointed a finger at Andy. "And no bloody Pom is going to hold me anywhere against my will."

Andy flushed and held his ground; the insult had found its mark. Until now no one had ever insulted him about being a Pom, in fact they had all thought that the Australians had accepted them for themselves, but now it became clear that some had longer memories than others. His fists clenched and he began to go towards Lee but was forestalled by Ray. "I'm going to tell you something now mate," he said, "These bloody Poms as you like to call them are a sight better than someone like you, after your performance yesterday I was bloody ashamed that I was Australian. These guys here have all come out here to make a new life and I take my hat off to them, every last one of them works bloody hard and they still find time to help other people." He strode over to face Lee and shook his finger into his face. "Now if you don't stay here and help get this place into shape and do your work I'm going to personally see to it that you never reach town. Now you can take that any way you like but I can assure you that that car you're so proud of out there isn't in a fit state to make it into town and no way are you going to make it by walking out. And don't start thinking for one minute about taking one of the Ute's because I took the precaution of taking out all the distributor caps so none of the vehicles on this place can be driven without my say so. You were brought in to help run the farm and that's your job, so do it."

Lee watched him through eyes that burned defiance but he was just clever enough to know when he was beaten, without another word he walked to the door and went out into the passageway that led to the rear of the living quarters and gave access to the nursery section, if he kept walking he would come to the far rear where the animals were to be kept. Ray watched him go and then turned to Pat. "When are those animals going to come out here?" He asked her, "It might calm him down if he's got something to do."

Pat looked at him with eyes that had a slight sheen of tears behind them. "I think the animals will come in the next couple of days if the guy keeps to the delivery date he promised. By the way, thanks for the vote of confidence just now, we appreciate it."

"Didn't do it for your sakes I did it for mine," Ray said gruffly, "We need the guy out there and it's too late to find someone else. By the way……." He grinned. "It'd be a good idea if someone went and took the distributor caps out of those vehicles out there before he takes it into his head to have a look."

Smiling broadly but with serious intent, Martin the Biologist asked. "I've got one thing to ask you now that these serious questions are out of the way. It's always puzzled me that you keep saying you might have to defend this place and I can see that it could be necessary, but can you tell me how do you intend to defend a place that's got a glass roof and a big windmill on top of the hill? It doesn't make any sense to me."

Jim laughed dryly. "It's quite simple really Martin, What happens if any attacker wants to get in here? Don't answer that, I'll tell you.

They want to use the facilities when they're in here, and it's going to do them no good to break everything to get it, because in that case they've got nothing for their trouble. The whole principle of this place is to survive and that won't happen if they trash it getting in."

"Yes, but." Martins face screwed up in concentration, "They might think they can just come in to the top floor through one broken window and patch it up when we're disabled in here, or even disconnect the windmill so we've got no electricity."

Jim shook his head in denial. "I don't think you've followed the idea right through to the end Martin, first of all we've got enough fuel to run a diesel generator for a year, second we can retreat down the stairs and drop a concrete beam into place where the staircase is now. So they can only access the top floor and without electricity and water, both of which we can cut off from down here, they can't use it for much longer than a couple of days anyway." He gestured round the kitchen area where they were standing. "This area's quite secure here, and they'd need some heavy armament to break in, it's all concrete and concrete block walls. The living quarters are another matter as they've been built on to the front, but we can abandon them when we want. Don't forget that time is against them, they won't have much in the way of food or drink; the air I think, will be unbreathable out there for some time as the dust can get in your lungs and clog them, so they have to have some sort of breathing gear or face having a lump of cement in their chest. But beside all that is the fact that we'll be using some pretty impressive arms and if they attack I intend that we'll use them to defend the place. I know that sieges generally work because the attacker can sit outside and wait for the defenders to run out of food, but in this case they have to get in quick or die outside."

He looked around at the assembled company and smiled ruefully. "I hope that answers any questions that you might be thinking of asking? Now lets snap to it and get those arms inside and ready for use, I want to be prepared as they say in the scouts."

They all stood and started to file out to do their various jobs, the men going with Andy to retrieve the guns and ammunition from their hiding place. It took most of the rest of the day and while they worked they kept an ear out for the latest news from America. The surprise for most of them was that two lorry loads of supplies were delivered. One was the medical supplies Colette had arranged and the other was the rest of the supplies that Pat had ordered the previous day in town, it was short of some items because they were unavailable at the moment but they were promised for a few days time. They unloaded them and carried them into the storage spaces. They had still heard nothing on the broadcasts so went about their tasks as usual. Jim gave Andy the job of unpacking the guns and checking them over. He had to get a lot of grease and preservative off them but it was a job he enjoyed and by nightfall they had everything they needed inside and ready. They had still had no word from the Prof and Colette even though they tried all day to get in touch with them.

That evening they all sat down together in the huge kitchen and dining room to eat their evening meal and during the hubbub of conversation that was going on all around them Pat turned to Jim and asked quietly." Do you think something's happened to Colette and the Prof? I'm really worried about them; they haven't been in touch now for three days."

Jim nodded abstractedly, and would have left it at that but Pat was of sterner stuff, her elbow hit Jim's ribs with a sharp pain that made him grunt. "You'd better pay attention when I ask you something, this is our daughter I'm talking about and I want an answer from you about what you intend to do."

Jim blinked in surprise, this was a totally unaccustomed method of getting his attention than she usually employed. His ribs hurt and he felt bound to answer her question. "I don't know what to do," he answered, "Maybe they've been busy and haven't time to get to the phone yet."

She sniffed. "Huh, well let me tell you that Colette has never left me for too long without phoning me, she's always in touch and I think something's gone wrong for her to leave it for so long." She pointed a finger at him and wagged it. "If I don't hear from her in the next twenty four hours you're on the road to town to try and find her."

A shout came from the room where the TV monitors were kept

and someone called. "There's a car coming up the road." There was a general rush for the doors and windows to see who would be coming up the drive and when the car finally came into view it was recognised as the Prof's. It came to a halt and he climbed out beaming from ear to ear, and was nearly knocked over by Julia's welcoming hug. His children Kevin and Pauline ran out as well to greet him and it took many long minutes before Pat was able to get close enough to ask. "Why can't we reach you on the phone and where's Colette?"

He frowned and reached into his pocket to get his mobile out and looking at it he apologised. "I forgot to charge it before I left; I was in too much of a hurry." Seeing Pat's face he went on hurriedly. "She's OK, she wanted to get some last minute supplies for here and went to collect them at the only place she could be sure to find them, some place in Darwin she said to me, but I'm not sure where. But I have got a little surprise for you." He went on, and turning he opened the boot of the estate car and lying there tucked up in some blankets was Emma, her eyes opened and she blinked lazily and stretched her hands out as she woke from her sleep. Pat's heart gave a leap and she screamed in pleasure and reaching into the back of the car she picked her up blankets and all and hugged her to her bosom, then turned and went into the building oblivious to all the others who wanted to greet the newcomer.

Prof looked at Jim. "What's the latest news about this eruption then?"

Jim shrugged his shoulders. "I don't understand it, the eruption definitely took place, but it can't have been very large as nobody's saying anything about it at the moment." He gestured around them, "We got everything ready as we could and now we're just sitting here waiting for something to happen."

"So is everybody here then?"

"All except Colette, and now we don't know when she's coming."

The Prof looked at Jim worriedly. "I don't know how to put this but you know what she's like, I think she'll stay until she gets the supplies she wants and even then she might decide to go back and check on some of her patients."

Jim swore to himself, he knew well enough what she was like, but he thought she would have had enough sense to realise that if the eruption had been as large as predicted it wouldn't have mattered one way or the other if the patients survived or not. Then he cursed himself for being so selfish and wanting his daughter to arrive. Without his realising it Dick had been listening to this exchange and now he ran into the building and a few minutes later came out with some keys and started to go over to the Ute's. Ray came to the door and watched amusedly as Dick started turning the ignition keys to start the engine. It turned over without firing and Dick kept clicking it on and off until Ray strolled over and reaching in the window pulled the keys out of their slot. "You know we disabled these vehicles the other day, don't you?"

"I've got to go and find her." Dick said obstinately.

Ray tossed the keys back into his lap. "You can go if you want mate, but tell me where you're going to look, because this country's a bit too big to wandering off on the off chance you might run into someone, and anyway that makes two people missing if you don't see her. Now why don't you wait another day and see if she rings in, her phone could have run out of credit, or it might have broken down without her realising it. She might even think its better not to ring as everybody's going to want her to do something she doesn't want to. Now why don't you come in and wait for her the same as the rest of us, we're all worried about her as well."

He pointed to the building behind them. "You've got a little girl in there who wants to see her daddy, if he can spare some time for her. And you'd better get a hold of her before Pat steals her straight out from under you. So go look after the one you've got, all the rest of us can worry about Colette. Although from what little I've seen of her, she's quite big enough to look after herself."

Dick looked at Ray despairingly. "You've forgotten one thing haven't you? What about the baby? How does she look after that with all the travelling she's been doing?" he crashed his hand down on the dashboard in temper. "Why the hell couldn't she let the Prof bring the baby with him?"

Ray looked at him compassionately. "She'll have had her own reasons for doing what she did, look, I promise if she doesn't show by noon tomorrow, or at least get in touch, we'll get a search party out and go and look for her."

With that Dick realised he couldn't do any more that night and climbed slowly out of the Ute and walked in slowly to try and prise his daughter out of Pat's hands. Ray looked around at the assembled audience who had been hanging on to every word and said defiantly, "I meant what I said, I'll lead the search party myself if she doesn't show."

He was rewarded with some smiles from the rest of them and Julia patted his arm in thanks. "We might make a caring husband out of you yet." She remarked as they all walked into the building.

Luckily for Ray they had no need of a search party as Colette rang through the next morning and confirmed what he had surmised, her phone battery had indeed run out and she had been too busy to try and charge it. She had bought the supplies she wanted and was just about to leave to come to them, both her and the baby were well and she expected to arrive there at about seven in the evening. When asked if she wanted Ray to come for her she refused, saying. "I want to bring the car out there; as if this doesn't blow up I can use it for transport." No amount of cajoling would change her mind so they had to allow her to have her own way. When she eventually arrived in her estate car they could see she had packed another large load of medical supplies in to the rear of the vehicle, the baby was alongside her in a carrycot strapped down on the seat. Jim breathed a sigh of relief when he saw the trail of dust coming towards them; finally everyone had come together.

The next few days were spent preparing the camp for the time ahead as everyone settled in and were busy making sure that when the time came they could close off the outside world and live the disaster out. The animals arrived the next day and brought some surprises with them. Two pregnant female dogs and a male dog of uncertain breed came with them, they looked to Jim like a collie cross, but he couldn't be sure. When he looked into the lorry to inspect the animals he found the same number of cats as well, he stared in surprise and then looked round at everyone there. It was obvious from the expression on Leah's face who was responsible for the extra mouths to feed. She smiled sweetly and said defensively. "If you thought we were coming out here and leaving pets behind you were very much mistaken, and anyway these pet's will earn their keep sometime in the future. The dogs will be needed for outside farming and the cats are going to catch the mice that get in here, and anyway," she went on, "If you can save horses, I can save these."

Jim smiled and took the wind straight out of her sails. "I can't imagine how I didn't think of this before, I think it's a great idea to bring them." He leaned forward and looked at her closely. "I hope you considered how you're going to exercise those dogs, because I think you've got a problem there."

She flushed, but being the woman she was, there was no way she intended to let him win. "I think this place is quite large enough for someone to run round the outside edge and give them some exercise." She smiled at him all sweetness and light. "Maybe you'd like to volunteer to give them a run; you look like you could do with something to tone you up."

It was Jim's turn to flush and he answered roughly. "I've got more important things to do than spend time running round taking dogs for their constitutional." He turned and walked over to the men standing waiting for him and they started the process of getting the animals inside and in their quarters. Whilst they were doing this, Jim kept an eye on Lee to see how he was reacting to staying there with them, but the man appeared to have settled down and accepted his lot. Jim supposed that the news of the eruption had had some effect on him, as it had certainly brought it home to everyone, that it was now a distinct possibility.

When they had offloaded all the animals and waved goodbye to the transporter, Jim had some of the men help him prepare some surprise defences that no one could possibly find out about now, as he felt that the element of uncertainty in any aggressor would help. He had waited so as to be absolutely sure that no outsiders were there to make sure the arrangements were a secret. He had decided not to take Andy up on his suggestion of claymores across the front of the building as he felt they were lethal things to use, and although defence meant using as many things as possible, he didn't want a lot of people being maimed from these to be on his conscience. He had seen too many pictures of innocents with no legs.

They had constructed the building on the ground floor with no windows because they had installed air-conditioning in to the area. When they built the living quarters across the front they had simply built them on the front and had constructed a passageway leading from the front rooms into the back where they were growing the crops. The passage ran at right angles to the main building and this was deliberate planning. They had always had a wooden floor as Jim had told everyone it was to facilitate running electricity and waste pipes through. But now Jim revealed its true purpose, it was about six feet deep and ran for a distance of ten metres, and then it doglegged and ran for another five metres till it reached the entrance to the main building. The wooden decking they had been walking across could be removed in an emergency and they could fill the passageway with water. It meant that if they took out the decking anyone wishing to cross from front to rear would have to swim. The passageway had one other use and that was the wall that ran on the side of the passageway had had some piers built on the other side so several people could stand above the wall and look down. Jim intended to position gunmen on them so they could fire down into the water filled passageway; it would be a lethal entrance should anybody try it.

The upper floor had a glass roof but he didn't intend to try and defend that at first, as it would be impossible. They could stay in the ground floor for some time and let the attackers beat themselves out trying to access the solid built bottom floor. Andy had watched these preparations Jim was making with some amusement, he knew there was no way that Jim would let him use his own ideas but had already decided that if push came to shove, he would solve the problem in his own way before Jim had a chance to stop him. If Jim thought that men would be willing to put their heads over the top of a wall to try and shoot someone in the water he was in for a rude awakening. Most men wouldn't risk anything if it meant they got hurt, or even worse killed.

He felt a tingle between his shoulder blades and with that sixth sense that people have he glanced over his shoulder and found Leah regarding him with amused eyes. "You don't think much of your Dad's preparations do you?"

He shrugged his shoulders. "It doesn't usually matter what I think, he never takes much notice anyway."

She put her hand on his arm and stroked it, and he felt the blood rush to his head; she said. "I want you to come and give me a hand while all these people are working on this."

"Doing what?"

She smiled mysteriously. "You'll find out soon enough, come on now before someone finds something for you to do."

He looked around from under lowered eyes, the others seemed to be occupied with working on the alterations and he felt they weren't doing it in the right way, so had little need to help them. Also he admitted to himself, he was intrigued as to what she wanted him from him. He turned and walked quickly out of the door in her tracks, but if he thought he had got away with it he was badly mistaken. Pat was watching him go.

When he caught her up she headed for the outside door, past one or two of the children playing outside. She looked round at him as he hurried alongside making her way across the open ground in front of the building. It needed a clearance, as the materials for the construction lay scattered around in haphazard piles, Jim had said some time previously that they needed to clean up but they still had to use some of the items. She made her way to the caravans that were lying in the same places they had occupied whilst the construction work had been done. When she arrived at the one she had occupied with Ray, she quickly opened the door and entered. The doorway was out of sight of the building and about two hundred yards distant from it. It smelt musty and unused so she sniffed and opened a window to let some fresh air in. Then she indicated a pile of sheets and blankets that lay in the sleeping area. "Those are the reason we came over here, if anyone wants to know."

The weather was warm and humid and she had the minimum of clothing on, and for Leah that meant a pair of shorts and a blouse, looking down he was extremely aware of her and wanted to reach out and touch her bare arm. He held himself in check and as he bent to pick them up he felt her cool hand on his arm as she stopped him from doing so. He stood and looked at her with a question in his eyes; her hand slid up to his chest and toyed with the buttons on his shirt. "How are you getting along with Victoria these days?" She asked.

He frowned; it was a question he didn't want to answer. The truth of the matter was that they were almost living separate lives. She had shown no interest in the sexual side of the marriage for some time now and he felt the need for some comfort badly. "What do you know about that?" He asked.

He could see in her eyes she knew something and she swung round to face the window so he couldn't see the expression on her face, she said over her shoulder, her voice slightly muffled. "Do you remember on the boat the night of the attack when you came down to my cabin when the men boarded us?"

He nodded, and she went on. "Why did you come then?"

"I think you know the answer to that without asking, don't you?"

"We got close on the voyage here as well didn't we?"

Andy went back in his minds eye and remembered the feel of her breasts when they had done watch keeping together in the evenings and early morning. The might have gone further then, but they was no way they could do anything on a boat with all the crew listening to the slightest sound and feeling the movement of the boat.

She turned back to face him again a different expression on her face, her lips were parted slightly and he could see from the blouse her breath had quickened, she stared at him through eyes that showed desire. "We've got unfinished business between us Andy, and I want it out of the way before we get stuck in that place over there for a long time. Now are you going to do something about it or am I going to have to drag you over to that bed and do it myself."

She reached up and put her arms round his shoulders and he felt her firm breasts press against his chest. He groaned in despair and couldn't stop himself nuzzling into her neck to smell the sweetness of her. He felt himself rising as the blood rushed through his body and the last thought he had before surrendering to passion was of Victoria.

Pat and Jim walked along in the cool of the evening, although cool was only a term here for not as hot as day. The air was still and quiet and as they walked through the orchard they could smell the ripening of the fruit on the trees. One of the dogs had adopted

Pat and now walked around them sniffing enthusiastically in the undergrowth. The rest of the dogs had taken to various people amongst them and although they allowed others to pet them, they tended to follow along with their chosen partner. The cats just went wherever they felt like and preferred to stay close to the kitchen where they watched all and sundry for any scraps that fell to the floor. They had grown fat and sleek with the amount of food they received and Jim was wont to say that it was about time they earned their keep and caught some of the mice that occasionally gained access to the building.

He looked at Pat and thought to himself that it was all a bit of a let down, it was now four weeks since the scare with the eruption and no news of the area was coming out at all. He wondered if it really was going to happen but knew the only thing they could do was wait. They walked a little further in the comfortable silence of their years, each busy with their own thoughts. Jims centred on his dilemma with food, they had a definite surplus and he wanted to get rid of it; he acknowledged the general feeling amongst the community that they should take it to town and sell it. The problem came with who he should send, some of the community wanted to have some of the money to buy luxuries with and also be there to spend it themselves. He knew he could trust Ray and Andy to go but he didn't want to send the farmer Lee as he expected him to give a repeat performance of the last drunken episode and it would raise a lot of questions in the town.

Martin had told him that he thought he could be producing gas in the next two or three weeks and he would have preferred to wait for that to fuel the Ute's but now they had no time so he intended to send the reliable people to town and promise the others a run later. The electrician had come out tops with the general electrics in the building and had now turned his talents to the computers. At least Ray seemed to have swallowed his dislike for the man and he was helping him with the programmes; he had been as good as his word and they had an extensive library of knowledge stored on CD's. The computers he had obtained had been some sort of general workhorse machines that he had recommended and had so far proved as reliable as promised. They had ample supplies of them and some in store if the original ones broke down. They had also procured a large library of films and general entertainment, and that alongside the large quantity of books that had been brought by various members should mean that nobody would be bored.

Pat's problems centred more on the personal problems of the members they had in the community, she had noticed several of them weren't speaking to each other and in particular she was certain there were problems with Ray, Leah, Andy, and Victoria. All four of them gave off the wrong sort of vibes to her, but the problem was that none of them seemed to want to talk about it. More and more she saw them sitting with the wrong partner, so Andy would be talking to Leah, and they sat far too close to each other. Then she saw Ray speaking and laughing with Victoria; she suspected nothing had gone on yet with them but it was obvious that it was only a matter of time. Victoria had had an air of despondency about her for some time now and she only seemed to pay any attention when Ray spoke to her. She worried about it and had spoken to Julia about the problem but Julia had thought the best thing to do was to leave them to get on with it. Some of the other members were starting to notice and speculate on the outcome, but Pat had determined that if she had anything to do with it her son and daughter in law would carry on being married to each other and raising her grandchildren. But she couldn't put her finger on the root cause of Victoria's unhappiness.

They both lifted their heads together and looked at each other, their eyes reflecting their troubled thoughts. "We're both worrying aren't we?" Pat said.

Jim grunted and nodded in the affirmative, and then he grinned ruefully. "Probably about different things I'll warrant," he answered.

She sighed and said. "Why is it that we can come all the way out here and yet our children who ought to be happy living in this near paradise are still causing us problems?"

"I must confess I wasn't worrying about the children love, I was worrying about the sale of the produce."

She groaned and grumbled. "Haven't you seen what's going on right under your nose? Andy's marriage is in danger of breaking up and all you can do is think about selling some veg in town."

He flushed under her onslaught and answered angrily. "That boy's got to make his own way in life, and anyway if the truth's known about that relationship the fault doesn't appear to come from him but from her, she's been mooning about for the last few weeks as if the end of the world had come." He stopped speaking as the import of what he had just said struck him.

He said wonderingly. "Now I can't think where that particular thought came from but it's very apt anyway."

She punched him on the arm half in anger and half playfully. "I don't know what I'm going to do with you, but we've still got to do something about those two, it's driving me crazy. I know that something's happened and I don't know what I can do about it."

There was a shout from behind them and turning round they found Jeannie, Ray and Leah's daughter running across the field towards them. She was turning into a pretty young woman who in a year or two would start turning heads, her breasts had started blooming and she was already starting to try out her new found feminine ways on the young men around the community. She reserved the best of the ways for Dick as she still kept a torch going for him. Colette treated her attempts with tolerance, while still keeping a watchful eye on her.

She ran up to them panting a little with the exertion and Jim tucked away a thought about creating an exercise programme because nobody thought about exercise unless it was absolutely necessary. "Mum and dad want you to come straight away, something's happening."

Jim and Pat stared at each other, then at her, "What is it?" Pat questioned her.

"I don't know," Jeannie gasped, "all I know is they said to come quick, it's serious."

They glanced once more at each other with questioning eyes, and then Jim decided that the best way to find out would be to go and see for himself, so started to run back to the main building. Pat followed him as quickly as she could and Jeannie ran like the wind and was back before both of them. She flung open the door and they both ran in to the main living quarters to find almost all the community clustered round the television set, it was set on one of the American news channels they could access via the satellite link. The newscasters were in a state of near panic talking about the loss of life in the millions, Jim pushed in to the front where he found Ray glued to the set. "How bad is it?" He asked.

Ray glanced at him with eyes full of sorrow. "Just as bad as you could expect, it really has blown, they heard the explosion all over America, and the sound might even reach the other side of the Atlantic, just like they predicted in that programme. The loss of life from the fallout of the dust will run into millions, the dust is choking them to death, it gets into the lungs and clogs them. Apparently the government knew about the possibility but concealed it to stop panic buying and people trying to make their own arrangements, but that's only made it worse as no one is prepared now so they're really panicking. There's hardly any power in the States and most of the news broadcasts are being made using back up generators."

Jim nodded and reflected on the selfishness of politicians who would manipulate the people for their own ends, he would place bets that the very same politicians would be making arrangements to save their own skin though. He wondered where the President of the United States was right now; 'Probably on a nuclear submarine out in the Pacific with the rest of his family if the truth was known' he answered himself.

His attention was drawn back to the television, they were showing a satellite picture of America and it had a big black cloud over almost half of the ground area, the whole of the east coast couldn't be seen and it was swirling round in a semi circle to cover the north pole and coming back in black streaks to fall on the west coast. There was a large section of it that had been caught in the prevailing wind and had swept out into the Atlantic and was heading towards the European side of the globe. It was menacing in its appearance and Jim shuddered as he thought about what it could mean for humanity.

The announcer who was plainly rattled, started saying something about people should stay at home and wait for the crisis to pass but Jim knew it would be to little avail. The mass of humanity would be out now looking for somewhere to find shelter but he knew that not one of them realised they needed shelter for maybe the next ten years.

"Have they said anything about whether they think it's going to spread to the southern hemisphere yet?" He asked Ray.

He shook his head. "They seem to have this theory that if it's above the 40th latitude it won't spread below the equator, but they don't seem to have thought it through, if enough gets into the atmosphere its inevitable that it will spread over the whole planet. There're having problems with the amount of fallout east of the eruption though." Ray added. "The build up of dust downwind to the main area of eruption is incredible, there're talking about maybe ten centimetres of dust falling as far away as Washington and the rest of the east coast."

Jim shook his head in disbelief, this was as bad if not worse than he had imagined it would be; he felt sorry for all the millions of residents in the path of this super eruption but at the same time he felt relieved to be on the other side of the planet to it. "They didn't realise how big it could possibly be." He muttered, half to himself. "The caldera is seventy kilometres long and thirty kilometres wide. Its also eight kilometres down, if that has blown its unimaginable force and size could mean millions of tons of debris and dust being blown into the stratosphere, and has to mean its going to spread over the whole planet and lower the mean temperature for years to come."

His attention was drawn to the television as the announcer started to repeat almost word for word what he had been thinking. The picture and sound on the screen started to deteriorate as he watched and suddenly switched of, cutting off the announcer in mid sentence. One of the others immediately started to search for other channels and eventually they found one in England. The cut glass accent and concerned face of the young woman said it all as they watched. The government had already issued emergency powers to deal with the situation in the short term but it was obvious they would only have at best a few days to come up with any solutions. They heard the announcer say that almost all communication had been cut off in America as when one electricity supply failed it took down the others with it too quickly for the electricity companies to cope by switching power. Government installations now ran the only news coming out of America and they held back on giving out the real situation, as they seemed to want to control the populace. There was also the possibility that the Nuclear Power Stations were going to have to close down to stop fall out spreading its deadly radioactive dust over the whole country.

They looked at each other in despair; although this was the reason they were in the community now, the women in general sat and stared, hugging their arms around the children as if to protect them from the news on the screen. As the announcer was only going over ground they had already seen covered from the American broadcast, Jim felt he could interrupt to say something to them. He stepped forward and facing them he said. "Well, I'm the first to admit it when I say I didn't really expect to see this day come in my lifetime, but now it's happened and we've got to make the best of it, we've prepared in every way we can think of, so we have to make it work by living and working here together."

One of the women from the farming team held her hand up slowly and coughed to get his attention; he looked at her and nodded to let her speak. She glanced quickly round the assembled audience and said hesitantly. "My sister lives in town, and I'd really like to see her and say goodbye before that dust cloud gets here."

Jim stared at her kindly, "You know that's not possible don't you? Can you imagine what's going to happen if you do that? You're going to have the situation where you'll want to bring her back here and you can't do that. Then she'll be off telling everybody else and before we know it we'll have every man jack in the Northern Territories standing out there wanting to get in. Not to mention that you aren't the only one in this situation, if you do this, all the rest of these people here will feel obligated to go and see their loved ones. And the whole things going to get out of hand; and the one thing that is certain is that we can't take any more people in at this time. This project was designed to cope with the amount of people we have here now, if we take more we could be in danger of killing every one of us into the bargain. So that's your answer and that goes for every one of you." He looked at them with a hard flat stare. "From now on every last one of you is confined to this compound till the whole thing blows over, and that could be for the next ten years. Are all of you clear on that? Are there any more questions?

One of the audience put their hand up and asked. "What about the produce you were going to send to town?"

"We eat what we can and either freeze or preserve the rest, from now on we save all the food we can in case we have a crop failure or something happens. Luckily we're a long way from the centres of habitation, which is why we bought this property in the first place, so we shouldn't get bothered too much by unwanted visitors. I hope that none of you have any means of communication with the outside world because if you do get in touch with someone you could end up killing us all, our best means of defence is keeping our heads down and hoping nobody comes out to see what we're doing," then he went on. "That's all for now, just remember, we stay here to live, or we leave to die." He stared slowly round at them as he took in the grim expressions of them all.

When he had looked at them all, he relaxed and said. "OK, everybody, lectures over for the day, shall we see about closing down the outside and starting to live in here from now on?"

Over the next few days they watched anxiously as station after station closed down and the news became ever more grim, Jim had expected that most people would die from starvation but it seemed that everywhere the dust clouds swirled over the countryside the dust penetrated their lungs and they either suffocated, or the dust damaged them and they couldn't breathe anyway. Panic had reigned for a long time and they saw the government trying desperately to issue breathing apparatus but it was all in vain as the dust clogged all the compressors used to pump the equipment. It seemed worse in Australia as they knew it was coming and were trying their hardest to make provision for the people, but it only served to push them further into despair as the populace searched desperately for solutions to the problem. Jim knew that breathing apparatus wasn't going to be the answer as nobody could expect to go round for the next ten years breathing out of them. And anyway the biggest problem was going to be how to feed them.

The supermarkets got rapidly cleared of food as everybody started to buy in bulk, but this only made the problem worse as the poorest families with little or no savings had no chance of buying food and so ran out of supplies very quickly, troops had to be put into the shops to keep order and a few days later the government declared martial law and took over the supply of food themselves. This only served to exacerbate the problem and rioting quickly followed as a population used to times of plenty tried to get supplies in any way they could. Jim imagined that someone like Blackie would probably do well in times like this and idly wondered where he was.

All this happened before the dust cloud followed its inexorable course down into the southern hemisphere, in that at least Jim had been proved right. The total amount of dust and debris thrown out had far exceeded the expectations of the scientists and as the northern hemisphere had been completely covered the dust started to swirl around by the equator and drift into the south day by day. It moved slowly at first but the pace accelerated as the weather patterns started to change because the north got progressively colder. Soon the hot air from the south got pulled over the equator and violent storms raged as the hot air mixed with the colder northern climes. News got very patchy from the north and the dust gathered along the equator until it started its inevitable drift southwards. The first signs that something was happening was when they saw a haze gather round the sun towards evening, but gradually it got thicker and the daylight seemed to glow a little less brightly. They had still not confined themselves to staying inside the building, as Jim wanted all of them to get as much pleasure from being outside as possible. But one day they tasted the first dust as it drifted down coating everything with a layer of fine powder; by now the sun had all but disappeared in the haze so they reluctantly decided to go inside and close the doors against the dust.

They had had to leave the vehicles outside and Jim had made some small covers to protect them against the worst of the elements, they weren't very strong and Jim doubted they would last for ten years but shrugged his shoulders as even when they emerged it would probably be years before they had any contact with civilisation at all. His one big worry had been that the air cleaning equipment they had installed would get clogged up by the dust, but Dick had solved this by a unique filter system they could change without going outside. The news gradually died out as the stations suffered from the lack of electricity and this had a knock on effect as the population started to slowly starve as no food could be preserved by freezing. Jim placed a ban on anyone using the radio equipment or communicating with the outside world at all. Some of the people with families outside still wanted to try and communicate with them but he pointed out that they had to make believe they were on a spaceship and couldn't go back at all.

They had started to get used to being cooped up all day and night and Jim allowed them to have all the curtains drawn open in the front so they could at least look outside. The windows were double-glazed and couldn't be opened so it was as safe as possible. The dust had started to pile up and now it covered everything with a fine powder like talcum. Jim marvelled at how one eruption so far away in America had managed to lay dust on the other side of the world to that sort of depth. The only problem with this that Jim could see was the fact that it was a decidedly gloomy outlook and it quickly palled as a means of entertainment. Some of the members started to get very irritable and they had problems settling down, especially at mealtimes when even the place they sat in started to get important. There were many of these niggling little problems to solve and deal with, and at first Jim was hard put to keep the peace. Colette started to run a counselling course in community relations and gradually the problems started to get ironed out.

The communications networks gradually closed down over the next few weeks and it soon became apparent that the dust was killing off all but the most organised people. The government had set up as many emergency shelters as they could with the limited resources they had at their disposal but from the news they were getting now it soon became obvious that many people were dying. By some miracle one or two news stations kept going and appealing for any person able to give them food to come forward, these gradually petered out until the last one finally said they were going off the air and wished any person out there who could listen the best of luck. It was a poignant moment when it stopped broadcasting and the newscaster said goodbye. They all sat and stared at each other and counted themselves lucky that they had at least survived so far.

Some of them kept on listening for news on the short-wave radio, but this means of communication died out gradually and Jim banned any use of the transmitter as it would only alert any potential intruders to their whereabouts. It became clear over the next few weeks that they were indeed alone and if anyone still survived they weren't in any position to use the radio. It was a distressing time for all of them as they knew that any relations or friends they had were almost certainly dead and they could do nothing to save any of them. Jim still wondered what would happen to all the world leaders who had made sure they could survive; he thought that most of them would try and stay alive by going out in nuclear submarines or ships as the land at this time couldn't support life. They still kept radio silence, as it was apparent that they themselves couldn't continue to exist if unwanted visitors came knocking on the door to be allowed entry.

Jim was staring out of the window at the dismal landscape when a voice spoke by his side. "How long before the last civilian dies then?" Jim glanced round to see Leah standing there. He shrugged and answered. "I really don't know, I think some of the Abbos might get by, they seem to have survival built in when there're not on the grog. But I think a lot of the white Aussies are going to go pretty quickly as they haven't had enough time to prepare. I reckon it'll have been dog eat dog out there for a bit, and I don't think there'll be much in the way of law by now."

Leah nodded in agreement. "That's about what I thought, if anybody is surviving by now they'll be getting pretty desperate."

"I'll guarantee that a lot of those who were supposed to be looking after the general populace are still alive in their bolt holes though," Jim said, "but I don't know how long they can expect to survive, I can't imagine many people had the opportunity to put the sort of supplies away that we did. And we managed to create a community that stands a chance of surviving this catastrophe."

Leah put her hand on his arm and smiled. "I thought you lot were nothing more than a bunch of crazy idiots when I heard the idea all that time ago, I never really thought it had any chance of happening. Now it seems like nothing more than a bad dream, and I feel I'm going to wake up at any time."

Jim smiled back at her. "I'll tell you the truth, I thought it had a chance of happening but I didn't think it would happen in my lifetime. But one of the main reasons I did it was to form a little community in the outback and bring the kids up without all the pressures of drink and drugs and maybe teach them to be better members of the community. Do you know that just before I left England they said they couldn't get enough teachers for the classrooms? But they stopped them even touching the children or they were charged with assault, it was crazy, how can you keep discipline without some form of punishment. The kids were allowed to hit the teachers though. How can you expect teachers to work in an atmosphere like that? Would you accept a job where the children you're supposed to look after know they can get you into trouble for anything they like to say and it could ruin your life? I take my hat off to young people going into the teaching profession nowadays; they've got more gumption than me. I've got a friend who was charged with assault because she stepped in between two children who were fighting and pulled them apart, it was physical contact and not allowed." He shook his head in sorrow. "What a strange world we live in, if I got hit at school for something and told my mother when I got home, she'd fetch me a clip round the ear as well because I shouldn't have been doing it anyway." Jim stopped speaking as he realised that the problem no longer existed, and his mood turned sombre as he thought of all the promising lives that had been lost

Chapter Three

It happened as Jim had dreaded it would, several months later when they had thought that nobody could survive outside any longer. They were eating the main meal of the day when a shout went up from the next room where they had the CCTV monitors set up. They rushed in to see what the commotion was and were met by an amazing sight. Three Utes were pictured on the screen groaning up the road, but it was the conversion that had been done on them that drew the eye. They had been totally enclosed like a van, the bonnets had been removed, and some sort of air cleaner had been mounted on top of the engine. At least Jim thought it was an air cleaner as it was quite large and had what appeared to be a side panel with a grill on the side, the grill was revolving and spilling out what appeared to be dust. He had expected that any engine would need a constant supply of fresh clean air so the cleaner had obviously been tacked on to ensure that.

The rear of the van-like body looked as if it was sealed to stop dust coming in and another cleaner like the first had been welded to the top. All three looked incongruous as they ground slowly up the road towards them; Jim sprang into action and shouted to everyone to get back from the windows and not to make any sound. He knew it was a vain hope that these people were coming here accidentally as it was too far off the beaten track to be anything else but deliberate. Ray appeared at his side, with Andy and Dick close behind, "Oh Christ!" Ray groaned when he saw the Utes, "They've got to be pretty determined to come out here; they must know we're here."

It wasn't long before the Utes ground to a halt outside by the caravans they had used whilst the building was constructed. The passengers all dismounted and after stretching to get the kinks out after what must have been a long journey they started to look around and explore their surroundings. It wasn't long before they tried the tap that had supplied water to them when they were building. As the water gushed out he could see the pleasure in their attitudes. They all swung round and stared at them, and two or three waved. Jin growled deep in his throat; he should have turned it off and now he couldn't without disclosing their presence here.

Then they were distracted by a shout from Leah who had been watching the outside. "One of them is coming towards us." She peered through her binoculars and went on. "He doesn't appear to be carrying any weapons or anything, he's holding his hand above his head and he's got some sort of handkerchief and what looks like a loudhailer in his hand."

Jim snatched up some gun sights and stared at the man approaching. He was tall and something about his way of walking made him think he knew him. As the man got closer to them he couldn't see his face because of the breathing mask the man wore. He put down the sights and waited until the man was standing directly in front of the doors about twenty yards away. They had fitted an intercom unit when they had installed the security cameras but Jim waited for him to speak first. The man still had his hands higher than his shoulders and now he lowered them and spoke through the loudhailer in a slightly muffled way because of the mask. "Hallo inside, can we have a little talk?"

Ray gasped aloud, he knew that voice well, and it was the voice of one man he had thought he would never hear again. It was Sulim! The gunrunner! He thumped Jim on the shoulder, "That's Sulim," he cried. Jim stood in shock for a moment while his brain tried to absorb this new information. This put a whole new perspective on any dealings with the newcomers! He wrinkled his brow as he wondered how this of all men came to be here; he would have understood if the man had taken over some installation in Thailand, but to come here to the outback of Australia seemed impossible. Glancing past the man he speculated who else he had with him, as he knew that men of Sulim's ilk always travelled with like minded people. Then it came to him; it had to be Diman! He was the only person who Jim knew that could connect what they were doing with what had happened. First the guns and then the building here. He was brought back to the present by Andy, who had been peering through some binoculars. "I think they've got some sort of Rocket Launcher they're bringing up. It's got a long tube and they're carrying several cases of shells for it. And all that lot out there are carrying arms."

Jim could see that several men were walking slowly towards them carrying some items as Andy had said. He glanced quickly back to Sulim, who in his turn looked over his shoulder at his followers; then he turned and raised his hands palms out in universal appeal. "Don't worry," he said cajolingly, "It's just some of the men being a leetle impatient."

This last was said sarcastically, and Jim didn't believe a word he said. They were preparing to enter the building whatever he or anyone else said to the contrary. He leant forward and switched the outside loudspeaker on. "Go away," he said with the speaker full on. The words reverberated over them stopping the Rocket Launcher team in their tracks. "There's nothing here for any of you, we can't feed you because we've only got enough for ourselves. We can't let you in because this facility is at full stretch now."

The man Sulim used his hands once more to illustrate peace and goodwill. "Can't we just have a little talk about it, why don't you open the door and only myself will come in so I can talk to you man to man."

Jim sneered. "If I open those doors Sulim, I reckon you lot will be in quicker than a rat up a drainpipe."

Sulim shook his head. "So you know who I am Jim, but it's not true, we only want some food and a bit of comfort for a while."

Jim started to get angry with this man; He knew full well what would happen if they managed to set foot in there with them, and he wasn't about to let it happen.

Ray was standing next to him with Leah. "If we let him in….." He said warningly.

Leah broke in. "He's going to take over if we aren't careful. And if he does we'll all die, because he won't share with what we've got, he's the type that wants everything."

"Come on Leah." Jim exploded, "You've never even met the man, and both of you have got me wrong; I've got no intention of letting him in here at all. And anyway it's too late to worry about now." Jim said grimly. "We've got to go with what we've got, so I want you lot to break out those guns and get them ready for action; I think these people are going to be knocking on our door in a few minutes."

He decided to play for time and turned back to Sulim. "Just give us a few minutes to have a vote on it and then we'll let you know."

Sulim shook his head. "I know you're armed in there but let me warn you that I'm a professional man and my guns are bigger than yours; if you try anything funny I will wipe you out quicker than an ant under my foot. I'll give you ten minutes and then I want an answer."

He walked off and shouted at the men with the rocket launcher who laid it down and walked back with him to the caravans.

The women by this time were rushing around collecting all the children and Jim shouted to them to take them to the back of the building. Then he called the other men and instructed them to take the covers off the passageway and make sure the pit was as full as they could get it.

Jim had sense enough to know that none of the measures they were taking would be enough to stop a determined attacker but the idea behind them was mostly to deter anybody trying and maybe they could inflict some casualties on them and act as a deterrent. Jim glanced around to see the state of readiness they were in now. He was standing in the front looking out of the windows at the compound and he had Ray, and Dick alongside him and they were armed with the Heckler and Koch submachine guns while Andy had his automatic shotgun out. The other men were busy preparing the pit in the passageway to the rear, he had told them to leave several of the balks of wood to allow them to run across when the time came, they could then be pulled in with some ropes attached leaving the pit full of water for the enemy to try and cross. Jim knew Leah and Pat had the automatic pistols and were prepared to use them. He was unsure how many of the others would fire but he hoped if it came to it and they understood what the penalties for doing nothing were, they would take up arms to help.

He called out to Martin and Lee to take up position on the top of the wall leading into the back. He wanted to have someone up there so as to be able to direct their fire down if the enemy tried to cross the pit. They had placed some wire mesh across the top to stop anybody in the passageway below from tossing grenades over the wall and he made sure they had holes to fire through. He went back to the front and peered out into the gloom. He could see some small figures walking around and by their gait he surmised they were women. They were all wearing some sort of breathing apparatus with a filter on the side that could be unscrewed and emptied which he saw one of them in the process of doing. They wore coveralls that appeared to have no openings and these were tucked into boots so the whole ensemble had no way for dust to penetrate. At this range it was impossible to identify any of them, especially as they wore the masks constantly. Andy, standing beside him, asked. "Well, come on Dad, tell us who it is and how many of them are there?"

Putting down the scope, Jim handed it to him. "I think there's about fifteen or sixteen out there, it's impossible to tell which sex, but some of them appear to be womanly in the way they walk, and they are carrying some sort of weapons, but the worst thing is that they seem to be geared up for living out there. I don't know if they've got food, but they certainly have water now."

"We can cut it off from here any time we want to, can't we?" Dick asked.

"True." Jim answered. "I think it'll be a good idea to get on that straight away, I don't see any reason to help them do you?"

Dick said, "I'll get on to it right now. They aren't going to disappear for a long time I can see that, if you look at what they're doing you can see they're settling into the caravans."

This was indeed true, they were carrying bags and other items into the caravans, and a bulky figure had started to cut a hole into the rear of one to fit something he had in a box beside him. Some of the others seemed intent on clearing them out and fitting up some more screens on the windows. Sulim; if that was him just waved his arms about and gave the others orders.

Some of Jim's company had gathered round to see what was going on They were speculating as to whom the visitors were, and the general consensus of opinion was that they must be people who had had some contact with them recently as the very fact that they knew where to come had proved. Jim had a sudden thought, and turning to Andy he asked. "If I wanted to go outside for a time, what could I wear so I don't get any of this dammed dust in my lungs?" He reflected that as much as he had tried to think of everything, there were still some things that got forgotten.

Andy grinned in triumph. "I've got the very thing." And he went off to his room to fetch it. When he returned he was carrying a box in his hands, and setting it on the floor, he proudly opened it and produced a basic breathing apparatus. It had goggles and a mouthpiece, which were in two sections, these were held on to the head by rubber straps. The mouthpiece had a filter that unscrewed to allow the wearer to empty it without taking the whole thing off. It strongly resembled the masks that visitors were wearing, and Andy smiled when he saw the look on Jims face. "Army surplus store." He said. "They probably shopped there as well."

Jim was intrigued. "When did you get these, I never knew about them?"

"When I went down to that store and bought those meals ready to eat, I saw them on the shelf and figured we could use them sometime. I hope you don't think you're going out there to talk to them."

Jim shook his head. "I thought that I'll have to go out sometime or other, but I always imagined we'd have that breathing apparatus to do it."

"It's a good job some of us think about what we're doing isn't it?" Andy said. "You had too much on your plate when you were building this place and stocking it. I've got half a dozen scuba outfits in the back, just in case we need to go outside, but I think these things are going to be better, because with scuba you have to have a tank strapped to your back and you stand the chance you'll run out of air. These can be cleaned even if you're outside. There're basic but they do the job just as well."

Jim nodded his approval; he was pleased his son had shown some initiative. "OK son, well done; if you keep them handy we can maybe use them when we find out what's going to happen with this situation."

One of the women brought Jim a sandwich which he ate without tasting and drank something that tasted of tea.

Andy disappeared for a while and shortly after there was a

grunting sound behind Jim and Andy came through the door with Dick lugging the machine gun that had done such sterling work on the boat. Andy caught his eye and grinned. "I'm not taking any chances this time Dad." He said. "I'm going to have this set up in a few minutes and then we'll see about them breaking in here."

Jim opened his mouth to protest and then had the thought that he always gave the benefit of the doubt to people and without fail they always took advantage of his good nature. Some of the other men standing there glanced at each other and Martin the biologist said. "You can't use that on them, there are women out there."

Andy nodded to Dick and they placed the gun on the centre of the floor, then he stood and faced Martin. "Before you start saying things like that, let me put you straight on a few things. Do you realise that even before we got here we were attacked at sea; I think that these people are probably the same and they have got guns out there, and in my experience I've found that people who carry guns are inclined to use them to settle disputes. Now if they point a gun at you what do you intend to do? Do you think if they get in here there're going to let you live? Why should they do that? They'll have to feed you, and you know there isn't enough food for them, and us as well. And one last thing, usually when someone invades a place they usually try to kill all the defenders because prisoners can be a pain in the neck, and what do you think will happen to the women in that sort of situation? Do you want me to spell out what I think will happen or have you got enough imagination to think it out for yourself?"

Martin looked at Andy with an ashen face; he had never heard Andy say very much and this was the longest speech he had ever made. And then the content was completely foreign to him. Living in the world of plants had sapped the pioneering spirit out of him, and now he was being forced to come to terms with some very difficult concepts. It was all very well watching films of men fighting and dying in the best Hollywood fashion but when it came back to him and it might be his life on line he found it very difficult to accept that it might be him that died. And also he had never known any situation where the police weren't within easy reach. Up until now the very thought of killing another man was abhorrent to him and

The Survivalists, Book 2, **The Finale**

Andy in his way was forcing him to face up to the realities of the situation. He sank back into his seat and looked despairingly at Jim, who for his part added. "If you think that the fact that there are women out there should in any way influence us in not shooting them, I should tell you that those women are quite capable of killing you to get in here. That is if they want to enter, at the present time they've made no attempt to do that. Now what I want you to do is make up your mind; you either defend this place in any way you can, and that is why you came here. Or you might as well go out there with you're hands up and let them kill you anyway. Because if you hesitate in any way; you will lose either your life or your freedom. Now I suggest you pick up one of those guns over there and have Andy familiarise you with it."

Martin stared at Jim for several seconds until a dry voice came from behind them. "Come on, be a man and stand up for what's yours, I'll be using this gun if they try to force their way in here." They all swung round to see Leah dressed in fatigues with a gun belt over her shoulder and carrying one of the sub machine guns in her hands. She looked tough and ready for action with her hair pulled back into a ponytail on the back of her head. They all involuntarily grinned at the spectacle and Jim muttered. "Shades of Lara Croft," to himself at the sight.

Ray stepped forward and looking her up and down said tightly. "What do you think your game is, I thought we agreed you were to stay in the back and look after the defence of the growing area with the women?"

She sneered back at him. "It's OK lover, they can look after themselves, I want to be out here where the action is; don't forget I was on that boat when they tried to kill us, and from now on I want to be in control of my situation if it comes to defence. I don't want any man trying to put me in the 'little woman' category. And anyway, from what I've seen of you lot out here and this so-called man here." She indicated Martin. "Some of us women are going to make better fighters than you, and….." She leaned forward and put her face so close to Martin that he flinched back. "If there are women out there, I don't think you're capable of trying to fight them. You're going to flinch back and they'll kill you without a moment's hesitation."

Martin looked around desperately at them for support, but they all stared back bleakly, they all knew he wasn't capable of pulling the trigger while pointing a gun at the enemy. Jim held his hand out to him and relieved him of his gun. "Why don't you go out back and help the women? There's no shame in not wanting to kill another person, but you might get in the way if something happens quick out here."

Martin nodded dumbly, shame and despair written all over his face. Then he turned and with bent back and slumped shoulders walked slowly through the door and down the passage to the back. When he had gone Leah seemed to brighten up and said. "Right you lot what's the sit-rep here?"

The remark broke the ice and they all grinned together, except for Ray who was still feeling aggrieved at her treatment of him. He thrust his head forward pugnaciously and said. "I don't want you out here while there's any chance of fighting going on."

Her head came up with her usual defiance. "I'll be a lot more use to you than that sorry excuse for a biologist that's just gone out the back. Do you think for a moment that I can't handle myself in a fight? Well let me tell you I can shoot a gun just as well as you and I've got as much determination as any man here." She pointed a finger at him. "And don't forget that most of you men will still hesitate before you shoot a woman. And I'm here to tell you that if they do attack you'll all get caught out if you know the enemy is female, but I'm here to level the playing field, I won't hesitate for a second to give a woman a chance. If she's got a gun, I shoot." And she stared round at all of them waiting for someone to gainsay anything she had said.

Ray and Jim stared at each other in embarrassment, until Jim shook his head in wonder and said to Ray. "Better make sure she takes a prominent position if she feels like that."

Visibly relieved that this episode seemed to be over, Andy and Dick started to set the machine gun in a good firing position, Andy had a large bag with him from which he produced several belts of ammunition.He and Dick began to put the machine gun up on a table to give themselves a good field of fire.

Peering out Jim he could see in the gloom of the day that the visitors had got a generator running and they had power to the caravans. He could hear the steady thrum as it powered the various pieces of equipment scattered about. Looking around him inside he counted eight defenders including himself, he had Dick and Andy on the machine gun that had been set up to give the maximum field of fire. Ray, Lee, the Prof, and Leah were armed with the Heckler & Koch short-barrelled rapid-fire guns. These were supposed to be deadly at short range as long as the trigger was used sparingly; the fire rate would use all the ammunition in seconds if pressed too long. He himself had Andy's prized shotgun, although he would have preferred something else. It had an eight round magazine and at short range could blow a hole the size of a dustbin lid in a man. He knew that any hit on any part of the body caused such trauma that the man would be out of action from that moment on. He hoped he wouldn't have to use it. Roy the electrician had drawn the short straw in the arms department and was carrying a Kalashnikov. It didn't seem to bother him though as he had commented that if they were as close as they expected it could be an advantage.

He called out to Andy. "That machine gun isn't going to be any good at short range, so why have you got it out?"

Andy grinned. "If they start anything at all, I'm going to destroy all their living quarters and equipment; they won't have a thing left after I start on them."

Jim was appalled. "You'll condemn every one of them to a slow death if you carry out that plan, and anyway you'll probably end up putting shells through every one of the women out there as well."

Andy was exasperated and it showed. "Don't you think there're going to try and do the same to us, so why can't we do it first? Why does it always have to be the good guys who have to suffer? If they go away now and leave us alone they won't come to any harm at all."

Jim would have answered this with some more of his own arguments but was distracted by a shout from Leah who had been watching the outside. "One of them is coming up towards us." She peered through the binoculars she had and went on. "It looks like that Sulim again. And he's got two men with him who are heading for that rocket launcher."

Jim looked out of the window until Sulim stopped outside the door.

"Are you ready to talk Jim, and let us in?" The loudhailer called to them.

Jim watched the Rocket Launcher team stop about a hundred yards away and start to unpack the various items with them; he turned to the others and said. "Spread out into the other rooms along the front and watch for me to start shooting; wait for me to signal." He looked at Andy and Dick. "Can you take out that Rocket Launcher team if I give the word?"

Andy nodded, not taking his eyes off them for a moment. "From here I can get every last one in a few seconds."

"OK." Jim answered. Don't forget you might only have a few seconds, if they let loose with that thing out there it's going to kill most of us and take out the front of the building."

He turned back to the mike and switched it on. "Why do I get the feeling that if I open the door Sulim, I'm going to regret it."

Sulim shrugged. "You know full well I can break in here with no problem."

"I don't doubt that you can get in Sulim, but if you break in with the force you've got out there you won't have much to live with because we intend to destroy it all before you get inside."

Sulim gestured angrily; "Empty words Jim, you aren't going to destroy that facility, if you do, you die as well as us."

He turned and shouted to the men on the Rocket Launcher to give these idiots a taste of what could happen. They switched their aim to Jims Utes parked off to one side, and after a moment's hesitation while the operator lined his sights, there was a whoosh, and a trail of smoke sped towards one of the vehicles and as it hit, the Ute exploded in a ball of flame. Sulim nodded in satisfaction and turned to them again. "We've brought a lot of these things with us, and you must know that the range is long on them. We can stand off and destroy you and everything here without a single casualty amongst us; now I'm an easy going man so I'll give you one last chance and then I'm going to attack." He sat down on the floor and called out. "Five minutes."

Jim strode to the door and called out along the corridor to the others. "Get in here quick for a conference; we don't have much time."

They all came running and quickly assembled in the main living room, Leah reached into her rucksack and handed them all some small bottles of an orange drink. Then she and the rest looked expectantly at Jim. Some of the women from the back building had heard Jim call and came into the room as well. He looked around at them and rubbed his hands over his mouth as he thought about his next words, then said. "Well its crunch time now, he wants to get in here and use this place as his own, he's got a lot of fire power out there and he looks willing to use it. From here on we've only got two choices, we either stop him the best way we can, and I think some of us will die if we do that, or……" He looked around again. "We open the doors and let them in, I don't know what the outcome of that action will be, but I don't think it's going to be easy. There appears to be about sixteen people out there and this place at a pinch could support somewhere between twenty and thirty, so he might want to keep some of the experts alive to run the place, but I think it's going to be on a basis of slave labour because he can't trust anyone here, so it probably won't be much of a life. I'm going to give you the chance to vote on this but I warn you that if you vote to open the doors I for one am going to go out and try and fight on my own if necessary, because I don't think for one minute he's going to let me or anyone else who runs this place live anyway. Are you all clear on what you are going to vote for now?"

They all said yes in their own way one by one as Jim looked at them, so he said. "Hold your hands up if you want to fight him." He watched as without looking at anyone else, Leah, Andy, Dick, and Ray, put their hands up followed a little more slowly by Pat and Julia, then the rest of them followed suit. The only abstention that Jim could see was Martin the biologist which wasn't in Jim's eyes entirely unexpected.

"Almost unanimous." He commented. "Martin, I can see you aren't very happy about fighting, and if I could, I'd say you're excused but under the circumstances that's impossible. I can't let you go out to them because I don't think you'd live very long with them and you know a lot about our defences which I want to be a surprise to them, so you'll have to stay here with us and take your chances."

Martin had started frowning when Jim spoke and now replied. "I don't think you understand, I only voted against fighting, I find it abhorrent to kill another man but I don't mind helping out here if you want to fight." He shrugged his shoulders and said apologetically. "I'm sorry about the fighting but maybe you can find something for me to do like tend to the wounded."

Colette spoke up. "I think that's a good idea, I need somebody to help with the stretcher carrying, and general first aid like cleaning wounds." She looked at Jim. "I think you ought to get ready to defend this place Dad, don't worry about the casualties, I've set up a field hospital in the back."

Jim smiled his thanks and turned to the first team of defenders. "Well you heard her, let's tell this Sulim where to go, and good luck everybody." He added under his breath. "We're going to need it." Then slightly louder he said. "Lets get into position now, and I'll say it once more, wait for my signal."

He watched as Sulim stood up, waiting expectantly. After a few moments when the door failed to open he called out. "Come on Jim, don't be stupid; open the door."

Andy called out to Jim. "They've started to rig that rocket launcher up again dad."

"Watch them closely and if they look like firing it, let loose yourself."

As a precaution he called out to everybody to move away from the front doors. As the building was so long on the front edge they had only built one corridor behind the rooms that faced on the front. Some of the rooms were large, like the living rooms where they congregated, and others like the sleeping quarters were fairly small. The problem with this sort of building was the distance from the end rooms to the central passageway that ran to the main building at the back, the corridor was probably about 100 meters long, so the rooms at the end were at least fifty meters from the centre. With so few defenders it meant they were spread thinly on the ground, Jim thought about the implications of any one trapped at the ends so he moved into the corridor and called out to the end defenders to close up more and take rooms that were nearer.

By this time he had a very agitated Sulim outside the doors and he heard the muffled rage of the man as he went back into the centre room.

"Jim if you don't open these doors in two minutes I'm going to blow them off their hinges." Sulim was getting shriller as he stamped his foot in anger.

Jim called out calmly. "Why don't you tell us again what you want to do with us if we do open the doors, and while you're at it, tell us why you want to get in here anyway?"

This was probably a mistake as Sulim by now had completely lost his patience and wanted nothing more but for them to do what he wanted, he held his hand up above his shoulder and said. "If I drop my hand now, the attack starts and I will not stop until every person in there is my prisoner or dead. And I will destroy the whole of your fine building as well."

Jim spoke rapidly. "If you destroy the building you won't be able to use it yourself will you?"

Sulim shook his head in sorrow at Jim's remark. "You refuse to understand, don't you Jim? If I can't come in and use it then I will not let you use it either."

"That's crazy Sulim. "Jim responded. "You know better than me that if we let you in it means we're going to die as there's no way this facility can carry the amount of people here, so what's going to happen?"

Sulim shrugged expressively, it was obvious from that he had no intention of letting them stay there. "Maybe I can let you have the vehicles out there and you leave." His voice dropped slightly and an air of menace crept in to his tone. "But if you don't let me in very soon I think I'll kill all of you then you aren't any more of a problem. Now my arm is getting tired and I want to put it down, so what are you going to do?"

Jim opened his mouth to speak but Sulim disappeared from sight and he heard voices shouting something unintelligible from quite far away, suddenly there was a loud bang and then another from each end of the building and they heard the sound of breaking glass, followed a few seconds later by the muffled sound of a small explosion. Jim heard the defenders at the end cry out in surprise and the sound of feet running along the corridor towards them. Leah burst into the room followed by the Prof; they had been guarding the rooms furthest along the corridor.. Leah had a handkerchief over her mouth and there was a smell that followed her into the room. "They've just fired teargas into the room at the end." She shouted, and the Prof cried out as well. "They've done both ends then."

Andy shouted. "They're going to fire that rocket launcher; they've started to aim it." He cocked the machine gun and fired it straight through the window shattering it and Jim saw his bullets biting into the two men on the launcher, who were knocked back by the force of the shells hitting them and lay sprawled on the ground.

Jim sensed immediately what would be coming next and bawled as loud as he could for everyone to retreat back into the main building. Andy started to pick up the machine gun with Dick to take it with him but Jim shouted. "Leave the bloody thing there; we haven't got time to take it with us now." Andy stared at him wordlessly for a few moments then bent down and deliberately, removed the firing pin and picked up his sniper rifle which had been lying on the ground nearby and started to run towards Jim and into the rear of the building. As he ran there was a flash from about three hundred yards away and Jim could clearly see a trail of smoke arcing towards them. It hit the front doors and then came an almighty explosion as the rocket exploded. Luckily for them they had just passed into the passageway to the back, and the force of the explosion was diminished as it followed them through. It still threw them to the floor but did no serious harm.

Jim and Andy picked themselves up and as the smoke cleared they heard the shouts of men trying to enter. They stumbled along the passageway after the others and ran onto the wooden decking they had placed over the pit. As they ran over the planks they heard someone pulling them out as they raced in to the solid cover of the main building. They weren't a moment too soon as they heard a triumphant shouting from behind them. Jim glanced over his shoulder to see what had happened and saw the attackers standing behind them levelling guns in their direction. He dived for cover round the corner and Andy tried to follow him as they opened fire, the bullets slammed in to the wall a few inches from him and then he had turned the corner out of the line of fire. Andy was a fraction later and it was to prove unlucky for him because a bullet clipped him in the leg. Jim looked back when he heard a cry, to see him holding his leg where blood had started to drip down his trousers already. He started to go to him but Andy waved him away and bent down into the corner to pick up the rifle from where he had dropped it on the planks. Some more explosions came as the two men tried to hit Andy as he ran forward into the safety of the brick built corner. Jim heard a splash as the two men following them ran into the water thinking it was a puddle only to find it went over their heads. Suddenly all the lights were extinguished as those inside threw the switches. Then the passage was lit by torches being shone down from the wall above. Jim could see by their light that Andy had turned round and he was holding his sniper rifle in front of him. The triumphant cries of their pursuers had now turned into howls of rage as they realised they had been duped; he heard the shots as they tried to fire upwards at the torches but to fire a gun from their position was almost impossible and they endeavoured to go back towards the entrance. Jim was suddenly shook by the blast as Andy fired from the hip at them, the water churned around one of the men but this ensured they doubled their efforts to escape back to the safety at the end of the passage until a shout from above stilled the torches and two shots rang out and a man collapsed back into the water as he died. Jim heard more people running into the front of the building; he could hear men shouting to each other and the sound of feet approaching the passageway. They both ran into the back building with Andy hopping along as best he could. Behind them they heard the angry shouts as the dead man was discovered then the sound of some more shots as someone on top of the wall opened fire. The last of the planks were dragged inside as they stepped off them and thrown to one side.

Pat came running over to see what had happened to Andy, with Victoria in hot pursuit, they started to fuss and cluck over him but he was having none of it and simply sat down and said. "It's OK; just put a bandage over it for now, it's only a flesh wound."

Jim ran over to the higher position to assess the situation and found Ray and Leah standing on the top peering down, they were both holding guns and endeavouring to pick out any movement below. It had gone quiet for a while as the attackers probed about in the darkness to try and find out what defence they had.

Leah spoke in a whisper. "Shall I shine a torch down there for a quick look?"

Jim shook his head as he tried to make out her face in the gloom. "If you do that you'll show them what's in front of them and I want them guessing for as long as possible." He kept his voice low and his mouth close to her ear to keep anyone from hearing.

Looking around to get the situation into his mind he said to her. "Can you keep an eye open here for a bit I want to have a conference?"

She nodded and asked. "What happened out there just now?"

"It was a feint, with that first rocket launcher, they intended for us to watch it all the time, it took our eyes off the other one they positioned further out, that bastard just got two of his men killed so he could try for an advantage. We nearly fell for it as well; if we hadn't been prepared to retreat we would have been wiped out with one rocket."

He climbed down from the platform and called everyone to him, and one of the women produced a small battery operated lamp with a very dim bulb and in its gloom he motioned to all the men standing there to gather round and listen. He spoke rapidly and gave the orders as he thought of them. "Lee, I want you to go up on to the next floor and call out if you think they're going to come down through the glass. They might leave it for the moment as if they break it they mightn't be able to repair it. Call out if you see anything and come down, we'll drop that cover into place when you're down here."

"I want you Ray, and Dick on top of the defence wall with Leah, if you hear anything unusual, one of you shine a torch down and the other two can open fire. Make sure you keep the torch well away from yourself as they'll certainly try and shoot at it, and well done also for getting one of those two who followed us into the passage."

Ray shrugged. "Wasn't me who got him, I was still trying to get set up, it was Leah."

Jim was impressed, and reflected that a good fighting woman was a hard act to follow. "Well tell her from me she did extremely well, I'll have a special medal struck for her when this is all over, I can probably run one up out of an old tin can when I get time." He grinned to indicate it was a joke and waved Ray and Dick on their way.

He looked back and saw he now had Andy, the Prof, and Roy left with him, they had a variety of weapons between them, Andy still had his sniper rifle, the Prof had a Heckler and Koch, Roy still had the Kalashnikov and he himself was armed with Andy's shotgun. Andy reached out and gently took the shotgun from him saying. "I think that's better in my hands dad, I'm more likely to use it than you."

Jim handed it over wordlessly as he knew how much Andy prized it and went over to the other weapons stacked against the wall, he pondered on his choice for a moment and then chose one of the Kalashnikov's with some spare magazines. Going back to the rest of the men he looked at them steadily and said. "It's down to us to guard this passageway for the time being, from the ground level; I deliberately didn't put in doors so we can fire into it at will. Now you know they have got to get across that water and that makes life pretty damn difficult for them for the moment, I think there're eventually going to give it up as a bad job and try and force an entrance somewhere else. The first place will probably be the glass roof but they don't know we can close off the top floor yet. After that it'll probably be a rocket into the side of the building somewhere but that'll be the last resort as they know if they breach it they've got to repair it and they can't assess how much damage they'll be doing to the fabric of the place."

Andy held his hand up for permission to speak and Jim nodded to indicate he could; his leg had been bandaged now and he hobbled over to say. "I think we should do what we agreed before, let's go out and tackle them there; they aren't all that skilled as soldiers."

Jim smiled at the sight of him, hardly able to walk properly with bandages on his leg and he wanted to go out and run around playing soldiers. He shook his head and said. "I'll wait and see what develops before I start running around outside, I think that maybe if they lose too many men they'll call it off."

It was Andy's turn to smile. "You can't believe that, can you? You know as well as I do that if they lose too many men that guy out there is going to try and destroy this place, just out of spite….. And." He added. "He's got the means out there to do it."

His face started to go blank and he slumped down and would have hit his head on the floor as he went if Victoria who was standing next to him hadn't put her hands out quickly and grabbed him to lower him to the floor. Pat grabbed his other arm to help and Victoria rounded on Jim.

"Now see what you've done." She accused him. "He's got to get some rest; he's lost a lot of blood with that wound."

Colette came running from the small room at the back that she had been converting into a makeshift hospital with aid of Martin. "What's going on here? Can't you call me if something happens?" The blood drained from her face when she saw it was Andy who had been wounded, and she rushed over and took charge immediately; they made a stretcher out of some timber they had spare and saw that he was carried into the hospital room as quickly as possible. All the while she walked alongside checking him for any further injuries. He came round and started protesting that he was OK but she was having none of it and despite his protestations she insisted he went into the hospital and got a thorough check. When they had disappeared Jim turned to the others. "Now." He started to say when a shout of alarm came from above, and Lee came to the top of the stairs leading to the top floor. I've got some of them outside the windows looking in, and I think they're contemplating breaking through." The sound of breaking glass accompanied his words and he turned and fired the gun and then ran down the stairs. "It's happened." He gasped as if nobody had heard anything in the last few seconds.

Julia looked at him as Jim and the others ran to lower the concrete plug to seal the hole over the stairs. She shook her head in wonderment and commented. "Never fails to surprise me how the men folk of this world feel able to say the stupidest things as if there're the assembled wisdom of the ages."

There was another shout from Leah. "There're trying to get in here as well." She shone the torch down into the passageway and there was the sound of shooting as Dick and Ray opened fire. There was a new sound now as the fire was returned accompanied by men's voices shouting to each other as they tried to get across the water, it was evidently deeper than they expected but they could be heard making progress through the passageway. Jim looked desperately over his shoulder to see to his dismay that no one was guarding the entrance as everybody who should be there had come to help place the plug of concrete into its resting place in at the top of the stairs.

Julia and Pat saw the situation develop and ran to the guns that Jim and his crew had placed on the floor, and picking up a Heckler and Koch Pat ran to the doorway to the passage, Julia picked up Jim's Kalashnikov and took position on the other side, quickly opening fire. Shouts of alarm and pain echoed out of the blackness and slowly died out as the attackers started to retreat from the hail of fire.Both women forgot in the heat of the moment to conserve their ammunition and the guns ran empty in seconds. The plug fell into place and not a moment too soon as steps sounded on the top floor as the attackers rushed over to try and stop it being lowered. The locking bars were quickly shoved through their slots and they all stepped back.

There was the sound of women screaming in anger and then the thump of a heavy object landing on the floor right by Julia and Pat. Someone on the wall shone a torch down to the ground and to Jim's horror he saw a grenade lying there, he tried to scream to the women to get down but Julia was quicker by half and took a flying kick at it. It spun across the floor and somehow plopped into the water a second before the explosion came. There was a feeling of hidden power first as the water absorbed the expansion of the explosion and then a curtain of water rose into the air as it burst out. There was a gurgling sound as someone flopped in the water and then silence as the attack died down. Jim ran back to the two women and prised the Kalashnikov out of Julia's hands and quickly reloaded it in case of any further attacks. The Prof did the same with Pat's gun and then Jim handed the gun back to Julia. "Stay here for a bit, I'm going to get Andy's shotgun out." He said.

She nodded without speaking and he caught the shaking in her hands as he gave her the gun. He put his hands round her shoulders and hugged her; she laid her head on his shoulder and sobbed. "I was so scared; I didn't know what to do when I saw that grenade. I thought right then I was going to die."

"I'm proud of you Julia you saved both your lives and maybe the lives of all of us because if that had gone off I think it would have been the end of our defence as they could have come in here with no opposition. If it hadn't killed us it would have certainly stunned us and they would have got in when we were dazed."

She nodded and looked up at him with tear stained eyes, then making a visible effort to control her feelings she wiped her eyes and sniffing said. "Thanks for that Jim; it makes me feel a lot better now." Then with back straight she walked over to Pat on guard at the entrance and took up position alongside her, Pat reached out and put her arm round her shoulder and patted her on the back.

Jim ran back to where he could get Andy's shotgun and found it with a pouch containing the shells; quickly checking it he found only one had been fired so he replenished the magazine and went back to find the Prof and Lee in consultation with Pat and Julia, Leah was bent down from her platform listening and Ray was alongside her. Dick was still on the high platform keeping a lookout for any movement. They all turned when he approached and Pat said."They think there's a body in the water and they want to retrieve it."

Jim frowned. "I didn't think we got any in that last attack."

The Prof answered. "I think it was when the grenade went off in the water, there was one of them who must have thrown it and been too close to the explosion and it crushed them."

Jim strode to the opening to the passageway and peered round the corner, sure enough there was something in the water; he turned and nodded to them. "Have we got a long pole or anything to pull it in with?" He asked.

Lee stepped over to the storage racks and picked up a length of batten, he drove a nail down through it with a hammer and brought it back to Jim. "Keep an eye open for them." He whispered in case they had someone listening also. Then reaching round he poked the batten towards the object, when it snagged, he pulled gently until he could reach down and grasp the object. It was a body and he grabbed it by the collar and pulled it on to the dry concrete. The rest of them helped him manhandle it further away to the benches used for working on machinery. They lifted it up on to the bench and something in the composition of the body and facial characteristics made Jim take a closer look. He unzipped the coverall and gasped in surprise as he found he was staring at a pair of breasts. He closed the jacket and looked up at the faces surrounding him; they mirrored his feelings as they saw that Sulim had put women into his attack and not only that but in the vanguard.

Jim realised she wasn't wearing a mask and deduced that they must have repaired the front doors so that the air could be cleaned in the living quarters at the front. He looked more closely at the woman's face and saw that it had a definite eastern cast about it. "She must have been one of Sulim's wives." He said. "But why the hell did he send her in to the attack when he's got men out there? Surely the men are capable of attacking without using women."

"Thank you very much for the vote of confidence." The dry voice of Leah said sarcastically. "He's only taking a leaf out of your book, or does defending the place come into a different category."

'Oh, Oh.' Jim thought to himself. 'Made a mistake again.' Smiling apologetically he turned towards Leah and admitted. "You're right Leah, I made a gaffe, we are using women for our defence, and it's much the same thing isn't it?"

They heard a voice calling to them from outside the passageway, saying 'Jim', 'Jim'. It was Sulim's and Jim went over to the passageway to answer. "What do you want?" he called.

"What happened to the woman who was in the water?" Sulim's disembodied voice asked.

"She's dead; we just dragged her out, why are you sending women in to attack us?"

"She volunteered to do it, and volunteers make the best fighters." Sulim's voice had a quality about it that grated on Jim's nerves, as an afterthought Sulim asked. "Will you give her a burial?"

Jim thought this over for a moment before answering. "We don't know how to bury a Moslem, so she would only get a Christian burial." Some devil played tricks on Jim's brain and he went on. "Maybe we can do what we always do with waste products; we could recycle the body and feed it to the pigs, that way we can create a cycle of regeneration."

He heard the gasp from Sulim when he said this and not only from him but from his own followers as they contemplated the awful prospect before them. A cry of anguish came from outside the door and Sulim begged Jim. "Please, please, as one man to another, don't do this horrible thing."

Jim was touched but decided that if the man was off balance he wouldn't be thinking straight, so left him in limbo to think about it, turning to the others he winked to show he wasn't serious and said loudly. "Take that cadaver down to the farm, we'll cut it up later, it'll give the pigs some much needed protein."

He was rewarded with a shout from Sulim. "If you do that, I promise you I'm going to destroy you and the entire building around your ears."

Jim was thankful the passageway was built on a dogleg principle, as he was sure that if he could have, Sulim would have come running in with guns blazing. He called out to him. "I haven't done anything yet, but annoy me any further, and you'll know when I do it."

A few minutes of silence came after this and then he heard the voice once more. "Why don't you surrender Jim?" The voice asked. "You can't get out, and we can't get in without a lot of bloodshed. You are trapped and we can wait you out until you have to come out."

"I think you're forgetting something aren't you?" Jim called. "We've got the food in here and we can wait here until you starve out there."

He could hear a muffled conversation coming in from the outside and then he heard the sound of a fist striking a face, someone sobbed in pain and then Sulim called out. "It appears some of my information was incorrect but we can destroy the windmill that gives you all the power if we want, without that you won't be able to survive."

Jim knew that this would prove impossible to carry out because as soon as the windmill ceased to exist so did the community. But he didn't want Sulim to know they had a generator for back up so merely laughed and said. "If you destroy that you'll surely die as well as us."

"I can destroy this place around your ears if I want to." Sulim replied. "I've got a lot of firepower out here, and if you don't open up I will use it."

"If you destroy this place Sulim, you're going to die yourself, your only hope of life is to take it over intact, because if you use those rockets on us we'll destroy every crop that's growing so you'll get in but then you'll starve."

"Come on Jim, we both know you aren't going to destroy the crops, you want to live as much as we do. Why don't you let us come in and we can try to live the rest of our lives in peace together?"

Jim shuddered at the thought; he knew what the outcome of letting a man with Sulim's mentality into their community would do. He called back. "I don't think that's a good idea, you couldn't live in a community like this without trying to form a dictatorship all of your own, we'd all be slaves in a few weeks. Anyway, we haven't got sufficient resources to keep a large party like yours in food."

He heard another voice talking to Sulim and something about it brought back a time in the town; it had a quality and accent that reminded Jim of someone familiar. The conversation ran on for a few minutes and Jim strained to hear what was said between the two of them but the voices were too indistinct. They had a heated quality about them as if the two men were arguing over some point. One of Jim's party had put the lights on but very dimly so he could see the people standing around behind him waiting for the outcome of this talk. They could hear knocks and bangs coming from above as the attackers tried to prise the plug out of its hole, or knock down through it, but the thing had been made with just this emergency in mind and they knew that the only thing which would penetrate it was explosive. His mind was brought back to the problem at hand by the sound of another voice.

As it called softly and with menace Jim knew it belonged to Schoonheid, and a glance at Leah confirmed this. It had a quality about it that made Jim cringe inside. "You've forgotten one thing in all you're planning you supercilious bastard." The voice said. "We can cut off the one thing you need and there isn't a thing you can do about it." It was followed by a mocking laugh that chilled them all. It was the laugh of someone who sounded deranged and mad enough to follow any course of action. "We're going to cut off your air supply." The laughter continued and faded in the distance as the speaker walked away. Sulim had evidently stayed because they heard the sound of his voice next. "Jim, I tried to get you to see sense but now he's got his way, I wanted to join you but he is determined to kill you now. It will be better for you if you come out; I think I can persuade him to let you drive off in the Utes if you capitulate now."

Jim was surprised with the reaction from the other members, a chorus of angry shouts came telling Sulim to get lost, and someone fired their gun into the passageway to underline their defiance. After the yells died down Sulim shouted back. "You've only got yourselves to blame now, when you're gasping for breath, remember you were given the chance of life."

Jim turned and ran back to the air vent they had installed when they were building the air conditioning into the building and arrived just in time to hear it start wheezing as the blowers fought to suck air into the unit. He shut it down to stop it overloading and turned to look at the others, they stared back with various expressions on their faces as they contemplated this move. It would take a long time before they ran out of air as the area was so large but eventually they would have to face the fact that it would run out. They had taken the trouble to seal every possible entry for air so the air conditioning could scrub all the air that entered. Pat followed more slowly because she had stopped to guard the passageway. "I can hear them sealing the entrance now, they seem to be sealing it with boards, and I heard one of them say they could silicone over the cracks."

Jim cursed under his breath; he had hoped they would forget to seal it, as that would have allowed enough air to enter to keep them alive. The noise from above stopped as the people trying to break in were evidently told of this new development. They were left in silence to think about the fate that awaited them. Jim snapped his fingers as he thought of something and he ran over to the corner where the electricity cable came in from the windmill. When they had laid it they had placed it down under the ground about three feet as protection from the elements, and it was in a large pipe with a diameter of eighteen inches. The inlet had been placed at the back of a cupboard and Jim almost tore the door of its hinges in his haste to access it. When he could see it clearly, he saw the water pipe from the tank above ran down it also. According to most regulations that Jim knew, it was illegal to put both pipes in proximity to each other, but cost had dictated their actions and so both pipes ran down into the building together.

They had no worries about water as the borehole and pump were inside the building with them and they could soon isolate the water tank from above and use the water direct from the borehole. The pipe stretched away sloping upwards as it went and Jim stuck his head into it to peer upwards. It was black inside and impossible to see but a draught of air came down and blew over his head. He grinned and sat back on his haunches to say that it was clear when to his horror smoke started to curl out of it, he sniffed and immediately his eyes started to water and the breath caught in his throat. It was tear gas! He slammed the door to the pipe closed and stood with streaming eyes, coughing and wheezing. When he finally got his breath back with some slapping from the other members he sat down and thought about what to do next. It was obvious that they had somebody posted at the top to guard it and they had had the idea of rolling a teargas canister down the pipe to clear it in case they tried to climb up, it also meant they couldn't use it for air as it could be contaminated very quickly. He hoped the attackers had no access to any of the nerve gases that the military used as they would have no defence against anything like that.

Ray and the Prof had been talking while he was getting his breath back and now suggested they went to the emergency kitchen they had set up whilst building had been going on. It had been equipped in the same way as the large kitchen at the front but left for this very purpose. Jim had always thought they could be attacked and had incorporated it in his original plans. Now it came into it's own as some of the women started to prepare a snack. For the moment Julia was left on guard at the passageway entrance but it was low key, as there seemed little likelihood of any more attacks coming from that direction. They all gathered round the table in the cramped kitchen and started to eat ravenously; while they ate the Prof asked Jim about the construction of the exterior.

"That's the problem." Jim answered dolefully. "We built it to be sealed from the outside, so we could have the air conditioner going. It was never intended to have air coming in to it. So we have to face the fact that for the moment we can't get any more air in."

"How long can we survive without air coming in to replace the oxygen we're using now?"

Jim looked over at the questioner, it was Ray, and shrugged. "I don't know the answer to that." He replied. "You'll have to ask the expert." He indicated Dick.

Dick looked down at his feet and shuffled them, then glancing up he admitted. "I don't know, all the programmes and charts I need for that are in the front, and even if I had them it'd take me ages to find the answer. My best bet would be several days, but it's only a guess."

Ray made a gesture of annoyance and said to angrily to Dick. "Do you mean to say you're an expert on civil engineering and you can't figure out how long the air's going to last in here? Can't you hazard a better guess than a few days?"

He strode to the door of the kitchen and looked out at the vast hall, it was at least a hundred meters long by as many wide, and the ceiling was two and a half meters in height. Then he turned to them and said. "There's approximately twenty five thousand cubic meters of air out there, now all we need is to know how much air does the average person consume every hour, simple maths will give us the answer then."

They all looked at each other in puzzlement, then Leah spoke huskily. "So much for how clever we all are, not one of us can give an answer to a simple question like that. I'd have thought that one of you two would have some inkling." She indicated the Prof, who looked surprised to be singled out for attention.

He answered. "Why do you think that Julia or myself should know the answer, I know she can't speak for herself right now but if she could I'm sure she'd say it's not the sort of information anybody is expected to know. The other item I should bring up is that since we've been inside I've tried to use the computer we put in here and it's been shut down from outside."

Jim groaned inwardly, aloud he said sarcastically. "Whose idea was it to link the two systems together?"

They all looked at each other in consternation, then the Prof spoke hesitantly. "It was agreed by everybody so the information in one could be accessed by the other."

"Can we separate them?" Jim asked.

The Prof shrugged. "Maybe they could but it'll take a lot of time and I don't think we're going to get too much of that, do you?"

Before Jim could let go and start on one of his legendary rages, Dick interposed. "Two things that haven't been thought about yet, the first is that we've still got a monitor working in here so we can access the cameras to the outside and the second is nobody's thought about the cavities on the outside walls."

Jim looked up from the table when he said this."Where's the monitor?"

"In the cupboard over there." He pointed in the direction of a small cupboard just outside the kitchen. "It was put there because we couldn't figure out where to put it, and we wanted some means of keeping a lookout in case this sort of thing happened. They all rushed to the door and for a moment everybody was jammed in trying to get through, finally they got it sorted out and when the door was yanked open they were confronted with the monitor, a computer, and a small joystick to turn the camera when they switched on. With a trembling hand and praying it would work Jim reached out and pressed the switch, it hummed for a few moments and then slowly before their eyes a picture started to form on the screen. The camera was on the hill directly opposite and about seven hundred meters away, Jim moved the mouse and brought up the magnification to full and was rewarded with a view of the front of the building. There were no people in sight and Jim surmised they were all inside. He turned to them and breathed. "I don't know who installed this here but whoever did it deserves a medal."

The sparks Roy leaned forward and offered. "I'll take that if medals are being given out."

"Well if you want one when this is all over I'll make sure it's gold." Jim answered.

"Yeah then you can flog it off for an exorbitant sum to some collector to pay for your retirement." Lee joshed.

They all grinned in appreciation of the attempt at humour and then the thought struck Jim. "What did you mean about the cavities?" He asked Dick.

Dick grinned in pleasure at the thought of giving some good news. "We installed air bricks to the outside so the cavities could breathe; otherwise it was going to get very damp. But we didn't bring them through into the inside as that was against the principle of sealing the walls. I know roughly where they are and if we cut a hole into the cavity we can get air into here from the outside, we'd have to install something in here to scrub the air clean but it would mean we don't suffocate."

Jim could have kissed him, but then a sudden thought sobered him. "If we cut holes from in here it's going to make a lot of noise if we use hammers and chisels, we'll have to figure out a way of cutting without making any sound." A thought struck him as he spoke and he realised with a sinking feeling that if he were outside the cavities would be blocked by now. He went on to say. "We'll hold back on trying that course of action, for now anyway."

Colette walked into the room and glanced around at them. "I know the defence of this place is important but do you realise what the time is, if you lot don't get some rest you'll be like a lot of zombies."

Involuntarily they all looked at whatever they used for telling the time, there was a general air of surprise as it was now ten in the evening, the dim lighting and lack of something to relate to, like the passage of the sun overhead had thrown all their body clocks out of kilter, Jim immediately started to think about what could be done about keeping guard. If they took three shifts through the night they could easily guard against a sudden attack. Sulim had said he wanted to suffocate them but Jim wanted no surprises. He divided them into three teams and set the first watch to stay on for three hours; then the other two could take the same, that would take them through till eight in the morning. He didn't think they needed to be later than that.

He told them especially to watch the monitor in the cupboard, it was particularly important as he wanted to know if these people were going outside. The night passed comfortably enough and the next day everyone was up early and after breakfast Jim called a conference in the kitchen. The children were directed to go and help Lee with the animals in the farm at the back. Although the air quality was still quite good it would soon be difficult to breathe. Jim started to ask them how they were going to make holes into the cavity when Ray spoke up. "I've got one observation to make about this; don't you think this guy is going to get suspicious when we aren't gasping for air in a couple of days?"

Jim conceded the point and after agreeing with him said. "This is only in the short term, you know the only way to stop this guy is to face up to the fact we've got to kill him, because he sure as hell is going to kill us if he gets the chance."

There was a babble of sound as they all tried to speak at once. Leah managed to shout the loudest and got her voice heard. "If what I can figure out is right, there were approximately 17 people out there and I count four possible dead, which means if we take them on in a fight some of us are going to get killed. Now I'm not that scared for myself but what about someone like Alison there?" She pointed at Roy the spark's wife. "She's going to have that baby soon, are you willing to risk her life in a fight?"

"Of course not." Jim snapped. "But the only way to survive now is to get out of here and attack them; that comes later though, our first priority is to get some air coming into this place. Now has anybody got any ideas about making holes quietly?"

"We don't have to do that." Dick said calmly, I thought it over last night when I was trying to get to sleep." He looked around. "The best time to think when there's no distractions to worry you."

"Oh, get on with it." snapped Victoria recklessly, the tension had made itself felt in her demeanour and she found herself with less and less patience.

"OK, OK." Dick was enjoying his brief moment of keeping them all puzzled. "It's really quite simple, we put in a waste pipe to outfall down the valley if you remember, for stuff we couldn't recycle. It's doubtful anybody's been down there to check, as it's probably about five hundred meters away, and not immediately obvious it's there. We decided that although we wanted to recycle everything it just wasn't possible for some things."

Jim slapped himself on the head. "Of course, we sited it in the corner of the farm by the recycling room, why didn't I think of that?"

"There is a problem though." Dick went on. Jim's head came up and he stared at Dick with an expression that said. 'Here we go again, why is nothing straightforward for us.'

"Two problems actually." Dick was enjoying himself. "The first is easy, there's a trap in the pipe to stop smells coming back up. That's only a simple water trap so we've only got to drain the water out. The other problem's a bit harder, we can suck air through the pipe easily but we've got to expel the same amount of air as well, and that's where the problem lies. How do we do that?" The Prof's head came up. "Simple really." He said. "Exhaust the generator through the pipe

Before they could go on with the discussion there was a shout from the guard Liz on the monitor. "There's something going on out there."

They all rushed round and tried to crowd into the small cupboard to view the monitor, there on the screen they could see several figures dressed as usual in one piece coveralls and with breathing masks on walking round to the side of the building and starting to climb the hill towards the windmill. Jim watched aghast as he realised what was going to happen. They intended to shut down the electricity supply; he also knew what would happen when that happened, the diesel generator would kick in and within a short time the whole place would fill with choking fumes. His mind went into overdrive as he considered the options.

"Right." He said. I want everybody working on this; I think the Prof's idea stands up so we'll use it. In a few minutes the lights are going to go out, before we allow that generator to start we've got to get a pipe into that exhaust and it has to go through that waste pipe, right out to the end. If that happens the exhaust fumes get expelled and the drop in air pressure means that the fresh air will be sucked in."

He turned to Dick and Ray. "Tell me we've got enough piping to carry right to the end of the waste pipe."

They looked at each other for confirmation, then nodding Dick said. "Yes I think we put enough in store to reach." He shook his head in despair. "The problem is, how do we make sure we can push it through that far?"

Jim was beginning to intensely dislike the word 'problem' coming from Dick. He leaned forward and poked him in the chest. "The 'problem' is yours to solve. We'll cope with the mechanics of it when we have some answers. He turned to the rest of them and said. "Let's start on the easier parts first while this guy has a good long think."

Everybody started to run around to work out the best way of doing something when with a suddenness that took everybody by surprise the lights blinked out. Before the generator kicked in to supplement the power, someone had it switched off and torches started to gleam in the inky blackness. A voice came out of the gloom. "Not very considerate are they? You'd think they could wait until we had sorted out some emergency lighting."

"OK, knock it off and let's get some work done." Jim snapped before everybody started to get in on the act and tried to see who could be funniest.

Jim and some of the others dragged over the tubing to be used and Dick, who had been staring at the equipment they were using, snapped his fingers and broke into a huge smile. Then he went rushing off to the storeroom and came back bearing a small brass fitting. He held it up triumphantly and exclaimed. "This is going to get us out of trouble."

Jim and the Prof stared at the item and Jim shrugged his shoulders. "You'll have to explain that one." He said. Dick smirked at Jim's lack of knowledge. "It's a high pressure drain cleaner, we rig it up to a water pipe and through that compressor over there, which incidentally runs off the gas we've been producing to run the Utes. That means it won't pollute the atmosphere down here as much as diesel."

He pointed at an item of equipment Jim had never really noticed. "That puts out up to 3000 lbs PSI when its working, we connect it up to the pipe, and when we switch on the water the jets on this drain cleaner point slightly backwards and they will pull the pipe through, it's designed to clean the pipe of scale as it goes through. All we have to do is make sure we feed it in gently and hey presto, through it goes."

The Prof frowned, and pointed at the jet in Dick's hand. "You've forgotten one very important thing."

They all watched as he reached out and took the jet from Dick, and held it up for all of them to see. "These jets are designed for high pressure work and so they're very small, I can understand that the exhaust gas can push the water out of the end but these holes are never big enough to let the exhaust gas out quick enough to run the generator."

He handed it back to Dick. "Nice try mate, but think again."

There was a dry cough behind them and turning they saw that Andy had somehow managed to come out of the hospital room and join them. He sat down on a crate nearby and waved away Jim who went over to help him. He looked pale and weak in the torchlight and sagged visibly from the effort of walking over. "I've been listening to this problem and I think I've got an answer for it if you let me have Ray for bit to fix something up." Jim nodded and Ray went to Andy and helped him walk over to a small workshop they had in one of the small rooms near the farm. They could be heard talking as Andy explained and then Ray came out at a run and dashed over to the weapons store. He came back after a few minutes carrying some packages and re-entered the room.

The Prof stopped working for a moment and stood next to Jim and made one of his periodic observations. "We've got a problem Jim old friend." He said. Jim stared at him unblinkingly, the Prof went on. "I had this problem once with a car I had, and it was a pretty basic car really, anyway, the difficulty was that the exhaust had to give a certain amount of back pressure for the engine to work comfortably. But the problem here is that I think you're going to have too much back pressure and the gases won't travel out through that length of pipe." Then an afterthought struck him and he stood again. "I suppose you know we've got to clean the air when it comes in as well, it'll be full of dust won't it"

Several of the others had been listening to this and now Jim glanced resignedly around to see what the consensus of opinion was. Ray looked up from where he was busy with the work and growled. "I think he's got a point."

By this time Jim had had enough of problems caused by this and looking around at the assembled crowd, he snapped. "Solve it."

His words galvanised them into action and before long a simple contraption started to take shape, it consisted of a large drum to take the exhaust gases and an air pump connected to the waste pipe to force the gases through the long polythene tubing to the outside world. They then got ready an air conditioning unit to fix to the waste pipe to clean the air as it entered, they made sure that the filters were replaceable easily and when they were finished it looked like something out of the museum of crazy inventions but had a good chance of working properly.

By this time Ray and Andy had finished their project and carried the result out proudly to show them, at first glance it was just some wrapping round the polythene tubing just behind the nozzle, Jim looked at it in puzzlement and waited for Andy to enlighten him. Andy sat once more on the box and pointing at their handiwork, said. "It's simple really. It's a little bit of plastic explosive connected to a radio-controlled detonator. When you've pushed the pipe through to the outside I'll blow the thing up and the nozzle goes leaving the pipe wide open."

"It'll work?" Jim queried grimly. "Because if it doesn't we'll have wasted a lot of time and effort, and what about the noise alerting those out there?"

Andy shrugged. "It's better than to try and use the pipe with the nozzle on the end, and it's got every chance of success. The noise is too far away from here too be noticed, it'll only be a small bang after all."

"OK." Jim answered. "Let's give it a try."

They threaded the nozzle down into the waste pipe and nodding at Dick Jim said. "OK, switch on when you're ready."

The compressor burst into life and a small splash back from the pipe indicated they had pressure, the pipe immediately started to disappear down the hole and the Prof stood by with a measuring tape to estimate how much had gone down, they had made measurements when it had been installed so had a good idea of how much tubing to push through. They all watched with baited breath as it threaded slowly through and Dick who had taken over the job of guiding it paid it out hand over hand. After a while the Prof called out. "That's three hundred meters."

They stopped the compressor and fitted the next piece of tube onto the other with a brass fitting, making sure it was rock solid tight. Then they started once more, it had not gone more that a few metres when it stopped suddenly, Dick looked up and observe."There's a bend about two thirds of the way down because we hit some rocks and went round them."

Roy the electrician stepped forward. "Can I have a go?" He offered.

Dick stepped back reluctantly and let him grasp the pipe, Roy took hold of it and tensed his body, then pulled it back about six inches and thrust it forward eighteen inches with a twisting motion. It seemed to snag for a moment and then went on with its journey through the pipe. He grinned and looked up at the assembled company and said. "We get a lot of that in the electrical business; it's just a matter of technique."

Jim looked at the Prof whilst this was going on and said. "I want you to get this measurement dead on mate, because the outfall is at the top of the bank on a stream and we want to have the exhaust gas go into the open air."

The Prof didn't take his eyes off the pipe and nodded silently as he carried on measuring it. Finally a while later he tapped Roy on the shoulder and stood saying. "I think we're out in the air now."

A small cheer went up as he said this and several of them clapped each other on the shoulders. Jim looked over to where Andy was sitting waiting for the outcome, he smiled wanly at his father and picked up the little transmitter to make it ready and pressed the buttons until it gave him a light to say it was armed. Holding it in front of himself he crossed his fingers and pressed the button, they heard nothing but a moment later the compressor changed its note and raced rapidly in revolutions. Dick closed it down instantly and turned round and said. "The pressures dropped a mile; it must be open at the end."

Another cheer went up and they started to connect all the pipes together as quickly as possible. When they had finished Jim could only smile at the mass of tubing and wires they had assembled to gain some air in the building. He once more thought of Heath Robinson, but turning to Ray he said. "Time to give it a go then."

Roy looked up from his seat on the floor and said. "Don't forget we've got to switch off all power to the other floor and the front or they'll know instantly that when the electricity comes on, what we've done."

"OK, Roy. "Jim offered. "You're the sparks around here, why don't you switch off the things yourself, you'll know better than anyone which ones they are."

Roy nodded and walked over to the switchboard; he busied himself for a few moments with some levers and then turned to Jim and said. "Its all clear now, the only electricity is in here."

They all looked at each other, some with fingers crossed, and then with a nod from Jim they switched on the generator. Luckily when they had installed it they had placed it on a solid block of concrete for stability so combined with the silencing system and the fact that the generator ran quietly, they could hear almost no noise, or feel any vibration. Jim knew that there was a possibility the attackers would find the exhaust pipe or hit upon what they were doing but resigned himself to waiting to see if they did. The lights came on and the air pump hummed into action pumping the exhaust gases out on the long journey to the outside world. They all stared at the generator as if hypnotised whilst it ran for several minutes, then the piece of cotton they had placed across the end of the waste pipe started to flutter as the air began to come back into the building through the pipe. Gradually they accepted the fact that it was going to work and they visibly relaxed and started to go about the business of cleaning up and putting all unnecessary tools away.

With these problems over, they decided to eat something and all of them except Andy went to the kitchen to get some food. Colette took Andy back to hospital and it was about two hours later that Jim got himself some free time and decided to check on him and see how he was recovering. He walked over to the room they were using as a makeshift hospital and into the room expecting to see Andy but found the bed empty. Glowering around he could see no place that Andy could be, so went to the door and called Colette who had wandered over to watch the progress with the generator. She came as soon as he called and he asked. "Where've you hidden Andy?"

She looked at him in puzzlement then walked into the room herself to check; she came running out and ran over to the single toilet they had built for anyone working at the farm end, but it was empty. She came back to him and gasped. "I don't know where he could have got to; you can see he isn't anywhere here."

Jim stared at her. "Then where the hell could he have gone then?" He didn't wait for an answer but ran into every room at this end of the building, with no success. He looked out into the main hall and peering into it he asked her. "Was he fit enough to move around much today?" I thought that wound would keep him down for a bit."

Colette pursed her lips and confessed. "It was only a flesh wound, a good bandage and he was OK, I thought that a days rest would do him some good so I told him to stay in bed today to give it a chance to heal. The only time he got out was when he helped Ray with that problem with the pipe."

Jim walked rapidly over to the crowd that was still gathered round Dick and Ray discussing their work. "I want several of you to go round and have a look to see if you can see Andy, he's disappeared."

Leah looked keenly up at Jim from her position on the floor where she had been helping to clear the debris from the work on the exhaust system. "Jim." She said hesitantly. "I think I know where he is."

"Well spit it out then Leah." Jim exclaimed. "I don't like the sound of this."

She began. "We were talking while I visited him last night and he said he fancied going outside with his sniper rifle and seeing if he could pot one or two." She spread her hands helplessly and went on. "I said to him that it was a crazy idea but he kept on telling me that if anyone could do it, it was him. He said he had experience of sniping because he had done some training in the army; he just wouldn't listen to reason. I would have said something to you sooner but I didn't think he had any way out of here."

Jim glanced around at everyone. "Well." He demanded. "Just how the hell did he get out? With all of us here trying to get a simple pipe through another one for some air, how did he manage to get out of here?" a thought struck him and he asked. "Is his sniper rifle here? Has anyone seen it?"

They all stared around at each other with guilty looks on each face as if Jim had accused each of them with an offence. Lee held his hand up and gestured to Jim. "I didn't pay any attention when I saw it because I didn't think it was important, but I saw him a couple of hours ago, going into the room where the cables come in. He had a scuba tank with him, but I thought he was just checking the pipe out and a lot of people have been round here just lately." He shrugged his shoulders. "I've got used to being down here on my own, now everybody's here."

Jim stared at him with icy eyes. "Why didn't you tell me this when it happened? Instead of leaving it this length of time."

He knew deep down it would be too late to stop Andy but still started to go over to the cupboard where the pipe connections were. Ray put his hand out and held him back by the arm. "Let me look." He said. He strode over to the cupboard and looked up the pipe and then signalling to them to be quiet he bent his head so he could listen, then standing up he said. "I think I can hear him, the sound carries quite well along the pipe." He took off his coat and placed it over the end of the pipe, while the rest looked at him in puzzlement. "To stop anybody hearing what we say, if we can hear them they can hear us." He shook his head in sorrow. "I can't call out to him; the others will probably hear it."

He pulled Jim by the arm and when they were out of earshot of the rest he said. "I think it's quite likely they're going to be waiting for him when he gets to the top, I'd put a permanent guard on it or block it off completely if I was outside."

Jim nodded; worry had etched deep lines down his face and he felt as if every incident that happened was the gods conspiring against him to make life as difficult as possible. He gnawed his bottom lip and scratched his head, as he thought about the possible options open to him. He considered it extremely likely that Andy would get himself captured and looking at Ray with a determined glance he said. "Give me a hand; I'm going up that pipe myself."

His voice had carried over to the rest and several stopped what they were doing and came over with Pat in the forefront. "You're going to get yourself killed if you go up there, I know Andy's my son and I want him to be safe but if you go I'll lose the two of you. And that's not going to happen if I have anything to say about it."

Jim put his hands on her shoulders. "I'm not going to get myself killed just yet, but think about what happens next." He pointed at the generator behind her. "How long do you think we've got before they discover that pipe? He held his finger up. "One potato is all that's needed to shut that thing down. One, that's all, they only have to stuff it up the end and the exhaust won't work any more."

Ray looked up at this and attempted to lighten the atmosphere. "It's doubtful they've got one to spare old mate, we'll probably only rate an apple off one of those fruit trees out there if they're fruiting which is doubtful."

Jim grinned weakly. "OK, I get the point, but it is serious and we aren't going to win this war by sitting around here waiting for their next move, now it's my idea that we have to carry this fight to them or next time they might come up with something to shut us down completely. It seems that they've probably got about thirteen people out there and they're bound to be well armed, so if any of us go out its likely they could die." He looked around to make sure his words were sinking in. "But it won't do any good sitting around down here waiting for something to happen." He pointed at the contraption they had erected. "That thing there is only going to buy us a little time, Sulim will want to get in here pretty quick, I can't guess how much food he's got but it won't be very much as we all heard how everyone was starving before they died. He'll also figure that if these crops here are to survive they need light and cultivation, and he knows they aren't getting any at the moment."

At that moment Lee walked in from the farm, he was holding Andy's sniper rifle in his hands. "I found this hidden by his bed." He said. "But I think my Kalashnikov's gone from the other room where I left it."

Pat snatched the gun from his hands. "Give me that." She said heatedly. "If anyone's going to use it in future it's going to be me."

There was a cry from Liz who shared her husband's pacifist views and so had been detailed to watch the monitor. "There's something going on out here." They all rushed over to where the monitor had come to life with the fresh surge of electricity that had been injected into it. On the screen they could make out some figures walking round to the side where the glass had been broken and allowed access to the upper floor. They appeared to be carrying some tools and they climbed up the ladder that had been placed against the outside wall. It looked as if the party was four in strength and they disappeared into the interior and were lost to view. After a few minutes they were startled to hear a great deal of banging on their ceiling. They looked at each other in consternation; it was obvious that the attackers were trying to make a hole down through to them.

Dick stepped forward. "Before you all start getting worried, I mixed a lot of that concrete up there myself, and I can assure you that some people with chisels and hammers aren't going to make a hole down through there easily, I'm not saying it can't be done but it will be very difficult by hand. There aren't any electric tools up there to my knowledge, and anyway I laid a mesh of reinforcing bars through there so they won't get in without our say so."

Lee sniffed. "They don't have to get in, they can put plastic explosive into the hole and blow it and we're finished."

"All the more reason for us to carry the fight to them, I'd say." Jim said.

Ray said to the assembled company. "Look, there are ways of combating any measures they take to get at us in here, don't forget they don't want to die any more than we do. That's why they stopped trying to rush us, because they could see we were determined to fight them. This isn't like one of them American movies where the bad guys surround the shack and keep on firing until everyone's dead. They've got to break in here and expose themselves to return fire when they do, and we've at least got concrete around us and that makes it difficult for them to get in without casualties. But Jim's right, we aren't going to win this one without taking the fight to them, because sitting here gives them an advantage."

He turned to Jim and asked. "You've been thinking about this a long time, now what plans did you make for this situation?"

Jim smiled. "First of all I want to ask for volunteers to come out with me and try and deal with this menace to our lives." He held his hands up to forestall anybody coming forward yet. "I also want you to know that if you do want to do this, you stand a good chance of getting yourself killed."

Ray stepped forward. "I'd rather die doing something than sitting around here waiting for them to kill me anyway."

One by one most of the others stepped forward, until with the exception of Martin and his wife Liz, they had all volunteered. Jim looked at them all in turn and said. "Thanks for volunteering, but I don't think it would be a good idea to have us all out there so I'm going to choose four of you to come with me, and the rest have got to guard this place." He looked around and discounted some because he wanted people who had fighter's instincts, he chose Ray, Roy the sparks, Lee, and finally to a gasp from the rest he chose Leah.

She looked as amazed as the rest and said. "I want to go out with you, but what made you choose me?"

Jim rubbed his chin and scratched himself on his stubble, then said. "You've already proved you've got what it takes, by pulling no punches earlier when you defended this place on the first attack, and by your attitude, there are women out there and us men have got this stupid thing that we'll try and capture them rather than shoot them. It might just happen that you can help us to do the job properly."

Pat sniffed at this. "You men, when it comes down to the nitty gritty's of life, you all want to back down and let us women do the work for you. Some of us women could do the job of fighting better than you any day."

Jim rounded on her with scorn. "You find it hard to kill a spider, so how can you claim to be better suited to do what we're doing.

Now why don't you get this place organised for defence and let us get on and sort out what we want to take with us."

One thing about Pat was that Jim had never been able to browbeat her and now it was as if he had never spoken for all the notice she took of him. She held a finger under his nose. "And another thing." She went on. "I want my son back in one piece."

She glared at him for a moment, then turned and marched away with the defenders, her back straight and if it could have talked Jim would have quailed before the onslaught. With a sigh Jim gazed at his volunteers. "The first thing I'm going to say is this isn't going to be easy, and the second is thanks for volunteering. Now lets get organised, I want every one of us carrying the same sort of weapon because then we can carry one type of ammunition and we can reload each others weapons. I think the best thing is to take the Heckler and Koch machine guns, they're ideal for the type of fight we'll be having."

They all busied themselves readying the guns and before they had finished, some food arrived from Pat, and Julia came with a small package of food for each of them to take with them. He told Ray to get the breathing masks out from where Andy had placed them and made sure they all knew how to operate them; they were the most basic type and only filtered the air to make it breathable. The filter on the side unscrewed to allow cleaning. This had to be done on a regular basis, judging by the amount of dust in the atmosphere outside. They had to hold their breath as they did this but it only took seconds to shake out and would save them from breathing the air with its deadly dust.

They also got out and put on the coveralls they had stored for the purpose of going out into the atmosphere. These buttoned up round the neck and had Velcro strips on the sleeves and ankles to stop dust penetrating inside. They felt warm and restrictive but at least they protected them while they were outside. Once they were clothed and they all had their packs ready, Jim went over to a chest in one of the rooms and produced some grenades from it; he solemnly handed each of them three and took three for himself. Ray shook his head when he saw this and said. "I'd forgotten all about these, it seems so long ago we got them."

Jim nodded in agreement, and replied. "I don't know whether you've noticed but we bought some claymores as well and they've gone missing."

Ray snapped his fingers. "Yeah, I remember those, what do you think happened to them?"

Jim shrugged. "I don't know, but I reckon Andy knew how I feel about them and decided to put them somewhere safe, but I've no idea where that would be." He looked at the team and asked. "Is everybody OK about this?" He thought about trying to teach them some hand signals in case they should be quiet but decided that it would only confuse matters in a fight. He got various assents from them and then led them over to one of the rooms at the back. They stood in the room and looked at each other in puzzlement. Unnoticed to them Jim had picked up a hammer and chisel and now stepped over to the wall; it had been plastered over in sand and cement and looked much the same as all the others. Jim tapped with his knuckles along the back wall while they still looked at it with bewilderment, suddenly instead of a solid sound it came back hollow;he continued tapping along until it sounded solid again. He put a mark on the wall where it had sounded hollow and then tapped gently on the chisel with the hammer, it went straight into the wall and Jim hooked his hand behind and pulled. A gaping hole opened up in front of them and with very little effort he opened an area about two-foot square. When it was open, he glanced over his shoulder. "I put this in when nobody was about just in case this situation happened. It looks solid but it's safe as long as nobody knows it's there, it's the same outside, the problem is, I've got to push out and I don't know if anybody is standing out there, it should be quiet but we can't tell from in here. Has anything been reported on that monitor over there?"

"The only people that have moved are the party on the floor above and I think they'll be stopping soon as its getting dark." Martin offered, he carried on. "I'll be glad when it is dark because that noise is going to drive us nuts if it carries on much longer."

In this he was right as the sound of hammering had carried on incessantly and was by now getting on everyone's nerves. Jim hesitated as he couldn't be sure if the people above were taking it in turns to walk around inside and peer down to see if there was any movement below. Ray glanced at his watch and said. "It'll be dark in a few minutes, especially with the atmosphere out there."

Jim nodded and said to them. "Take it easy for a bit and we'll see if they intend to carry on, they probably won't have any lighting up there, so they won't be able to see very much in a little while."

They waited and after a few minutes the banging started to peter out and then stopped, the silence was beautiful after all the clatter and a sigh of relief went round the assembled community. Most of them had by now wandered over to see what was going on and Jim felt a hand touch him as Pat came and stood next to him, he touched her back to show there was no hard feelings from their harsh words to each other, and reflected that most marriages were probably like that, with each partner arguing with the other over trivial things. A shout from Martin who had taken over the duty of watching the monitor broke into his thoughts and he called out. "I've got four people coming down from the top floor and they look like they're going to go into the front." He went silent and then a couple of minutes later he said. "The top floor is clear now, they've all gone inside. By the way Jim, they seem to have fixed one of those air conditioning units on to the front and they've repaired the doors where they fired that missile. It's not the best repair but it seems adequate to keep the dust out."

"What are they using for power out there?" Jim called.

The reply when it came wasn't too much of a surprise; "They're using the old generator we brought up here to power the caravans when we first started."

Jim sighed, he knew it would have been better to either bring it inside or destroy it but he had wanted to keep it for a back up if anything happened to the large one they had now. They had also left quite a large amount of diesel out there to be used on the Utes if they ever wanted to go anywhere. 'This is going to prove a costly mistake' He thought to himself. But a further thought came to him. 'Maybe if they hadn't had these things they might have attacked more eagerly, and that could have proved fatal for us.'

He called out again. "Can you see anybody out there at all?"

Before he got an answer he decided to go over and see for himself.

When he arrived it was to find Martin staring intently at the screen, he turned to Jim when he got there and said. "I haven't seen anybody out there at all, but that doesn't mean they aren't because the monitor wasn't working for some time when the electricity went out, there could be maybe four of them up in the windmill, I haven't seen anybody come out of there since they switched off."

Jim cursed under his breath; although he had been expecting something like this it still galled him to think that all the cards seemed to be in the other mans hands. Using his sense of what people were like he tried to guess what he would do in their position. Keeping four men on guard in the windmill wouldn't be an intelligent use of manpower. He thought they would probably try and have two there, as one man on his own would tend to skive off and if anybody came into the windmill they would want to overpower them as easily as possible. He turned to his team of fighters who had followed him over and said determinedly. "I'm going to guess they've got two men guarding the windmill and no men on any sort of roving guard. I'm going to break out of the back as quickly as possible; taking a chance is all we've got, so let's do it."

He got some grim smiles from them and Leah actually broke into a beaming smile and said. "Wow! Let's get going."

They all strode over to the back wall and Jim picked up the hammer and chisel and placing it against the opening he gave a full shouldered smash on it. The two-foot panel shot out and landed on the floor behind the building and Ray scrambled out as quickly as he could levelling his gun in front of him. The precaution was unnecessary as the area was completely deserted. They all followed him out and the people inside quickly closed off the opening behind them. Jim picked up the fallen panel and placed it back where it had been and then rubbed some dirt into the joint, when he stepped back and looked it was almost indiscernible and would need a close inspection to find it. He knew that when the attackers found out they were outside the first thing they would do was look for the exit hole. He then peered around and felt depressed at the sight that greeted him. It was dark and for the time of the year when they should have been enjoying long warm evenings, the air was chill and gloomy. No stars shone in the heavens and Jim knew they stood little chance of seeing any for a very long time. He looked up the hill to where the windmill turned uselessly in the wind and regretted the fact that for the time being the electricity they could have been using was being poured into the ground. He thought also about Andy and wondered for the hundredth time where he had got himself to. He looked at the others who had assumed the guard position about them, they all glanced bleakly back at him and nodding in the direction he wanted to go he stepped carefully off to go round the building to the front.

As they walked he felt surprised that the ground felt soft and spongy and looking down he could see the whole floor was covered with a layer of dust that billowed round them in a cloud as they walked; he marvelled again at the fact that one single eruption on a volcano thousands of miles away could produce so much outfall and wondered what the ground in America would look like now. It was hard to comprehend how many people this one single event had killed. He knew that in earth's history it had happened before, with the dinosaurs, but they had lasted millions of years and man had lasted so little time in comparison.

He hefted the gun in front of him and walked carefully to the corner. When he arrived he poked his head round to check and was rewarded with a view of the side of the building stretching away into the distance, it was deserted and he stepped out and walked along the building to the front. Looking over his shoulder, he saw the others had followed in his tracks. He glanced carefully round the corner expecting at any time to see one of the enemy, but he was relieved to find the front was devoid of life. The generator gave out the familiar noises as it ran almost silently powering everything at the front of the building. The air conditioning unit they had brought was fixed now into one of the window spaces, and Jim could make out the strange filter on the side spinning whilst it took all the dust out of the air intake. Something made him look up the slope in front of him and he waved to a camera he couldn't see and hoped they could see him.

Luckily for them the invaders hadn't bothered to draw the curtains, probably because as far as they knew there were no other beings for hundreds of miles. He went back to the others and made them huddle round him on the corner, he spoke to them in the muffled speech they all had from wearing the masks. "I want you all to wait for me here; I'm going to do a quick recce along the front."

Ray touched his arm. "Let me come with you, I want to have a look at who that guy's got with him."

Jim nodded and then added. "Make sure you don't get trigger happy before I say so, I want to mount the best attack possible and not to go in prematurely."

He got a thumbs up from Ray in return and together they set off to reconnoitre the front of the building; as they passed each room along the front they slid down and crawled along under the window; just raising themselves sufficiently to see who was in the room. They all seemed to be occupied by one or more people in various stages of living together. The first room they passed, they looked in and Jim gasped when he realised who inhabited it. He could clearly see it was the electrician who had left in such strange circumstances. He glanced quickly to one side to se Ray's reaction, and was rewarded with a rising of the eyebrows; he didn't recognise the woman with him and left to go along to the next room.

The next room held another surprise, as it was the supermarket owner; he appeared to be on his own. There were guns in the room, stacked along the wall. He carried on to the next room, which was in darkness and looked deserted. He had by now started to see a pattern to this and when he reached the next window, his suspicions were confirmed. He could see it was the Belgian he disliked so much, Schoonheid. There was a woman in the room with him but Jim didn't recognise her, but assumed it was either a companion or his wife.

The next room along was the central recreation room and there were several people in there. He peered through the window in shock as he recognised a man tied to the chair. It was his son Andy and by the attitude of the men clustered around him he could see that he had been undergoing some serious questioning. His head hung on his chest and as he watched one of the men grabbed a handful of his hair and slapped him across the face, his finger tightened on the trigger of his gun and it was only Ray's hand clamped tightly round his arm that prevented him from pulling it and blasting his way into the room. "Back off for a minute mate." Ray whispered. "He's not been hurt too badly yet, we can attack in a few minutes, but let's get a better idea of who we face."

Jim slowly subsided and studied the other men in the room. Sulim was there and with no surprise Jim recognised Diman, the third man came as no surprise either, it was the policeman who had visited them looking for the guns. Ray practically scuttled along the rest of the windows past the filter mechanism and came back a few minutes later to say. "I think there're three coppers with their wives. They're all armed. Then in one room there seems to be four women but they don't look western they look eastern."

Jim speculated momentarily as to who these women could be and surmised they were probably with Sulim, and maybe one could be the policeman's wife; he couldn't imagine Diman having anyone as he probably liked to play rough when he had a woman. He looked through the window at his son and raised his gun to spray the room with bullets but Ray pulled him back saying. "It'll do no good to attack just like that; we've got to make some sort of plan to take the maximum possible people out while we still have the element of surprise. They don't know we're out here yet so let's capitalise on that. Andy can stand just a little more while we make a plan."

Jim slowly turned his gaze from the tableau facing him in the room and looked at Ray with anguished eyes. "How would you feel if it was your son?" He whispered vehemently. "If this goes on much longer they'll kill him or maim him."

Ray looked into the window where Andy had just received another blow to the face. "Just a couple of minutes more and we'll attack, I promise." He grabbed Jim's arm and pulled him along to the end of the building where the other three were waiting for them. When they arrived Ray spoke rapidly to them. "They've got Andy in the recreation room; they're beating up on him so we've got to go in quick." He pointed at them. "We've got to hit them as hard and as quick as we possibly can. Roy you take the first room, Lee, you take the second room, and Leah takes the last room. I'll go to the other side and take the room just past the recreation room. I'll have to try for three rooms as there are possibly three people along there, with their women. We'll have to ignore the room with the rest of the women for the time being as we haven't got the manpower out here to cope. Jim you take the room Andy's in; we're going to toss grenades into each room. When that happens on my shout I think they'll run out to the passage to see what's happening, you'll have to try and get him out at that point in the confusion. Now, I think we'll have the element of surprise for a minute or so as it's almost certain they don't know we're here. When you get in position, wait for my signal and then smash the windows with your guns and throw the grenades in, don't forget to duck down. When they go off stand up and fire half the magazine in the window. Then stand to one side and wait for anyone to stick their head out and shoot it off." He grinned as he said it; although they could only see his eyes in the ridiculous looking masks they were all wearing. "And one more thing, don't forget Jim's going in to get Andy out, so don't blast off without checking who you're shooting at. And remember, be strong and do your job, now get along there and take your positions."

He took hold of Jim's arm to stop him from running along. "You'll have the worst job because you can't fire until Andy's safe, don't forget that Diman's a trained gunman, he's going to catch on quick to what's happening. I'm going to come to you as soon as I know my coppers are finished."

Jim nodded, his mind in a whirl, all he could think off, was to get back to Andy's window and try and stop the torture. He scrambled along on his hands and knees as the others had done to reach the window and when he arrived he slowly raised his head until just his eyes were over the windowsill. He was worried and reassured at what he saw inside as Andy had obviously passed out and the torturers were taking a break while they studied him. He glanced from side to side and saw that everybody had taken their positions, Ray was a few feet from him with a grenade in his hand and the rifle, butt first, aimed at the window, they nodded to each other and Ray pulled the pin on the grenade while holding it, they saw the rest mimic their actions and Jim raised his gun to smash the window when they threw the grenades into the room. He had inadvertently stood up to give himself some more leverage and something made Diman look up. Jim saw the look of total surprise appear in his eyes when he saw Jim outside the window before he opened his mouth to call a warning. There was the sound of smashing glass and shouts of alarm from the windows alongside Jim and he started to smash the gun into the window, after that events started to move rapidly. Someone, he didn't know who, at this time, dropped the grenade outside their window and started to run away from it. Ray smashed his window and threw the grenade but the person inside had run through the door before it went off.

Jim crashed the gun butt through the window and saw that Diman had dived for his gun, which was lying against the wall; he reversed his gun and fired as quickly as he could but in his haste he missed him completely. The policeman had clawed his pistol from his holster and Jim fired in his direction. He saw the shot hit but the man turned and ran for the door; the delay had given Sulim time to get hold of a gun, afterwards Jim had no recollection of where it came from only that bullets shattered the rest of the window by his side. He turned the gun towards Sulim to try and shoot him but to his complete surprise all the lights went out. He was temporarily blind as he peered into the room and Ray appeared alongside him. "Where's Andy?" He whispered. Jim stared into the room trying to make sense of the blank space in front of him.

More bullets whipped past him in the darkness and he fired back at the flash hoping to get the person firing; he felt rather than saw Ray slither over the windowsill into the room and held his fire for fear of hitting him. Leah appeared on his other side and whispered. "I think I got one but I missed the other." She looked quickly around and almost shouted into his ear. "Where the hell is Ray?"

Jim stared back at her now with his night sight starting to come back and indicated the room. "What's he doing going in." She would have said more but Ray appeared in the window with his arm round Andy, he pushed as hard as he could and Andy fell out of the window into Jims arms. There was a howl of rage from inside the room and someone fired a gun, Ray gasped and fell back onto the floor. Leah jumped up and fired over his head but suddenly there were two people firing automatic weapons and a hail of bullets shot out of the room. She spun round with a small scream and dropping the gun she clutched her shoulder. Jim pushed her in front of him and dropping his own gun he picked Andy up and threw him over his shoulder and ran for the corner as quickly as possible. She stumbled alongside him until they reached there. They passed the body of Lee lying on the floor outside the window he had been assigned. The window was still unbroken and Jim assumed his own grenade had killed him when it didn't enter the room. He dumped Andy unceremoniously on the ground round the corner and went back quickly to retrieve Lee's breathing mask and placed it on Andy's face. As he did so Andy started to show signs of coming round and flailed his arms in protest at Jim touching him. Leah saw this and bent down to stroke Andy on the cheek and said soothingly. "Its OK lover boy, you're safe for the moment."

Jim glanced sharply at her for the choice of her words but he heard a noise and looking round the corner he saw several torches flashing as the figures holding them were coming along the front wall. He looked desperately round and saw the nearest cover was about fifty yards away where they had parked their Ute's. He tapped her on the shoulder and said sharply. "On your feet, they're coming out to look for us and we aren't going to be safe here for more than a couple of minutes."

She winced at the touch and Jim saw that she had blood seeping through the fabric of her coat. She stood and he pushed her in the direction he wanted her to go and she started walking towards the Utes. He dragged Andy on to his shoulder and went after her in a shambling run. The mask made breathing difficult and he was sweating even though it was cold when they arrived at the cover of the Utes. They slumped down beside the wheels and Jim peered round them at the torchlight bobbing around along the front of the building. They had stopped at Lee's body and were obviously discussing what their next move would be.

Taking a moment he checked Andy and could see that he would be useless to them for some time, as he was still groggy from the beating he had received. He then went to Leah who had opened the top of her jacket to inspect her shoulder; he couldn't see anything and had to feel gently to see if any bones had been broken. She gasped when he touched one spot, and held his hand away from her. He persisted and grabbed one of the field dressings that Andy had thoughtfully provided when he had bought all the supplies and wrapped the arm up tightly to staunch the flow of blood. Then nodding to himself said "I think it's only a flesh wound, I can't feel any broken bones"

He reached into his pouch to get an ampoule of morphine but she stopped him and said. "Don't give me any of that, it's not too painful and I'm going to need to be thinking straight without being drugged up." She smiled gamely at him and went on. "Not many men get asked this, but can you put my jacket back on, we've got to get going soon, it won't take them long to figure out where we are."

She looked over at the building they had just left and said with a catch in her throat. "I wonder if Ray managed to get out before they got to him?"

Jim pulled her jacket over her shoulder and helped her button it up. As he was doing this he could see the torches start to travel along the side of the building, and knew they were going to look for the bolthole they had made. He took hold of her good shoulder and stared deep into her eyes, she looked wonderingly back at him. "For the moment there's not a thing you can do for Ray, so try and forget him. We'll be going back as soon as we can, but a lot of shots came out of that room so it's possible he didn't come out. On the other hand, remember he's pretty resourceful so he might have made it, either way we've got to fight on or we're all going to lose."

She took a deep breath and nodded that she understood, she wiped away the tears that had started to form and sniffled. Jim looked around and frowned. "Did you see anything of Roy?"

She shook her head, wincing a little as the pain shot up her arm with the movement. "I never saw anything of him, but if you remember, the window you allocated to him had been broken and the grenade had gone in."

Jim shook his head in despair, until he found out what had happened to Roy he was down two men and had a fighting force of only three people, two of whom were unfit right now. He looked at Andy who was sitting comatose and prayed he wasn't too badly hurt to fight. He reached out to pick up his gun and with a sense of shock remembered dropping it to pick up Andy. Leah saw his look and glanced around for a minute and then looked at Jim in surprise.

"Where's your gun?" She asked with panic rising in her throat.

He looked at her sheepishly and hung his head. "Dropped it when I picked Andy up."

"Aw, Christ." she hissed vehemently. "Can't we trust you men to do anything right? You know how important it is and you go and throw it away. Now what are we going to do?"

Jim mind was racing under the reprimand and he replied nastily. "Maybe if you still had your gun we could have done something. It's too late now for recriminations, we've got to do something to create a diversion or that lot are going to be attacking though that hole at the back that we came through. How many grenades have you got left?"

She reached painfully into the pocket of her jacket and pulled out two. "That's what I've got, what about you?"

He nodded in satisfaction. "I've got a couple as well, so let's put them to good use." He glanced round and saw the lights were still bobbing along the side of the building and then looked the other way towards the caravans parked a few hundred yards away; he could just make them out through the murky blackness and right alongside he could see the converted Utes that the attackers had arrived in. Turning back to her he said musingly. "I wonder if they've had time to unload them yet?"

The mask she was wearing mostly hid her face, but he could see the sparkle in her eyes. "Now you're talking." She answered. "Even if they have, it'll give them something to worry about."

Jim reached down and picked up Andy once more with a little help from her and when he was on his back they started to shamble over in the direction of the Utes, it took several minutes and when they arrived Jim collapsed on the ground breathing hoarsely through the mask. She bent down beside him and held her hand out to take the grenades from him, then reached into her pockets and produced a ball of twine and unwinding it slightly she pulled it to check how strong it was and nodding to pronounce it was strong enough she said to him. "Get your breath back and be prepared to move when I say."

Jim watched for a few moments and then turned to Andy to check on him. He was showing signs of coming round and he pulled him upright against the side of the Ute and ran his hands over his body to see if he had any external injuries. His arms and legs appeared to look OK and apart from being sensitive to being touched he didn't appear to be severely hurt. Jim thanked his lucky stars, and then suddenly, Andy opened his eyes and looked groggily around. His eyes were still a little out of focus and he winced when he moved his arm to rub the back of his head. He came to with a start and said to Jim. "What happened?

Jim grinned in pleasure and answered. "We got you out is what happened."

Jim looked around and took in their surroundings and then peered over to see what Leah was doing; by this time she had connected three lengths of twine to three of the grenades and had started to walk over to the Utes, she glanced inside and nodded in satisfaction at the contents and then opened the filler cap on the petrol tank on the nearest and gently wedged the grenade in the top with some rags she had found. She then wiggled it to make sure it was tight and leaving the twine lying on the floor she moved out of sight to go to the next one. By now he had recovered his breath and standing up he peeped into the door of the Ute. He could see now that it was loaded with boxes of weapons and supplies, it caused him to wonder why they hadn't moved them closer to the main building for protection. But realised they probably hadn't had time or the energy after the days fighting. He felt the presence of Andy standing next to him and felt relieved he could at least stand.

He went to the end of the Ute and from there he could see that the torches by now had almost reached the back of the building, he knew if they turned the corner they would almost certainly find the hole at the back and that was going to spell disaster for them because if they got inside they would have hostages to hold against them. The rest of the community although willing, wouldn't be able to stand an onslaught for very long. Leah materialised by his side and she pulled his arm and hissed. "I'm ready now, we've got to get out of here, and quickly too." Nodding to her, Jim turned to help Andy to find him almost recovered, he asked. "Can you walk any distance?"

Andy nodded but winced a little as the movement caused him

some pain. "Don't make me run too fast for a bit though."

"Come on." Leah said urgently. "They've almost reached the corner and I want them to see this before they turn it." She went to the central place she had put the twine from the grenades and picking it up she joined all three and then tied the remainder to the knot. Then started to walk backwards with her hand paying it out as she went; they walked backwards in the direction of the slope leading to the hill and when they were about fifty metres away the twine ran out. Jim looked over his shoulder at the relative safety of the crevasses on the slope and then at the others. They were standing by his side looking at him and Leah was smiling evilly. Jim said regretfully. "This twine could have been a bit longer couldn't it?"

She shrugged and answered. "Spoil all the fun though wouldn't it. Now when I say go, I'll pull the string and run like hell, we've got five seconds after pulling before that lot goes up, and some of the pyrotechnics from those petrol tanks are going to be dangerous to say the least." She looked at Andy who was standing looking at her with a grim expression on his face and said. "Ready?"

He nodded and looking at Jim she nodded and said. "Go."

She pulled on the twine and then turned and ran as fast as she could, Andy started to lose ground but limped along with them. Jim was counting in his head up to five. "One thousand, two thousand, until he reached five, then he dived to the ground and pulled Leah down with him, the explosion came instantaneously, and he felt the shrapnel going over his head in a shower of metal. Andy had dived down as soon as they had and now they looked back. The explosion had set all three vehicles on fire and one had been thrown on its side. They stood and started to run away from the light and Jim could hear shouts of alarm and anger coming from the group by the building. They were too far away to make out the individual voices but by the sound of them someone was really angry. They ran for several hundred yards until suddenly the flames reached the ammunition inside the Utes and with a blast one of the rockets exploded, this set off a chain reaction and they were treated to a display of pyrotechnics as the rest of them blew out and sprayed the night with bright explosions. Some of the bullets overheated, ignited and they fired out in a random pattern, and one or two came close as they hurried out past the caravans to take refuge in the shrubbery on the hill. Looking back Jim could make out the torches approaching the Ute's. They had gone about five hundred meters when a final explosion rocked the Ute's and for a moment or two they were deafened as it blew them to smithereens.

They stopped and surveyed the damage they had caused and grinned at each other in triumph, the odds had been considerably reduced now as the enemy had lost a lot of their armament, and also the use of the Utes. Jim felt a smothering sensation in his mask and realised that the filters were becoming clogged and unscrewed it to empty it. The two others saw him doing it and did the same; they only had to take them off and tap them on the ground and then screw them back in place. The time taken was only a few seconds and they could then breathe easily. Turning, Jim led them away from the scene of devastation out into the wilderness; he knew where he was going and slowly trudged in that direction.

Chapter Four

Jim stretched and tried to get the kinks out of his legs, he must have dozed for a while, as it had got a lot lighter than he remembered. The air was cold and a chill wind blew round him, he looked down the hill to where the buildings were and saw that the Ute's still had some smoke drifting away from them to be dispersed in the wind. His gaze took in the surrounding area and was relieved to see it empty of people. The building as far as he could see hadn't been too badly damaged and some repair work had been done to the windows on the front. He looked down to see Leah and Andy stretched out on the ground under some shrubs, they were still wearing their masks against the dust in the atmosphere and he reached down to shake their shoulders to remind them to empty the filters on the side. As he touched Leah her eyes flew open in alarm and he could see the pain she was feeling in them. She turned her face to him with a worried expression and her eyes formed the question without speaking, almost imploring him to give her the right answer to the unspoken request. He shook his head sadly as he clasped her shoulder gently and then turned his attention to Andy. The movement had awakened Andy and he stretched and ran his hands over his body to check how he felt; then satisfied he looked over to Leah and nodded sympathetically. Then stared at his father and asked. "No sign of Ray then?"

Jim shook his head and sat down between them, they both swivelled in the earth to face him and Jim said. "We haven't got much time, first of all, Lee bought it last night." He waited for the look of surprise on Andy's face then went on. "I've had a look at the rations we brought with us and I think we've got enough for the present, but after that we'll have nothing. Now we've got to try and get something done today and my suggestion is that we have something to eat and drink then we go and get something to fight this war."

He looked at Andy. "You know what I mean? Don't you?"

Andy nodded and Leah raised her head. "You're going to get those crossbows?" She asked.

Jim looked at her quizzically. "Ray told you about them then?"

She shrugged her shoulders and gave a little gasp as the pain shot across her arm. Jim went to her quickly but she put her other arm up to stop him. "It's OK; it's only a bit stiff. I'll be all right if I exercise it for a minute." She rubbed her hand over it but couldn't quite reach the place so Andy stood and going to her he knelt beside her and gently massaged her arm until she smiled her thanks and stopped him. She moved her arm in a circle to regain some use in it then said to Jim. "Let's get a bite to eat, I'm bloody starving, my stomach's beginning to think my throats been cut."

They sat in a circle and attempted to eat by pushing the food into their mouths with the masks still on, Andy smiled and said. "Next time I go out and buy some masks, tell me to get one designed by a man who wants to eat without taking the things off. This food tastes as gritty as hell."

"Yeah." Leah said dryly. "That's if you can still find the shop open."

"Gallows humour." Jim commented. "Think positive, we don't want to be out here too long. Work on a plan to take out some of the enemy down there. We gave them a lot to think about last night but it's not going to take them long to figure out what we're up to, How many do you think there are down there now?"

Leah stared at the ground as she did some mental arithmetic and when she looked at Jim she said, with puzzlement in her voice. "I make it that we've only got four definite kills, the rest can only be speculation. We killed two definitely on the front of the building with the rocket launchers, one in the passage, I think I got one more last night with a grenade, but for the rest I couldn't say with any accuracy if we got any."

Andy nodded in agreement and Jim looked at them in dismay. "Do you realise what that means? He counted on his fingers as he went over the figures. "Martin won't fight, Lee dead, Ray missing." He shook his head in annoyance. "We won't find out yet." He looked at Leah who stared stonily back at him with no emotion on her face. Then he went on. "Roy, I don't know where he is, he just disappeared, and you two are both injured. That leaves me as the only one who can say he's fit to fight, and they've got at least nine men down there right now." He stood to walk around in agitation but Leah stood and confronted him.

"I suppose you're going to do the giving up bit now are you, you'd better start thinking of the advantages we've got here, first we've got us three and all of us can fight well enough, we might be a little injured but not enough to stop us. Some of the women you've got down there can fight as well; don't forget what Julia and Pat did when they stopped that attack with machine guns. At least three of those women they've got are Moslems and the men never allow them to have any say in fighting. And those men down there don't know we've got access to anything to fight with, they think we dropped all our weapons on that useless attack. Now I suggest we get off and find those crossbows before that lot down there find us here unarmed."

She stopped talking and glared at him waiting for his reply, Jim looked back crestfallen, to realise he had almost been on the point of giving in to his despair. Then he straightened his back and said. "Well that told me didn't it?" He smiled at her. "What are you waiting for? Let's go and find some weapons and come back fighting."

They all stood, and with Andy favouring his injured leg they shambled off in the direction of the first hidden crossbow.

Looking up as they walked slowly along Jim had a thought and stopped abruptly, then turned to Leah and Andy who were looking at him in puzzlement. "I've only just had a thought." He exclaimed. "That camera on top of the hill, the others must have been watching on the monitor last night, they would have seen everything that went on. They might know what happened to the rest of the team."

Leah looked at him in dismay and then said scornfully. "You don't get it do you? Even if that camera has night vision onit; the dust wouldn't be good for sight would it?How the hell do you think they saw anything at all?"

Jim shrugged defensively. "It was only a thought, I wasn't thinking straight." He brightened. "Maybe when we get back we can go over there and show them we're still alive, I know we can't talk to them because it hasn't got sound either but we can at least show ourselves."

Andy coughed. "If we use our commonsense, we can communicate with them."

Leah frowned. "How in hells name are you going to do that?"

Touching the side of his mask Andy said. "Leave it to me, I'll show you a little trick I saw once."

They trudged on in the gloom; everything around them looked grey and dismal and looking around Jim could see much of the plant life had died back as the cold and dark had killed it off. At this time of year the landscape should have been bursting with life but the outfall from the volcano had killed most of the plants that relied so much on sunlight. It would be many long years before anything grew properly again and he imagined what it would be like over the rest of the world. He thought that some people would be surviving like themselves and others like the nuclear submarine crews had a chance of living. He didn't think that many would live as long as ten years, which was how long he imagined the winter would last, they had deliberately not tried to communicate with any other people to avoid the very situation they found themselves in now. He could understand why people tried any means at their disposal to survive and knew that only the really selfish people could do it. They had managed it so far, but now they needed to go one step further and hunt down and kill the intruders to ensure their own survival. He smiled wryly to himself and thought. 'The world of nature again, the strongest live to breed and make their race better'.

He stopped and gazed around; they were nearing the place where one of the crossbows had been buried, but now it had all changed. It was gloomy and dark and nothing like the day when he had buried them. It took him some time to find the tree he had used as a marker and Andy was no help as he merely slumped on the ground and waited for him to find the spot. Leah watched in some exasperation as he paced backwards and forwards until finally he arrived at the spot where he had buried the first crossbow. He stared down at the ground unbelievingly; the bow had been dug up and taken! All that was left was a depression in the ground and some earth scattered round the hole.

He turned in despair to Leah and said through gritted teeth. "Some bastards been out here and taken it."

She joined him by the hole; then knelt down to examine the ground, she looked up at him with a curious expression on her face. "This digging is still quite fresh, see how the earth is still piled up and not rounded down." She took a quick look over her shoulder. "Who else knew about this place besides you and Andy and Ray?"

Jim shook his head. "No one, we kept it a secret to give us an edge if anything happened."

"So that only leaves one other person who could have been out here doesn't it?"

She smiled joyfully at Jim. "It has to be Ray doesn't it? They couldn't have found it because they didn't even know about it did they?"

She walked away about five metres from the depression and began to walk in a circle around the perimeter, after a few steps she bent down to peer at something and then called Jim over, pointing excitedly. "See here." She indicated the ground. "That looks like a footprint there."

Jim looked intently where she was pointing but apart from a little scuffmark he could see nothing. Putting his hand on her shoulder he said. "Don't get your hopes up Leah, it could be anything."

She shook his hand off angrily. "You aren't thinking straight are you?" If it wasn't Ray digging that up, we could be in serious trouble." She looked at the direction from the depression to the footprints and turning in that direction she asked. "Have you got another one buried on that bearing?"

Jim stood on the depression and looked on the bearing, he could see that if it was a footprint it would lead directly to the next crossbow, he knew the distance would be about one and a half miles over to the next one and if the footprints went there, only one person could have made them. "You know, I think you may have a point Leah." He muttered; he held his hand up to stop her shout of pleasure and went on. "If it is him we'd better get to him before he loses us."

He looked up at the sky; it was still as gloomy and chill, and large clouds gathered above them threatening to bring rain at any time. He shuddered to think that they could be in for ten more years of this sort of weather. "We'd better get on; he can't be too far ahead of us because he couldn't have found them at night so he must have left in the morning."

They shouldered their packs with the small supplies they had and pulling Andy up they started to walk in the direction of the next cache. As they walked it became obvious that Andy was flagging, and finally he sank to the earth and sat disconsolately down with his head between his legs. Leah sank to the floor next to him and the pair of them leaned against each other tiredly. She looked at Jim and whispered. "I think this has taken more out of me than I thought; you go on and try and catch him, you can walk faster than us two, I'll stay here and look after Andy. I think the rest will do him good."

Jim had been dreading this, as he prescribed to the view that you should never divide your forces. But looking at the pair of them he could see they would only hold him up and maybe make him miss Ray, if it was him in front. He reviewed the situation in his mind and knew there was only one answer so he reached into his pack and handed her his bottle of water. "Keep plenty of fluids going down him; I'll be back as soon as possible."

With this last admonition he turned and marched resolutely away, pausing only once to look back as he went over the crest of the next rise, then they were lost and he was on his own in this vast wilderness. He found that without them he was able to make good headway and soon he was approaching the next hiding place; as he neared it his heart leapt and then as quickly his hopes were dashed as he saw that the ground where it lay had been disturbed. He ran forward quickly to see if anything remained but it was empty. He stood over it and looked wildly around, wondering how anyone could have unearthed the crossbow in its wrapping so quickly and get away before he caught them up. He was about to turn and go in the direction of the next one when a voice called out from some rocks about thirty feet away.

"Hold it right there." The anonymous voice said. "Put your hands up."

If the situation hadn't been so serious Jim would have burst out laughing at the old cowboy saying, it sounded totally preposterous and turning Jim raised his hands and searched the rocks to see who could be holding him up. A man slowly stood up and Jim could see he was holding a nasty looking gun on him, the ugly hole at the end pointing right at his chest and it loomed larger than it really was as his imagination took over. "I'd be careful of that gun if I were you." He said. "You could end up hurting someone with that."

The man smirked. "Even if I killed you right now, no one is going to come and punish me are they?" He carried on without waiting for an answer. "And if I did, it'd be no worse than you throwing a grenade through my window last night would it?"

Jim had no answer for this but the man was waiting and he decided to play for time. "Maybe it was because you fired rockets at us the day before that, and if it comes down to it you were the ones who attacked us in the first place, we didn't ask you to come here and try and take over did we?"

It was the wrong thing to say; the man's face hardened and the gun was raised and Jim stared at that ugly hole as he squinted along the barrel. He could see the finger on the trigger whiten slightly as he put some pressure on it and closed his eyes in expectation of the pain. He knew that from the point of view of the attackers it was better for them if he was dead and now he had no defence. The wait was interminable and at last he opened his eyes again, the gun was still pointed at him in the same position. Slowly the man took control of himself and lowered the gun slightly. "I think it'll be better if I took you back with me."

He lowered the gun even more and Jim relaxed as he saw that the man couldn't kill him in cold blood; then the unexpected happened. The man was unskilled in the use of guns and forgot to flick the safety on and as the gun reached the downward position the pressure on the trigger was too much and the gun fired in a shockingly loud explosion, Jim dived to the side and the man raised the gun to his hip and fired a shot at him as he thought he would be trying to escape, it missed by a long way but that did nothing for Jims peace of mind and he scrambled to reach some sort of cover before another load of shot came his way. He knew he had no chance of reaching anything to hide behind, but survival took over and ran for his life, another explosion came and hit just to one side and Jim knew it was all over as the man was taking control of the gun and aiming now. He jinked desperately to one side to throw his aim off and then jerking the other way; he continued to run straight hoping the man would expect him to jink again. All the time he was expecting the thump in his back to come but nothing did and he dived over the top of a rock and lay flat for a second before wriggling away as fast as he could. He was brought up short by a gust of laughter behind him, and Ray's voice shouting. "You should see the way you ran like a scared rabbit; any decent gunman would have had you in a minute."

Jim stood slowly, shaking like a leaf; Ray was standing by the gunman who lay at his feet with an arrow sticking out of the side of his neck and a surprised expression on his face. Ray had a crossbow in his hand,. The gunman was very dead and looking down Ray poked him with his toe. "Nearly had you didn't he? Good job I saw him stalking you or you'd be lying there instead of him."

Jim looked at him; he had torn clothing and scratches on his hands where he had scrabbled in the earth. "How the hell long have you been there?" He demanded angrily.

Ray could see what was coming, and stepping back he raised his hands. "Hey, hold on there." He said. "I didn't put you through that deliberately, I could hear what went on but I had to get this crossbow up and running. That wasn't easy, don't forget you didn't show me how to use it; you only took the time to show Andy." He looked around. "Speaking of him, where is he? And for that matter, where's my wife."

Jim sank down on the ground to get some rest, only partly mollified. It seemed to him that Ray could have interfered a lot sooner than he had, then decided to try and forget it. "They're safe for the moment." He answered. "They're both injured but nothing that won't heal."

Ray looked concerned but Jim waved him down and quickly brought him up to date on the night's events. Then he asked. "How come you got out in one piece? The last I saw you I thought you'd bought it. Or at the least were wounded."

Ray shook his head in wonderment. "I must be the luckiest man walking around." He answered. "When I got Andy out, some guy came in the room spraying bullets everywhere and I tripped over something on the floor, the lights had just gone out and I couldn't see a thing. I bumped my head and passed out for a minute. The guy obviously thought he'd killed me and ran out of the room, and when I came to I was alone and just scrambled over the window cill. When I got outside they were chasing you down the side of the building, so I hot footed it in the other direction, then ran up into the hills and hid all night. I saw what you did with those Utes though, made quite a good fireworks display." He grinned suddenly. "I heard them shouting. They were really pissed off about that, I reckon you destroyed a big part of their ammo."

He indicated the man lying on the ground. "Do you know who this is?"

Jim shook his head in the negative. "Take a closer look." Ray said. Jim bent over the man and could see some thing familiar about him and reaching out he took the man's facemask off. He could then see clearly who it was; it was the supermarket owner who had supplied them with a great part of their supplies. He heard Ray speak. "I've seen a few familiar faces out there and I reckon they got talking and cottoned on to our plans, that's why they all arrived here together."

Jim nodded. "I've seen some of the men myself, that Schoonheid feller for a start, then there's Sulim the gun merchant." He looked up. "Is that Diman there?" Ray nodded in affirmative.

"I thought I saw him when we tried to ambush them. He's dangerous, that one." Jim commented. "The electrician who left so quickly, he's there as well, isn't he?"

"I still think there's something fishy about him." Ray nodded again.

"There's a few ex-police guys out there as well, isn't there?"

Ray looked grim and then blinked his eyes with a nod of the head. Jim counted mentally and cursed life. There were probably about seven or eight men available to hunt them and he had only four in total and two hurt, one badly, although Andy might yet recover, given time. Jim looked once more at the body on the ground. "Reckon we ought to bury him then?"

This time Ray was more definite. "No time mate." He answered. "They're all out there looking for us and those shots just now are going to bring them running and at the moment we aren't in any position to defend ourselves." We've got to get out of here pretty damn quick or face getting caught, oh, and by the way I saw Roy, over there on the way to find that first crossbow, looks like he got hit by shrapnel from that grenade he lobbed in."

He shrugged. "He was dead, must have lost too much blood."

'One more piece of bad news.' Jim thought, then went on with his original question.

You've seen them out there have you?" Jim asked.

Ray said. "Watched them leave this morning, they split up and went in all directions, and they're all carrying guns like this one. So far they haven't thought to go round the back and look for the escape hole, but it won't take them long to figure it out." He bent over the body and wrenched the arrow out of the mans neck and wiping it on the ground thrust it into the holder on his shoulder. "That's one good thing about this ammo, its reusable, and they won't know how he died when they find him."

Jim looked down at the gaping hole on the side of the man's neck. "They might have pause to wonder though, with a hole like that to look at."

A bloodthirsty smirk passed across Ray's face. "Nothing like putting the shits up em though is there? Now, let's get out of here before they start coming over that hill there and catching us."

They quickly stripped the man of anything useful they could find and took his gun and all the ammunition he had on him, he had some small rations on him and Jim knew they would provide some welcome energy in the day ahead. Then they took off at a run in the direction of the others. When they arrived back where Leah and Andy had been; they found they had moved about a hundred metre's to better cover, and when they approached, Leah stood and waved. When she saw Ray her hand flew to her mouth and she ran forward and clung round his neck for a minute with tears coming to her eyes. Then she stepped back and said. "I suppose you think you're clever putting me through all that misery thinking you were dead. Well let me tell you I'd have carried on without you even if you were." She wiped the tears from her eyes. "Now tell me where the hell you got to?"

Ray grinned happily and brought them both up to date. Andy seemed to have perked up a little and they sat and ate the few pieces of food they had taken from the dead man. While they were eating they reviewed the situation and decided to move out and try to circle round to get the next crossbow. Jim gave the gun to Leah, who seemed fitter than Andy for the moment. Then took the other crossbow for himself, he took the wrapping off and was relieved to find it in good working order and working as fast as he could, he assembled it. While he did this he told them what he wanted to happen.

"As I see it." He said. There are probably about seven or eight men out there at this time and they're well armed, not only that, they'll find that dead guy soon and they'll know we're out here and capable of killing them. So don't look for any mercy, they'll shoot first and ask questions later. Don't put your hands up and expect them to let you live, all you're going to get from that is a bullet in the back of the head." He looked around bleakly. "If you see any of them in any position at all, shoot, whether it's in the back or front. We have to kill them to survive ourselves. Do you all understand that?"

He waited for them all to acknowledge what he had said then nodded. "OK, lets go and give em one up the jacksy."

Grinning they all set off in single file following him to find the next crossbow. Andy was second in line with Leah following him so she could watch him and Ray brought up the rear. Jim had told them to keep a close watch out for any movement in the bush but they passed the next hour quietly enough. By now they were behind the hill where the windmill stood and Jim saw it was motionless although a good breeze blew across the blades. They could see no sign of life around it but he still gave it a wide birth. Jim looked over his shoulder as he walked and was pleased to see that Andy seemed to be keeping up with them as they marched, he also looked a little more alert and was now taking an interest in their surroundings, so much so that a few minutes later he heard Andy call softly to him.

"Dad, I want a word."

Jim stopped and waited for the rest to catch up with them, then squatted down in the cover of some shrubs. They hunkered round and looked expectantly at Andy. He rubbed his hands over his forehead and started. "I'm only just now coming round after last night and first I want to apologise to you all for going it alone, it was stupid. But I thought I could get the drop on this lot before they had time to organise." He grinned ruefully. "They were waiting for me when I poked my head out of that tunnel, they must have been laughing their heads off when I went up it. They probably heard me from a mile away scrambling up."

He looked around at them and then went on. "Anyway, all I can say is thanks."

There was an embarrassed silence for a moment and then some mumbling as everyone started to say it didn't matter. Except for Leah who came right to the point. "Well, I hope this teaches you a lesson, it was bloody foolhardy to go alone, and you broke one of your own rules. That we do things around here as a team, that way we can cover for each other. What you did was stupid and I hope you don't do anything like that again, because you could have got some of us killed trying to rescue you."

She sat back and still looking annoyed, unscrewed the filter on the side of her breathing mask and tapped it angrily on a stone alongside her. It was a signal for the rest of the to follow suit and for a while no one spoke, then Andy screwed the filter back into his mask and breathing hard he said. "OK, I admit I was wrong but so are you lot now, I've been a bit dazed and not thinking straight for a bit, but now I'm getting it together. I wasn't aware of where you're going, and I just walked along with you. Now it's got to stop."

He pointed at Jim. "You're walking around in a circle; don't you think that these people are going to figure out what you're doing?"

He drew a plan in the dust on the earth a square in the middle to represent the building and then three points joined by a line round the outside. "You started here on the front of the building, then you travelled to the first point for the crossbow then on to the second point for the next, now you're going in a straight line for the third, and that leads you in a circle right round the perimeter." He jabbed a finger at a spot and said. "You're going to get ambushed there."

They all sat and contemplated his map, Jim looked up.

"What would you do then?"

Andy looked triumphantly around. "Ambush them myself."

"How?"

"Create a diversion and draw them into where we want them to be."

Leah gestured with both hands splayed. "OK, OK, I can see what you're getting at but what about weapons? We've only got two crossbows and one gun between us, how do we fight seven men with those?"

"Easy." Andy looked at her as he spoke, then pointed over at the windmill. "I bet they've got a man in there on guard for a start. If we can take that and fire some shots they're bound to come running to see what's going on."

Involuntarily they had all looked at the windmill and realised he would be right; it made sense for the attackers to leave someone there. It still provided an escape route out of the building, and they would want to keep it intact so they could use it themselves later. As if to prove him right there was a movement near the door as something moved. It was only slight but they all saw it for what it was. There was someone inside!

Each one of them reacted differently to the sign but it was Andy who gave vent to their feelings. "Right, now we know what's up there, let's go and see if we can set up our own ambush. Take your lead from me, and no one pulls a trigger until I give the go ahead. Understand?"

As they neared the windmill he signalled to Ray and Jim to take a position to the side behind some shrubs and then whispered to Leah. "Do you think you're brave enough to go up to the door unarmed, I'll be right behind you, I don't think they'll fire straight away as they never leave the best fighters behind on guard."

She looked at him in disgust. "Trust a man to think of a plan like that, why don't you do the walking and I'll stand behind you?"

Andy sighed impatiently. "Why do I have to pick the most bolshie woman living to try and set up a trap, I said that because I think I'm better with a gun than you, now are you going to do it or not?"

She stared at him for long seconds, emotions flitting across her face. Finally she poked her finger at him. "You miss him and get me killed and I'll be coming back to haunt you, I promise."

She handed the gun over then turned and started to walk slowly towards the windmill, it was by now only a hundred meters distant and Andy stepped to one side to get a clear shot, then followed her towards the door keeping in the cover of the shrubs as he did so. When she got to within twenty meters the door swung open slightly and a gun barrel poked out.

"That's far enough mate, I want to get a good look at you." The disembodied voice came from the gloomy interior. Andy tried in vain to see the man behind but without looking round Leah stepped to one side hoping to give Andy a better sight but moved right into his line of fire.

She raised her hands and called out. "Hold your fire, I want to come in, I can help you catch the rest of them, I reckon they've had it."

"A bloody woman." The voice said. "What the bloody hell are you doing out here?"

The limited use of expletives marked him down as uneducated but he still proved crafty, the door swung even wider and the gun barrel waved as he indicated with it. "Lie down on the floor while I check this out."

She had no option left but to do what he said and lay down in the dirt, the door swung wide open but it was still too dark to see anybody inside and Andy couldn't risk shooting yet as the man still had the gun pointing at Leah. It took several minutes of silence before the voice said. "OK, crawl towards me slowly and one false move gets a bullet right in your head and I can't miss from this range, now do it."

Leah raised her head and looked directly at Ray on her side, then deliberately signalled 'no' with her eyes, because she knew that he would be the one to rush forward and try to save her. Then she started to crawl forward on hands and knees to the door, the voice came once more.

"That's right come to daddy; I'll take care of you." The voice had a hint of menace in it but Andy was still no better placed to take a shot and had already started to regret this course of action. The voice mumbled something but it was too quiet for Andy to hear and

Leah had now come within five meters of the door. She stopped and started to stand. Andy screamed inside himself for her to lie down and let him shoot but she continued to get up. He heard the voice again saying something unintelligible and Leah faced the open door then started to walk forward.

Andy groaned inside, he had no way of getting a shot now as she blocked his sight completely, he thought of spraying the interior with bullets but was scared of hitting Leah accidentally.

The door swung shut behind her and Andy stared at it in despair, He glanced to both sides quickly and saw both Ray and Jim looking at him unbelievingly, he had let her just walk into a trap, and now they had no way of rescuing her without rushing in and shooting indiscriminately. He raised the gun and started to walk forward grimly, Ray and Jim had to stand and wait, as a crossbow would be worse than useless in this situation. He had walked as quietly as he could about halfway to the door when it started to open slowly; he stopped walking and kneeling down pointed the gun at the opening.

Leah walked out with a ghastly expression on her face. She had a knife in her hand and looking down she raised it to examine it. Blood dripped from the end and she shuddered when she saw it. Then she lifted her head to look at Andy. "You bastard, why didn't you shoot him like you promised." The knife waved in the air. "Look what you made me do."

She sank to the floor and was violently sick; Andy went to hold her but was pushed aside by Ray as he rushed to her. "Get out of the way you useless bastard." Ray snarled. Then he bent down to put his arms round her shoulders.

"It's OK darling, it's OK." He said ineffectually. "It wasn't really Andy's fault. When you went forward you got in his line of fire and he couldn't shoot because he was scared of hitting you."

Andy mentally thanked his lucky stars after the words that Ray had just used when he pushed him out of the way.

She raised her head with tears glistening in her eyes. "Do you think I care about your problems? Do you know what that bastard tried to do in there? He was going to rape me; that's what he wanted to do. He made me put my arms in the air and then tried to have a good feel while he said he wanted to find any concealed weapons.

If I hadn't had that knife up my sleeve he might have done it as well. I got him in the back of the neck when he bent down to feel me between the legs."

She shuddered slightly and readjusted the front of her coverall buttoning it up. Ray looked downcast at her and Andy couldn't look at all as he felt guilty enough but had to try and make things right. He walked quickly to her and said.

"Look Leah, I'm sorry it happened like that, I just couldn't see him and then you walked right in front of me. I was coming in when you came out."

"On your big white charger, I suppose?" She raised her hand as if to slap him but thought better of it and contented herself with saying. "Next time you promise something when you put another person in danger, you make sure you keep that promise or you'll have me to deal with." She looked around at them. "For the sake of unity in this team I'm going to forget about this incident but don't any of you ever put me in that kind of position without back-up again, do I make myself absolutely clear?"

Jim had still not moved from his place in the shrubbery and now he stepped out. "Well said Leah, I agree with that, but we're in a vulnerable place here and I want to get to a safer spot before long, I've got one question though. Who was that guy in there?"

"You might well ask." she answered. "It was that copper who came out to search the place with the abbo. He thought he was on to a good thing then, and he still wanted to carry on where he left off."

"Well you did good to keep your head when he started." Jim praised her. He looked at the other two men. "You'd better take his gun and any ammunition he's got, and see if he's got any food there as well."

He turned to Leah. "We'd better get down the path a bit and keep a lookout while they're in there."

She nodded and then walked slowly away from the windmill with him. They had gone down the path about a hundred metres and Leah bent down as they walked and cleaned the knife on the wispy grass bunched up alongside them. Jim glanced down to watch her and heard a voice say. "That's far enough mate, we don't want to lose sight of everybody do we?"

He looked back up in surprise and saw the man he probably hated more than any man in Australia; Schoonheid! He stopped in his tracks and glared at the ambusher. He was accompanied by two other people, dressed as he was, in shapeless coveralls. From the look of them they were feminine as they had about them a certain way of standing and holding their weapons. He heard Leah gasp and had his suspicions confirmed. Schoonheid gestured with the gun in his hand. "Lets wait for the other two to come out, and then we can all sit down and have a confab eh? Oh, and lets have the weapons on the floor shall we."

Jim bent and laid the crossbow on the ground and Leah dropped her knife alongside it. The man gestured again with the gun and one of his companions scuttled forward to pick them up. The way she walked confirmed Jim's suspicions that she was indeed a woman as the difference was clear. She carried the crossbow back to the man and he bent and examined it closely. His eyes narrowed and he looked up at Jim.

"I wondered what killed Arthur and now I know, deadly these things aren't they?"

Jim nodded dumbly, not that it mattered to him but he knew now that the man Ray had killed was Arthur. Still keeping them covered the man examined the crossbow again, then stared at Jim. "Maybe I'll use it to kill you two when the time comes, I'll be able to get in some target practice at the same time."

Jim cleared his throat. "You'd have to be really dumb to need target practice with that, its more accurate than a gun."

Schoonheid raised the gun again at the implied insult, and then grinned evilly. "You know, I think I will kill you with it but slowly so you can savour the full irony of your position. You always tried to put me down before and now you can pay for every little insult you laid on me." He pointed to Leah. "And that goes for you as well little miss smarty pants; I've got certain plans for you as well."

One of his companions leaned over and said something to him and he answered angrily in a low voice that didn't carry to them. Then he raised the gun and fired a shot into the air, he smirked. "That ought to bring them out in a hurry."

It did, and Ray and Andy came out of the windmill at a run to find them with their hands in the air and a gun aimed at them. They stopped suddenly uncertain what to do but Schoonheid held the gun steady on Jim and Leah and called out to them. "Its OK boys, come and join us, and don't try anything or these two get it, right."

He indicated to Jim and Leah he wanted them to sit on the ground and waited for Jim and Ray to come and join them. When they arrived he indicated to them to sit alongside the others and then told one of the women to relieve them of the gun and the crossbow. With that accomplished he told the two women with him to keep an eye on them and walked forward a little to stand in front but to one side so they could see the prisoners. He stood grinning at them in triumph and then gloatingly said to Jim. "I've got you right where I want you now mate; the rest of them are going to hear that shot and come running to find out what's up. Then the fun can start."

He looked up at the windmill and asked. "Is he dead?"

Jim nodded at him, and he shook his head. "You make it worse and worse for yourself don't you? The boss isn't going to like that, I reckon he's going to let me kill you really slowly when he finds out what you've done, I think I can let you have about twenty of these bolts before you die, and I can let you have them slow, so you've got time to think about the next one before you get it."

Jim felt sick as he contemplated the fate the man had in store for him but he would never show his emotions in front of him. Schoonheid kicked him on the leg to force him to look at him. "Did you hear what I said, Mister. You're going to pay for every time you insulted me."

Jim refused to acknowledge his insults and losing interest the man moved on to Leah, appraising her. Then making up his mind he turned to the two women with him and said. "Keep an eye on these men here I'm going to take this one in for questioning."

He bent down to lift Leah to her feet and Ray started to stand. Quickly the man swung his gun and hit him on the side of the head, knocking him back down. He snarled. "If you know what's good for you, you'll stay down there until I get around to dealing with you as well."

The two women looked at each other worriedly, it was clear from their expressions they didn't approve of the way he was handling this situation. One of them stepped forward and started to remonstrate with him. "I don't think this is a good idea, we should wait for Sulim to get here and let him deal with this."

Her voice had a foreign twang to it and Jim surmised it was Sulim's companion or wife; Schoonheid's next words confirmed this. "You can think all you like but it was my wife that got killed the other day and I want some revenge for that from this lot. And I want them to think about what's happening to her while they can't see her. OK?"

He bent and grabbed Leah by the arm and yanked her to her feet, and then turning to the two women he said menacingly. "Now do what I say, guard these here and I'll be back in a while."

He turned and dragged Leah by the arm towards the windmill; she gasped in pain and let him take her with him. He pushed her in front of him and held the gun in her back as they walked. Leah deliberately stumbled to try and get him off balance but he easily stepped around her and pushed her further in front of himself, poking the gun in her ribs until she gasped once more in pain. The two women guarding them looked at each other with a question in their eyes but Jim knew they would do nothing as it wouldn't be easy for a woman who had been brought up to obey men to go against one now.

He waited until the Leah and the man had gone far enough that they couldn't hear then asked Ray. "Are you OK?"

Ray was holding his head in his hands but nodded miserably when spoken to. Jim turned his attention to the two women. "You know what he intends to do don't you?"

The pair of them stared at Jim; something about her eyes made him think he could detect a weakness in the one who had remonstrated with Schoonheid, it was faint but she didn't seem so sure of herself. The other one refused to answer but stared at him malevolently, then she spoke. "Who was it who shot my husband with one of these bloody things?"

She touched the crossbow lying at her feet, with leather-clad boot. Ray raised his head slowly. "That was your husband?"

She ignored the question. "I said who killed him?"

Ray could sense the danger he was in and decided discretion was the better part of valour and sank down to contemplate his feet.

"You." The command rang out loud and clear.

"You knew he was dead, you must have been there, who killed him?" She raised the gun and pointed it directly at his head. "Answer me right now or I'll shoot you where you are and your wife will hear me do it while she's getting her sex life improved."

By now Leah and Schoonheid had almost reached the windmill, which was about a hundred metres distant. She could be heard arguing with him and trying to persuade him to stop this thing he was doing but it appeared to have no effect on him. The other woman turned to her and said. "It'll do no good, trying to have all this revenge; we can't live our lives with bitterness."

"Why don't you shut up and do what you were asked, we're the law here and we can do what we like." The woman said menacingly. "Or maybe you'd like to join this lot here." She pointed at her prisoners.

"Well all I can say is, my husband will be here soon and when he comes I hope you've got your story straight for him, because he doesn't like this kind of thing." Her voice rang with a belief in her husband and his ability to sort out any troubles.

The woman looked at her with disbelief at these words written all over her face. "Do you know what your husband does for a living, you stupid cow?"

The other woman looked at her with despair in her eyes, it was clear that she did know but had never had to face the truth before, she had somehow convinced herself he was just another honest business man, and right now she didn't want to have to face the fact that her husband was a vicious gun runner. They were set to go on with this argument for some time and Jim said desperately. "Rape isn't a good idea in any society, if he gets away with this now, who knows who he'll try it on with next? It could be one of you two who take a turn if he thinks he can get away with it."

The words grabbed their attention and the gun swung back to cover them once more. The more assertive woman started to reply angrily to Jim but her attention was drawn to Leah and Schoonheid, who could be heard arguing heatedly from the top of the rise by the windmill. They all looked at the spectacle of Leah in full flow shouting at Schoonheid who was desperately trying to get her inside the door, out of sight. He reached out and tried to grab her arm again but she shrugged him off and attempted to hit him in the face. At that point he plainly lost his temper and dropping the gun by his side he punched her in the face, she went down as if pole axed and lay inert on the floor. Before Jim could stop him Ray had jumped up and started to race towards them.

One of the women shouted at him to come back and raised her gun to fire but he ignored that, and Jim thought he probably didn't hear it anyway. She fired a warning shot after him without bothering to take aim and Schoonheid glanced up to se what the problem was. When saw it was Ray he picked up his gun and aimed at Leah lying on the ground at his feet, and shouted to Ray to stop. Ray ignored this also and continued to race towards him. From his viewpoint Jim could see that he had no chance of reaching them in time but he could only watch with his heart in his mouth as Ray went on with his hopeless charge.

Andy had bided his time and now took his chance and jumping up ran toward the assertive woman. She saw him coming and swung the gun round to fire at him but it was too late and Andy hit her in the stomach hard with his shoulder she crumpled up under the onslaught and Andy grabbed the barrel of the gun to stop her using it. Jim was taken by surprise by the events but saw his chance and raced towards the other woman who saw him coming and dropped her gun and ran. He picked it up on the run and turned it on Andy and the woman who by now were wrestling for possession of her gun, they both fell to the floor and the gun exploded between them. Jim stared in dismay his heart in his mouth, as they both lay the floor, inert for several moments until Andy raised an arm and shoved her slowly off himself. The bullet had hit her in the chest and travelled upwards into her throat, she fell back with the first trickle of blood coming from her mouth and a shocked expression on her face.

Jim had no time to look and see what happened after that, because he had to try and save Ray who was staring death in the face as Schoonheid cocked the gun and prepared to shoot Ray. He dropped to his knee and tried to line up a shot on Schoonheid but try as he might Ray kept coming between them. Schoonheid raised the gun and took careful aim at Ray and Jim could almost sense his finger tightening on the trigger. He still had no chance of a shot and Ray still had forty metres to go to reach him. As Jim watched he knew that Ray was about to die and he was helpless to stop it.

Andy shouted to him. "Shoot for Christ's sake, and put him off his aim."

Jim fired quickly but the shot went far too high as he endeavoured to aim past Ray. He shouted back. "I can't see Schoonheid to get a shot." But by now it was far too late as Schoonheid obviously enjoying himself, held his fire to make Ray think he had a chance of getting to him. Then his finger tightened on the trigger and Jim knew beyond all doubt that Ray was about to die.

Another shot rang out and Schoonheid stiffened and his gun rose slightly as he tightened his grip on the trigger. The gun fired and the shot intended for Ray hit the ground about a metre past Leah's head; she moved in surprise and Jim saw she had been playing possum hoping to delay Schoonheid in his intentions. Jim stared in amazement at the scene. Schoonheid crumpled slowly to the ground and lay face down in the dust.

"Where the hell did that come from?" He asked Andy, who looked as puzzled as he did, and shook his head.

"We'd better get up there and see what's going on." Jim said.

They both quickly looked at the woman lying on the ground in front of them but it was too late to try and save her as she had stopped breathing and lay still. Jim could see the blood had pumped out and stained the front of her coveralls. He bent down quickly and felt her pulse but the skin under his fingers was lifeless. Shaking his head he looked at Andy and they both nodded then wordlessly they picked up the remaining weapons and ammunition and started the long climb to the top of the hill. Jim had a sudden thought and said to Andy. "We'll have to get out of this area pretty quick because the other guy's will be arriving soon."

Andy grunted in reply, preferring to conserve his energy for the climb. It took only a few minutes but Jim was breathless when they arrived. As he approached he could see another person had joined Leah and Ray at the door of the windmill. On a closer inspection from the back it looked like a woman, but when she turned round to his amazement it was Pat!

Her eyes lit up over the top of her mask a she regarded his face with amusement. "What the hell are you doing here?" He questioned her. "I thought I told you to stay inside and guard the building."

"It looks like I chose the right moment to come out and get into the action." She replied hotly. "If I hadn't arrived when I did I think we'd be missing a few members of our team by now. We decided that with you lot scattered all over the place it would be better if I tried defending from outside rather than wait for them to try and force entry to the building." She looked at Leah who was standing with her arms round Ray and looking up at his face with pride. "Those two would have been dead for sure if I hadn't managed to get up here as soon as I did."

Jim grumbled an acknowledgement and looked down at her hands, she was carrying Andy's prized snipers rifle and had an ammunition belt round her chest; she was completely covered by the overalls and looked the part of a guerrilla. Andy leaned forward and touched the rifle. "You'd better look after that gun; I want it back when this is over."

She flared at him. "If I had my way, all the guns in the world would be destroyed, this one included."

She looked at all of them and said. "There's some food down the bottom at the back of the:" ¾ She would have finished but a shot rang out and a bullet snapped past them and ricocheted of the side of the windmill. They all dived for cover and Jim fell to the ground and scrambled for the shelter of a clump of bushes, there was a thump as another body fell beside him and Jim looked to see it was Leah. Ray fell down a moment later and for a moment they lay listening to a hail of bullets whining past them like an angry swarm of bees. Jim looked down and with a sense of shock realised he had put the crossbow down momentarily and now it was still where he had left it, a few metres away by some bushes. The fusillade stopped as suddenly as it had started and Jim peered out from the side of a convenient rock to see if he could glimpse anything. A bullet suddenly spanged off the rock only inches from his face, showering him with dust; followed by the crack of a rifle.

"Shit." He cursed. "Someone out there's got sharp eyes."

He rolled onto his back and called out. "Is anybody hurt?"

Andy and Pat called back they were OK. He looked at Leah and Ray. "Are you two alright?"

They nodded back and Ray said laconically. "I wish we'd gone sooner for that grub."

Jim ginned weakly and rolled back on to his stomach. "I wonder who's out there." He mused, I think it can only be about five or six at the most if my arithmetic is any good. Although it's possible they could have some women out there as well."

Leah snorted. "The women they've shown so far don't seem to be much use."

Jim glanced at her sternly. "If they point a gun at you and it fires, you'll still be dead even if they are no good. That one who was holding a gun on us when you left almost killed Andy."

She snorted again, but said nothing. He made up his mind quickly. "Ray." He said. "I want you to go over to Andy and Pat and see if you can flank them, right now we've got a little advantage as we're higher than them but they'll probably try to get round the side of us pretty soon. So keep a sharp eye out and shoot first. Leave Pat to guard the centre if she's got good cover and take Andy. We'll go the other way and try to get a crossfire going. Now go."

The orders shot out quickly and authoritatively and Ray nodded and was crawling on his way before he had time to think of coming up with an alternative plan. Leah grinned at Jim. "You got away with that one mate, and he's probably wondering right now what he should have said to change things."

Jim grinned back. "The plans the best we've got in the circumstances, all he could have done was change the characters."

He looked to see what weapons Leah had with her and was relieved to see she had a gun in her hands. "How much ammo have you got for that thing?" He asked.

She shrugged dismally. "Only the clip it had in it when I picked it up."

Jim swore softly. He had the same, as his ammunition had been dropped when they were fired on. By now only a few minutes had passed since the last shots from the enemy and Jim thought they were probably trying to get a better position for an attack. He turned to Leah and asked her, have you seen any movement out there?"

She shook her head but said. "I can hear some movement, but I can't place where it's coming from."

Jim nodded. "I think the best thing to do is to try and draw some fire and see where they return the shots from, I'm going to let off a round and see what happens, you keep a watch out for muzzle flashes, they'll tell us where they are."

He fired a shot at random, merely pointing the gun straight forward. The effect this had was instantaneous and terrible. There was a thunderous roar and a hail of bullets came their way, biting their way through the bushes snapping of twigs and showering them with leaves. The only thing they could do was keep their heads down and wait for it to stop. It finally did and Jim looked at Leah and said. "Did you count how many?"

She looked at him in surprise. "If you think I'm going to raise my head and try and count how......" She started to say hotly. Then saw the look on his face and realised he was kidding her.

"I reckon there's about five of them out there, with automatic weapons." She finished lamely. "But the way they opened fire I don't think they've moved about much at all. I think they must be about fifty metres down the slope."

"That's the way I figured it." Jim agreed with her. He glanced over his shoulder, they had a few shrubs behind them and a cleft in some rocks led over the ridge. It was only about five or six metres but the way they were pinned down it would be a very long run to reach it.

"We've got to get over that ridge behind us." He said. "But we don't want them to know we're going until it's too late, what do you reckon?"

For answer she rolled over and faced the direction of the windmill. "Pat." She called softly. "Pat."

"Yes." the answer came back as softly. "Are you two all right?"

"Yeah, we're fine. Have you got good cover?"

"Yes." Pat replied sotto voiced.

"Can you fire of one shot at them and then keep your head down? We want to make a move here."

"OK." Came the reply. "But whatever you do be careful. Ray and Andy have gone off to the other side."

Jim was pleased she had sense enough to impart the information as it gave him an indication of the situation. She went on. "I'll fire in about ten seconds so get ready."

They counted to ten slowly and it was a tense few seconds more before the shot came. Once more the hail of fire started but in this instance it was directed to their left and they both jumped up and ran for the gap; they dived over the ridge just as one of the enemy spotted them and fired in their direction. As they hit the safety of the ground some shots kicked up dust at their heels, but the fire was hurried and before they could take aim they were safe behind the rocks.

Although they had only run five metres, the effort involved, had them both breathing heavily and it took some moments to get their breath back. Finally Leah turned to Jim and said. "I wish we could take our exercise some other time, I'm getting tired, hungry, and thirsty."

"I agree with you wholeheartedly Leah." Jim answered. He was thinking that Pat had said there was some food down the hill and he assumed she meant by the hole in the back of the building. He also knew that to try and go there would be madness in their present position.

"This won't go on much longer." He went on.

She stared angrily at him. "Don't try and comfort me." She replied with an edge to her voice. "I'm a big girl now and as you expect me to fight like a man give me the same respect as you would to one of your macho mates."

She pointed back the way they had come. "We've got to get in a position to flank those bastards down there and then we can go for something to eat and drink. Now what do you suggest?"

Jim looked at her; he was suitably chastened and hurried to make amends. "Your right, we have got to flank them, but we've got to go carefully because if they get the drop on us we haven't got a lot of ammo to try and fight our way out."

She had been staring back down the slope as he spoke, trying to see if the enemy were moving, after a moment she snapped her eyes and came to. "What did you just say? No ammo? There's loads of it just along in front of that gully there." She pointed to where Pat was hidden. The shooting had stopped now and silence reigned. "All we've got to do is crawl over there and rescue some of it."

Jim was appalled. "Do you know what that entails, that ammo's in full view of about five men with automatic guns and you want to crawl out and get it. They'll cut you down before you've gone one metre."

"We could start a diversion." She replied defensively.

Shaking his head in disbelief Jim said. "They'll be expecting you to do that, that's why they haven't rushed us yet. They can afford to wait and let us make a stupid move. It's always harder to attack a defensive position so they want us to make the first move and they're hoping we'll make a mistake." He pointed at her. "And if you do that, it will be a mistake."

"All right clever sticks, what are you going to do?"

Jim grinned at her. "That's the best joke of all, I don't know yet."

He looked back down the slope over to his left and wondered where Andy and Ray had got to. They should have got themselves into a good position by now, but try as he might he could see no sign of them.

He was alerted by the sound of a low call and then peering round the bush he was surprised to see a missile in the air coming from the direction of Andy and Ray, it curled over in the gloom of the day and landed just short of a clump of bushes about fifty metres down the hill. He just had time to think that it was a fairly good distance to throw a grenade when shouts of alarm came from there and suddenly three men burst out and ran further down, it wasn't a moment too soon as the missile exploded in a shower of hot metal and Jim could see puffs of dust where they burst into the ground. Raising his rifle he fired a couple of shots at the fleeing people joining Andy and Ray as they emptied a clip in that direction. As far as he could tell no one was hit but it did his morale a boost to see it happen. He wondered where Andy had managed to get the grenades as he had left before they were handed out.

He looked round to say something to Leah and with a sense of shock he realised she was nowhere to be seen. Suddenly she burst out of hiding along the gully a few metres from their hiding place, she ran forward and falling to the ground she scrambled in the dust and placed some things in a bag she had with her. He knew instantly she had taken advantage of Andy creating the diversion she wanted and had rushed out to gather as much ammunition as possible. One of the people in the bushes had seen and fired a hurried shot at her. It kicked up some dust near her and glancing up she turned and ran for her life. Several others now joined in to fire shots at her but she ran sideways back towards Jim and before they had time to line up on her she had slumped down alongside him.

She was breathing heavily and lay there panting for a minute and then started to laugh hysterically; she turned back to Jim still laughing and shouted triumphantly. "I did it, I bloody did it, and you said they'd get me."

Jim was angry; he knew just how close she had come to being killed, but he also knew that if he tried to reprimand her now she would only take offence at what she perceived to be an act of bravado in the face of the enemy.

He swallowed his anger and asked. "How much ammo did you get?"

For answer she turned the sack over and tipped it out; she had done well, there were nine clips of bullets and she had picked up the rest of the bolts for the crossbow. Jim looked at them and shook his head in despair; she stared at him until it came to her. He had dropped the crossbow when they were in their ambushed. She turned her head and looked the other way, then put her hand up to her face, Jim knew she was trying to hide her disappointment and that tears had come to her face. To take that chance and then find it had been wasted.

He put his hand on her shoulder only to have her shake it free. "Come on it isn't that bad, we've still got these clips." He said. "The crossbow isn't important."

She turned on him fiercely. "You know damn well it is important, don't you? People dodge bullets and think they can make you miss, but that crossbow puts the shits up them, because they know if you use it you have to take very careful aim and it seldom misses the target. So they get frightened if they see you using it. Now, how much chance is there that we can get that bloody crossbow back?"

Jim looked speculatively at the spot where it was left, by now the enemy must have realised that whoever threw the grenade had no more of them and had crept back to their old hiding places. Some sporadic shooting was happening, but only from the other side as Andy and Ray were doing the same as Jim and trying to conserve their ammunition. He looked at the sky and saw the light had started to fade and he knew with the daylight going they would loose the advantage of their defensive position. He wished they had some flares or lights so they could surprise them if they tried to creep forward. But that was an impossible dream now; he knew the others had had some lights the previous night because they had used them to hunt for them. But it was probable the batteries would have worn out by now and they had no chance in the present circumstances to charge any.

"How far over is Pat?" he asked.

Looking at him speculatively, she answered."Maybe ten or fifteen metres."

"Mmm, it's not far under normal circumstances but miles under fire." Jim was talking out loud. He made up his mind. "It's going to be dark in about thirty minutes, and if we can get to her we could maybe try for the crossbow."

Leah nodded. "We can get to the end of these rocks here and it's only about six or seven metres across open ground to reach her, we can set up some covering fire and maybe one of us can get it."

She grinned, her face was coming alive, and Jim started to worry that she would get over enthusiastic and risk that extra pace too far. She saw the look for what it was and shook her head. "I'm not going to risk any more than is needed to carry out the mission, Mr Boss man sir."

Jim's mind had started to wander and he wished he had some night sights but the thought discomfited him, it was entirely possible the others had some. He shuddered at the idea, and then calmed himself. If they had had them they would have used them last night to find them. He turned and Leah looked at him. He nodded in the direction of Pat and they both moved along the line of rocks until they reached the end. He looked at the distance; it was about five metres, 'Not far,' He thought. Then said to Leah. "When I say go, I want both of us to go, if only one goes they'll see and wait for the next one, OK?"

She nodded and he called out softly. "Pat."

The answer was equally soft. "Yes."

"We're coming over to you, so be prepared."

For answer Pat loosed off three shots in a row to encourage the enemy to keep their heads down, even so, it was a close thing and the bullets came just a fraction of a second too late, kicking at their heels like angry wasps. They landed in a heap alongside her and she merely glanced at them and fired once more at a flash she had seen. Jim stared in surprise at her; she had outfitted herself with straw and vegetation to break up her outline. It would be difficult to spot her at five metres, unless you knew exactly where she was. He reached over and squeezed her shoulder to try and give her some encouragement; she acknowledged him with a shake of her head but didn't take her eyes off the bushes downhill. She had the telescopic sights on the rifle and whispered. "I've got one spotted, and if he pops his head up once more it gets knocked off."

Jim did a double take; this was the wife from England who carried spiders out of the house so she didn't hurt them. "What's got into you?" He asked. "You don't turn into a sniper just like that."

"These men are bastards that's why." She laid the rifle down with a sigh. "It's too dark to get a clear shot now anyway. The light had faded rapidly with the amount of dust blocking out the sun. It had turned chill and Jim was glad of the thick coveralls he was wearing. Pat sat hunched up on the ground and looked at them.

She thought for a moment and then came to a decision. "Jim, what I'm about to say goes no further than us three, although Leah knows what I'm going to say." She glanced at Leah for confirmation and received a blink of affirmation. "I had a talk with Victoria before I came out as she felt it best that I knew the truth, I admit I suspected something but not this."

She looked at Jim in the eye. "She was raped by that electrician who left in a hurry, that's why she was so off with Andy afterwards. Leah helped her and stopped it before it went too far, that's why he left so quickly and we couldn't get to the bottom of it."

Jim sat back on his haunches and put his head in his hands, this explained so much. Especially with the way Victoria had been withdrawn and moping around for the last few months. He looked from one to the other, pain for Victoria in his eyes. "Why didn't she confide in us? We could have helped. Trying to keep it all to herself isn't the right way to handle the problem."

Leah looked at him and sneered. "You men, you all think you've got the answers to all the problems of mankind, well let me tell you. If she had told everybody, what do you think the men here would have thought? Every time they looked at her it'd show in their eyes, and not only for her but for Andy as well. He'd have thought about it every time they made love; did she encourage him? Why did she let him do it? The questions would never have been solved." She poked Jim in the chest. "I know because it happened to me, and if this gets out from you I'll make you suffer. I told her to keep quiet about it and until now I kept the secret. One thing I will tell you, she must have had some good reason for telling Pat."

They both looked at Pat who had been waiting for their response, she nodded agreement. "She was sure she caught sight of him when she was on duty on the camera on the hill and she thought it was better to come out and tell us in case anything happened."

Jim looked over his shoulder although he knew nobody was there. "We'll have to keep this quiet for a bit until we get this problem under control. Then we can sit down and have a good long talk about it."

The two women glanced at each other and it was plain that they thought the idea was useless but they were in no position to dispute it right now. There was a low sound as someone whistled and they looked over in that direction. They all made sure their weapons were handy and waited, a few moments later Andy slid into the hollow. He grinned when he saw who was there and with eyes dancing he said. "Don't worry, I won't tell the headmaster you're all goofing off." They grinned sheepishly and he went on briskly. "Ray's got an eye on them for the moment; if they want to move they'll have to do it under the cover of dark. They've got to cross open ground to get out of the bushes they're in, and if they do that he'll get one at least. What I want to know is before we were so rudely interrupted, you started to say there was some food down there mum, is that right?"

The question reminded them of how hungry and thirsty they were; Pat smiled. "Trust you to be the one to remind us of that. Yes, there is food down there but how do you propose to get it?"

He looked around earnestly. "To be honest, I don't think this is the best place to make a defensive stand. If we sit here I think they can overrun us in the night when they can move around easily, I reckon the best thing would be to go and get some food before they know we're gone and then split up and wait for them to go to the back of the building. They'll only figure we'll have gone inside anyway, that's the way people think. If they do we can blast them from the flanks."

He poked a thumb over his shoulder. "I've got some things in here that mum brought out and we can leave them out when they come for us."

Jim's head snapped up. "What do you mean? You've got some things for them."

"Calm down Dad, These people are trying to kill us, if we disable some of them, so what. All we have to do is remember where they are and stop innocent bystanders treading on them."

Jim caught on quickly and said without waiting for an answer so you've got some landmines here "Before all this happened, they were trying to get landmines banned and now you want to start planting them again."

Andy stared at Jim his eyes glinting. "The reason they were trying to ban landmines was because innocent people trod on them, now that lot out there aren't innocent, and after it's all over we'll come out and dig them up, OK?"

Pat rolled over and fired a shot in the direction of the enemy, then rolled back to speak to them. "Just to keep them thinking we're still here." She said conversationally. "Now the way I see it is this; we have to stop them anyway we can and if these do the job well and good"

Jim had started to lose his temper and poked his finger at his wife. "Just as long as you know what happens when people tread on them."

"Don't you point you're finger at me." She snapped.

Leah stepped in before it turned into a royal argument with neither side giving in because they were too angry. "Calm down you two, we aren't going to solve anything by arguing with each other. Now do we plant the damn things or not?"

Glancing at each other they all nodded assent; Andy looked satisfied and reaching over his shoulder he took off the pack and took out the claymores. Jim watched him feel inside and take out a trenching tool. He recognised it as one they had bought years before for the camping trips when the children were young, and reflected on the strange things people saved from their past. Andy must have kept it when he moved out and brought it with him.

Silently they watched as he surveyed the ground and then buried the mines on the easiest path through the bushes and rocks, in an effort to trap them unawares. He armed each one as he buried them and looking at the deadly mines Jim thought to himself that if anyone was going to disarm them it wasn't going to be him. As Andy finished it got quite dark and turning to them he said. "I think we'd better call Ray in now, so we can show him where they are, in case he decides to trample all over them."

While Andy crawled away to bring Ray Jim turned his attention to the problem of the crossbow. He could see the spot where it was lying and Leah watched him as he prepared to go and get it. He took his pack off and laid it down then kneeling down he adjusted his headgear so that only his eyes showed through a slit. Then looking at her and Pat he said. "Cover me." And was gone.

Crawling rapidly he reached the bushes in a few moments and scrambled in, it was the work of a minute to find the bow and then he turned to return. Then disaster struck! As he left the cover of the bushes a light shone out from the enemy position, blinding in its intensity. Jim lay on the ground as still as he could but a cry of triumph from the enemy gave him away. A shot rang out, followed by several more, and dirt kicked up around his prone body. He was only moments away from death as they zeroed in on him and he looked despairingly back at them. Leah opened fire and got off several shots but they continued to fire. Jim was in a dilemma, if he stood and ran he would present an even bigger target so he lay as still as possible. Andy and Ray opened up and fired some shots at the enemy but suddenly there was a crack from Pat's position followed by a cry of pain from someone. The light went out with a suddenness that surprised Jim and taking his chance he stood and ran back to them carrying the crossbow.

Diving thankfully to the ground he looked at Pat and gasped. "Thanks darling, I reckon you've just saved my life there."

Pat acknowledged this with the comment. "I wonder why? The way you treat me sometimes, I ought to have let you lie there."

Jim laughed. "You know you don't mean that love." He looked at the smoking gun in admiration. "I think you got one with that there gun, you'd better not let Andy know or he'll take it off you."

They heard some footsteps and Andy and Ray dived into the hollow. They were smiling as if they were having fun, and Andy lay down next to Pat. He touched the rifle and said. "Good shooting, I heard one of them complaining about a hole he acquired. I'm starving."

It took a moment for it to sink in that he had mentioned food as it was said with no change of inflection. When it did, Pat started to say where the food was but Jim interrupted her. "We were thinking of going back down and getting something to eat before this lot find out what we're doing." He nodded at the ground. "At the least they'll get a shock if they come in too quickly."

Ray looked from one to the other and asked. "What's going on?"

Andy quickly brought him up to date about the claymores and Ray raised his eyebrows at the mention of them, but refrained from any comment. Jim asked them all what they thought of going to get something to eat and looking down the hill which was by now in pitch blackness Leah said. "If they come in and use that light again, we're going to get in some serious bother; I think it'll be better for us if we aren't here when they come over that hilltop. Anyway it could be an hour before they try it because they'll think we're still waiting for them here."

Pat coughed and cleared her throat. "Before we go down there, I've got an announcement to make."

Jim frowned and waited for her to speak; the rest stopped what they were doing and waited with him. She quickly glanced around and taking a deep breath she said in a rush. "We did a deal with the women who were left behind when these men came after us, they had kids with them and we couldn't bear to leave them there to die."

"How many?" Jim asked coldly.

"Three women and two kids."

"Christ Almighty, what the hell were you thinking of, they could be using sympathy to try and finish us from the inside."

She faced him with back straight and a defiant look on her face. "Don't be so bloody stupid, they were on the verge of starvation, and another thing." She went on. "You might think that that Sulim is the leader, but he isn't. That Diman is. And he's a bloody sadist. It him who made those women fight and get killed. Now you tell me how many women are out there now, he took two with him."

"One's dead." Jim said tersely. The news had upset him. He knew that there was some spark of humanity in Sulim, but Diman killed for the pleasure it gave him. His blood started to run cold as he thought of what would happen if Diman won this battle. A life of misery faced every survivor. He went on. "The other one did a runner, and we haven't seen her since."

"Humph." Pat was disdainful. "She's probably too scared to come back, how many men are left out there?"

Jim shrugged. "We aren't sure, we think maybe five, but we haven't seen them to make a count,"

"Well." Pat said. "I think there are only four out there now, if there are five it's probably a woman with the men."

Leah leaned forward and interrupted. "Look, I know you lot like to gab about things but I for one am bloody starving. Why don't we get back while we've got time and get something to eat? You can gab all you like then."

There was a general agreement with these sentiments and they gathered all their equipment together and started down the hill to the building, treading as quietly as possible. In a few minutes they were standing at roughly the same spot as Jim had left from previously. When Pat had left earlier she had taken the trouble to cover the hole up and a large hamper of food had been hidden nearby under some shrubs. They tore it open and devoured the contents ravenously; it contained some bottles of water and these they drunk with pleasure. It was left to Ray to comment. "Never thought to say it, but this water's welcome as a bottle of beer."

There was a general air of disbelief when he said it but Pat silently approved. When they had finished, they sat for a while and listened to the night sounds and tried to hear any strange noises. All of them were worried about the others and wondering if they were moving around out there. Finally Jim said. "The way I see it is they'll probably try and come down here and see if we've gone back in. Especially when they realise we aren't guarding the windmill. What I want to do is set up two guard posts about a hundred metres out on both flanks, that'll give them space to enter into and we can maybe get them in a crossfire."

He gestured in Ray and Andy's direction. "I want you two up over there on that slope." He pointed in the direction of some low lying shrubs near the top, if you set up there we'll know where you are in case our fire strays off a bit." He pointed to some more shrubs on the opposite flank. "Leah and me can set up over there."

Pat looked at him dangerously. "Where are you going to put me then?" She demanded.

Jim could sense what was going to happen and desperately thought of some way to avoid it. She was having none of it. "If you think I'm going inside with all this going on you're very much mistaken." Jim spread his hands innocently. "I thought it was going to be better if you set up a guard post inside in case they get past us for any reason."

Plainly displeased, Pat knew he was probably right and nodded, she turned to go and uncover the hole but Andy stopped her and said. "If you go inside you can leave that sniper rifle out here with me, you won't need it in there."

She glared at him and reluctantly handed it over, taking his automatic from him. He smiled in pleasure as he felt the polished wooden stock and frowned slightly as he noticed some soil on the stock. He would have commented on this but was forestalled by Ray saying. "Why have you taken Leah with you Jim? Don't you think she'd be better with me?"

Jim took a deep breath, he had hoped to avoid the question, but now it was out in the open. "If you have her with you and anything happens I think you'll do all you can to save her without regard for the greater good. We all have to be a bit dispassionate when it comes to a fight."

Leah was on him like a cat striking. "So now we have it, you'll leave me to die if there's any trouble."

"That's not what I meant Leah and you know it. I just happen to think that if someone too close to you is there it could complicate things in an emergency." He gestured in the direction of Ray. "What do you think he's going to do if he hears you cry out in pain in the middle of a fight? Do you think he's going to ignore that? Or is he going to run to help you, even if he should concentrate on fighting them. In a situation like that you could both end up dead."

"Mmm." Leah was decided about her reaction. "If I'm left like the last time you'll live to regret it."

Jim smiled, shaking his head. "It won't happen again, I promise."

"Better not." She sniffed, and bent down to pick up her belongings. Pat went to the wall and prised the panel off with a knife from her pocket. When she opened it, she called softly and Dick's face appeared in the opening. He smiled when he saw that they had Andy with them and then he was pulled to one side from the back and Colette thrust her head out to welcome them. Pat pushed her back a little with the words. "OK, darling, we haven't finished the business yet so let these guys get away and do their job. We've got to do the same job we've been doing all along, that is, guard this place."

Colette shook her head. "We don't need any more guards in here mum, if you want to go outside and help we can look after this place, especially now those women are here helping."

Jim reached out and touched his daughter on the shoulder. "Don't go letting those women take the first line of defence, some of them still have men out here and they won't shoot them, that's for sure."

She looked at him with disappointment. "You don't know how they got treated before they got here dad, I think they'd like to get out there with you and a gun in their hands. They've got no reason to protect any of those thugs out there I can tell you. She bent down when someone pulled her from the hole and passed out some boxes of ammunition. "Dick said you might need some of these." They took them greedily and filled their pockets. Then she looked at them all. "Good luck to you and don't worry about us, we've got enough in here to protect this place."

She withdrew her head from the hole and Pat turned to them and said. "Looks like you're stuck with me for a bit." She held her hand out to Andy. "Do you want to hand that rifle over?"

Andy glanced down at the rifle with regret. "Do you really want it?" He asked reluctantly. "I can put it to better use than you now."

She smiled grimly. "I'm sure you can son but it's a better rifle for a woman to use than those ugly automatic's you keep trying to foist off on me."

Andy would have answered hotly but he never got the chance, a shot blasted out and Jim felt a thump in the shoulder followed by indescribable pain, it knocked him to the floor and he heard Andy screaming. "Scatter, scatter." He felt a hand pull him to the side and then for a few minutes the world went blank. He came too to find himself being pulled along up the slope he had intended to set the ambush on, bullets were still pinging around them but there seemed to be no direction to them. He could feel his arm was wet and the ache hurt. He could feel that he had two people with him but he had no way of knowing who they were. They seemed to stumble along for hours until finally they threw themselves down on the earth.

The two people lay for a while getting their breath back, then sat up and regarded Jim with worried eyes, Jim could now see he had Ray and Leah with him. He felt faint and blinked his eyes rapidly to clear them. Leah saw the signs immediately and took out a bottle of water from her pack; she soaked a tissue and wiped his brow then dribbled a little into his mouth. He sipped hungrily and when he could move his mouth said, "What happened to the others?"

"I think they got away." Leah replied. "But you're the one we've got to worry about now, you took one in the shoulder and we've got to get it seen to. It's a pity we couldn't shove you back in that hole but we didn't get the chance as it happened too quickly. We should try and get you in there now."

Jim knew what she meant and shook his head. "That's going to make it too easy for them, if we go back that way they've only got to wait for us, they'll pick us of like flies." He grinned ruefully. "Sort of comes back to me what I said, you've got to be a bit dispassionate in a fight like this."

He only had one thought in his head right now and the question there remained unanswered, 'How did they get past the claymores at the top of the hill?' He surmised they had probably gone to the flanks to try and trap them and missed the mines altogether.

Ray grinned and said hoarsely. "Only one thing for it mate. We'll have to get that slug out of there, and now."

Leah looked around. "We can't do anything here, and we're still too close. We'd better get a bit further away and wait out the rest of the night; we can only do something when we can see what we're doing. And anyway, that lot'll be hunting for us right now so let's move." She looked down; blood was dripping off the end of Jim's fingers on to the ground and staining it. "We'll have to stop that or it'll be a dead giveaway."

She pulled her pack off her shoulder and felt inside, finally pulling out a field dressing. "Good old Andy." She smiled. "He bought these when he went to that supply depot." Working rapidly she took his top off and stared at the wound in his shoulder. He gasped when her fingers touched the raw wound but smiled when she said. "Come on, don't be a baby, I got one of these a little while ago. It's better than dying."

She bound the wound as best she could then took out an ampoule of morphine and thrust it in and squeezed. Jim could feel the warmth coming and the pain subsided. Nodding in satisfaction she helped him back on with his top and said. "Right, let's get going before that lot find us."

They both helped him to his feet and taking his good arm Ray started to walk up the hill. Jim looked down as they walked and couldn't believe his eyes; he was still clutching the crossbow! He glanced to one side and noticed for the first time that Ray had the case of bolts over his shoulder; he sighed with relief to know that all hadn't been lost and they still had some means of protecting themselves. A thought occurred to him and he asked Ray. "How did I keep hold of this crossbow? I must have passed out."

"Ray glanced at him and answered laconically. "Couldn't get it out of your hands mate, must have wanted to keep it pretty bad, stuck like shit to a blanket." He held the quiver of bolts up. "I thought I'd better keep these cos that wouldn't be any good without em."

Jim thanked his lucky stars that something had gone right for them. He started to feel a little better and knew the morphine was spreading throughout his body, he hoped it wasn't going to slow him down too much. After some time they reached the top of the rise and Jim wondered what the time was and how long it would be to daybreak. They had heard no sign of pursuit in the last hour or so and finally Leah who was in the lead turned and said. "I think we can stop now, we're far enough away that they'll find it hard to search for us."

Thankfully Ray let Jim slide down and lay on the earth and squatted down beside him; he reached into his pack and took out a bottle of water saved from the previous meal and opening it he offered some to Jim. As it was offered Jim realised just how thirsty he was, and taking it he drunk greedily. Ray reached over and snatched it from his hand. "Hold on mate." He said meanly. "That's all we've got to last us for a bit."

He took a small swig himself and gave some to Leah, she drank and then looking at both of them in turn she said. "We've got to get some rest, so I suggest we kip down for a bit here; then in the morning we can have a look at that shoulder of yours Jim and make up our minds what we're going to do."

"What do you reckon about them having torches then?" Jim asked.

Leah sighed. "If they have got torches they don't seem to be using them, I reckon the batteries are flat and if they're rechargeable it'll take time to charge them up and if they aren't they haven't got anything to light the way."

Ray agreed with her and offered to take the first watch, Jim's eyes closed almost immediately. Leah and Ray watched for a while then Leah whispered to him. "It's going to be a bastard trying to take that slug out you know, we've got no medical equipment out here worth a light, I wish we could get him into that bloody building over there so Colette could have a go."

Ray nodded. "No chance of that love, they must know they put one into one of us, they'll be waiting if we try anything like that."

Leah lay back and closed her eyes. "Wake me in a couple of hours; I'll take a watch then."

Chapter Four

Jim woke to a dawn that was anything but good. Cold dark winds blew around them and dismal clouds scudded across a desolate landscape. He sat up and clutched his shoulder in pain, he had stiffened up during the night, and the morphine had worn off. He groaned slightly and attracted the attention of the other two; they were busy scouring the landscape with binoculars. From their position on top of the rise they had a perfect view of the whole valley. From here it stretched for about two miles with the building in the centre, it was about a mile from their position and they could make out a small campsite about five hundred metres from the back of the building in a line to the windmill.

Some small figures were huddled round a fire with some smoke rising from it and blowing away in the breeze. "Why can't they have gone round the front and tried to get in to rest and get something to eat?"Jim asked.

They both looked at him and smiled condescendingly, and Leah answered for them. "We talked that over last night while you were having a good kip. You've got to remember there's no one in the front now so they probably figured we took it back after they left. They were maybe scared of the reception they'd get if they tried to get in. Don't forget what we're playing for here, the losers are going to die, so a mistake here is going to be fatal."

She came over to him and said. "I've got to get that slug out of your back as soon as possible."

She bent over him and undoing his coverall pulled it down to his waist, his shirt came next and then his vest. She wrinkled her nose a little at the smell of BO that emanated from his unwashed body, he grimaced in embarrassment, and she said. "Nothing a good bath won't cure, I smell just as bad. Bags I the first shower when we get back in there."

He grinned and said. "Leah, I'll let you have the first three showers if we get back in there after we solve our little problem out here."

"I'll hold you to that." She replied.

She frowned when she went to his shoulder and took off the field dressing to examine the wound, it had reddened overnight and looked inflamed and sore, a small amount of pus was oozing out of the surface and it looked unhealthy. As Leah looked at it, some dust blew up in the wind and stuck to it. She wiped ineffectually at it with a tissue but only succeeded in smearing it further. Putting a temporary plaster over it she sat in front of Jim with a worried look on her face. "The outlook isn't good Jim; you really ought to be in that building over there getting some better medical attention."

"You know that isn't possible for the time being, why don't you just bind it up give me a shot of morphine and we'll go hunting for that lot." Jim said.

She shook her head. "It doesn't work like that, if we don't get that seen to in the next few hours, it'll be going gangrene, and you'll end up losing the arm if it don't kill you."

Jim cursed under his breath, of all the things to happen now, just when he needed all his powers. He made up his mind quickly. "I've got some morphine in my field pack, put some in and cut it out; it's the only way we can do it right now."

She looked at Ray and he nodded agreement with Jim, so she shrugged and said. "OK, let's find somewhere a bit more sheltered and get on with it."

They pulled Jim to his feet and set off, away from the building, looking for a hollow sheltered place, they found a spot about three hundred metres away and Ray took out a poncho that he had carried rolled up on his pack. He quickly made a shelter out of some brushwood and draped the poncho over it. They laid Jim down in the shelter and made him as comfortable as possible, Leah took the phial of morphine from the small medical pack Jim had, and looked in despair at the tools it had in it. A pair of scissors and some tweezers. "Some chance of major surgery." She commented to herself with a shake of the head. At least it contained some bandages, antibiotic powder, and sterile dressings; she looked around at the dust blowing around the shelter and hoped against hope that when she cut him open that none of the dust had infectious bacteria on it.

She took her knife from her sleeve and studied it, bits of dirt and rubbish still clung to it, and she could see some dried blood on it from the previous time she had used it. She shuddered slightly as she remembered the circumstances and the feeling she had had when she plunged it into the neck of her attacker. She cleaned it as best she could with a tissue and as she did so Ray said. "I think I'll go and have a look round to see if anybody's moving around out there."

Leah looked up at him and said through gritted teeth. "You move one muscle mister and you'll regret it, we can see for two or three hundred metres from here so have a look and come back in, I need a hand here and you're it."

Ray looked dismayed. "I can't stand the sight of surgery on the TV and you're telling me I've got to help, I'll probably pass out if he starts bleeding all over the place."

She sneered. "Thanks very much macho man, now I can't do this on my own so you're down to help and no arguments. Now get outside for a quick look round and then come in here ready to help."

He ducked down and went out with a woeful expression on his face and she bent to the task of cleaning her knife. She rummaged into the medical pack and found a small tube of sterilising fluid, and spread a little on some cotton wool. She then rubbed it all over the knife and tested the blade with a finger. Nodding to herself she turned to Jim to find him watching her with guarded eyes. He indicated the knife and asked."That thing sharp enough?"

She shrugged. "I sharpened it before I left and it's all I've got, it'll have to do in the circumstances."

She heard Ray returning from the scouting trip and said to Jim. "You'd better turn over and lie on your stomach."

She quickly laid his clothing on the ground so he had something comfortable to lie on. He lay face down and she pulled the plaster off and looked at the wound apprehensively, it had festered some more since she last looked at it and pus had formed a hard scab on the surface. The area round the bullet hole showed an angry red and she knew that unless it was treated very soon it would turn gangrenous. Ray looked over her shoulder and whistled. "Don't like the look of that mate." He said to Jim, and then grunted as she drove an elbow into his ribs. The breath wheezed out of his lungs and he turned angrily to her and hissed. "What the hell was that for?" She glared at him and understanding her suddenly, he coughed and looked shamefaced at Jim. "Sorry mate." He said. "I didn't mean to upset you by blurting that out, but it really don't look very good."

Leah's eyes widened as she listened to him make mistake after mistake. "Have you got anything there to clean up as we go?" She asked him to take his mind off his big mouth, and he rummaged in his pack to produce a packet of tissues. They were rough round the edges from being carried around for a long time but still serviceable. She grunted in disgust but nonetheless put them down to be used later.

"Right then, might as well get started." She said and reaching out she picked up the last phial of morphine and pushed it into the shoulder just above the wound so the blood stream would carry the drug to the site of the trouble. She waited a minute then touched Jim there. He flinched a little and then muttered. "I can feel it working now, give it a moment."

Nodding, she pushed him down until his face was facing the floor and he lay with arms under his face on the ground. She looked at the meagre tools she had to work with and sighed. She had a knife, some tissues, some antibiotic powder, a bandage, tweezers that were plainly meant to get splinters out, and a pair of scissors that would be hard put to cut through butter. A thought struck her and she delved into her pack and triumphantly pulled out a needle and some cotton. She waved them in the air with glee until Ray commented sourly. "I bet that cotton's stuffed full of infection coming from that pack."

She waved him quiet. "It's all I've got, so it'll have to do."

She turned to Jim who had by now closed his eyes as the morphine took hold and made the pain easier. She touched near the wound again and this time he made no complaint. She then looked at Ray with a determined expression and said. "Let's do it then before this morphine wears off." She could have added, 'Because we've got no more.' But refrained and picked up the knife.

She gripped the knife firmly and placed it over the wound ready to cut, then closed her eyes and said a short prayer then cut down swiftly across the hole; blood and pus spurted out as she did so and

Jim writhed in agony, almost throwing her off. Ray leaned forward and held him firmly by the shoulders to stop him moving but he still said. "Christ Leah, I thought that morphine was supposed to stop the pain."

Sweat had broken out all over Jim's body despite the cold and his skin became slippery to the touch. Leah brushed a strand of hair from her eyes with the back of her hand, and saying nothing more she pushed even harder with her next stroke. She penetrated into the muscle trying to follow the path of the bullet, the blood was flowing freely now, and she attempted to stem the flow with one of the tissues. It was sodden within a moment and she flung it away as useless. She cut again and was rewarded with the first touch of something hard under the knife, probing deeper in the area she encountered more resistance but it was bone and cutting round it she saw that it was chipped where it had deflected the bullet. She picked up the tweezers and teased out as much of the bone as she could see. The bullet had lodged just under the bone and now she could see it lying there, surrounded by pus and chips of bone. She opened the wound as far as she could with her finger and reaching down with the tweezers she attempted to get hold of it. Jim moved suddenly as the pain was too great and he tried to pull away. She hissed. "Hold still for Christ's sake I nearly had it then." And looking at Ray she went on. "Hold him firm for a second till I get hold of it." Ray looked sick around the gills and swallowed before taking a firmer grip. She picked up the knife again and cut a little deeper to allow more room to manoeuvre and gasped in triumph, as she was able to reach in and grip the bullet firmly. It came out with a slight sucking sound and she thrust it under Ray's nose to show him. He flinched back and she jeered at him. "Mr macho man in action; can't even stand the sight of a bit of blood. Wouldn't be any good you having babies would it?"

She laid it to one side and concentrated on cleaning the wound as best she could with the materials at hand, some of the chips of bone she removed but some were too small to be gripped properly so she decided to leave them in the hope they would work their way out themselves. Blood kept flowing steadily as she worked but until she had finished she made no attempt to staunch it as it helped to clean the area. The wound had had pus in it before she started but by the time she had finished most had been flushed away. Finally she sat back and looked at it and decided it was time to close the hole, she picked up the antibiotic powder and sprinkled some in the wound and the rest around it, then picking up the cotton she threaded the needle and sprinkled some powder on that.

Grinning at Ray who had started to look green again she bent to the task of sewing the wound as neatly as she could. The flesh slipped and moved as she sewed but she managed to grip it until the first stitch was in and after that she was able to sew the two sides together. At last the job was finished and she sat back and considered her handiwork, then nodding to herself she pronounced. "Not bad if I say so myself, I think you'll manage soon, it'll be a bit stiff but I don't think any lasting damage was done. You'll end up with a scar but that'll be too bad"

Picking up the bandage she quickly wound it round the wound and tied it off under his arm. Then she looked worriedly at Jim who turned slightly to see her. "That morphine's going to wear off soon though and we've got no more. I reckon we've got to get this business sorted out pretty damn quick so we can get you some proper medical care."

Jim sat up and slowly bent his arm to test it out and winced when he lifted it up. It felt as stiff as a board and he knew it would badly affect the way he could operate. She helped him put his clothes on and then stood and glanced at Ray who was looking round to see if any of the enemy had found them yet. "Any sign of them?

He shook his head and turned to look at her; it was the last thing he did before he died. The front of his head blew off in a spray of blood and bone and he collapsed to the floor before even a look of surprise could cross his face. Blood and bits of brain exploded all over her face and she felt sick as she realised where they had come from. She shuddered and stared in horror at the spectacle and would have screamed if Jim hadn't reacted swiftly and pulled her to her knees. A bullet snapped through the air right where she had been a moment before followed by a second bang. The explosion reverberated through the air and Jim estimated that the shot had come from behind them, about two hundred metres away.

The realisation swept through his head that while they had been concentrating on his medical care they had been flanked and now they would have enemy on both sides of them. 'But where?'

The question was solved soon enough as more shots rang out from the other direction but they bounced harmlessly several metres away as if the persons firing had no control over the gun. It seemed that they had three people firing at them, one behind, and two in front. Another shot came from behind them, and the bullet dug a small sand pile by Jim's face. 'Too close for comfort.' He thought, and pushed Leah hard on the shoulder. "We've got to get out of here and quick." He cried. She was still staring in horror at the body of her husband lying in the earth with blood seeping from under his head. He had collapsed forwards and Jim was surprised to see that the entry hole at the back of his head was so small. She laid her hand on him as if she was trying to lift him and bring him back to life, her other hand was over her mouth and she had started to weep.

"Get moving you stupid bitch or you'll get the same as him." He shouted and slapped her hard with his good hand.

She looked at him with pain filled eyes and he knew he would have to be tough with her or she would either grieve, and let herself be killed or make a run to try and kill their opponents. Neither way would allow them more than a few minutes life so he pushed her hard in the direction he wanted her to go and snarled. "Get moving or we're both dead, now move." This last was shouted with his mouth a few inches from her face.

She stepped back and Jim saw that spark in her eyes that told him she was about to explode in his direction, he pushed her again, and this time she turned in the direction he indicated. He picked up as much of their weaponry as he could and handed her a gun. Then they stumbled a few steps to a gully that ran sideways to the ambushers. They dropped to the ground when they got there and with Jim pushing her from behind they crawled along until they met another gully that joined them diagonally. Jim turned her into this and they crawled some distance into it and went up the side of the slope. No bullets followed them and Jim could only hope they were out of sight of the sniper.

As they crawled Jim's brain had been ticking over the possibilities and he came to the conclusion that the first shot had to come from someone who could handle a gun extremely well and his mind went back to the time they had bought the arms on the freighter. Possibly Sulim, but his bet was on Diman, he was the assassin and wouldn't hesitate to fire at someone from ambush. The other two were harder but if he had to bet it would be a woman and another man, but not a natural killer, maybe the electrician. That left two others hunting Andy and Pat. He knew that the direction they were heading in now would take them to the top of the bluff where they had hidden the guns all those months ago, but he also knew they had no alternative at the moment, as they had three people hunting them and they would have to find a way to set up their own ambush.

They crawled another few minutes and by now the shoulder that Leah had mended was beginning to pain him badly. At last he judged they were far enough away to call a halt and get their breath back. He stopped and held Leah back by her leg; she sat and stared wordlessly forward, her face full of despair. By now she was in shock and looking down she tried ineffectually to brush the gore from the front of her coverall and took no notice as Jim checked their weapons. He still had the crossbow and the bolts for it and the guns had enough ammunition. Ray's gun was gone with no chance of retrieval and his ammunition was still in his jacket pocket. Jim shrugged and wrote it off in his mind.

He handed her the gun back after checking it and said grimly. "I know you want to sit and grieve for him but we've got no time for that now, and it'll get you killed as well. We've got to fight on and beat these bastards or they win and we lose; now I think the one that hit Ray is Diman. He's the only one I can think of who could hit a man from two hundred metres, that was quite a shot and I don't want to let him take a pot at us. Now they'll be looking for us and it's not going to take them long to find this gully, and when they do they'll be following us up it."

He tapped her on the shoulder as her eyes had glazed over as she thought of Ray again. "You'd better pay attention to this, it might just save your life and if I'm right it'll give you an opportunity to get revenge on that bastard."

She looked at him when he said the word revenge and paid

attention for the first time. Her face was bloodless and gaunt He could see she was only just holding herself together by self-will. "You've got to put this aside for now and try and go on as if nothing has happened, if we can set up an ambush somewhere we can at least get a shot at them. We'll have to watch out for that Diman, he's a devious bastard." He put his arm round her shoulder. "If you can pull yourself together we might be able to win this war, we've done quite well in the battles so far."

She smiled wanly as he mangled the old saying and then shook herself. "If you promise to stop trying to get me to forget Ray for now and pull I myself together, I'll try and do what you want, but…." She said harshly. "Some one's going to pay for this and with their life." Her face took on some of her old determination. "Now what plans have you managed to make?"

"Apart from thinking we've got to ambush them somehow I haven't thought of anything." Jim had to confess. "I had a vague thought that maybe we could get them up to that butte and if we go over the top they'd be forced to follow, I cut some footholds up there when we hid the guns on the cliff face." He finished lamely.

He could tell by the look on her face the plan was a no go, she pointed back down the slope they had just crawled up. "I don't think this Diman is going to come up that gully there, it's too easy to see him coming, he'll be climbing that slope over there trying to get above us. I think the best bet is to try and get over that way towards the other two and try for them." She pointed in the direction the other two would be if they tried to head them off in a pincer movement. "We can use those two to draw him to us if we can get near them and put them under some pressure with a few shots."

"Expose ourselves and make us the target, that's great thinking." Jim said scathingly. To his ears the plan was no better than his.

Her face hardened as she heard the sarcasm and she faced him, the piggy mask making her eyes stand out from her face. Jim knew the saying that the eyes are the mirror of the soul and hers were portraying the hurt and anger she felt right now. He felt sorry for the person she was directing this anger at, and knew she would carry it until the man who killed her husband was dead himself. "Look over there." She answered, pointing in the direction of some rocks further round the slope, there were some small shrubs clustered around the outcrop.

"They'll make an ideal hiding place if we can get there unseen, and over there, if I'm right is where the other two will be coming." She pointed back up the slope. "See that bulge in the hill above the rocks; that means that someone higher up the hill can't see anyone in the rocks, so they've got to come over the top or round the side to get a shot in but then they won't have any cover themselves. That means they get exposed and not us."

The idea had it's merits, it still left the possibility that their pursuer could choose any direction of three to come at them, but to try and reach the butte Jim had mentioned meant covering at least five hundred metres of open ground to get there and Jim didn't fancy his chances of reaching the butte alive with a sniper like Diman behind them, whereas the rocks were only a hundred metres away. He nodded and together they stumbled across the intervening ground as fast as their legs could carry them. Once there they quickly picked up some of the smaller rocks and closed any gaps between the larger ones. Finally they sat down and looked out of their makeshift ambush, it wasn't a moment too soon, from exactly the direction Leah had indicated; they could make out two figures. They were approaching cautiously and would be abreast of them and in five or six minutes at the present rate of progress.

There was a barrage of shots from the distance and they looked in that direction. "Andy and Pat." Jim breathed in her ear quietly. "Hope they're OK."

She nodded and looking down Jim could see she had crossed her fingers in the age-old gesture. The two down the slope had stopped and they could see from their vantage point that they were arguing hotly, and they were waving their arms and gesticulating wildly at each other. Jim could see now that it was a man and woman. The man pointed towards them and said something to the woman and her shoulders sagged as she nodded her head in agreement then they started up the slope carefully towards the rocks where they were hidden. Leah turned to Jim.

"They're coming straight at us, I don't think they know we're here yet and want to use it themselves for cover." She picked the crossbow up and loaded it, adjusting the sights as she did. Jim felt the pain in his arm momentarily hurting, and then it was forgotten in the heat of the moment. He picked up his own gun and checked it as quickly as possible; by now the two people were approaching to within a hundred metres and he could see that the woman was probably the one who had run from him before. 'Maybe Sulim's wife or woman.' He thought to himself as he watched them approach.

Leah breathed quietly. "I'm going to take the one on the left. You take the other one, fire when I do."

Jim sighted on the one on the right, and saw he had drawn the electrician to fire at; he smiled grimly as he recognised that Leah had done that deliberately, so he wouldn't aim off, because he would be too soft on a woman. He held his fire until the two of them were within fifty metres, and heard a gentle twang and the bolt from the gun sped on its deadly way. Before he had time to fire himself, the woman flung her arms up in surprise and shock as the bolt hit her full in the chest high up near the throat. He fired in reaction to the events and even as he fired he knew he had missed, the recoil from the gun hit him on the shoulder in a shockwave of pain and the last thing he knew was a black cloud passing over his eyes as he lost consciousness.

He opened his eyes slowly, coming out of his stupor, he was lying on his chest with his mouth on the ground, his back hurt painfully and he wondered idly how long he had been unconscious. It was almost too much effort to move and he relaxed to avoid the pain that any movement would give him. He became aware of a man speaking in a low tone and as he listened he could recognise the voice, but he couldn't put a face to it. The voice went on talking but Jim couldn't distinguish any separate words in the pattern of speech. The last thing he wanted to do was raise his head as the effort was going to be too hard, he tried to raise his hands to pick himself up but they wouldn't move. His brow frowned as he endeavoured to work out how to move them and moving his head slightly his eyes widened as they took in the scene in front of him.

Leah was lying on her back with her hands tied under her, the front of her coveralls were open and the electrician had his hands inside fondling her, and as he watched the hands went to her waist to undo the belt and give him entry to the lower regions of her clothes. The man was sitting with his legs astride her and as Jim watched he slid backwards a little to allow himself to pull at the trouser legs. Jim became of Leah staring at him fiercely and then she let her gaze drift down to her right. He followed it down and looked puzzled, as he saw nothing there, the electrician was still talking and Jim began to make some sense of the words the man was saying.

"To the victor the spoils, eh Luvvie, I don't forget what happened the last time we were in this sort of situation, that won't happen again. This time you're going to pay for hitting me like that and spoiling the fun. Come on now; just open those legs a bit so I can slip these trousers off easy like. I don't want to hurt you but if I have to do it the hard way I will."

He bent to nuzzle her on the neck and attempted to roughly kiss her on the mouth, his hands still busy with her clothes, he had managed to open the fly of the trousers but she had her legs clamped firmly shut and he found it too hard to pull them down. As he fumbled again with the fasteners, attempting to open them some more she kicked as much as she could to try and unseat him. It gave him his opportunity and with a cry of triumph he pulled her trousers off. He stared in fascination at the spectacle in front of him and she took the opportunity given to her when he was looking down, her gaze came back to Jim, and once again she directed his gaze to her right side. Jim looked down once more in puzzlement and the shock hit him, her knife lay in its scabbard just under her waist on the ground; it must have fallen out in the struggle. Her look turned to pleading as he watched and he tried again to free his hands. She kicked once more but this time when she did she turned slightly to take the electricians sight line further away from Jim. He was now at a quarter turn to him and if he had wanted to see Jim would have to swivel his head.

Jim had still not regained all his senses yet and struggled a minute more before he realised that the reason his hands wouldn't move was that they had been tied with plastic police handcuffs, fortunately they had been tied quickly with little thought and were in front of him. If they had been tied behind he would never have been able to budge. The electrician by now had lost patience with the struggle and reaching round to his belt he unclipped a hunting knife and waved it under her nose. "Right now, we'll see who's going to win this one then, shall we?" He laughed. "Struggle now and see what happens."

He reached quickly forward and slashed quickly, Leah's breath exploded out in terror as she thought he intended to stab her, but instead he swiftly cut her bra straps and pulled it off exposing her to the air. He did the same with her panties and smiled as she tried to force her legs together to hide herself from his staring eyes.

He sniffed as he did so and said. "So you've been a couple of days without a shower have you? Don't worry we're all in the same boat, I won't hold it against you." And he laughed at the irony of the joke.

Jim kept his head down and tried to free his hands but to no avail. He looked once more at the knife and saw that in her struggles Leah had managed to wriggle it a little further from her and nearer Jim. She tried kicking once more but this time the electrician was ready for her and he grinned as he held her still.

"Ooh, carry on Luvvie." He said. "It just makes it more interesting." He laughed evilly. "You're really turning me on; I reckon you'll be better than your friend."

Leah was panting hard now and her breasts were heaving with exertion, he eyed them and reached down to touch them, relishing the movement as he fondled her. He thrust a grubby hand down between her legs and roughly pushed his finger into her causing her to cry out in pain. She jerked once more to try and dislodge him but he rode her and held her knees between his legs. She had jerked just a little more to the side and now his back was almost facing Jim. Her eyes fixed again on him and the message was clear, 'Get the knife!' she had not uttered one word from start to finish and Jim marvelled at her control. The electrician moved himself slightly and pushed his knees down between her legs in an effort to force them apart and now Jim had to make his move. As the electrician stared down and felt between her legs she suddenly stopped struggling and opened herself voluntarily, the man stared in pleasure at the display and said. "That's better Luvvie, now it won't hurt quite so much." he was completely oblivious now to what was happening around him as he only had eyes for her. With his hands still bound Jim lurched forward and grabbed the knife in both hands, awkwardly he held the scabbard between his knees and pulled the knife out.

By some sixth sense the electrician knew what was happening and started to turn to confront him. Jim pushed forward awkwardly with the knife held in front and tried to thrust it into his neck, it missed and opened a gash on the mans shoulder. He cried out in pain and reaching back he pushed Jim to one side and then grabbed his own knife from the ground alongside him. Jim had fallen painfully to one side and now tried to gather his feet under himself, this proved to be so difficult without his hands to push with that he had no chance of regaining his balance before the electrician was on him. The man drove the blade in front of him, aiming for Jim's chest and he was barely able to twist in time to deflect the knife. The electrician couldn't stop himself with the power of the thrust and stumbled forward hitting Jim on the shoulder and throwing him back down on the ground.

The man paused momentarily as he surveyed Jim who was at a disadvantage for the minute and said. "I should have slit your throat when I had the chance matey, then you'd never have come back to haunt me again. Well I'm going to rectify that little mistake now and dispose of you properly."

He started towards Jim with the knife held in the classic pose of the street fighter with the blade ready for the underhand sweep. The most dangerous move in knife fighting; Jim struggled to get to his feet to meet this attack grasping the knife in both hands as he did. The man grinned at the prospect as Jim presented a sorry sight, his wound had opened again, and blood dripped down his arm making the blade slippery to the touch. He knew he had little chance against this much more powerful opponent but held his ground as the man approached him with both feet splayed for balance and the deadly knife always pointing at Jim's belly.

A movement over the man's shoulder caught Jim's eye and he stared open mouthed at the spectacle of Leah standing now, naked with hands behind her back, incongruously she still had her boots on and her socks hung round her feet. Even in their present peril Jim felt a flash of admiration for her as he saw her body in all its glory. The electrician smiled and said, you won't catch me out with that old trick matey, I'm too old in the tooth for a sucker play like that."

They were so close now that one split second would make all the difference, and Jim smiled superciliously as if he knew something that the other man didn't. He could see he wanted to take a look over his shoulder but if he did Jim would be able to thrust this knife forward and cut him. He decided to ignore the possibility and feinted forward with the knife, Jim swayed to one side to avoid the blade and Leah jumped and kicked the electrician in the back of the knee. He grunted and surprise and shock flashed across his face, he sank to one knee almost landing on Leah who now sprawled on her back behind him. Before he could regain his feet, Jim pushed forward with both hands and the knife went straight into the man's neck. He opened his mouth to cry out but only blood spurted out and he gurgled incoherently as he gasped and drowned in his own blood. He feebly attempted to catch Jim with the knife but it was in vain and he slumped forward dying on the ground. Jim held himself quite still as he waited for the man to die and when he collapsed forward in a heap Jim withdrew the knife. He stared down at his hands and saw they were covered in blood and he shuddered in horror at what he had been forced to do. Leah took the look in and said. "Join the club mate, now you know what I went through. Only I had two attempted rapes in twenty four hours." She turned her back to Jim and held her bound hands towards him. "Will you cut these off, I want to try and get some clothes back on before I catch my death out here."

Jim looked down at her bare back and sliced the plastic cuffs from her wrists, she was filthy from lying in the earth and bits of dirt clung to her buttocks and almost without thinking he started to brush her down before realising what he was doing and stopped. She glanced over her shoulder and smiled when she felt the touch but said nothing and bent to retrieve her trousers, she quickly donned them and then took the knife from his hands and cut the bonds on his wrists. Jim looked at her puzzled and asked. "How did he get to you from down there?"

She shrugged her shoulders drawing his attention to her breasts, which jiggled as she did so. "It was bloody stupid, I didn't know how to reload the crossbow properly, and by the time I did he'd got too close and was holding the gun on me."

She then walked over to get her top which lay screwed up where the electrician and thrown it, putting it on she dressed herself in the rest of her clothes and put the piggy mask back on. Jim did the same and she said in her muffled voice. "Hope we haven't been too long without these and the dust gets in our lungs."

They both rubbed their wrists to get the circulation going and she went forward and put her head on Jim's shoulder and hugged him. "That was too bloody close." She said with her cheek pressed against him.

A voice spoke from behind them. "How very touching, to see such expressions of affection between good friends."

Jim swore and jumped to get his gun but the voice said. "Don't even think about it Jim, old friend, or I will be forced to fire this weapon. And please drop those weapons I don't like the way you use them."

Jim stopped and spun round to see the hated face of Diman. He dropped the knife and looked regretfully at the rifle and crossbow lying where they had been dropped earlier. The man was standing a few yards up the slope from them, and he held a gun casually in his hands pointing in their direction. Jim knew what it was even before he could examine it. It was the gun that Sulim had offered to sell to Andy when they had been in his arsenal. Diman caught the look and smiled superciliously. "Your son would have done well to take the job when he was offered it, then it could have been him standing here instead of me."

"I'm happy he didn't." Jim replied. "If he'd turned out like you I wouldn't want him for my son."

Diman's face darkened but he ignored the insult. "Now what am I going to do with you?" He mused, half to himself. "I don't think I can let you live my friend, we are too alike, you and I. We both want to be king of the pile and there is no room for both of us. You have caused me a great deal of trouble and you are going to pay for it." The menace in his voice was unmistakable; he spoke almost dispassionately, as if the outcome was of no interest to him. Jim recognised the signs and knew with a certainty that this man would kill him without a second's remorse, as if he were a bug that got under his feet.

Diman went on. "When I came here, I intended to take over this place and kill everybody, except some of the women in case they were needed." He indicated Leah, who involuntarily clutched the jacket tighter to her chest. "Oh, don't worry my dear you have nothing to fear from me, I don't have to rape women to have them, like him." The gun pointed down at the body on the floor between them. "Women always come to me when I want them."

"This one wouldn't." Leah spat out the words. "The last man I'd want is a backstabbing slimy bushwhacker who kills from ambush. Why don't you face up to fighting like a man."

His face tautened and now they could see the evil written on his face. He leaned forward and snarled. "Have you forgotten so soon the actions of your man, he shot a man with a crossbow from ambush in the same way, or doesn't that count."

She jumped at him with fingers outstretched to scratch his eyes but he easily sidestepped her and hit her on the side of the head with the butt of the rifle, she went down like a sack of potatoes and the gun swung round to cover Jim who had started his own move. "One more step Jim and you're a dead man."

The words brought Jim up sharp, he knew the man intended to kill him but decided to wait until a more opportune moment arrived. He held his hands in the air to signify he wouldn't move, and nodded at Leah lying on the ground. "Can I have a look at her?" he asked. "Just to check her over."

Diman shook his head. "No." He said shortly. "She's going to be all right, I didn't hit her very hard, just a tap to teach her a lesson."

Sure enough after a few seconds she started to stir and then sat up clutching her head, she examined her fingers and saw the blood smeared on them from her scalp and then remembered what had happened and groaning she looked at Diman. Her face contorted and she swore at him. "You'll pay for that you scumbag, just turn your back for two seconds and see what happens."

"On the contrary my dear." He smiled. "If anyone pays for anything round here, it's going to be you, for spoiling all my plans."

He leaned forward so his face was close to hers. "Do you realise what you've done, you two between you. You've killed all the people I recruited to run this place for me. Now I've got to find another way of making it work, but I don't think I want to include you two in those plans. Somehow I don't think you would give me a minute's peace."

He stood up and gestured with the gun. "Walk over that way if you please, I want everybody to have the pleasure of seeing my next actions."

They turned and started to walk in the direction he had indicated, it was out to the front of the building and up the hill facing to where the camera was situated opposite the front door of the building. On the way he said conversationally. "I figured it out that you had some way of seeing what was going on, and took a quick walk round, someone inside made the mistake of following my movements with the camera and lo and behold I spotted it. The only problem I had was where did the electricity come from? But it took only a few moments to stand in the building and feel the vibration in the floor. I let you think you had me fooled because I wanted you to keep the plants in good condition for me."

Jim seethed inside, all this time and the man had been playing them like a fish on a line, to be hooked and reeled in when he said so. He had also thought it through and he had a good idea what Diman intended to do to them. As he had said if he wanted to take over he had to be rid of the two worst protagonists he faced. Jim glanced over to where Leah was striding alongside him and she looked back grimly with no expression on her face. He cast around in his mind for a way out of this predicament, but could find no solution and resolved to try and turn the tables at the first opportunity. Diman was walking behind them with gun trained on their backs, and a hand knocked against his. He glanced down to see Leah's hand swinging backwards and forwards as she walked, then his heart leapt, somehow she still had the scissors from the medical kit and as her hand swung forward she turned her palm up to show him.

In the next few seconds, Jim had made and discarded a dozen plans to get the better of Diman, but not one would work unless they could get the jump on him and at all times this man was at least four or five metres away. Much too far to even try, if they had, he had ample time to kill them before they took two or three steps.

"They won't let you take over you know." He called over his shoulder. "You'll end up with no sleep, trying to figure out which one might jump you."

He heard a muffled chuckle come from Diman. "You don't know much about human nature do you Jim? If you did, you'd know that when it comes right down to it, people would rather live unhappily than die. And with me there, they won't be unhappy, because I am going to be a benevolent ruler."

Jim stopped and swung round, the other two stopped as well, and Diman raised the rifle slightly in alarm. "You don't get it do you? But the clue was there in that statement." Jim raised a hand and pointed at him. "You just said you're going to be the ruler, but that's just what I'm not. It's a democracy, and everybody gets a chance to have their say. If they didn't want me in charge all they had to do was have a vote and I would step down."

Diman sneered. "You're wrong my friend, people want to be told what to do, that way they feel safe and secure in the knowledge that their leader is looking after them. Now turn round and start walking, it's not far to go now."

Jim turned and started to walk again in the direction Diman indicated; his heart felt heavy as he knew what Diman intended to do. He was going to kill Jim and possibly Leah in front of all the people inside. That way he could make them all afraid of him until he was securely in charge and then he could produce a regime that would allow them more freedom to do what they wanted. It could work, but it still stood the chance of failure because most of them, and especially Andy and Pat, would stay fiercely loyal to Jim, even if he were dead.

Jim saw a movement out of the corner of his eye and looked round to see the camera swivelling round to point in their direction. He wondered idly who would be manipulating the controls but gave it up as he had to try and think of a way out of this situation. They slowly climbed the hill towards the summit and Jim's mind carried on racing and trying to puzzle his way out. He knew that Leah beside him would be doing the same thing but Diman kept his distance to their rear as if expecting them to try something.

They neared the summit and without looking Jim knew the camera was following their every move. As they breasted the top of the slope and reached the brink of the chasm Diman called to them to halt and ordered. "Right there my friend, kneel down facing the edge."

Jim reluctantly knelt down facing the gorge below; if he was to make a move it had to be now, as time had run out. Diman let him stay there for a while to see if Jim would beg for his life but he resolutely refused to even turn in his direction. He then proceeded to turn the screws to reveal the true horror of his intentions. He produced a pistol from his pocket and emptied it till only one bullet was left, he cocked his rifle and trained it on Leah and handed her the pistol. She stared at it in puzzlement and he smiled. "Don't think you can use it on me my dear, I'll kill you like a dog if you even turn it in my direction. I'm going to give you a chance for life, if you kill our friend here, I'll allow you to live. If you refuse I'll kill the pair of you."

He stepped back a few paces keeping the rifle trained on her. "In your own time dearie."

Leah stared in horror at the gun in her hand, and shook her head. "You can't expect me to do that." She gasped.

The smile on Diman's face became merciless; he was obviously enjoying the moment. "I not only expect you to do it:"…….. He would have gone on but his attention was drawn to Jim, who had stood and turned to face them.

"If you want to kill me, I can't stop you. But if you do, I want you to look me in the eye when you pull the trigger." Jim spoke to Diman.

Diman sneered. "So you want to act like a man do you? Well look at this gun when I fire it. I wonder if you'll see the bullet coming at you?" He raised the gun and aimed it between Jim's eyes.

Momentarily his attention had focussed on Jim and Leah saw her chance and jumped forward, she still had the scissors in her hand and she dropped the pistol because she was unsure if it would work and had no time to find out. She had covered half the distance to Diman before he had time to react. And after that things went rapidly. Diman started to swing the rifle in an arc to aim at her and at the same time Jim jumped from the other side. Leah reached Diman before the rifle could come to bear on her, and got under the barrel. The force of her impetus forced her hand with the scissors into Diman's chest and his eyes widened in surprise. The wound they caused was minor but Diman reacted with a bellow of rage and tried to hit her with the rifle. He succeeded in knocking her to one side but as she fell Jim managed to hit him a glancing blow on the side of the face from the other side.

They fell in a heap and for a moment struggled there as each of them tried to extricate themselves without conceding any advantage. They were too close for the rifle to be of any use so Diman let go and hit out at Jim's face. He missed but hit Jim on the wounded shoulder, the pain was agonising, and Jim pulled back slightly as he attempted to absorb it.

Diman punched again, this time aiming for Leah. Jim had felt his body tense and pushed out against his arm so the punch scraped over Leah's shoulder. They were still lying on the ground and finally Jim managed to disentangle himself from the melee to find Diman had done the same and they both scrambled to their feet facing each other. Diman tried to pick the rifle up but Leah was lying on it and gripped it ferociously; he gave up the struggle and kicked her viciously on the side of the head, and she fell back unconscious on the ground. Jim jumped forward and attempted to punch Diman but his reactions were too quick and Jim only succeeded in connecting with the side of his chin. They turned and faced each other with fists held in front of them but then Diman smiled, his face evil and triumphant. He reached to his side and pulled a knife out of his belt, Jim stared at it. The knife was big and the back of the blade was flat until about two inches from the end, then it turned to a blade near the point. He recognised the type as a Bowie knife and his stomach shrivelled at the thought of the blade entering his body.

He cast around desperately for something to defend himself with but there was nothing to hand and now Diman had started to stalk him weaving the hypnotic blade gently in front of him as he came. He had adopted the street fighters stance with feet splayed and wide for balance, knees slightly bent and left arm out to the side either to grip or push as the occasion demanded. At first Jim made the mistake of looking at the knife and when Diman got a little closer he struck. Jim jumped back and twisted but the knife still scraped down his ribs raising blood. He knew he should look at the man's eyes but the blade mesmerised him and it was only with a force of will he made himself look at his face.

Diman's lip curled at something he perceived in Jim's face and he smirked and said silkily. "You don't like my little toy do you? Well it won't be much longer before you can sit and watch your stomach spilling its contents on the ground. Just one little cut and it's all over for you."

He slashed again but this time with no attempt to cut Jim but to make him squirm away and show him the power he held over him. Jim jumped back and as he did so he saw a movement behind Diman. He stared in amazement and his eyes were drawn away from Diman for a moment. It was enough! He felt the blade enter his chest as Diman thrust and luckily for Jim it hit a bone near the shoulder. The pain shot through his body and he struck out as hard as he could with the other fist. It was on the same side as the bullet wound and although he hit Diman it was as if he had tapped him with a sponge, it did no damage. Jim stumbled back and almost fell over Leah lying behind him. She hadn't moved since being hit and as Jim stepped over her she lay still. Diman stopped for a moment to look at her and ascertain if she could use the rifle, which still lay under her.

Jim took a break while he did this and glanced down the hill, he could see almost the entire population of the farm hurrying up the hill towards them. They must have been alerted to what was happening by the camera operator. Diman caught the look and stared down the hill as well. His head swung back to Jim and he grinned maliciously. "They've all come out to see you die my friend, you'll have a good send off."

He stepped over Leah to get to Jim and her head swung up and she buried her teeth into his leg near the knee. He bellowed in pain and struck down with the knife, it cut into her neck and she relinquished her grip but not before Jim had stepped forward quickly and kicked him between the legs. The blow had the entire strength that Jim could muster and Diman buckled as it struck home. He dropped the knife and folded his hands over his manhood.

He looked up at Jim with eyes that held all his agony but burned bright with the lust for revenge. Jim tried again to kick him and Diman ducked as the strike went over his head. He reached down to grasp the rifle but Jim stamped down on the barrel to deter him from getting it. Leah was bleeding profusely from the cut on her neck but still managed to hold on to it. Jim bent down and tried to hold it as well but he had no strength in either hand now and his grip was nearly useless.

Diman gathered his shoulders and with a mighty bellow he pushed the two of them away from him. Leah still clung like a limpet to the gun and Jim landed on the ground on his back. Diman picked up the knife and once more started to stalk Jim. His eyes were filled with bloodlust now and Jim knew that nothing would stop him until he himself lay dead before this man. He could hear the cries and shouts of alarm now from the rest of the company, but had no time to see what was happening as Diman leaped again at him. The knife flashed towards him again and he grabbed the arm as it lunged at his belly. He felt the knife cut his arm as Diman twisted it on contact with his fingers. He held on and pulled the knife arm towards himself in a circular motion swinging Diman towards the brink of the chasm; he then clasped the other man round the arms and held him with his back towards himself. For the first time Diman showed alarm as his feet scrabbled on the edge and Jim kept up a steady pressure forcing him to choose between freeing himself and trying to stab Jim. Finally Diman pulled the old fighters trick of collapsing down as if finished and dragged Jim to the ground. Jim's hold was broken and Diman spread his arms to free himself, he scrambled to his feet, knife still in hand and as quickly thrust again with the blade.

Jim rolled to the side and avoided it, and somehow struggled to his feet, they came together and clasped each other round the arms to prevent any movement, Jim had the knife arm under his armpit and he could feel Diman trying to turn the blade and stab him. Her clung on desperately but knew his strength would soon give way and let Diman have the advantage he sought. They swayed together and Diman heaved Jim round until his back was towards the chasm, he scrambled with his feet, trying frantically to find some purchase for them but it was hopeless and he knew that very soon he would hurtle to the bottom. He felt the despair and sorrow in his heart as he thought of all that he had done to make this venture possible and now this man was trying to take everything from him.

Diman's eyes gleamed in triumph as he felt the weakness in Jim and started to bend him backwards over the cliff. With the last of his strength Jim pushed back but it was no use and slowly he felt himself going past the point of overbalancing backwards. Diman grunted in his ear. "You lose my friend, prepare to die." And he stood straight to give the final push. Jim felt a thud in his chest and Diman's face took on a look of horror and pain. He slowly let go of Jim and collapsed gently backwards away from the cliff pulling him with him. Jim stared down in puzzlement until he saw the point of a crossbow bolt protruding from Diman's chest. It had penetrated right through from his back and on coming out of his chest had struck Jim. The man died as he looked at him.

He stared down at his own chest and saw that he had been lucky enough to only have the bolt hit after the force had been spent and it had struck his chest bone and hardly entered his body. He massaged it gently as he gazed over Diman's body towards the approaching company. In the van Andy was waving the crossbow a smile on his face. "Not a bad shot, eh Dad. I thought for a minute I wouldn't have time to make it."

His looked alarmed as he saw the bolt had hit Jim. "Jeez Dad, I didn't expect it to go right through him, are you OK?"

Jim nodded, too exhausted to speak, and sank to the floor to rest; from that position he watched as Colette ran towards him and gave him a cursory examination, she pronounced him not badly injured and ran to Leah, she immediately shouted to someone else to help her and placed her fingers over the cut on her neck to staunch the flow of blood which even now was pulsing out as the cut Diman had made stayed open. Jim saw Pat hurry over and sink to her knees beside him, she put her arms around his shoulder, and the tears came to her eyes as she saw the damage he had sustained. "It's all right now darling." She whispered in his ear. "We'll soon have you better."

Andy came to them and began to help Jim to his feet, Pat saw what he was doing and took the other side, putting her head under his armpit. Jim looked over her shoulder and his eyes widened in surprise, she felt his body tense as he stared into the brown face of Sulim, the gunrunner. The only place he could have been hidden was down the face of the butte where they had hidden the guns all those weeks ago. Now he confronted them with a machine pistol in his hands. Andy could see by the size of the magazine that it held about fifteen shots. Quite enough to cause some serious damage if he started to fire it; he was holding it with two hands in front and looked like he meant business. Dimans' rifle was by now hanging from a strap on his shoulder.

"I want you all to stand quite still and lay down your weapons." He growled.

By now Andy had the full weight of his father dragging on his shoulder and wanted nothing more than to lay him down and be free to take some action. One of the other women must have been reading his mind as she took a step towards him and supported the other side of Jim. The movement was small but Sulim saw it and growled. "Nobody moves another step or I shoot; now lay down all your weapons and stand with your arms raised where I can see them."

After they had all reluctantly laid down the weapons, he nodded silently to himself and gestured with his pistol. "All you members of this community, who are allied with Jim, step over to that side there, and I want you." He pointed to his wives. "To go over there, out of the line of fire."

Pat asked. "What do you think you're going to do right now? You can't run this place alone and you need people here to work, but I don't think they'll volunteer to go in there with you."

Sulim smiled evilly. "If people are given the choice of living or dying they will always take living, and they will find that I can run a benevolent society as long as they do as I wish."

Pat gasped. "But that's nothing more than dictatorship." She replied angrily. "That's the one thing Jim wanted to avoid. We wanted to form a democratic society where everybody had the right to speak their mind and all of us could live peacefully together. Not some." She paused for a moment to think. "Tin pot banana republic dictatorship; where the top guy sits on his behind all day issuing useless orders."

"Shut up." The words were rapped out from Sulim's mouth, he swung his pistol in her direction and as it passed the other members of the community they cowered down as if to avoid the possibility of being shot.

The pistol swung back in the direction of two policemen who were standing passively waiting for events to happen. "You two make your minds up now, do you want to live in this community? Or do you want to take your chances outside?"

The two men glanced at each other and as one they stepped to the same side as the two women. Sulim grinned derisively. "Wise choice." He commented. The rifle swung once more in the direction of the original members of the community. "Now what do we do with you lot?" He murmured, almost to himself.

One of the policemen waved a hand in his direction. "I think you're forgetting something mate." He commented. Sulim's eyebrows rose questioningly.

The policeman gestured in the direction of his two wives. "You've got two women here and they belong to you, what do you reckon's going to happen in the future? We haven't got enough people to run this show and not enough people to breed for the future. You'll have to get some more bodies going in there or the whole shooting match is going to collapse round your ears."

Sulim glared at him for a moment, he knew the truth of what the man said but he also knew that all the women that were left must hate them violently, and the situation would only get worse in the future. "You want to take some of these women in with you?" He asked disbelievingly. "You'll never get any sleep at night, worrying whether they're going to go gunning for you after you kill their men."

The two policemen both looked shocked and turned to look at the assembled crowd a few yards away; then one took a pace towards Sulim. The gun came up threateningly, but he stopped and asked. "What do you mean, when we kill their men?"

Sulim's lip curled in contempt at these men's apparent stupidity, and lack of thought. "You don't think that if we take over this building that those people over there are just going to ride off into the sunset do you? What would you do if you were left on the outside? Do you think you could avoid taking some action to sabotage the place? I tell you, if we enter there and leave this lot outside, it'll probably be about an hour before they start destroying it."

Andy, by now, had turned a little with Jim's arm over his shoulder and he gestured to Alison who was supporting the other side to lower him to the ground. The movement though small attracted the attention of Sulim, the pistol swung once more in a small arc and rested on Andy's chest. "Be careful, sonny, I'm holding this trigger very tight and I don't want you or anybody else upsetting my concentration for the moment." The voice left Andy in no small doubt as to what would happen if they tried to rush the man.

He simply stared back and tried to assess the situation they were in, there was no doubt they all had access to weapons; but by the time they picked them up and levelled them, Sulim would have time to kill maybe three of his friends. These odds were simply unacceptable. He could only hope for something to change the situation and it seemed that if the policemen tried to take some women out of their side it would maybe create a diversion to give him a small chance of surprise.

For the moment it was stalemate and both sides eyed the other while they tried to work out their next move. Steve and Arthur; the two policemen had been thinking things over while this had happened, and now Steve commented. "One things for sure mate, if we only go in there with three men and two women, who're both your wives it won't be a very happy ship. But I don't fancy too much the idea of taking in two of these women here against their will. That'll be just looking for trouble won't it?"

They all stopped and contemplated the women who were left. They in their turn stared balefully back at them. In all there were eight women facing them, Pat, Victoria, Colette, Julia, Bev, Alison, Liz, and Leah lying injured. "Right." Sulim snarled. "Your times up. We aren't going anywhere with this unless you two get on and choose. I'm going to count up to ten and if you haven't made up your mind by then it's all over, and you do without."

He started to count slowly aloud and with an apologetic shrug to the rest of them Steve walked over and grabbed Alison, she gasped aloud as she read his intentions and tried to pull away. She resisted for a moment but he leaned over and whispered in her ear and she stopped struggling and went with him as he yanked her over to their side and stood holding her arm tightly.

After a moments hesitation Arthur went over and grabbed Bev by the hand and pulled her into their line. Sulim's lip curled. Neither of the women was pretty or even young. "So why did you pick those two?" He asked. "Neither of them would get entered into a beauty contest, even if it was held now."

Alison flared at this and snapped back at him. "You ain't got the brains to see it have you? We've both got kids and our husbands are dead, so we ain't got anything to lose have we?" She swung round and stared at Steve. "I suppose it's better than dying." she said. "But only just, if you don't treat me right mate, you'll be waking up one morning with an extra smile under your chin."

She was rewarded for this with a baleful look from Steve, who wisely said nothing. Sulim spoke, his voice full of silky menace. "Now you've made your choice, take them inside and start getting things organised in there, and if that guy they left in there gives you any bother get rid of him. There must be several children in there, don't harm any of them, but at the same time leave them in no doubt about who's in charge in there."

The two men took the two women by the arm and started to march them back towards the building, they in turn stared mutely at the rest of them left waiting there. Andy stepped forward towards Sulim. "You're not going to get away with this Sulim." He said his voice firm and disciplined.

Sulim turned his deadly black eyes towards him, his face set grimly and smiled mirthlessly. "What makes you think that? He asked. "Have you got some sort of crystal ball that you can see that far into the future."

Andy stared back, he knew it was time for the showdown and mentally girded himself for the coming task. "Simple." He said.

There are eight of us left here who are capable of fighting, and you, and we all know that you've got to kill all of us to be safe, and even then it could still go wrong, especially if those kids in there find out you killed their parents." He grinned with humour. "Kill the parents and the children will take their revenge when they can, and they have the rest of their life to wait."

If he could have, Sulim would have thrown his head back and roared with laughter, but that being out, he laughed, his shoulders heaving at some secret joke. Finally he stopped, the pistol still trained on them, he was about ten metres from them with the weapon on automatic. One squeeze of his finger and bullets would spray out. The magazine, Andy knew, held fifteen rounds but something made him look a little closer and he could see that the magazine itself was slightly longer than normal. It could probably hold twenty rounds and with one loaded that meant he potentially had twenty one shots at one time.

"I'm not going to kill any of you; I want you to do it yourselves." The words fell like icicles. There was a gasp from his captive audience, and one or two would have rushed forward there and then but the pistol remained firmly held in their direction. Andy glanced to his side to see what the reactions of his friends were and was reassured when he saw the anger on several faces. His mother Pat was tensed already, alert for the first opportunity to rush in and disarm this madman. Colette was still kneeling beside the stretcher with Leah, and although she appeared to be taking no notice of the proceedings he knew she was tensed as well. Dick and the Prof were both standing with clenched fists ready to go in at the first sign of weakness in Sulim's guard. As if he could tune into their thoughts, Sulim stepped back one or two paces to give himself another second to defend himself. Andy gauged the distance to Sulim but in his heart he knew that although it was only about ten meters, it was as far as a deep chasm. With the automatic on his pistol Sulim could easily cut down three or four of them before they reached him. That made the odds impossibly long; if they rushed him and he cut down that many, there wouldn't be enough people to run the farm. He was still running the possibilities over in his head when events took a turn, at the time he wasn't sure it was for better or worse.

Sulim gestured with the gun towards them; then he pointed to a spot about ten meters in front of himself. "I want you all to form a line there." He said, the harshness in his voice, underpinning his intentions. He waited until they had all shuffled forward and formed a rough line from left to right. Andy seethed inside, all the weapons were now out of reach and they had no chance to grab anything to defend themselves.

"Now lie down face down on the ground, with your arms behind your backs." This last order snapped out, and made matters even worse. How could they defend themselves now? Suddenly the situation took on a whole new meaning; a shot rang out sounding incredibly loud in the silence of the countryside around them. Some dust spurted up just by the side of Sulim's foot, he jumped about a foot in the air and landed with the gun at the ready in front of him, glaring wildly about. It was the diversion that Andy needed and he shouted as loudly as possible "Scatter!!" then without waiting he sprang to his feet and raced for the protection of a small depression in the ground, as he ran he noted the position of the crossbow he had been carrying and thought with regret, of stopping to pick it up. Luckily he didn't stop and just as he reached the relative safety of the cover several bullets hit the ground around him, he swerved and jinked until he dived into the hollow.

As he dived for the cover he lay for a moment panting for breath then attempted to see what the rest of his companions had done, his view to the front was hindered by the top of the hump and for the moment he didn't wish to poke his head up to investigate. To his right he could see Julia, lying in the same depression as himself, and wonders of wonders, she had a gun!! She grinned when she saw him and pointed at the gun in triumph. Another shot barked out and a spurt of dust spat sand into her face, she had raised her head a few inches and it was enough to give Sulim something to shoot at. From the noise of the shot Andy surmised he was probably only about twenty metres away. Julia faced him with her head on the ground, her ear pressed against the dirt, and Andy lowered his hand palm down to indicate to her to keep her head down. Then he called out. "Sulim, why not give up now and save further bloodshed, we've got at least two guns in action now and we'll treat you well, if you don't hurt any of us. You know we'll get you anyway, you can't fight all of us at once."

"Very funny my little blond Englishman." Sulim said, his words laced heavily with sarcasm. "But I don't think I'll live long if I do that. But I will tell you that if any of you think you can kill me with none of you injured you'll be mistaken. The first one of you to poke his head above the cover is going to get it shot off."

For answer a shot blasted out from somewhere behind Andy and he heard a muffled curse from Sulim, he raised his head quickly, just a few inches to try and assess the situation, what he saw made his blood run cold. Leah and Jim were still lying where they had been dropped, but Colette hadn't moved and was still trying to tend to them. Pat was also there but lay about five metres behind them as if she had been undecided about running for cover or staying to help Jim. Now they were in the most dangerous position of all; trapped between two opposing enemies, both of whom were armed and willing to kill. He frowned as he thought and then tried turning over to find out who was firing from the back of them. He knew that there were three men there; Martin, who surely wouldn't shoot anyone after his pacifist views were known. The other two were the policemen Sulim had told to secure the building. He didn't think that any one of them could have tried shooting Sulim without the cooperation of the others, so he had to assume they were all supporting this rebellion against their erstwhile leader. Sulim must have deduced the same as Andy because he heard scuffling from that direction and trying to get a view of events nearly got his head shot off. The gun barked once more as Sulim fired at his head just poking slightly above the hump. He was lucky as Sulim was at that moment trying to distance himself from the predicament he now found himself in.

They were on a slope that led down to the building and the ground at their point was on the lee side of a low foothill that led upwards to the butte where the camera was. If Sulim kept up his progress for another fifty metres he would be over the brow of the slope and be out of their sight for another hundred metres, he was backing up and keeping a watchful eye open for any signs of them following. Andy had no intention of following, but something made him question why he hadn't shot Colette, who had presented an easy target. He wondered in passing if Sulim had intended to let her live in case he needed medical assistance in the future.

He heard a shout from behind and Steve the ex policeman came running up from the rear of the building. He was panting a little and flopped down beside Andy who had moved over cautiously to reach Colette who was still busy tending to his father and Leah. Andy stared hard at Steve, and said. "Whose side are you really on mate? First you side with him then you change again, what the hells going on with you?"

Steve smiled ruefully and shook his head. "Look, the only way I knew to get the upper hand with him, was to pretend to go along with him. I'm surprised he swallowed it really; I suppose he thought we wanted to take over like he does. He forgot that you chose all the members here for their professions and not for how well they could fight."

The explanation satisfied Andy for the moment, but he made a mental note to keep a close watch on the two of them until he was happy with them settling in with them. At this time he needed them, and turning he glanced up and spotted Sulim with the rifle levelled in their direction. He screamed. "Dive." At the top of his voice and shoved Julia to one side just as the gun belched smoke in their direction. The bullet pinged just to one side of him, right where he had been standing a moment before. He hit the floor with a thump and quickly glanced round to see what had happened to the others. Colette was still out in the open, with the two wounded, she was trying to drag Leah back to cover with the assistance of Jim, it was an almost impossible task for her and Andy rushed out to help her. As he ran he glanced across to where Sulim was backing rapidly over the ridge to get access to the hollow. He seemed preoccupied with making progress and missed the chance of a shot at them.

As they struggled to carry the wounded back to the low ridge, which was their only cover, the rest of the team rushed over to help and within a few moments they got to the shelter provided by the fault in the ground. When they arrived, Andy glanced round to ascertain whom he had with him, and more importantly, which was able to help him. He could see four men able bodied enough to carry on with the struggle. They were, Dick, The Prof, Steve, and Arthur, who had come out to join them, with himself this made five men. He shrugged to himself, 'It's going to have to do,' He thought. They were armed with an assortment of weapons, he counted two crossbows, a Kalashnikov, his snipers rifle, although Pat seemed to have taken control of that again, and two of the machine guns. "Has everybody got ammunition for their weapons?" He asked.

Steve held his hand up and answered. "We can get some more from the store if we need it, I checked with that Martin guy when I went in with the women."

The rest of them swiftly checked and nodded in affirmation. "Right." Andy went on. "We'll have to get everybody inside and get some food and drink inside them, I want one person to stay out here and keep a look out for Sulim in case he decides to try something. Prof, I want you to do that, you can get something later."

The Prof smiled and answered. "Leave it to me." He took a quick look over to where Sulim was making his way out past the old caravans and trucks, now rusting away about five hundred metres away on the far side of the compound. "At least I can still see him." He said, and frowned; "Get down." he said urgently, and flung himself down. It wasn't a moment too soon, because no sooner than they had all got down on the dusty earth than a shot rang out and dust was blasted into the air round Andy by a high velocity round.

"Nobody move." Andy yelled. "There's more coming from him soon. He won't stop there."

Sure enough, the bullets started to bounce and ricochet around them, this went on for a few moments and then just as suddenly they stopped, as Sulim realised he was wasting ammunition. Andy thanked his lucky stars that Sulim wasn't as good a shot as Diman. "He's moving round the hill right now." The Prof said sotto voice, although with Sulim at least five hundred metres away it was probable that he couldn't hear anything they would have said even if they had shouted. Andy gritted his teeth and gave his orders. "I want everybody over to that building as quickly as possible, get in the lee side now."

For the next few minutes it was a grim slog to move Jim and

Leah over to shelter, all the while keeping a watchful eye open for any shots coming from Sulim's direction. Fortunately they managed it without mishap and they gathered together with grins of triumph for the achievement. The Prof took up a position from where he could peer round the corner at Sulim without being seen himself and waited patiently for any sign of movement. The rest of them struggled along the side of the building and went in through the hole at the rear that they had created only a short time ago, although to Andy and some of the others it seemed a lifetime.

When they entered they found Alison and Bev waiting for them along with Liz who had stayed inside to look after the children, they were standing with a tray full of drinks and Andy tore of his mask and grabbed one and gratefully sank it in one gulp. The others followed suit and then Colette took charge and ordered the stretcher-bearers to take Jim and Leah to the small hospital room. At first Jim protested that he wanted to carry on as he felt better but one look at Colette's determined face and he subsided and let them carry him to a bed. Alison spoke up and said. "We've prepared some food in the mess room; it's been repaired enough to use it for a while, and it's time you lot got some inside you, you must all be bloody starving. As if to prove the point, Andy's stomach gave the first warning growl, it was loud enough to raise a smile and they went straight to the mess room to eat. Andy gave a sigh as he sat down at the table, it had been a long day and he for one would like to see an end to the trauma they were all going through. He knew that any rest they were trying to get would be short-lived and he intended to get back out and hunt Sulim down as soon as he had eaten.

He looked over to where Sulim's two wives were sitting in a corner, with one of the older children, George; squatting on a table in front of them ready to shout a warning if they tried to move. An arm carrying a plate came across his vision and Beverly plonked the plate in front of him. "Get that down you son." She said. "They tell me you bought the bloody stuff so you can be the first to eat it. Personally I think it's a load of rubbish, and I wouldn't touch it with a bargepole but apparently until we get more established here it's going to be the main source of food hereabouts."

Andy stared down at the plate lying on the table in front of him;

it contained an unidentifiable mass that resembled nothing more than gravy with bits of vegetable floating in it. It looked disgusting and if he had had any sort of say in the matter, he would have walked straight over and dumped it in the slops bin but he glanced up and every eye in the room was watching him furtively. 'MRE.' He groaned silently to himself. Meals ready to eat, courtesy of some unnamed fighting force. 'Probably from the USA, or UK.' He thought silently to himself. 'Doesn't make it any easier to swallow.' He mused, then taking a deep breath he plunged his spoon into the gooey mess in front of him and raising it to his mouth he swallowed it on one gulp. It tasted absolutely disgusting! But he raised his head and smiled as he said. "Great, if there's any more I'll have seconds."

The rest of the company stared in amazement and a lone voice was heard from within their ranks. "If you believe that you need your head testing." It broke the silence and to a general muttering of jocularity they proceeded to start eating.

Suddenly one of the windows in the mess room shattered with terrifying noise and glass flew throughout the room, a shot was heard from a high velocity rifle a second later. For the next few moments' pandemonium reigned as some of the women screamed and everybody cowered on the floor. Finally everybody calmed down and stared fearfully at each other, the women hiding behind the upturned tables the men had thrown up as a temporary measure. Andy hissed. "Is anybody hurt?"

After a moment Dick answered. "Julia got some glass in her face."

Just at that moment footsteps sounded in the passage and Colette rushed into the room. "What's going on?" She shouted. "We heard a shot from back there."

"Get down." A chorus of voices yelled. She took in the situation at a glance and asked. "Anybody hurt here?"

Dick motioned her over and she bent to the task of examining Julia. Andy meanwhile had slithered over to the window and risked a quick glance over the cill, it was almost his last act as another shot pinged of the wood alongside his face and ricocheted into the room. Once more the sound came a second later. He knew now that they were being shot at from a distance, his mind racing now, he called out to Dick. "Dick can you get down to the end of the passage and call out to the Prof and find out this guys position, the rest of you men get hold of a gun and if he fires again try to spot the smoke from the barrel and fix a place for him. If any of you see a movement call out. Now go!"

They all scattered to do his bidding and none of them at this time questioned his right to give them orders. He felt a tap on his arm and looked round to see his mother Pat, lying next to him with his sniper rifle cradled in her arms. "Thought you might need a hand from a good shot." She smiled.

Smiling back he stretched out his arm and took the rifle out of her grasp. "How much ammo have you got for this thing then?" He asked.

She glared at him in chagrin. "What do think you're doing? I'm a good shot with that and I want to have a go at that scoundrel out there, I've got a score to settle with him."

"Maybe you have Mum, but you're needed in here, for the moment you can tend to the wounded far better than I can and that's what I want you to do."

She stared for long moments at his grim face and then in a characteristic change of mood she nodded in affirmative and reaching into her pocket she pulled out a box holding about a hundred shells, she placed them in his hands and crawled away to assist Colette.

Andy turned on to his back and keeping his head below the window cill, he called out. "Anybody see anything yet?" He glanced to both sides of himself to ascertain their answers but everybody shook their heads. He waited a minute and then heard Dick pounding along towards them, he stopped outside the door and bending down he scuttled over to Andy. "Prof says he's about five hundred metres out to the right and he's hunkered himself down behind some scrub there. Andy knew exactly where he was as he had done the same thing himself previously when he had been struggling for survival. He would be almost to the top of the headland and looking down on them with a perfect view of the whole building, and with the rifle he had he would be able to pick them off with ease. Andy knew he was lucky to be still unwounded; Sulim must have taken a quick shot at him when he had poked his head up for a look. If he had taken the time to aim better, Andy would have been hit.

He raised his voice and called out. "I want all the men here to come with me, we've got to go out and finish this off for the last time."

"What are you going to do?" The voice came from Liz. She and her husband had displayed a streak of pacifism when they had had to defend the building and now it was coming to the fore once more.

Andy sighed and looked at her lying on the floor next to her husband; neither had any weapons, and stayed as much out of sight as possible. He knew deep within his bones that they were never going to accept what he said but he said it anyway. "We're going out there to kill him."

The reaction from them was all that he had expected, they started to get up together and protest at his reply, another shot came through the window as Sulim saw some slight movement. This time the bullet ploughed into the floor, just by Liz's foot and she slumped back to the floor drawing in she curled into a foetal ball and moaned. "Oh God, make all this go away."

Andy's lip curled and he would have replied sarcastically had Pat not taken it out of his hands. "Shut you're moaning mouths, and think about these men going out there risking their lives to save your skin. Now get down to the hospital and make yourselves useful by tending to the wounded."

Her words had the desired affect and they both crawled out of the door shamefacedly. Pat turned to the rest of the company and said. "Is there anybody else who thinks we have to try and pacify this man?"

They all shook their heads and Dick said. "We might as well get started then."

"No." The word came out like a bullet from a gun. "I don't want anybody going out there except me." It was Andy speaking with the voice of authority. "I don't want anybody risking their lives any more to defend this place, I'm going out there on my own and I'll take him out myself."

"But." Several of them started to say, Andy held up his hands to stop them going any further. "That's an end to all the arguments, there's only one man out there, and." His lips curled in a small grin. "He's not that great a shot anyway."

Pat raised her head with an appalled expression on her face. "Why does it have to be you?" She asked plaintively. She had seen her husband almost die and now in the worst situation that can happen to a woman, her son was volunteering to go and face death to save them all.

Andy faced her, his face grim, he knew that as with all women she couldn't bear the thought that she might lose him. But something stronger drove him to do what he thought was right. "Mum, we can't afford to lose any more people; he's only one man and if I'm careful nothing's going to happen, trust me."

As if to emphasise his words, another shot tore into the room, this time they all exited as fast as possible and gathered in the corridor outside. Andy thought regretfully of the food he had left on the table, but put it aside to concentrate his mind on the task ahead. "Right." He snapped. "I want food and ammunition enough to see this job out, and first of all I want an update on his position, we'll have to create a diversion when I go out so I want you Dick, and Steve and Arthur." He indicated them as he spoke. "To get in position in the mess room and start firing on my command and I'll get out the back and up the hill towards the windmill. When I'm gone I want someone to keep an eye open for any movement in that direction. You must preserve the windmill at all costs as it's our source of power in the future, and if he can this guy is going to try and shut it down, everybody understand?"

He got the replies he was expecting and nodding silently to himself he started to prepare. For a short while the place was a hive of activity as everybody chipped in to equip him for the task ahead. Finally he was ready, with a pack of provisions and ammunition on his back. He had the crossbow hung from a strap over his shoulders, with a quiver full of bolts. The sniper rifle he held in his arms for instant use, and a bandolier of ammunition hung round his shoulders. They had arranged for two of the children to run between the Prof and themselves to keep up to date with any movement from Sulim, he had been quiet for an hour now and Andy suspected he was probably busy changing his position. He wondered for the umpteenth time why he would want to try and destroy their community rather than join it but could find no sensible reason for the man's actions. He knew he would have to go back up the hill towards the windmill, as it was the logical place for anyone to go to if they wanted to cause any hardship to the community. He looked round and his eyes widened as he saw Victoria marching towards him with a rifle in her arms and dressed to go outside. "I'm going with you." She said determinedly.

He shook his head and snarled. "I don't have time for this, take all that rubbish off and get back to guarding this building; I don't want to be looking out for you while I'm running around out there."

She stared at his face for long moments and he noticed that she was doing something he had never before seen her do, she normally acted quiet and compliant with his wishes, but this time her eyes started to flare and her whole demeanour changed. Finally she leaned forward and poked him in the chest with a long slim finger. "Don't try and tell me what to do, it wasn't me that went out without telling anybody and nearly got myself killed, and, had to be rescued. That was you, and you made a complete mess of that, so don't you try and set yourself up as the saviour of these people."

Andy was visibly taken aback at this attack on him, especially from his wife. He would have taken the matter up with her right then and there but events were suddenly taken out of his hands, one of the children set up as runners came in and said excitedly. "Prof says he's spotted that man on the move and he's heading back out to the windmill, he's on the east side of the building and he'll get there in about ten minutes at his rate of walking."

Andy stiffened and swirled round to run to the door shouting to the company to close all exits after he left. He ran along the passage and out into the main growing area, he crossed this at a busy pace and when he arrived at the hole in the wall at the back to go out, he found Victoria standing there with a defiant look on her face. She was dressed similarly to him and carried a crossbow and bolts and one of the smallest arms they had, a sub machine gun with a pack weighing down her side carrying he supposed, some ammunition for the gun. His face set and mouth closed in a grim line he bore down on her ready to give her a dressing down. He opened his mouth to snap at her and stop her from going outside but she forestalled him from this course of action by holding her hand up and saying. "You can stop me from going outside to help you if you want, but I'll still be coming out anyway, I'm not letting you try and get yourself killed without me there to help prevent it."

He would have stopped her even then but something told him that this time he would lose and if she decided to come after him without his knowledge they might get into further trouble. It had to be an instant decision and he made what he thought was the right one. He nodded his head and said forcefully; "You stay near me at all times and don't try anything without my say so."

She looked at him sombrely for a moment then smiled her acquiescence. "Promise." She said. "I leave all the orders to you."

"Humph." Andy grunted. "Make sure you do, the last thing I want to do is try and protect you while I'm trying to kill Sulim."

She frowned. "You're really going out there to kill him?"

A dry voice came from behind them. "What would you have him do darling? If he doesn't die, he's going to try and kill all of us."

They both turned to find Pat standing behind them; to both their surprised faces she was dressed in the same way as themselves; in combat gear and armed to the teeth with a Kalashnikov and a large dagger on her hip, a bandolier of ammunition completed the ensemble. Andy groaned, this was the last thing he wanted, to have two women running around like loose cannon, but the real problem as far as he was concerned, was that he had no way of stopping them coming out. He stood contemplating them for a minute, and then said. "I don't have time for this, and you two should stay here and help in case I don't get him. I don't want to have to go round looking out for you and trying to stop you getting into trouble."

The two women looked at each other and smirked, then Pat said. "We shouldn't have to remind you, but as far as we remember, it was you that got into trouble last time and nearly got yourself killed."

Andy groaned inwardly, he didn't need reminding again of what he had done before, but in their way they were right, he had made a fool of himself last time by going out on his own and getting captured. Raising a shaking finger he pointed at them and ground out through gritted teeth. "I might have made one mistake here but it's not going to happen again; now I'm going out there and I'm going to kill that bastard, because if I don't he'll be the death of all of us, if either of you two get in my way you'll be the ones to suffer. Are you clear on that?"

He waited till he got the answer he wanted from them both and as they nodded their agreement he turned abruptly and would have exited through the hole in the wall but found Julia standing there with a package in her hands. "I've made some food up for you, I know you haven't eaten, and a bottle of something to wash it down."

Andy wanted to shove her to one side so as to get on with the job in hand but Victoria stepped forward and with a smile of thanks she took the package from her and thrust it into her bag hanging on her side. Andy said nothing and after a moments hesitation he pulled his dust mask down tight over his mouth and nostrils and scrambled through the hole, Julia stepped forward and hugged both the women, with tears brimming behind her eyelids she mumbled. "Come back soon and good luck."

The two women tried to smile through their tears and then followed Andy through the hole pulling their masks down over their mouths as they went. They arrived in a world totally different from the one they were accustomed to. The air was thick with dust that would have choked them and destroyed their lungs in a few minutes if they breathed it in and although they knew the sun was in the ascendant it was impossible to tell from the amount of light they received from it. The day was as gloomy as the darkest day in winter and they knew that it wouldn't get any brighter for some years to come. A chill wind blew past them as they came outside and involuntarily they all shivered. Andy looked up at the rising ground facing them and could see no movement anywhere; he hadn't really expected to, but mentally he shrugged and thought it would have been nice to have spotted Sulim straight away. He looked over his shoulder and muttered to the other two. "Ready?"

He received a muffled response from the both of them and then turned and started to walk up the rising ground, he heard a hissed shout to stop and swivelled round to see the Prof had poked his head out of the hole in the wall. "Last I saw of him he was up on your left about five hundred metres away on the ridge." the Prof called.

Andy waved in response and turning he took a few paces in the direction indicated. Suddenly he felt a tug on his shoulder and a bullet spanged off the wall behind him, followed a second later by the sound of a shot. He dived for the floor and tucked himself in behind a small ridge of rough ground left over from the building work at the same time as yelling to the women. "Get down and take cover."

When he was on the ground he glanced quickly round to check them and the small movement must have been visible from Sulim's viewpoint as another bullet smacked into the ground just to the side of his head spattering a stinging shower of sand and gravel into his face. He pulled his head down and this time checked cautiously if they were OK. He was rewarded with the sight of them staring at him wild eyed and scared and hugging the ground as if they were expecting it to open up and let them cower down even further. Something about their attitude made him start smiling and he almost laughed out loud at the predicament they were in. They had no sooner started to hunt Sulim, than he was on their trail and worse still he knew exactly where they were.

He heard a hoarse whisper from Pat. "He's using that bloody sniper rifle isn't he?"

The question must have been rhetorical as she had been there when Sulim had taken it. Victoria was plainly angry and said venomously. "You'd better wipe that smirk of your face and start to figure a way out of this or you could end up either dead or divorced."

This sobered him up and turning he inspected the ground before him as best he could. Another bullet flung up sand in his face and he whispered without turning round. "He's zeroed in on us, we've got to get out of here before he hits one of us. First can either of you spot where he is? And can either of you move without exposing yourself?" He felt movement behind him but no sound so he snapped. "Don't shake you're head, answer loud and clear."

He got a chorus of 'no's' for an answer and shook his head in anger, he tried to raise his head a few inches to give him a view and nearly got it shot off for his trouble. Inwardly he was seething, to be pinned down now and they had barely left the building. He also knew that with the rifle Sulim had, and especially the sights, he could take them out easily even though the range was at least five hundred metres. As he cast around for a plan to get them out of this difficulty he heard from behind a voice whisper. "We've got someone going out of the front to try and draw his fire or disturb him, when you hear shots and I give the word make a break for it."

Andy wasted no time waiting and said over his shoulder. "You heard the man, when I move you two get up and follow me, and run like hell! Understand?"

Pat asked plaintively. "Where are you going to run?"

"Don't worry about that for the moment." He snapped. "Just follow me."

The wait seemed interminable and Sulim was plainly bored as he loosed off a couple of shots to let them know he was still out there. Finally, after what seemed like hours but was probably only a few minutes, they heard a shot. It came from the front of the building but there was no shout from the Prof, at last they heard a whispered message. "They can't see him from there so they want you to draw his fire to give them a chance to spot his muzzle flash."

Andy grinned to himself at the black humour in the remark and turning slightly he said. "Does either of you two want to get out there and draw his fire?"

The pair of them stared back at him expressionlessly, neither moving a muscle. He sighed to himself and cast about for something to use, his eyes settled on a small piece of batten, discarded when they had finished the building, it was about a metre long and he reached out gingerly to take hold of it. He intended to use it to fix a piece of rag to it and wave it gently to encourage Sulim to shoot at it, but inadvertently he raised himself from the earth to reach and presented Sulim with a shot. It was taken! He felt the pain like a blow to the shoulder and it knocked him flying back. He became aware of Victoria screaming in shock and that Pat had turned to come and tend to him. They had both moved and now presented targets for Sulim who loosed off a volley of bullets in their direction. "Get down you stupid idiots!!!" He roared.

Luckily, Sulim had had no experience of sniping and so hurried his shots, and in doing so he missed with them all. Both the women now cowered down and Andy bent to examine the damage caused by the bullet. He groaned when he saw it, the bullet had hit him in the upper arm and feeling it tenderly he felt the bone move, the pain shot up his arm and he had to grit his teeth to stop himself from crying out in pain. He could hear shots coming from the front of the building and realised that for the moment they knew nothing of what had happened here at the back, and the two women were still staring back at him wondering what to do.

He made up his mind in an instant and then had to make the hardest decision in his life, he knew without doubt that he had a broken arm and would be no more use in this fight or at least for the next hour or so, even if he managed to convince Colette to patch him up and let him go out again. "There's nothing for it but for you to call out Dick and those two policemen, to try for him, and you'd better be quick about it or you'll lose the advantage of the diversion those lot at the front are getting for you."

The two women looked at him with eyes wide and an astounded look came over Pat's face. "Have you gone out of your mind?" She asked sarcastically. Look behind you, there's probably thirty metres of open ground there, that's why you collected that bullet if you remember. If we all start scuttling back and forth over it don't you think he might catch on to what we're doing?"

She turned decisively to Victoria. "Are you up for it dear?" She asked affectionately. As if she were asking her to go down to the local supermarket. Victoria nodded her face grim.

"Let's do it." She said. The two women stared at each other for a heartbeat of time. Then without a word to Andy they both turned and crawled off along the remains of a gully that offered a little protection from above. He raised his hand to say farewell but all he could see was the back of their heads as he crawled away. There was no fire from Sulim and Andy was left to his own devices for a while until he heard some rifle fire from the direction of the front of the building. He lay for a moment contemplating the events that had brought him here and then with a sigh he turned to crawl back to the hole in the rear of the building. As he turned he caught a movement out of the side of his eye and two figures thumped down alongside him, he turned and saw it was Dick and Colette. She had her medical bag with her and he was dressed ready for action, carrying a rifle and pistol with bandoliers of ammunition over his shoulder. Dick was also carrying a bag, which Andy surmised contained some food.

"What's going on?" Colette snapped, he voice betraying the anxiety she felt, her eyes shifted downward to take in the bloodstained sleeve on his coverall, and widened in astonishment. "What's happened to you?" she said next. "Can't you do anything without getting yourself hurt?" It was a rhetorical question as she didn't wait for an answer but reached out to touch him on the arm. Andy shifted painfully under her probing fingers, and gasped. "Take it easy, Sis. That's hurting enough without you making it worse."

"Where's Mum and Victoria." She asked, taking no notice of what he had said. "Don't ask." He answered. "They've gone off on their own, Christ knows what'll happen now, they haven't got the first idea of how to deal with this. Ouch! Take it easy." She had touched a raw spot on his arm and he winced as she tore his sleeve to get to the wound more easily. She glanced over her shoulder at Dick, who was hovering close by. "You'd better get after those two women before they come to any harm. And look out for yourself as well; he's got an advantage at the moment because we don't know exactly where he is."

"You going to be alright here with him?" Dick asked.

"I am here you know." Andy said sarcastically. "So there's no need to speak as if I'm not."

Dick's gaze settled on Andy's arm and he said equally sarcastically. "My, my, aren't you the one for getting into trouble, this is the second time I've had to bail you out, becoming quite a habit of yours isn't it? Getting yourself into fixes."

Andy would at that moment willingly punched him on the nose, but there was no way he could lift his arm for the effort. Instead he contented himself with saying. "Watch out for yourself, that guys toting that sniper rifle around and you know how accurate it is, especially at long range." As if to emphasise the point, a shot rang out from the top of the ridge and they could hear muffled curses from the two women about fifty metres away. Dick had stiffened when he heard the shot; he knew that in combat there is no knowing if you will be in the sights of the gunman or not.

Andy grinned from the cover of his prone position. "Don't worry Dick." He said sarcastically. "They say you never hear the one that gets you."

Dick threw himself down for a moment and looked pointedly at Andy's arm. "Did you hear that one mate or were you trying to collect enough lead to start a scrap yard?"

"Oh, very funny." Andy retorted. He would have said more but Colette had had enough. "If you two don't stop this bickering, I'm going to go out there and hunt that man myself." She snapped. Andy winced as she unconsciously pressed his arm while she said it.

"Maybe you'd better get a start Dick, before she really does do it." He commented, the apology for his sarcasm clear in his tone of voice.

Dick looked at him seriously for a few seconds and then nodded his head grimly, and blew a kiss at his wife who was still tending Andy. "See you soon Luv." he said. And would have gone if she hadn't clasped him to herself for a moment. "You'd better get back here in one piece, because if you don't I'll never forgive you." She answered, her voice betraying the emotion she felt.

They were interrupted by a shot followed by some cursing from the two women and raising his head in alarm Dick said. "I'd better get out there, something's happening."

He hugged her back momentarily and then wriggled off after the two women. Colette turned back to her brother and looked dispassionately at his arm. "If anything happens to him, I'm never going to forgive you, you know that don't you?"

She bent over him as she tended to the wound in his arm. He looked at her sympathetically as she did so and noticed she had tears in the corners of her eyes. Raising his other hand he poked her on the arm and then pressed gently to show her he cared, his face showing his concern. This from Andy the big macho man, who never showed his feelings, was a major breakthrough and she stored it away in the further reaches of her brain for analysis later, because she had never known him to display any such emotion before. He for his part felt only affection for his big sister and wanted everything to turn out right for her. He winced once more as she moved his broken bones to try and set them in a better manner, and said. "Don't you think we'll be better inside in the hospital, than trying to do it out here?"

She nodded and turning she called out softly to the survivors inside to come out and help her carry him in.

Chapter Five

Victoria turned to Pat alongside her and whispered. "Where do you think he is? I hate all this creeping about, hoping we'll see whoever it is we're trying to catch."

"Don't get too het up about that dearie." Pat replied. "Keep your eyes peeled and tell me if you see the slightest sign of movement. And never forget, if you don't keep your wits about you it could be you he shoots." She pointed up the slope towards the windmill, and went on. "See that slight hollow along the crest of the hill." She waited until she had a nod from Victoria. "Well don't go across that ground at all, because Andy laid some Claymores when we were last up there, they were meant for something else but it didn't work and I think they're still there."

She glanced round to see if the information had sunk in and was met with a blank look from her companion. "You don't know what I'm talking about do you?" she asked.

Victoria shook her head and Pat sighed, and gave a shake of her head sorrowfully. "They're land mines dearie so stay clear of that area, do you understand now?"

Victoria's brow furrowed. "But I thought they were illegal now." She said.

It was Pat's turn to respond, she made a show of looking round their surroundings. And then said. "Do you see anybody in authority around here to come along with a piece of paper and take us into court? Now listen to this, we're out here all on our own, if we let him, that man out there is going to try and kill us, if he steps on one do you think I'll worry one jot about whether it's legal or not. This is life or death here and if we don't kill him he's definitely going to kill us. Do you get the point?"

Victoria smiled in embarrassment. "OK Pat I think you've made your point, but had you thought about disarming them when the main battle was over?"

"Already thought about." Pat was happy to say. "In fact if this hadn't all blown up, it was going to be our first job before 'battening down the hatches', so to speak."

She raised a cautious eye above the surrounding gully to try and find a route out of the hollow they were in. She had been out here a few times when they were constructing the main building, but it all looked a lot different from the point of view she had now. At first glance she could see no way out but then she spied a small trench that had been probably dug for exploration purposes when they had surveyed the ground. It was small but she figured that if they kept all parts of their anatomy down they might be able to crawl up it. The trench ran for possibly fifty yards up the slope and was about eighteen inches deep. It culminated in a natural gully with a few scrubby shrubs round it; they were leafless and withered but should provide a modicum of cover if they could get there.

She turned to tell Victoria the plan that had started to form in the back of her brain and was surprised to see Dick making his way towards them, snaking along on his belly. He reached them a few minutes later and asked. "What happened just now, when that shot came, we could hear you cursing?"

The two women glanced at each other and smirked guiltily, and then Victoria pointed to her side, which had a damp patch on it. Pat had a similar patch on her other side. "He got the water bottle when I turned over and exposed it; we both got soaked and surprised at the same time." Victoria giggled nervously.

Dick closed his eyes in despair at their apparent lack of concern. "If you two had only stopped to think, you might have thought how close you came to being dead." He exclaimed, his voice rising as his anger at their apparent stupidity took hold. "Don't you know the danger you're in? That rifle he's got there can kill you easily at 1000 metres. And with the sights he's got, he can zero in on you from practically anywhere he likes. The only reason he missed is because he's been hurrying his shots, but he's going to catch on pretty damn quick soon, and he'll take his time, and that's when he's going to get you. Now smarten up and stop treating it like some big adventure, or you're going to get yourself killed."

The two women stared back at him in amazement, he hardly ever raised his voice to anyone, preferring the easy life, but this man was now a different person. Then as suddenly as it had started his anger subsided and he smiled at them. He beamed and said briskly. "Right, rollicking over, have you got a plan at all? Or are you planning on lying out here for the next few hours." His eyes started to roam over the surrounding terrain and he grimaced. "There isn't much cover out here is there."

As if on cue a shot rang out and a bullet dug into the earth, inches from where he lay in the small depression. He wriggled as if trying to sink into the hard packed earth a few more life saving inches. Pat pointed to the gully she could see and said hesitantly, as if expecting to be told off. "That's the only way forward we can see from here and it ends in that scrub over there, it's not much cover though, the branches are all bare."

Dick looked in the direction she indicated and nodded. "He knows exactly where we are for the moment." He answered. "If we could get over there without him seeing us, it'll worry him and that's what we need for the time being. Then he won't be sitting there waiting for us to put our heads up for him to take pot shots and after a little while he'll start thinking we could be anywhere. So let's try to get up there slow and easy, keeping our heads down the whole way."

He waited for them to agree and then wriggled off along the gully. For the next hour the only sound was panting and the scrabble of their bodies over the earth as they painfully pulled themselves with hands and elbows towards the meagre cover of the scrub. When they finally pulled themselves in to the scrub the found the gully underneath was deep enough to allow them to squat without being seen. Victoria tried to put her head over the lip to spy out the ground but before she moved too much, Dick put a restraining hand on her arm and shook his head. "Hold on for a minute." He whispered. "He doesn't know we're here yet, so let's keep it that way for a while."

He reached into the bag on his side and produced a bottle of water which he then opened and handed to Pat. "Take just a swig." He said. "We don't know how long we're going to be out here without any supplies."

Pat nodded and taking of her mask she took a sip of the water and handed it to Victoria, who did the same. She in her turn gave him the bottle back and he took a small sip before placing it back in his bag. He glanced in the direction of Sulim and said conversationally. "He hasn't got any supplies with him, so he'll be getting hungry and thirsty about now."

Victoria sniffed. "Much good that'll do us." She answered.

"Don't dismiss it too quickly." Dick snapped. "It makes a big difference to your moral, no food and drink makes you edgy and liable to make mistakes."

He reached into his pocket and brought out a small pair of binoculars, then taking off his bush hat he slithered over to the edge of the gully and cautiously peered through the shrubs. What he saw depressed him even further, he couldn't see a thing! There was no movement or any sign of their quarry. He put the binoculars down and shook his head sadly, then turned his head and found Pat regarding him with amused eyes. "You didn't really expect him to be in full view did you?" She asked sarcastically.

He shrugged his shoulders. "You never know your luck, do you?" He commented wryly.

He rolled over, the better to see them and said. "I've got something to say now and I want you two to listen to this carefully." He pointed up the slope behind them and went on. "This guy up there has been pretty quiet for the last hour, now that suggests one thing to me, and that is, he doesn't know where we are. So now he's getting really worried."

The two women glanced at each other and rolled their eyes, it was plain to see that they both were thinking, 'Here he goes again, macho man telling us what to do'.

Dick shook his head in despair and said sorrowfully. "I think you should listen to what I say, I might not have been in the army like your precious Andy." He ignored the look they both gave him and went on. "But I read a lot of books and play a lot of games on the computer. Now I know that's not going to put me in a position to dictate to you but I do know something about what goes on in combat. Right: -" He pointed once more up the slope. "This guy is an amateur and doesn't know how to fight, and I want you to listen to this because it can help us to win. The first thing a sniper should know is when to move position, now most good snipers stay in the same position until the last minute. But right now I can feel he's not sure where we are. He knows we're somewhere out here but he isn't certain just where we are. And he's probably thinking we're trying to outflank him so he'll also be worried that just maybe we've managed to do just that. And don't forget some of the others could have come from the front of the building and right now they could be working their way round to get behind him. That makes me think he's going to move soon and try for the one place around here that gives him a good field of vision."

Both women involuntarily looked over his shoulder towards the top of the hill where the windmill stood, its long blades whirling through the air, making a strange whump, whump sound as they spun round. He grinned when he saw they had both solved the problem for themselves. Then he saw both their faces, the first shadow of doubt cast its spell, and registered in his brain. "What's up?" He asked, his mind racing, wondering what the problem was. At least half a dozen different scenarios crossed his mind, but the answer when it came completely threw him.

Pat took a deep breath and answered for both the women. "When we were out here fighting before, Andy sowed some claymores up on that ridge, and: - er, they're still up there."

"What." Dick was flabbergasted. "What the hell was he thinking of, and come to that why the hell are they still up there? Why didn't somebody think to say, or, or, dig them up?"

He scratched his head turning the possibilities over in his mind. Pat in her turn shrugged, and looked disconsolate. "We haven't had the chance to take them out yet." She said despairingly. Her face brightened and she went on. "And anyway." She said defensively. "When we put them down, we had quite a lot of enemies out here, and if you take a good look round, you might notice that there aren't any police out here to protect us from these killers, so we had to take care of ourselves. In any way we could." She finished with a determined voice.

Dick contemplated his feet for a few minutes whilst trying to work out the best way to deal with this situation, then slowly raising his head he said. "What if we could use those mines to get a solution to our problem?"

Pat smiled, her eyes lighting up, as she knew that she had won an important point. "Now you're thinking on the right lines." She said, and went on almost apologetically. "I realise that they're a terrible solution but in our situation we don't have much choice but to use them."

"Yeah, I agree." Dick answered. "And when this is all over we can destroy them and ban any mention of them in the future, but for now this guy is going to kill us if he can and we have to win in any way possible."

Victoria piped up and asked. "How do you mean, use them to get a solution to our problems?"

"We've got to draw him into crossing the top of the hill there by the windmill and go through that gully." Dick answered. He scratched his head and said doubtfully. "But the only thing is that I haven't figured out a way of making him follow us through there yet. The main problem is that he's up there to there to the west, and the windmill is north. So he's got to come down the slope and then back up to go across the gully, that means we've got to expose ourselves and risk him shooting us to draw him down. But it'd be in his best interest to stay where he is."

They all peered up the slope in front of them, what they saw didn't give them much encouragement, it was almost barren with a few remains of shrubs scattered like dry twigs across it. There was hardly any cover and all of them knew that it would be the easiest shot in the world to hit them if they exposed themselves out there.

While Dick was casting about in his head for some alternative way out of their problem, Victoria asked. "How long till its dark?"

Dick spun round and looked at her appalled. "I hope you're not thinking of swanning around out here in the dark?" he asked darkly. "It'll be so black you won't be able to see your hand in front of your face."

"I know that." Was Victoria's scathing response. "But we've gone and got ourselves into a hole here and now we've got to get out without being shot at."

"Maybe I can help you with that." A strange voice said behind them.

As one, they all spun round to see that their worst fears were about to be realised. It was Sulim!

"What the……f."Dick couldn't repress the expletive. His mind raced and came up with the obvious conclusion. All the time they had been crawling painfully up the gully, Sulim had taken the initiative and sprinted round the top of the hill behind the windmill and come down behind them. That was the reason that The Prof and the others had not been able to spot him. Now he had managed to turn the tables on them with one easy move.

Sulim gestured with the rifle he was pointing directly at them, its meaning was obvious. To drop all their weapons. They complied slowly, piling them all on the ground in front of them. "And all the little extra things that you have hidden about, in your pockets and tucked down your trousers please." The command came brusquely with another wave of the gun. "We don't want you springing any surprises if my guard drops for a moment, do we?"

Another little pile of pistols and knives joined the rifles lying in front of them. "Is that all?" He finally asked roughly, when they stopped adding things to the pile. They were still lying prone on the ground and when they nodded, he strode forward and inspected the armoury he had suddenly acquired. He raised an eyebrow when he saw Victoria's crossbow but refrained from commenting on it. He looked up suddenly and frowned, then bent down and inspected her leg, then slowly touched a bulge at the bottom near the ankle. "And what have we got here?" He sneered. "Did you think to hold out on me?"

Victoria blushed, and bent forward to retrieve a small two barrelled derringer pistol, it fitted into the palm of the hand and the fingers could be closed over it easily. She handed it to him and he smiled malevolently. "A bullet this size is only useful to distract somebody, you know that don't you?"

She shrugged. "If you think so." She answered. "But I have been told that if it hits in the right place, it's capable of killing a person."

He stared down at the pistol for a moment and then leaning forward he held it about one inch from her eye with his finger curled round the trigger. "Right about there, that should do the trick." He whispered harshly. "Right where you would do it to me if you had the chance.

Victoria had little choice but to stare at the barrel of the gun

The Survivalists, Book 2, **The Finale**

and hope against hope he didn't pull the trigger, the blood drained from her face as she contemplated what would happen if he fired. Finally he stood back and pushed it into this pocket. With another gesture of the gun he waved them back from the pile of arms and then picked up the Kalashnikov which Pat had laid down. He also picked up the ammunition she had brought with her. When he had ascertained that the gun was in good working order he laid down the sniper rifle he had been using and grinning at them, he said. "Good job I managed to get hold of this little store, I was just about out of ammo."

Dick glanced over to Pat and Victoria, the look on their faces told its own story, all that hard work trying to get to him and they could possibly have rushed him! Sulim grinned again when he saw it and went on. "Right, let's get going then, stand up and walk up there." He pointed behind them up to the slope by the windmill; Dick stood and turned in despair. The way they were going now led directly to the claymores. The other two women stood as well, and began to trudge up the hill. All of them knew that to walk over the crest by the gully meant walking to their deaths. Dick tried to divert them from the course set by Sulim by walking slightly diagonally to the right but was soon brought back to the trail set by Sulim who snarled. "Not that way, up there to the windmill."

Up to now Dick had been worried about the claymores but a thought stuck him as he walked as slowly as possible in the direction indicated. "Why hasn't he killed us?" He murmured as low as possible to the two women. Pat raised her head and looked disbelievingly at him. "You don't know?She whispered. "Think about it"

She was stopped from saying any more by a command from Sulim, he hadn't heard what had been said, but knew they had spoken. "Next one to speak gets a bullet in the back." Dick glanced over his shoulder and was almost amused to see Sulim struggling under the load he had picked up, he had most of the weapons and their food bags over one arm and the Kalashnikov in the other. Pat's words still echoed through his mind and he pondered her remark until it hit him! He would probably kill Dick as he was a potential source of trouble, but women were different, they would be very useful in a new world which was underpopulated, he might have some difficulty in controlling them but without men around they could be more easily forced to comply with his wishes.

He heard some noise from behind and an oath, so looked around to see that Pat had stumbled over a stone and had landed on her knees, without thinking he turned and went to offer her a hand up. A shouted command from Sulim stopped him in his tracks and he had to wait until she had regained her footing, she took another step and immediately fell over again. This time he managed to get to her side and help her up, Sulim shouted angrily and waved the gun at him to tell him to get back in the front and walk over the brow of the hill, by now about 100 metres in front of them. He heard a whispered order from Pat at the same time. "When I say 'break' run as fast as you can to the left."

She patted herself down and whispered fiercely to Victoria. "You go to the right." Victoria showed an impassive face to her and turned round to carry on walking up the hill. Dick, by now, understood what Pat's plan was and knew it was decidedly risky, he also knew that anything was better than to walk meekly over the hill and get shot in the back. He walked on, his mind in a turmoil as they slowly approached the high point of the hill. By now they could hear the thump of the windmill on its unceasing journey round and round. He wondered what it would feel like to be hit by a bullet but the only thing he remembered was somebody saying it was like a good whack, but infinitely more painful. He also knew that now Sulim had a Kalashnikov, and that was a far better weapon for close encounters, and from the look of this, the encounter would be very close indeed. They were coming up to the brow of the hill now and the distance was probably no more than fifty metres, Dick stole a look at Pat but got no response from her as she trudged along just behind him. Victoria on the other side kept her head down and just walked, he put his own head down and carried on putting one foot in front of the other, pacing slowly to try and lull Sulim into thinking they had no thought of escape in their minds. He mentally counted how many metres it was to the top and hit the twenty mark and then ten, now his head was level with the top of the gully where the mines had been laid and he scanned along quickly to see if he could see any sign of them. There were lots of footprints in the sandy soil but not a glimpse of anything that looked like a buried mine, no humps or bumps in the level of the soil.

"Halt!" the command rang out from Sulim. They all stopped their movement and waited for him to say something. He went on. "I want you three to bunch up a little closer in a straight line now" They obeyed his command and bunched slightly together, still with their backs to him. And then he said. "Right now, I want you to walk forward slowly over the brow of this hill."

Dick gasped and swung round to face their tormentor, he had no need to say anything as the look on Sulim's face said it all. He knew about the mines! He was grinning from ear to ear in triumph. "I knew it, just where I predicted they'd be, you lot never thought once that I sold the mines to your little blond boy, and when we couldn't find any in the building we knew you'd laid them somewhere out here, and when we were fighting before, you laid them then, didn't it ever occur to you that we didn't follow you through that gully when we came over the top of the hill?"

He gestured with the rifle. "Now get on and walk through that gully or get a bullet in the back."

The command rapped out loud and clear. "Break."

For a long full second, Dick hesitated; it was almost to cost him his life as Sulim levelled the Kalashnikov in his direction and pulled the trigger. Nothing happened! And Dick took off like the proverbial scalded cat. He neither looked right or left but just ran for his life in the direction of the windmill, he jinked to his right and then immediately to his left; trying to spoil any aim Sulim was trying to take. He kept on dodging in his headlong flight and finally he heard a shot and felt the wind of a bullet whip past on his right, he thought correctly that Sulim must have had the safety catch on the Kalashnikov and it must have taken several life saving seconds for him to adjust and flip it off. But now it was off and he had it on automatic so the bullets came thick and fast. Luckily for Dick he was firing from the hip in classic western film stance and from there it was impossible to aim properly, and so the shots went wild.

After what seemed like a lifetime he reached the relative safety of the windmill and dodged round the side and fell to his stomach panting for breath. By now Sulim had turned his attentions to the other two and Dick squirmed round to see what had happened. He saw that the other two had done exactly as they had planned, except Pat had come off worst. She cried out in pain and sprawled about twenty metres in front of Sulim. She had tried to jump the claymores directly in front of herself, and had been successful but it had taken two vital seconds too long and he had caught her in the leg with a shot. Of Victoria there was no sign, and Dick breathed a sigh of relief, it was short lived though, as he saw to his horror that Sulim was headed directly for him, reloading the rifle as he did.

He had dropped the rest of the weapons on the floor to do so but they were completely out of Dick's reach behind Sulim. He glanced quickly round over his shoulder and was unsurprised to see there was no cover for at least fifty metres and even then it was only a few sparse shrubs. 'No chance of making it to there' he thought wryly to himself. He knew that the reason Sulim was headed for him was because he was male and probably posed the greatest threat. The windmill offered scant protection as it was one of the modern types which was round and tapered, he thought wildly of what he should do and decided to try and sneak round the other side from Sulim, and attempt to rush over to retrieve a gun of some sort from the pile that lay by the gully. It was a long shot at the best of times especially as Sulim would expect him to try and do something of the sort anyway.

He poked his head back out once more and several bullets spanged of the side of the windmill inches from his nose. He withdrew his head far quicker than he had poked it out and scrambled back down the slope a little to the other side of the tower. He stopped halfway down and considered his plan, if he went right round to the other side he guessed that Sulim would be waiting for him there, but if he went back the same way he could be caught by him anyway. Whatever he did would have to be in the next few seconds and the wrong move would end up with him dead. He listened carefully for footsteps or anything to give him a clue as to what Sulim was doing but heard nothing.

He decided to rush out and attack Sulim with bare hands, so his heart in his mouth he took a deep breath and ran forward screaming

The Survivalists, Book 2, **The Finale**

to unsettle him. And Sulim was nowhere to be seen! He was just in time to see Victoria rush past him with a surprised look on her face at his appearance; she ignored him and carried on with her run. She was carrying a knife in her hand! He had a split second's thought, 'Where did she get it?' Then he turned and could see that Sulim had taken the obvious route to try and catch him, he was slightly down slope and was at that moment spinning round to try and level his gun at Victoria.

From this moment on it was as if everything went into slow motion, Dick began to dash forward as he watched the two of them approaching each other, Sulim with the gun and Victoria with the knife. The gun raised as she got closer and Dick could see that she had no chance of getting to him before he fired and blasted her at close range. He cast about for something to distract Sulim and saw a rock lying at his feet; he scooped it up and threw it with the power and aim borne of desperation. Somehow, and later he would think it must have been divine providence, the rock struck Sulim on the forehead. It was enough to deflect his aim and the shot went wide of Victoria who managed to reach him and plunge the knife deep into his chest. She released her grip on the knife and sank to her knees in front of him, her strength momentarily spent. Sulim stared down in wonder at the knife sticking out of his chest, then placed his hand on the shaft and pulled it out!

It was the worst possible action he could have taken as almost immediately blood bubbled up out of his mouth. Dick had by now reached them and took hold of Victoria and pulled her back, away from her adversary. Sulim followed his actions with his eyes, and attempted to raise the gun once more, it got halfway up and then sagged as his strength gave out. The blood carried on bubbling in Sulim's mouth and Dick knew that somehow Victoria had managed to pierce a vital artery and the blood was flooding into his lungs, slowly drowning him.

He turned pained eyes to Dick that pleaded silently for help, but Dick was too angry to offer any sympathy to this man who had attempted to destroy their whole community with his dreams of grandeur. Sulim started to slump down on to his knees, the rifle still in his grasp pointing down at the dirt, and Dick carried on pulling

Victoria away from him. She allowed him to get her a little distance from him as they watched fascinated at the blood now dripping down over his neck onto his clothing.

He must have sensed his imminent demise and with one last effort he raised the gun once more, Dick saw the barrel of the gun start to point in their direction and began to rush forward to stop him firing, when a large body ran in front of him and kicked the rifle out of Sulim's hands. Dick looked up and saw the Prof grinning from ear to ear at his surprise. "Looks like I got here just in time", He boomed. "We had to run like the devil when we realised he'd moved from that ridge, if he'd stayed there we wouldn't have been able to winkle him out easily".

Dick glanced round to see Arthur the policeman standing behind The Prof, and then he bent down to help Victoria to her feet. "What are we going to do about him?" Arthur asked. Dick glanced down to see Sulim had slumped down and now lay face down in the dirt, his blood pooling under him, the rifle lying in the dust a short distance away. "We'll come out later and give him a burial." He answered slowly. "For now, he can stay where he is."

He turned and went over to the pile of guns lying a few yards away, and reflected that it was only a short walk now but it had seemed like an impossible chasm a few minutes ago. He was brought back to reality by a thump in the back and he was knocked to the floor with an agonising pain spreading over his shoulder and arm. He turned over and tried to scramble to his feet but his legs were like jelly and his vision blurred. He could just make out the figure of The Prof firing a rifle point blank into Sulim's chest and then he passed out.

When he came to, his eyes opened and he found himself in the room they had previously designated as the hospital room. Lying on various beds around him, with assorted bandages swathing them were, Leah, Jim, Andy, and Pat. They were all grinning as they watched him try to move and found it impossible with the efficient way he had been trussed into his bed. Colette came into the room in response to a bell someone had pressed and moved to his side to check his temperature and pulse.

Andy said; his face like a Cheshire cat. "Thought you'd have had more sense than to turn you're back on a man with a loaded gun."

Dick frowned at the recollection. "I thought he was dead, and he didn't have the rifle in his hands." He mused.

"And we thought it was because you wanted to get out of all the extra work that's happened because we're in here."

"That's as maybe." Colette snapped. "Now let him get some rest you lot." You've had your share of letting other people do all the work anyway." She pointed a happy finger at all of them. "Some of you are going to get up tomorrow and I'll be setting a course of physiotherapy, to get you fit and well and back to work. I've had enough of you all skiving in here while others do all the work for you."

Jim turned and surveyed them all when she said this, and nodded silently to himself in satisfaction, they had come through some tough times but now all they had to do was keep the community going and they were going to form the nucleus of the future population of the world.

The End

Writers Note.

Did you enjoy this book? Although it was intended to be written and finished when all their enemies were gone and they settled down to life in the complex, I got to thinking what would happen if this scenario really did happen. Particularly with regard to any other possible survivors. In any catastrophe there are bound to be some who manage to live. Who amongst us would be able to live through a Nuclear Winter for ten years? I thought that there would be at least one group of people who would manage to pull through. I have written one further book about this possibility. And with no leaders in sight what would the potential outcome be? It would necessarily be a group of people who had some means of survival at their disposal. You will be able to read about this possibility when I have finished the next book. Please keep an eye open and watch my website to find out about this interesting future.

As always with a project like this, typos are an inevitable problem. If you have read this far, thank you for taking the time. If you have any comments or corrections you wish to offer about the details of climate, weapons used or anything else of interest to other readers and myself please contact me at the following email address.   franciswait@hotmail.com

I will endeavour to reply to all comments.

Reviews are always appreciated and I do ask that you are kind enough to post one.

Francis Wait

The Survivalists, Book 2, **The Finale**

Made in the USA
Charleston, SC
29 March 2015